To
Happy Jack
Drive That Thing
Careful

Jack Cady
PT townsend

Singleton

JACK CADY

Singleton

A NOVEL

1981
MADRONA PUBLISHERS
SEATTLE

Published by Madrona Publishers, Inc.
2116 Western Avenue
Seattle, Washington 98121

Library of Congress Cataloging in Publication Data

Cady, Jack, 1932-
Singleton.

I. Title.
PS3553.A315S55   813'.54   81-8117
ISBN 0-914842-63-3
                                                            AACR2

For Pauline Cady,
WHO WAS MOTHER, TEACHER, AND FRIEND.

For every tree is known by his own fruit. For of thorns men do not gather figs, nor of a bramble bush gather they grapes.

Luke 7:44

Singleton

THE restless voices were tossed by the wind that had worked out of the southeast since early morning. The wind burst across the asphalted loading yard of the truck terminal. It smacked the tall forty-foot trailers and blew away pockets of dry crap and dust that had accumulated in corrugations of aluminum bodies. It dusted the vans like a broom, turning the equipment to brighter colors of silver, red and traffic yellow. The wind humped like it was trying to meet a schedule.

Singleton stood on the loading dock to catch his breath. His own rig was closed up. The men still on the dock hustled to secure a company truck, eyed the south with the clustered nervousness of horses that feel far-off lightning. Stiff-legged, loud, they banded together and moved too quick.

I like the two of us laying together like this, mixed, all mixed together

When you worked past the natural rhythm of a job it was easy to get busted up. Singleton watched the wind shred a newspaper. The paper was flat against a chain link fence. Beyond the fence a secondary leader from a tree was tumbled by the wind. Beyond that an American flag and a corporation flag cracked from the staff of an oil company building. The flags popped in tandem like small caliber pistols. From behind him there was a yelp of pain and indignation.

He turned easy because the yelp was not mortal. A tall man in faded khakis hopped up and down. He held his hand which had been caught in a trailer door, and he was swearing in time to the dancing. His long nose was wrinkled and his eyes were squinched. His long brown hair was blown straight back. It made his head look streamlined and Singleton grinned. Twenty-five years ago he would have looked almost like the guy and might have pulled the same fool stunt. He wrinkled his own nose in sympathy. The guy's hand would be sore for a couple of days.

The wind was hunting its howl. He listened carefully and thought about how you could be fooled with a wind. Guys at sea often underestimated what a wind was going to do, but a wind always told you when it started that low howl. Over the land it usually moaned. Coming off the sea that howl meant trouble. The wind ironed Singleton's clothing against his tall body and straightened his black-and-gray-streaked hair. It slapped his face, flattening the furrows of twenty years at sea and the general weather a man took in forty-nine years.

He hopped from the loading dock, to run his hand along the side of his trailer as he walked to the cab. The trailer rocked in gusts. Pat would have loved this wind. Singleton remembered Pat, a kid standing a pier head, dark-haired and laughing as he braced against the kick of a northeast storm.

"Southeast now," Singleton muttered, and wondered why no voice came. Of all the voices that should ride a wind Pat's would be the one. It would be a good thing to see Pat, good to talk after so long. Running south there was no chance. He did not like to think about it much, but still, he ought to go see Pat.

Blowing chief, going to blow

"Thanks punk," he said. Across the yard trailers were being pulled to the lee of the terminal, the landing gear dropped and the wheels chocked. The weather side would be deserted. He figured it was time to get moving.

The wind whipped under the van and snapped his pants legs. A burst of dust flew in front of the cab. Catherine would be waiting for him and had been since he left three weeks before. The road.

He climbed up, high in a twenty-thousand-dollar truck that was

[4]

his and paid for. The engine was closed down, the air pressure level at one-twenty. He held a brake check. Then he started the engine and climbed down to hunker under the truck and bleed condensation from the brakes. The water spat in a hiss of compressed air that blew hard against the asphalt in spite of the crosswind. The wind kicked gravel in his face. He wondered how far the wind had carried the gravel.

He returned to the cab and checked headlights, turn signals, fogs and markers; a climb-down each time to look. The truck flashed and glowed, yellow, red, white. Singleton entered the cab after checking the tires. He ran through the routine of wipers, washers, fans, horns and mirrors.

On the loading dock a small man appeared running jerkily against the gusts. He jumped from the dock and ran along the driving side. The man hopped on the bottom step, reached for the grab bar and steadied himself with one foot. Singleton pushed the heel of his hand against the trailer brake to release a hiss of air. He rolled the window. The man's face reached to his shoulder.

"What?"

The guy was panting. He had a tooth that was yellow and needed fixing but he wore a tie. "The boss says pull her over. It's moving in faster."

"Your boss." Singleton popped the trailer brake to hear it spit. "Not my boss."

"Gypsy or not."

"Get off my truck."

The guy tried it different. He started whining. The whine was funny. The guy was a bop guy, a greaser. "It's his load, man. His responsibility. I'm not tellin' you. He is."

"It's on my truck." He did not feel in any mood for argument. He did not give jackshit for talk, but it was like the little guy was afraid of losing and had to argue.

"Listen."

"You listen," Singleton told him, speaking just over the wind. "See that ground. See it there? In ten seconds you hit, either on your feet or on your can."

The man got down hollering.

"A friggin' hurricane."

Singleton found low and pulled. The engine roared and surged

[5]

forward. The trailer came along behaving pretty. He had been up half the night trying to keep a mechanic from dogging it while they removed slack from the fifth wheel. The smoothness of the trailer made the loss of sleep and the work worthwhile.

Nearly sixty thousand gross. Payload. A profit and a stable truck. In his mirrors he watched the little guy with the bum tooth do an angry dance in the wind. The window was open to the weather. A storm made him feel just fine, and he cleared the yard laughing at the little guy who was now giving him the finger.

The streets were almost empty, the warehouses galvanized and nearly lead-colored. The wind was blowing away the stink of petroleum, chemicals, lime, fertilizer, and sour tastes of wet cardboard and trash that were always in a loading area.

An occasional car wavered toward him but nothing appeared in his mirrors. Even on the low side of the gears the wind was knocking the van. He scanned the deserted streets.

Leave these blues behind me

There was strength in driving through heavy crashes of wind. It was special because it took a little more than just nerve.

Let that tandem call

Before he connected with the new interstate he idled down to look over the choppy water of the bay breaking in runs of building waves.

Start that road to windin'

The swells were cracked by the wind, gutted, pitched, the spume like a torn cover over the water.

From it all

An old, black-winged gull hung motionless in the wind, while around him the gray and brown gulls flapped or fell off on one wing between the gusts.

"Breezing to fifty," he told the truck. Singleton swung onto the interstate and pulled for the high side of his gears. The road was empty. Even the usual trucking had holed up. The interstate pointed north and away from the storm. New, good road. That was the trick, get the storm to the rear of the van and let it furnish some of the ride. He felt the thrust as his hand was steady near the trailer brake, moving from wheel to gears as the diesel roared and stuttered from the stacks behind him. Chrome stacks, almost a hundred bucks. Good resonance, booming like the heavy pipes of a big organ.

The tach rose and fell, to rise and fall, to rise. The gears dropped behind and moved to higher ranges. They tuned in with the high steady song of the tires, the whisper and yell at once that spelled running, the work a man could do in spite of the buffeting wind. Soon there would be rain. The wind was punching harder as he began to cruise. The speedometer read sixty-five, the tach twenty, and the gauges checked. The tandem moved to a higher pitch in the turbulence. At seventy the thirty-ton rig was a solid force that drove before the storm.

Beyond Columbia the wind backed off for fifteen miles of easy road, then came back singing. Hurricane force, sixty-five, Beaufort scale. He figured that it was not that much but it was bad enough. It was going to break his speed. He checked his mirrors with the usual regularity. The van was rocking over the tandem. Singleton dropped the speed to sixty-five and then to sixty, inching the wheel in short snaps to catch the trailer which was trying to take a walk sideways. He felt calm, but beneath the calmness was an edge of fear. A sudden gust could ditch him. He dropped to fifty-five and loafed.

The truck was again stable. He did the normal things, shifting his glance down the road, to mirrors, to roadside, to dials, to down the road, to mirrors again. The overcast sky was changing to black, the darkness in pursuit. The marker lights glowed amber in the mirrors as he watched empty road.

A state car passed from the opposite direction. It moved at high speed and staggered in the quartering wind. There were three cops. Singleton watched the car in his mirrors. A gust whipped the van and it rocked. He automatically corrected and watched the veins stand out on his hands.

"Going to a drowning," he told the truck. "Those guys will work all night and then catch hell for being late." The job was not much different from the one he had done in the Coast Guard for years. By now the coast would be a mess. There would be some guys lost. There almost always was one guy lost. Made no difference how good you were, weather was going to take somebody every once in a while. He had nearly lost a man himself, one time. Pat.

[7]

He thought about it, then tried not to think about it as he almost seemed to catch a glance of Pat grinning in the wind. The tach told him that he was bearing down.

"It's past," he said. He eased the power. In his mirrors the darkness, the black bellows of the sky, moved across the rise of land. The land was going black, the road inked in like on a blueprint. There was a trailing darkness behind the van. The road ran like a vessel's wake: running, a line, a course, compass-course, compass; when the rain arrived he had it pegged. He drifted left to meet it, running the left side of the road and laying the tandem six inches from the shoulder.

There was a fist in the wind. A rush of water took him from the left quarter, and he met it, hands slightly off the ten-two position so that the right could get the trailer brake. As the rain hit he tapped the brake gently. The tall truck backed against the blast that brought water flooding across the road. The van humped and made a small jump right but he caught it. The roadway was glazed. Singleton knew that no matter how bad the storm got, his footing on the road would be most skiddy in the first few minutes of rain. The dust on the road was mud, a thin layer, an invisible slick that could ditch the rig. He could feel the slip. The speed was down, dropped to hold back more reserve power. As he corrected he applied power and could feel a small spin in the drive. Because he did not want a sudden jerk on the trailer it was useful. The speed started to rise. At sixty the rig began a long drift right. He dropped back and eased up slowly. The point of drift came at fifty-eight. Singleton dropped it back to fifty-five and grinned.

"Naomi," he said. "Your dumb ass," he told himself. "Catherine Elizabeth," he said. He wished she had been there to see. True, she would not have understood five cents worth of what she was seeing, but he wished she had seen it anyway. "For the experience," he told her. He turned on the defrosting fans and rolled the window halfway. The high-speed wipers threw rain. He could see enough road in the day turned nearly night. There was yellow light in the blackness from the left bank of fogs. The right bank threw white. Most guys did not mix them that way, but the different bulbs had separate qualities.

The interstate jogged to the right below Greenville, and the wind followed more to the rear of the trailer. The road was washed

[8]

clean. He ran sixty in the decreasing wind and heavy rain.

The letdown. Singleton tried to remember that he had nearly been afraid and thought that outrunning the storm was not such a big deal. That was a trouble with fear. You remembered it different later. Even when you tried it was hard to be honest.

He yawned. The good part, the professional part was always awake and now it was taking control. It was his automatic pilot. The good part held the wheel, felt the roll of the trailer on curves, adjusted the speed, made the signals, allowed for normal winds. The good part felt for unwanted noise. The engine cruised steady. The good part became meshed and one with the engine, the wind, and the song of the drive.

"I miss you," he said to Catherine or Naomi.

"Then don't go," he heard Catherine say. He rubbed his face and welcomed her. Thinking of her made the voice disappear. He looked at her picture; her long hair did not show well in the photo stuck on the dash. Her hair ran past the small of her long back, and he liked to wrap her hair behind him, around his neck and pull her face to his with them all tied together . . . or bring her hair beneath her breasts to lift them; and that was one more thing he believed she did not understand. The heavy-lipped look was clear and her eyes excited as they occasionally were when he was lying beside her. It was a good photograph.

"I have to go," he told her. "You need some practice at understanding that."

He did not know why he saw pictures like those of Pat in the wind. He did not know why he heard voices, but they often came to him and sometimes they came over a long distance of memory. The voice might be that of his father or occasionally of his aunt who helped raise him. Mostly their voices were like memory and sounded only a few words. Others were not so plain. Some girl he had once known, or Pat, or Catherine, or Naomi or his brother. Occasionally a voice spoke, someone he had heard some place at some time and never heard again. Singleton did not understand why he heard voices, and he heard them just often enough so that they were no surprise when they came.

He figured it was the trucking. It had never happened much before the trucking. He figured it was the long nights and the loneliness, with the road winding silver and ghostlike under moon or cloud cover. It had to do with the shadows of shrubbery, signs and trees that fled backward before the headlights. Sometimes the road felt like a long corridor down which he hurtled, a passage that could move through space like the new Russian rockets, or through the center of the earth. The road. In the daytime it was different. He did not hear them as often in the daytime. Sometimes he liked to hear them. Sometimes they made him afraid. He occasionally wondered if other guys heard things and would admit it if the subject came up.

I want you to have it, take it, take it baby

"Get out of my mind," he told Naomi.

The worst of the storm seemed to be behind unless it was circling on some odd angle. The rain was much heavier and beginning to get ahead of the wipers. He dropped the speed and decided to leave the interstate for a short stretch. It was just past noon. Usually he did not eat a lot while driving, but coffee would help break the boredom.

He rolled the truck off a twister and ran two-lane. The stop was small but modern. Since the war they had been popping up everywhere. He eased the rig to the far end of the blacktop lot, headed into the wind and listened to the rain pound the aluminum cab. There was now a lot more rain than wind. It drummed the cab and tapped out a different noise on the sleeper. He smiled at the engine which continued trying to pull, running high. When it settled to a measured, steady surge, he turned to the sleeper. He reached under the pad for a raincoat folded in a small packet. The lot was level. There was no need to chock. With the emergency set Singleton took a weighted club like a policeman's billy and climbed down to thump tires. The rain got under the collar of the coat and ran down his neck. When he replaced the billy he looked for a cap, remembered having it in Ohio and figured that it must have been left at the next stop, probably in Lexington or maybe Knoxville. He brushed water from his hair and brows.

When he walked toward the restaurant, the shape of the protruding sleeper box on a tractor stopped him. He knew the shape. "Bull hauler," he said. "Using her to haul hogs." Instead of going inside he walked across the lot and approached the cattle rig from the rear. The trailer was a possum-belly, stacked in close with animals. The stench of urine and hog smell was thick and bitter-tasting in the fuming rain.

The animals were quiet. If they were not given a ride they would get sick. You had to have a flow of air when you rode animals. The trailer was red with home-painted, unprofessional yellow trim, like a circus wagon. The paint was new and the box seemed sound. Singleton watched water pouring down the slatted sides and felt as much as saw the occasional movement of heavy hog bodies in the truck. The lot was surrounded by mountain trees. He thought of a jungle and knew that it must be the steam and stench coming from the hogs.

The truck was a conventional Mack, almost new, a '55 or '56. There were a lot of them on the road but the sleeper had been his brother, John Singleton's idea. It was built with an extra compartment for storage shelves and that caused the irregular hump. He walked around to the lee side. Something pleased him. The truck was well kept up. His brother would have liked that.

"And that," Singleton told the wind and rain, "marks the end of a freight line and the end of a life." John was no longer in the hospital, but he was still the same as dead. He would be better off dead.

As he thought of John he also thought of Ben. It was funny. Ben was his nephew, but he never heard Ben's voice. He walked to the restaurant.

The waitress smiled as he entered. Full mouth. Young. Slim waist. She did not know his name but she liked him. Waitresses had a way. You knew how welcome you were. Singleton grinned at her and slapped water from the raincoat. She moved for coffee and it was on the counter by the time he was seated. She was only a kid, nineteen or twenty, but she was sharp. She knew exactly how to commit herself without offering sex. Most of them were self-conscious or self-admiring. The more experienced seemed convinced that they were the target of every guy who walked in and they were anyway ninety percent right. A good waitress made a chromed counter seem like a kitchen table.

"Bad," she said, talking about the weather.

"You'll get some rest. There's no traffic."

"Then it's not all bad." Her eyes were kind of gray-blue. Catherine's were brown, but the two women were built much

[11]

alike. This girl had more chest but not better. Good face. Smiling. "Match you for the juke."

"I'll buy." He hated jukeboxes. Singleton fished a quarter and shoved it across the counter. She walked to the far end of the room and started punching combinations. As a general thing they all had their favorites memorized.

"What'll you have." She was saving the last for him.

"Anything but truck songs." He turned. At the far end of the counter two drivers slouched and drank coffee. One was heavyset and wore overalls and a flannel shirt. He was young. He was fat in the face as well as the seat of his overalls.

"Coming from south?"

"Uh huh. South."

"How was it?"

Singleton paused. "You got that bull rig?"

"Him," the fat driver turned to the other man who was now staring at the rain.

"Don't go south," Singleton said. "It's going to make the head-lines."

"At home we got us a television."

That was worse than jukeboxes. He walked to the window where the other driver sat watching the rain. It was heavy and constant. Close up, the wind made the window rattle. There was a heavy draft around the frame.

"You got a nice rig."

The man turned. He was muscular. There was worry showing in his face. "I like it. About a year I had it. She's good."

"You keep it nice."

The driver looked at him carefully. "Use to belong to you?"

"I just saw them sell. Indianapolis last year."

"That's right. They had a bunch. One of them freight outfits went broke."

The rain slammed the window. "He didn't go broke. He went dead." The weight of what he said felt right.

"Yeah? Well, she's been a good truck." The man was plainly worried. "This don't break and pass off by night I'll have to unload."

"One of these farmers will rent you fence." He drank the rest of the coffee. "Don't go south," he told the fat driver.

[12]

"Keep it in the road," the bull hauler said.

The waitress still stood by the juke. The record was just noise, somebody wacking the shit out of a guitar. She waved.

"Drive careful yourself," he told the bull hauler. He went through the doorway and across the lot. When he climbed up he pulled immediately. Catherine lived not far from Asheville and Asheville was not so far away. As he settled the rig squarely in the roadway the cattle hauler showed small in his rain-covered mirrors.

2

Twenty miles before Asheville the rain pulled him down. His gross was high. The rig pressed against the grades and roared. In the hills the transmission put him to work, the truck booming as he clutched, catching the under gears on the high side, on tough inclines roaring on the low side past ditches of rushing water and tall, bending weed heads; the speed lower, the mud banks of red clay. The interior of the forests were still dry where the brush was knocked back and a man could get a look. The graveled shoulders which occasionally edged the road were like oily silver fringes bordering the macadam. His stacks gave the rushing crack he loved so well as the engine rode high on the gear, then settled in and pulled. The wind and rain were at the very heart of sound; the crack of the exhaust was sharp and went off like a forty-five.

The wind was tricky on two-lane. He was tired. The wind forced his attention. Sheets of water were blown across the road in the few flat areas where the land lay washed. Red and yellow streams in gullies carried small branches, clutter, occasional tourist junk of discarded milk cartons, wrappers, trash. The hills were getting a good cleaning.

The rig moved beside the flowing ditches, water bursting over the road in low spots. As far as he could see, the mountains looked like huge vessels awash.

Singleton was bending it through a gentle curve at thirty when he saw the tree. It was in easy stopping distance but the curve was grabbing the trailer. He popped the trailer brake, popped it again, caught it straight in the road and eased down. When he stopped, the branches of the tree were no more than a yard from his face. A bare branch pointed at the windshield, a spear that could have come through the cab.

Be careful please

The rain was heavy in the felled tree. It was an oak that had been killed up one side, not yet rotting, solid. The last thing he needed was delay. The last thing you wanted was the thing you usually got. He knew that he had to move the tree and that made his fatigue heavier.

"Up too late," he told the truck. "Too fast putting up the load. Maybe next time we'll have Ben." If he towed from a distance, got a chain on the butt and swung it around, the tree should come clear.

Singleton put on his jacket and found gloves. Then he climbed down. The water in the gullies was nearly road high. He did not have a hat and his head and hands were immediately soaked. He threw the gloves into a ditch. His boots were taking water.

From storage beneath the sleeper he dragged tow chain and muttered when he found rust. Beside him the diesel rumbled. He kept flares in the chain compartment. Another set of flares was kept in the toolbox, but they were not for use. They were for when the I.C.C. pulled you over and checked safety equipment. He crouched beneath the van so that the striker of the fusee remained partly dry. When it was lit he carried it behind the truck about fifty yards where it burned and sputtered in the rain. The four-way signal put flashing red lines down the rain-slick road.

"You're doing better," he muttered, talking to the storm. There was a fine tremble in his hands. He was getting cold.

The safest and strongest tow is the simplest. He made a turn on the tree and snagged back on the chain, took the other end around one towing hook beneath the bumper and led it back up the line. He climbed back up.

The cab was steaming. Singleton turned on the heater and checked his mirrors. The fans blew the windshields clear. The

[15]

fusee was dead. When the cab warmed he began to tow.

The tree lay across a fence and into the road. The chain slid, then grabbed on the butt. The tree came sideways and ripped out fence. He had trouble with his mirrors and pulled rags from beneath the sleeper pad. The gully was starting to overflow onto the road. His passing mirror, the mirror to the right, was useless. He rubbed the steam off the driving mirror. He could see one side of the road. He ran the trailer toward that side, backing slow so the wheels were not far from the ditch. He felt the tree coming. When he had backed twenty yards he stopped to check.

The tree lay in the center of the road. He backed more, then stopped and climbed down. Water was eating at the fill beneath the pavement, taking out grade.

There was a jog. He figured that backing around the jog would throw the tree right. He changed the tow from the left hook to the right, then climbed back up. In the rain the curve was hard to negotiate. He figured that few men could back that curve in such weather. The tree rolled right to open one lane.

When his gear was secure the cab was still cold. The water had worked beneath his coat. The powerful heater made steam. The interior of the cab was sodden, moisture collecting on the seats and sleeper curtains. There was a place not far off and he hoped it would be open.

Even by Carolina standards the truck stop was not much, not really a stop at all but only a restaurant with pumps and a trashy bunkhouse. The lot was mud and gravel with dirty water standing in chuckholes pounded by the rain. Beyond the bunkhouse was a house trailer with collapsed tires. The owner had not jacked it up and was living there until it fell apart, which, Singleton figured, would take another year. Junk cars parked beyond the trailer were rust-filled, glass-busted iron. A '40 Ford pickup stood by the trailer. It no doubt ran, patched together with parts from other junkers.

Parked in front of the restaurant was a state car with the engine idling. The exhaust fumed in the rain. The wipers slapped and threw water. Beyond the state car and parked between mud holes stood two coal trucks with hay racks butting over the cabs. Both were overloaded. Singleton held the same opinion of coal drivers that most truckers held. Their equipment was junk. When they bought new equipment they turned it into junk by overloading and neglecting maintenance. The overloads made the trucks labor in the hills and slowed other guys who had a schedule.

Nothing else was parked in the lot. He hurried to the restaurant, fumbled the loose and rattling doorknob, then stepped inside.

The off-red, bricky-colored linoleum of the counter matched the patched linoleum on the floor. It had yellow florals parched and cracked and blacklined with age. There was dirt in the lines and creases. Painted walls showed lumps where most of the paper had been stripped away and paint slapped across the rest. An ancient juke stood by the windows. An old counter rested across the room from the juke and three booths sat in an alcove. The woman behind the counter leaned a fat elbow on a grubby pie case that had peeling transparent tape over cracked glass. The Lord's Prayer in glittery gilt silver was tacked to a wall behind her, a pile of religious tracts was stacked near the old cash register. Common in the country. The thing to do was not get tricked into conversation.

"H'yah." She turned to pour coffee. She was fat and about his age. Sweat fat. The room was not warm but wet lines showed in the wrinkles of her arms. There was sweat on her mouth and hands.

"Wet," he told her and wondered how people could look at other people and notice nothing.

"Back up to the stove."

He turned to the alcove and saw the small monkey stove alongside the booths, red with heat at its belly and flickering yellow through the smoked isenglass windows. In one booth was a cop. A kid. He did not look up, only sat straight and braced both forearms on the table like he was trying to steady hands wrapped around a coffee cup. His uniform was a slick mess of water and mud.

"Somethin'?"

"Not now," Singleton told her. "Maybe after I dry off."

"Goin' to catch a cold." Her voice became mournful. He recognized the tone, had perfect pitch for that tremble of soothing fellow misery. He half turned. The two coal drivers were sitting at the far end of the counter.

[17]

"I already had one. Over it now."

"Goin' to catch another." The mournfulness was deepening in her voice. He turned from the counter to stare out at the rain.

"Goin' around. Seems like everybody got colds or flu or somethin'. My old man with flu last week, him down and me runnin' the place. Still ain't movin' good."

"More coffee," one of the coal drivers said. "Gimmie the board."

"An' now there's stormin' and rainin' all over. Flood, I shouldn't wonder." She took the pot and waddled toward the far end of the counter, raising her voice as she moved away. She poured coffee and returned. Singleton walked toward the juke, trying to get away without being mean.

"Floodin'," she said again, "and them fellas there tellin' about a big nigger fight up to Hamilton. An' more sickness ever' day. My old man—"

He found a dime and pressed a button, never mind what. It was bound to be hillbilly and loud. The cop was sitting quiet. The two coal drivers were hunched over the punch board.

"Jesus," she slipped in before the record. "I reckon Jesus's all the hope men's got no more. With fightin' and sickness and pushy niggers and what all." The record started and it was noisy and hillbilly. Instead of trying to out-testify the record she turned and went through a door into what must be the kitchen. He figured she probably couldn't do without Jesus. What was even more likely is that she could not do without hell. She was a doom-sayer, a punisher, and he had been raised by one just like her. For a moment he remembered his aunt's face, a face not much different from this woman's. Fat face with thin lips that preached the wrong of everything. His aunt specialized in making people feel guilty. This woman specialized in making them afraid.

To that kind of face there was no difference between swearing and murder, between prostitution and working on Sunday. Singleton grinned and thought of a woman he had met in Nevada on a Sunday and wondered what the fat face would have thought of that.

"Win me a shotgun," one of the coal drivers said.

Singleton turned. The drivers were from the mountains or from mountain towns. Their builds were different but the set of their mouths was southern and small-town mean. They looked like the kind of men who would work all day and then kick a dog because it had been sleeping in the sun.

"No shotgun on the board," the heavier one said. "Ain't but a nickel board. Win you a horse with a clock in his belly."

"Not here. Up the road. They got a shotgun on a board."

"To where?"

"To London, up by the bootlegger."

"More coffee," the cop said. His voice was low and strained. Singleton kept his back to the cop while he watched the coal drivers. They were baiting the cop with the illegal punch board. With his braced arms and his tight voice it was plain that the cop was not thinking of them. The juke stopped.

"Get him," one of the coal men said, nodding to the cop and speaking just loud enough that the cop might hear. "Pride of the Mounties. Sergeant Preston."

The other driver grinned and stood up. He counted up his punches and threw a dollar on the counter.

"We got to get goin'."

"Wait."

"Hell no. Bad as it is, I'm for home and bed." The man looked at Singleton.

"Coming from south?"

The man seemed eager. "No. Out of Manchester up to Kentucky. Hay in. Coal out."

"Coal down this way?"

"It's a back haul anyways. We sell to a small plant. Me and him," he turned to the other man, "we about got it sewed."

"A hard way."

The man grinned. He shrugged into an old coat and reached for a rain hat that was crumpled from hard use. "I carry a mouse. One to a pocket. A two-mouse man."

"How was the road?"

"Good 'til Knoxville."

"Tree down about three miles south." Singleton paused. "Drive careful."

"How else?" The two drivers left. When they banged the door the woman hurried from the kitchen, saw them leaving and scanned the counter. She walked to the end, picked up the dollar and shoved it in an apron pocket.

[19]

"More coffee," the cop said again. His voice was no better. The woman carried the pot to the booth, filled the cup and disappeared back into the kitchen. Singleton walked over to warm himself at the stove. Close up, the cop looked even worse. He had to be burning his hands which were still wrapped around the cup.

"You hurt?"

"I don't know. Took a bang a while ago." He pulled both hands from the cup and tried to appear easy, but his hands were trembling. He grabbed the edge of the table. Just a kid, twenty-three or twenty-four. Standing he would probably be six feet, but sitting there with water in his short brown hair he looked small. His uniform was soaked and a mess of red mud was caked on the side of his face. There was a tear in his shirt about the middle of the rib cage on the right side. His shirt sleeves were rolled. His wrists were too narrow, too light for a working cop.

Singleton slipped into the booth. "Busted rib?"

"Just took a bang."

"Something's wrong."

"What did they mean by mice?"

"Mouse in each pocket?"

"Yeah."

"They steal. Guys that haul grain. They get a weight ticket, scrape off a couple of hundred, then sell the weight that's on the ticket. Same with coal. They rake and rake. One day they make a load out of their back yard."

"A kid drowned," the cop said. "I've got him in the back seat."

"Oh."

"A little while ago. Just a little kid. I got sent to a secondary to mark a washout. He came right across the road. Like to missed catching him."

"Ribs?"

"Log rolled over us."

"Feel anything in your gut?"

"Sore."

"That's okay, wait here." Singleton stood and wondered if it was worthwhile to call the woman, decided it was not. He put on his coat and hurried to the truck. There was dry clothing in storage and a bottle some guy had given him for a couple hours help in running down a short in his markers. There was no wide tape in the first aid box. An oversight. He tucked the clothing under his coat and walked to the state car.

The body was in the back seat covered by a blanket. One tanned foot stuck out with a long scratch on it that was almost healed. You could tell, even though the scab was gone. The cop had said it, just a little kid.

He pulled the keys and walked to the trunk for a first aid kit, then returned to the restaurant.

The woman was still in the kitchen. The cop was still sitting, but trembling as he began to let go some of his control. Singleton walked behind the counter, found a glass and came to the table. He broke the seal on the bottle, poured a little of the whiskey, then pulled his dry clothes from beneath the coat and lay them in the booth.

"No."

"Sure. It's going to hurt."

The cop sipped at the whiskey. "Don't want to cough."

"Can you stand up?"

"I think." He started to raise himself. There was a gust of wind and another heavy burst of rain. The cop sat back down. Behind them was the tiny snap of burning from the monkey stove. "Hurts."

"We'll cut the shirt." Singleton bent over and felt the rib cage. There was swelling. "I can call in for you."

"They've got other trouble."

"Hit you pretty hard?"

"Yeah, a big log."

"I mean the kid. You're nerved up."

The cop's voice broke. "Wrecks. I've pulled them out all cut up, pulled one out dead, but nothing as bad as this kid."

"Popping up sudden that way. Drink a little more and we'll get the shirt off."

Singleton went to the kitchen. The woman was sitting at a small wooden table and staring through half a window at the rain. The other half was boarded with rags stuffed around the boards. An old monitor-top refrigerator stood beside a dirty stove. A few dishes were stacked in a galvanized sink which had a leak. A slow drip splashed on the bare wood floor, pooled and ran off through a crack. The place smelled sour. People, what they didn't have,

[21]

what they refused to ask for. She was reading a church magazine. It lay beside a couple of tomato slices and other slop on the table. She looked up.

"The cop. I think he's got a busted rib. You have any scissors?"

"That what's wrong?" She stood. Her gray hair was thin and stringy. It hung limp about pouchy cheeks that, fat as they were, somehow seemed deflated with fatigue or indifference. "Reckoned he's put Danny down. That big fella that was pushin'."

"Other trouble." Singleton sketched it quick and knew before he was done that it was a mistake.

The woman began to swell. She would scale three hundred anyway, flaccid with pale skin that was gray tinged and looked like it should be moldy. Swelling, color moved in around the corners of her mouth, her cheeks tightened, puffed out, made her face flatten and her nose look level with her chin.

Her face wrenched up more. "Our Jesus," she whispered, the sound barely making sense as it burped from her lined mouth. She continued to gasp and puff, inflating like a blowfish. From somewhere in the fat, muscles began to push a moan. "Poor thing, poor baby thing. Poor little thing." Her eyes disappeared into the fat. Tears came. Automatic. He had seen it before.

"Scissors." He stopped. She was really getting to him. She began to tap her foot. The moan seemed to take a shape in the air.

"Goin' home to Jesus, our Saviour's called it home; goin' home." The moan was in time, a hymn tune was appearing. She began to move. Before, when she moved through a doorway, she had caromed off the frame like a barge adrift. Now she took off with accurate steps that vibrated the dishes stacked beside the sink.

"Scissors," Singleton yelled. He followed her, only to see her disappear through the outer doorway. The cop looked up. "I fucked up," Singleton told him. "We didn't need that."

The cop grinned and nudged his glass. "Didn't need her to smell this, either."

"Kick us out?"

"And step on us."

Singleton walked to the cigar case and found a package of razor blades. It took them ten minutes to get the cop out of the shirt.

The rib cage was bruised and tender. The cop took it well, hanging onto the edge of the table and half rising so Singleton could tape in tight.

"Hurt?"

"Sure."

"Being as easy as I can."

"Take my mind off the other." With the pain the cop's voice sounded better. A lot of the nervousness was gone.

"You'll think of it from time to time."

There was a sound outside.

"For God's sake hide the bottle." The cop's voice sounded like a scared, guilty kid. Singleton looked at him and smiled. The cop looked back and thought of how he'd just heard his own voice. "Goddamn it, I can't afford to laugh." He held it in. His eyes showed fun and hurt at the same time. Singleton shoved the bottle beneath the cop's torn shirt that lay wadded in the booth.

A thickset man came in. He was wearing torn pants, dirty undershirt and an unbuttoned plastic raincoat. His hair was long and spiky. He paused inside the door to kick off soaking felt bedroom slippers. The slippers had tar on them. He was in his fifties or sixties, had been a coal miner at one time judging from the coal dust that still lay beneath the skin in the crevices of his face.

"I'm Strunk." He walked toward them. The woman came through the doorway puffing. She now wore a tentlike piece of canvas that probably had been the awning of the house trailer. The awning was green and white striped. Her face was red. The high spots of her cheeks were nearly yellow. She followed the man and sat in the booth next to the cop.

"Judgement," she said and panted. "There's them will say else but hit's a judgement."

"Git out a here," Strunk said. Singleton looked up.

"I'm goin'." Her face was still changing color. Now it was going white under the yellow, the flush fading and her lips drawing into a hard white line.

"Hit's one a the Sizemore kids," Strunk told the cop. "They nearly a mile off, back up the hill."

"Give me a hand," the cop said. "I'm going to try it."

The woman stood.

"Git back to the trailer." Strunk moved toward the cop. He propped him on one side while Singleton helped raise from the other side. The woman moved away and turned to watch the cop. "They's signs and judgements."

"Git," Strunk told her.

"All over. Triflin'. Sorry." She slammed the door as she left.

"Sizemores are Kentucky folk, Methodist," Strunk said. The cop grunted and made it all the way to his feet. "Least these Sizemores are. Smoke tight-rolls, hell around some, have a pretty nice time."

The cop was breathing heavy. "That's why the Lord judged 'em?"

"Shit, my old woman judged 'em." From the lot came the sound of the pickup. "Headed there now I reckon."

"That's not right."

"Ain't goin' to happen neither fer that road's a swamp."

"What's Sizemore's other name?"

"They's three families up there."

"Phone?"

"Shit again, how long you been in this county?"

The cop looked embarrassed. "I got to worry about all that later. Can you guys help me to the car?"

"Sure you can make it?" Singleton stepped away from the cop. He seemed okay.

"Sure."

"Want me to follow you?"

The cop was embarrassed for a second time. "You've done enough."

"We'll get you to the car."

"Wait," Strunk said. He walked outside to the car, found the cop's jacket and brought it in. He draped it over the cop's shoulders. "Now try it."

They walked slowly. The rain was still heavy but slacking. Singleton dug for the car keys and managed to get the door open and the keys in the ignition without looking in the back seat. He helped the cop into the car. Helping him, he looked.

The woman had left the body uncovered. A little boy with brown eyes, maybe three and a half or four. Drowned. Death by strangulation was something he had seen before. Singleton opened the back door of the car and covered the body.

[24]

"Thanks again," the cop said. "I can make it."

"You've got the radio."

The cop got the car started and in gear with his left hand, looked up at them and then pulled out.

"Who is he?" Singleton turned to Strunk who stood in the rain indifferent to the soaking they were taking.

"One a them new hot rocks they hired. College boy. Drives the old woman wild." Strunk wiped rain from his heavy eyebrows. "Let's get the hell outta this here." He walked back to the restaurant. Singleton followed.

He was shivering. His dry clothing was stacked in a corner of the booth. He picked it up. Strunk moved to shake down the monkey stove. He opened the door and added slack coal. Then he looked up. "Change right here, ain't nobody around." He walked behind the counter and rummaged until he found two ragged dish towels. "Here, dry off."

"How about yourself."

"I'm goin' back to bed. No business in this weather."

"How about your wife?"

Strunk grinned. He closed his eyes like he was imagining something. Then he started laughing. "She's to the preacher's by now. Got the pickup stuck along the hill road and walked there because hit's closest. They'll dry her out. She'll tell 'em all about it."

"Seems kind of hard, no offense."

"Well, hit's what he gets fer bein' a preacher."

"I mean your wife."

"I reckon I know what you mean." Strunk lost some of his smile. "But, she's been a good woman. Old now, and fat. Kinda hard mouth but she's had hard times. Been a good woman."

"Want a drink?" He was buying off, knew it, and was disgusted with himself. He knew country ways and knew that you didn't talk about a man's wife. A good thing Strunk was easygoing.

"Well, hell yes. You got some?"

"Under that shirt."

Strunk got the bottle and went behind the counter for two glasses. Singleton felt warmer. He was dry and getting into dry clothes. A drink would take the edge off his fatigue. He wondered

[25]

for a moment if it was time to break one of his rules. There was still an hour to drive. He had to come off one tough mountain. It was not time.

"Still have driving, but give me a little coffee." He drank coffee and tested himself. He had seen too much death. Either that, or he had not seen enough. It was a shock every time.

Strunk was quiet and polite about the bottle. Singleton had to force it on him, finally gave it to him. They thanked each other, Strunk saying a word about the whiskey, Singleton saying that it was little enough for the help. He wondered if he should call Catherine. Overdue. She would worry. He was bound to sound bad on the phone. Better to let her worry a little than have her find that he had been shaken up.

He finished the coffee and stood. The rain was still slacking and was no worse than a heavy shower. The storm had done itself proud. For a moment he was filled with a familiar grief, then fear, the way he used to feel on search and rescue. The feeling rapidly changed to anger. He wanted to strike, hit, swear at the storm, curse all the sorry rednecks and their redneck God.

Maybe everything was judgements. If that was true then those judgements were piss poor. He wanted to tear somebody's head off. He wanted to yell, but when his voice came it was softer than usual.

"We'll see you," he said to Strunk.

"Drive that thing careful."

"Like always." He walked into the last of the storm, his feet still wet, sinking in the mud. It was better to think of Catherine. Maybe she did not always understand about these sorrows that you ran into on the road, but she would always listen. That is, she would listen if he told her but he almost never did.

The engine was still surging. The cab was warm. The mirrors were fogged again. He used more dry rags to clean them, not trusting the airstream to do it in time. When he was settled and feeling the truck with his hands and mind he pulled it roaring into the road.

3

SINGLETON slumped and drove. Sorry. The fat woman had said it. There was a difference between hill people and hillbillies, and that difference had to do with pride. To not know where a kid was playing when that kind of wind began.

It was the worst reaction in a long time. Usually he felt the initial anger and sorrow. There was something else as well, a darkness of mind that made him vulnerable to other bad feelings. It was like the dead were blaming him, but there was no blame. Some people did not care for their own. Sometimes it was like nobody was willing to try to care for anybody. He thought of his brother John. Helpless. Should he be doing more for his brother? What the hell should he do?

The rain was nearly gone. Visibility was improving. It would be dark by the time he arrived. There was enough water to keep the badly worn macadam slick. The trailer kept trying to make a side trip. In a way that was fine because it gave him something to think about.

His mind was full of things he did not want to remember: bodies wrapped in canvas, a burned skull eyeless and hairless bobbing in a life jacket. "Le savetiuer," some Canadian guy had called them and retched diesel oil and puke across Singleton's foul-weather gear. That was during the war. There had been worse times; worse because they made no sense at all, just death by indifference or error. Things were not so goddamn hot right now, to tell the truth. It seemed like the whole country was restless. People moving, people afraid and calling each other hard names. Nigger fight up to Hamilton. He could tell that fat lady a few things.

Death was the absolute worst failure. Living was how you did not fail, but no one seemed to understand that. They did not seem bothered by people dying as long as it was not done in front of them. They wrote stories about it. They acted it out on screens, and hardly anyone who wrote or acted understood how death looked or what it meant.

It always looked small. That part never changed, whether it was a man or a rabbit or a fish. Everything dead seemed to lose weight. The truth was that it was the man watching who shrank. Inside his head, that was where the weight was lost.

Take it to the fantail

He grabbed at the voice. Angry. It had been small and shaky. Who? From what ship? The voice had come and gone quickly. He ran through his memory seeking the owner of the voice or the job. Then he stopped. He did not want to remember the jobs. He could count the big ones the way some men counted women, at least the important women. Like he could count women for that matter. The difference was that the jobs were still real and all but two of the women were faded and unreal. That did not seem right.

Do you think about it

"Like a damn fool," he told her. He did not have to catch at that one. That was Naomi, a young voice from twenty-one years ago; and of all the voices that was the one that always remained in his mind. It hung in the wind or murmured through clear nights at sea. Always there.

She had claimed to be Portuguese. They had lived together in New Bedford for almost two years. That was back in the days when people got in big trouble for such stuff.

He still loved her, whatever that meant, even if he was smart enough to know that both of them were so changed that the memory was the whole thing now. He wished it would leave, but other times, awake but dreaming over the wheel, he was glad that it stayed with him.

[28]

Singleton pictured her the way she had been and did not try to remember the rest. The rest was kid stuff, anyway. She left for Boston saying that she must figure herself out. After a month he had known she would not be back, that in spite of hurt and loneliness and confusion there was nothing much left if she did come back. Naomi. Bible name. A Bible-pounding preacher had caused part of the trouble. Her family had not helped, and neither had the First Coast Guard District—shake it off, and fuck them all.

He had seen her for a few minutes five years later and there were changes. Married to a jackleg lawyer. Her face had looked sharp. Still beautiful, more cultured, and had herself a lawyer and not an enlisted man.

The crest of the mountain was still a thousand yards off. John had been busted up in rolling terrain. If it had happened here he would not have been hurt at all, or else he would have been killed. Either would have been better.

The rig was walking along at twelve miles an hour, the engine riding easy and high. When he reached the crest he drove into the pull-over at the top of the mountain. It was built so trucks could get off the road and allow stacked-up traffic to pass. A view of miles. During the summer there were usually so many tourists parked in the pull-over that a truck had no space. When that happened other tourists tailgated, blew horns and yelled because you could not get over. This time the area was empty. Singleton parked, climbed down and walked fifty yards in front of the truck and looked down into the valley. He was standing on about the same spot that Catherine had stood when they met.

The valley was a long way down and lay in beginning darkness. Her house was a white spot in the gloom. The valley spun out between the hills in a kind of dogleg, narrowing where it seemed to enter a hollow in the distance, and then spreading a few miles further under the face of another range. In dry seasons the stream puddled along a broad channel and seemed ridiculous. Now Singleton was glad for the channel. There was enough water running off that it would otherwise flood.

The hills rose in long chains. They were not very high, the range from Canada all the way down was nothing for height compared to the Rockies, but they were better mountains. The

[29]

Rockies always looked scalped.

Mist hung across the tops of the hills and sealed the valley which lay like a huge room walled by hills and roofed by cloud. There was misting rain. The valley was dark but still green. A warm smell of plant rot and plant growth filled the air. It rode an updraft. He watched for movement and thought that there was a smudge of smoke coming from the chimney of her house. Mist, maybe. The fireplace would feel nice.

Singleton realized that he was standing hunched over, his shoulders down like an old man. He snapped them back, explaining to himself that he had not been so tired in years. He thought again of the fireplace. He was not sure that he wanted to go down into the valley, or sure that he wanted to see her. He was not certain that she could even arouse him, at least not for the right reasons. He wanted to love her, and if a fireplace was all there was to it, he had better keep going on down the road.

Sometimes when a man was tired he got sort of calm. Nothing much mattered either good or bad. Death did not matter and neither did going to bed with a woman. Maybe what he was feeling was all reaction. For the last hour he had thought of nothing but death and sex.

Death and a couple of women, not sex.

He held one of his hands before him and saw that it was not shaking except for a fine tremor of fatigue. A good thing people could not see each other's thoughts. He took a last look at the valley from the place where she had stood. Then he walked back to the rig and climbed up.

As he came off the mountain he gripped the wheel too hard and his arm began to shake. He eased up. The night seemed to come fast as he headed into the valley. He rolled it against the gears, tapped the brake, the air hissing in bursts because only a fool braked straight away on a mountain.

"Catherine," he said. Her voice did not come and he did not feel much. He tapped the brake too hard and had to catch the trailer with both the wheel and the trailer brake. The beginning jackknife frightened him.

Her house was at the mouth of a hollow. The forest surrounded it, and downhill to the left was the stream. It was nearly flooding the road. The good part was the small concrete bridge. Before he crossed he stopped the truck. It looked as strong as ever.

The worst part was the driveway. It took a long bend across what had once been a lower pasture. If he pulled in he had to back out, bending the entrance to hook the trailer onto the road. If he backed in the getting out was easier. He made it with only one pull-up and was glad that he was not backing blindside. His depth perception seemed off. He did not know if he could have made it blindside.

Once the rig was straight it was easy to follow the gradual bend of the road. He did not see Catherine until he was stopped and closing the rig down. She was there, smiling, waiting for him in the light mist and rain.

She looked like an awkwardly tall young girl. Her coat was bulky around the narrowness of her face. Her black hair was swept back along the sides of her face and tucked in under the coat. It was mostly covered by a rain hat. He worked quickly. She was on her toes, looked to be dancing in the rain. Some of the feeling he had needed to get him off the mountain finally arrived.

He climbed down and turned to her. Her face was wet from the rain and her mouth was wet. She kissed him and he found a reserve of strength and picked her up, holding her and pleasured by the touches. Her hat fell off and the rain misted about them. For a moment it seemed to him that they nearly merged. It was a feeling he remembered from a younger time, before the world got old with dead dreams and broken men and pavement and mistakes. The shake in his arms seemed about to start back up. He stood her on the ground and she leaned against him.

"I love to see you, I do." Now she was holding his hand and at the same time pulling away, reaching down to retrieve her hat. It made him lonesome and he did not know why.

Always they were a little formal at first. It took time to get acquainted, to accept the motionlessness of this place, the feeling of intelligence about this place that he did not understand. You could remember that she was beautiful while you were out there. You could remember her need and her openness. What took time, every time, was the incredible fact of her, her presence, and that she wanted him. He had no words that he could put to it because the experience went beyond his words. The memory of the dead child came and went, and the memory of rain. Years of weather.

[31]

Years of wind. He pulled her close to him like he was afraid of losing her, and then he made himself hold her easy because he was afraid of frightening her.

"Welcome home," she said. She pulled at his arm and then took his hand and laughed more than talked as they walked toward the house.

THE voices talked across his sleep. Often he lay half in and half out of dream, feeling and analyzing at the same time. He would find words that he could not speak later, because the words were also pictures. The feelings would ride high through the pictures and kaleidoscopic faces; places and thoughts would range and he would understand things about himself that he did not understand while waking. Sometimes he was right in it, and at other times he was an observer, outside and watching himself. When that happened he felt that he was smiling and the smile was ironic.

He had done every goddamn thing in the world that he was supposed to do and he had done it right. No wonder he was ironic; because what was really *right* was something you could never explain to anyone, maybe even yourself. You tried to love them right, and you worked; you made the ships run and the trucks, and you saved people from dying so they could take time to die someplace else, and you hardly ever bitched about it, and you lent people money.

"Catherine Elizabeth," she had told him laughing. "It sounds grim. Don't use the Elizabeth."

He did though, under his breath, or muttering it to himself down the deserted midnight roads with the song of the tandem humming against the blow and roar of the diesel. In a way the whole story was the road, maybe the whole story of the whole country was the road, and he said the Elizabeth into the whistle of the night wind around the west coasts. He said, "Catherine Elizabeth," holding it as a shield against the vibration that meant tire or wheel bearing about to go. He loved her better than he had hoped. Every time you lost a woman you lost something permanent, even when you gained something else.

Sometimes he tried to tell her about that one important and loving thing. It had to do with magic. Of all people she should understand magic, but then, he was too embarrassed to ever use that word.

She tried to understand. When he stumbled for words while lying beside her the trying made both of them sad. He saw her separately then, not with her usual tall beauty, dark hair flying and the smile that could come with a sudden flash and glow. On nights when they lay warm together she seemed like a different woman.

How to tell it?

You woke and sometimes it was dark out, sometimes dawning. Usually it was dawning. He did not know why. He was always sleepy just before dawn, all guys got sleepy then. Once the sun was up it was okay.

It would either be cold with snow, or hot if you were south in summer. The cold was better. Your belt would be loose and you had emptied your pockets and stuffed your money under the pad of the sleeper. The rough blankets brought from the last ship were scratchy against the scratchiness of your face. When you rolled over and looked under the curtain the wheel would be standing lonely sentinel without you—and the wheel was alive. Through the windshield was the snow. The chill of the cab bit you as you stretched an arm, then rubbed sleep from your eyes.

It took a minute or two every time. L.A., Denver, Minneapolis, New York? The veined red and blue lines of the routes, emptying you here, there, thrusting to the heart of Oklahoma or the cold face of Vermont.

He would remember where he was and lie still. There would usually be a truck pulling from the stop. The roar of the gas or diesel engine was easily defined.

"That one's a Cummins. Mack, most likely. Sounds like a triplex. That one's a little Ford." He would lie there loving it and then would climb down into his own cab and slap himself awake. Then he would jump down in the snow and run to the restaurant of the stop in whatever part of the country he had landed.

Sometimes you thought you lived on coffee and he liked it in the big mug-type cups. It came to you steaming and you passed up the handle so you could warm your hands. If the dawn was only just coming you left the restaurant and walked outside to watch, over the plains coming, or over the eastern run of the Appalachians. The mug was a warm spot in the hands, a glow, and the dawn was like quiet music. That was the job, what he felt, could not explain. She tried to understand.

Mystery always hovered about her. He needed no picture pasted to his dash to summon a feeling of actual presence that was never quite as shocking as her actual presence when they met. In that way he saw her often. Because of the job he actually saw her seldom.

"Why? Are you running? Why are you running?"

He would lie silent and hold onto his anger. He would stare into the dark and sort answers and try to be fair and wonder if he really was running.

He remembered men in many stops. Half-recalled conversations, dreamlike always, songs and stillness would finally combine with the road in front, the lights of the truck changing it into a black-and-silver ribbon. Running?

"Do you run from me?" That was her question.

It was a good question. Guys tried to explain. He remembered a man like a thoughtful preacher. In where? West, it had been west.

"Guys like us have something wrong. Something wrong with them. I figured it out."

"Bullshit, I'm okay."

"Sure. But how long did you ever work indoors? Ever have a job where you went in at seven or eight and worked all day and went home?"

"I spent most of my time at sea."

"I don't mean guys are crazy. I mean there are different kinds of guys, and if a man has this thing, this thing to go, I think he'd ought to just quit fightin' it like guys do."

[35]

"I don't fight it. I'd die if I was tied down. I got a feel for the road."

"Everybody says that, and maybe some do, but it's something they learn."

There was always a lousy juke. Jazz, hillbilly, pop and that noisy rock and roll crap that was the latest fad. When it was late and the sleep came at you, you turned on the radio. Through the static out of Tennessee or Georgia a rocking voice combined with a drawl to sell you classical records and pills for female troubles.

He remembered things he could not explain. The sadness, the thin and unforgiving look in an otherwise fat waitress's eyes, or the joy that took men sometimes when the weather was hell and it was everybody pulling his own red wagon. Like, he would think, a guy jackknifing on a long grade, and you going by with the snow a forest of white, singing your fool head off because your drive was spinning and you did not dare stop. Knowing with the laughing as you watched the guy walk around his rig that at any minute you could be the next one setting out flares.

He remembered things he wished he did not know.

Other conversations. In stops all over the country, and especially the big ones going in up north, lonely men came in and eased themselves along counters and sometimes talked too much.

"I go five, maybe six weeks. Just hate to get laid while I'm on the road."

Sometimes the girls were in the restaurants or bars just waiting. You found a girl more quiet than the rest and spoke polite and careful. That almost always got it. Then dinner, a show or drinking, but you steered away from too much drinking. Sometimes the girl did not.

And once, which was plenty, there was the girl and himself and Naomi seemed there too. And he imagined that the girl's skin did not glow white in the dark and that that small curl belonged to Naomi. He shut his eyes and touched the curl. Then the woman did something real peculiar and particular, and then cried and took him inside her. And he knew that no matter what it said on the register he had signed, there were four people in that bed.

Others just talked too much.

"Had a girl in Toledo, looked like my old lady. She came in all dressed up, stockings and hat and all, and sat by herself and I thought it was her and saw finally that it wasn't. I took her out of there and spent company money keeping her away until the weekend was out and we dropped on south."

Sometimes you got into a city you knew and went to a whorehouse. That was easy but it did not hold you for long.

So that when he lay beside Catherine, loving her and knowing that she was the best part of his world, he often wanted to stay. It just was not that easy. A man did not travel so far and work so hard only to quit before he understood the reason for it all. Yet, he wanted to stay. It was only in the mornings, waking, that he knew he could not. The thing about movement was back, the drive was there, to be up, and going, and gone.

He slept beside Catherine and knew that the road continued to run as he slept. The road, if he thought about it, would seem to him the way a trail might seem to her. Or, the road wound out as certainly as did the wool yarn that somehow magically appeared in her hands when she worked at the stubby-looking modern spinning wheel. The yarn itself was like a small trail. In her work area, yarn lay beside the wheel as Singleton slept.

The trails ran around and across the mountains, overgrown sometimes, leading to clearings and abandoned coal roads and mines. The trails seemed to make old etchings across the hills. At times, although Catherine did not suspect it, an occasional hunter or poacher might stand high on the coal roads and look onto her house and pasture. The man would be distracted from the hunt, or perhaps lonely. He would shuck the load from the chamber, leave the lever dangling, and look through the telescope toward her. The house would focus then, like a single spot of directed energy in the great wilderness of the hills. Catherine, had she known it, would not have been the least disturbed. There was no harm in such men for her. The harm was elsewhere, not in North Carolina. She could lie dreaming, as she lay dreaming beside Singleton, in the tranquil belief that life had already offered her all of the harm that was likely to come her way.

She liked the color of dreams. It was almost worth having a bad dream just to see the mixing, swirling, clean-lined and distinct persons that color could be, the voices it could be and the sounds. Color held its own mysteries, more subtle than language. As often as twice a year Catherine would dream dreams in which color talked about itself, explaining and nearly diagramatic. She would wake from those dreams with a sense of loss. What she knew when dreaming did not translate into waking knowledge; and for the past year her dreams had been dull and uncolored.

And when she dreamed of her man, if he was her man, then the impressions doubled up and so did the frustration. In your dreams you could have it all sometimes; the man and the forest and the work. Once she even dreamed that all of it existed and was real and they were making love and talking about whether they should buy a dog, now that he, Singleton, did not have to go on the road anymore. When she woke up that time it had seemed like an almost scandalous dream, but it had made sense while she was dreaming it.

Catherine had pinned her hair before they slept. Now some of it had worked loose and the discomfort woke her. Usually she wore a braid. She rolled over on her back and looked at Singleton who slept facing her. Men were not supposed to be very good looking when they were asleep but this one was beautiful. Even relaxed his mouth was a firm but almost easy line. His hair was thick, graying heavy at the temples and gray-streaked through the middle. She touched his hand beneath the sheet.

It was heavily callused, certainly the biggest hand, thick and strong, that had ever touched her. The best part was that it was a gentle and exciting hand that moved exactly right—or else she was exactly right for the way it moved; a good big man who went his own way, and that was all right as long as that way kept leading home, which she was, if only he could see it. She even expected that she loved him, and sometimes she actually thought that she did love him. It was hard to tell when you did not see the man often, which meant that you always had knots in your belly when he did get there. If she did love him it was altogether different than what she had felt with her first man. Two men were not very many cases to make any firm judgements off of—from—it was hard to judge.

She unpinned her hair and the sheet fell partly away. She watched the movement of her breasts, which were probably too small but he liked them a lot. She moved her arms. The breasts moved, the small nipples erected as she watched. She ran her right hand across her stomach which was flat and tense. Last night had been pretty good, but it was probably not as good as she could do for herself, by herself. He had been exhausted. The lovemaking had not lasted long. He had evaded her with his body in the same way he evaded her when they talked. A good man, but sometimes he either lied or kept things to himself. What he should do, right now if he was honest, was wake up and make love to her until she was sore, the way it had happened once, and then they could go for a walk when the sun was higher. The valley would be filled with light steam. He would hold her hand and help her over logs that blocked the slick trail and they would probably slip and get muddy and clean themselves by the stream and then—even if she was sore—she had to reject the thought. He would not be comfortable without clothes if they were not inside the house.

Maybe she could get out of bed without waking him. She could make coffee. By then the sun would be coming through the window. She could sit beside him with the sheet falling any way it wanted. They could laugh and drink the coffee and he would take his large, callused hands and move them on her. She would hold his head with her fingers in his thick hair and pull it down between her legs like she had done that one other time that went so well. Her mind was as tense as her belly. She wished she knew more about men. She wished she had known a hundred of them instead of having been so shy. She would not have taken a chance with this one except she was so lonely; and because he talked not just quiet, but easy, and because he did not make her self-conscious, and because he liked her hair, which she could tell even before he said it.

She brushed one of her nipples with the back of her hand. The world was changing, wasn't it? Of course, and so all of this would never do. She placed one hand on the inside of his leg and pressed easy but firm. After a few seconds he woke up but he did not seem startled. Then he smiled, which he did not do very much, and reached to pull her close.

She had been bold, and it seemed like life was going to charge her for that. Now she felt shy.

"Can you stay," she said. "Can you stay for awhile with me?"

Maybe he was not yet really awake. His eyes seemed nearly fearful for a moment. His hand that touched her gently along the small ribs momentarily stiffened, and then his touch was again gentle; but then he began to move his hand, like he was drawing away.

"I didn't mean that," she whispered. "What you think, that I'm charging something for loving you."

"Yes," he said. "No, I mean. I mean yes I understand." He was suddenly as shy as she was and it gave her confidence. She laughed. "We're silly. Touch me here."

When you were loved, and when things had gone all right after all, the coffee tasted better and the morning was more alive. By the time the sun was fully over the hill they were together in the kitchen and Catherine told herself that she felt nicer, more comfortable with him than ever before. The kitchen was a special and personal place. Working spaces were like that, sometimes. The curtains were faded blue, made of remnants. The patterned linoleum was worn, experienced looking, and a rose-colored piece of fabric served as a cloth for the pine kitchen table. Wild roses in a dimestore vase dropped petals on the table. The funny, almost gimmicky wallpaper she had hung so many years ago was flaking behind the high-oven gas stove, fading windmills of red turning pink; and a sidearm bookcase held a tumble of patterns, graph paper, partly completed and abandoned notions for weaving; the whole a random design of work that pleased her. He would not understand what he was seeing, and she wondered if he was even seeing it, but she was glad it was happening.

He looked quite rested this morning, and yet the fatigue she always saw about him, accepted as part of him, lay on his face like the ease of wisdom. The only time she ever mentioned anything about it, he had reckoned it was the road. The miles made it seem that way, he thought.

And he was always more distant or more formal when he was dressed. He was in charge of something, even when nothing was happening. Right now he wasn't in charge of anything but a coffee cup, and yet, watching him, she could see motion. Like going to a museum and looking at Flemish painters who could put movement into a moored boat. Her mind automatically registered the lines of the face, used mental fingers to guess the experience that lay behind the weathered furrows. Old farmers got this way sometimes. Weather and wind. She thought of her own face, knew that it would be this way someday, but she hoped that day was a long way off.

"My work is going well," she said. "How's yours?"

"Just busting gears." He was looking through the window, sitting at an angle where he could see the back end of his truck. "Something came up, though." She watched his face, saw concealment, and then saw the concealment lift as he said what he obviously did not want to say.

"I have to go in tonight. I'll be back as soon as I can."

Tonight. She had counted on three days, at least. She stood staring at him and wondered why he bothered to stop at all.

"That's close to being insulting," she said. "I hope there's a real good reason."

"There is."

It was a good reason to him. She already knew something of people named Grace and John and Ben. She knew of a wreck, and that John was disabled, and Ben was having a hard time. Now Singleton was being called home. It was real to him. As she listened she understood more and more how unreal it was to her.

Her true home was the forest. When she was in the forest she did not have to take the rest of the world seriously; the traffic and radio chatter and the churches and banks of a world that was constantly threatening to set itself aflame. Usually she controlled her dismay pretty well. Sometimes she did not control it at all, and when that happened then only the mountains and forests could calm her.

Most days she did not even think of confusion. Most days she could remain in her private self, and so most days could be lived moderately well.

But he was sitting there bossing a cup of coffee and talking in perfectly normal tones about grown up men playing with oversized toys.

5

ON 127 south of Lawrenceburg, Kentucky, Singleton's rig lurched heavily as it crested a rise. He caught another gear while the van jumped behind the tractor like a rolling vessel with the sea on its quarter. His truck straightened out howling and fled north down the empty road, silhouetted against the coming dawn.

He rubbed his eyes. The coffee was not helping. His time was good.

He rolled the window for the cool air. Later it would be hot. He turned on the radio. A Louisville station broadcast fair weather. He switched to another station. News. Congress had the hots to build some kind of new rocket because their first one broke. He secured the radio.

Far down the road another truck appeared oncoming. Before he could read the lettering on the van he had the line marked by the color of the rig. As they approached Singleton eased slightly back on his power. Meeting the truck he hit the power full. The crash of air rocked the van. You could get dead, quick, if you met another rig without applying power. It was automatic, something you knew all of the time without thinking about it. He grinned and thought that the other driver had not answered his hello. A new man. A guy who was rocking over the two-lane scared, his truck driving him, so that he had no time to lift the necessary finger to wave. So many guys were turnpike cowboys. Get them on a regular road, there was a kind of dirty humor to it. Singleton thought he would like to give the guy a ride. There were pictures in his mind of how his rig must have looked, running the four-lane above Knoxville, fifty-five in a forty-five-mile zone.

A police car had been waiting. At another spot a state car was parked. He had not cut speed and the police did not follow. Good cops never bothered you for speeding. As long as you were not weaving they figured you were just doing a job and knew how.

The night spots were closing down. An all-night restaurant was a blare of light. Singleton dropped a gear and coasted. It was a good spot for a wreck. The juicers would be out.

Above Knoxville the road changed to narrow two-lane except for broad passing areas on the mountains. In those places he moved the gears down, then further down. The truck roared like it was boasting. He moved up the mountains, sometimes at no more than twenty miles an hour. On the downside the sound was different and there was a drum in the exhaust. It rattled into the valleys.

In his imagination he traveled in a deserted park. The mountains hulked on each side, dark with pine, oak and maple. Occasionally he met other trucks. There was a rise of yellow light beyond a crest and a burst of headlights on low beam.

Had it been day Singleton would have waved his left hand to the oncoming trucks. In the darkness he did not wave, but twice when a truck passed that he recognized, he flicked his markers after the truck was going away. Had he flicked them before passing it would have meant the same thing as a right-hand wave. Slow down, or road not clear. It might have meant roadway wet, or police ahead. But the night had been free of hazard and he made only the friendly wave with the lights.

His truck thundered across the tops of ridges and dived screaming into deep valleys as he built revolutions to throw against the next grade. He ran Knoxville to LaFollette. After LaFollette the bad road became worse. The night was clear but for the next twenty-six miles Singleton sat a bit higher in his seat.

He checked the night and the nighttime road. From the top of the cab his spotlight swept, searching, probing, as he asked the nature of curves. He inquired of the road surface. He hunted animals. A cow or horse was dangerous. A large dog or deer was bad. A full-grown hog was suicide. He walked the spotlight up and down the road reading the night. On downhills the rig fell screaming into the black valleys at seventy.

He lived with Catherine's smile for minutes. With her sorrow. She had not wanted him to leave. Then, on a short but fast downhill, he caught Pat's excited grin.

Blowing Chief, going to blow

The voice was all through his mind. The wind blasted the mirrors like a hurricane wind. Like the wind when Pat was hurt and Singleton was only maybe not to blame. He tried to push it away, the tall form of the kid held by the collar with a boat hook, face washing blood into the sea and Singleton struggling to help, trying to get out of the blankets they had wrapped him in. Those guys had almost lost Pat. And Pat permanently blind. And Singleton not able to do a thing. Because what could you do when you could neither bury a man, teach him or give support. "We did some good," Singleton told him. A surge of emotion caught him. He kicked the rig hard into a curve knowing that he was a fool. The trailer started walking. He caught it and his throat was tight. Close.

Above LaFollette he bypassed Jellico and left Tennessee, remembering that he had forgotten to fuel but would be charged for the tax anyway. There were more and more regulations lately. Now the states were checking your logs so they would be sure to get their share of tax. With that kind of business it was not like him to slip up. With people it seemed that just living meant mistakes.

And the biggest mistake was not getting over what was done.

"It's blown and gone," he told Pat. His voice was loud. The tires thumped and sang. It was good to be with her, Catherine, but it was good to be alone. You could admit that Pat had been like your son. He shook his head. He thought that a lot of times. It was embarrassing even in the presence of nothing but the truck.

You could still think it though, like you thought so many private things when you were unwinding the narrow, nighttime road. He had never really had a family, never met any interesting woman who even wanted a family. A ship's crew was not a family. A man spent too much time alone. No surprise that you sometimes had private thoughts.

He rapped out a short strip of interstate and the diesel settled to a steady, driving throb. The interstate did not last.

Singleton reeled off the night-covered towns. He boomed into Williamsburg following the river. There was a long pull to the top of the hill and then a long run of fair road. Corbin folded behind his driving wheels; and above London he drove through Bernstadt to swing high left, then right, and pushed over the long, eighty-mile-an-hour run of Dive Bomber Hill where other men in other trucks had died. There was a long pull on the next mountain and the next jump to Livingston.

He tallied the towns. Mount Vernon and the brightly lighted stop; he blew on by and down the hill to gather in Crab Orchard, Stanford, Danville. For a time, outside of Harrodsburg, he stopped.

The stop was on the left at the top of a hill in the manner of rolling country. From a crest two miles away he could see the blue-and-white glow of the signs. The paler glow of the town lay at the top of the next series of hills. He pulled onto the graveled lot. A freight was pulled over by the road, a furniture van was parked further down. He rolled his truck to the pumps.

A crippled man limped across the lot. He came from the shed and moved with a raggedness that showed he was not used to going slow. This was raw and new. He picked a tire billy from the pump rack and began hammering on tires. Singleton climbed down and estimated the amount of fuel he would need for Kentucky. He did not recognize the attendant. The man was wearing a red plaid shirt, one shoulder riding high, bunching up under the fabric and pulling the shirt sideways.

"I check my own," he told the man. He took the billy and walked around the truck.

"Fuel," the guy called. Under the fluorescent lights he did not look old. Maybe thirty-five. Maybe been in a wreck. Was everybody in the world hurt?

"Forty in the right tank. She'll take it."

"Do you want a slip?"

"Two copies." Singleton knelt beside a tire on the rear drive axle. There was a dark stain. He rubbed it. There was no petroleum smell when he held fingers to his nose. Animal. He had felt no thump. A glancer.

"These Kenworths are nice," the man said. He had fuel going in and was between the trailer and the cab checking the air lines. A good, careful guy.

"I like it." Singleton turned to go.

"Had an Emeryville, myself. She was pretty good."

"They are." The guy wanted to talk. Singleton backed off. There would be a story. He did not want to hear. He turned quickly.

"Show discount?" The guy was starting to write in the receipt book. His voice sounded like he was backing off from telling stories.

"Let the bastards sweat for it." He called it to the guy. Truckers got anywhere from two to five cents discount on a gallon, and the tax boys knew it. They couldn't prove it if it was not on the receipt. It was a few hundred dollars a year saved. Congress would just buy more busted rockets, anyway, to scare Russians.

The restroom was clean. The poets had been at work. A dark crayon had been used to letter a sign that read, "Coal drivers, earn while you learn. Call Roadway Express, Winston-Salem." He grinned. A coal guy had crossed out "way" and written in "hog." Over the sink was a reminder of the long pull approaching the stop from the north. It said, "Goddamn my truck." In a way it was pretty funny.

The restaurant was large. He stood outside wanting to go back and ask the crippled guy if he would have coffee—didn't want the story—guy probably had to stay on the islands anyway. Inside two drivers were sitting at the counter. He recognized one of them. A girl named Shirley was behind the counter. Each time he stopped it was a surprise to see Shirley still there. She was a good woman who was having a hard time and he figured it would beat her. The truth was that she attracted him, and he could not even say why. The truth was that he figured he would get this woman thing settled when he was dead.

It was safe to be attracted to Shirley, though. She was married. Singleton had a rule about married women. They had to have a note from their husbands.

He opened the door. She smiled at him and waved. The guy he knew turned. He was husky with corn-colored hair tangled

[46]

around his ears, eyes thin blue under yellow brows that bushed out. His lips were thick like a Negro. There was sleep around his mouth and he drank at the coffee like he was trying to wash the sleep away. His chambray shirt was a mess.

"I ain't seen you in one hell of a time."

"Rusty," Singleton said. "You look rusty."

"I overslept. I got to git."

"Shirley would have waked you."

"She was busy." Rusty shifted his glance to the other driver, then turned to face Singleton and wrinkled his nose like he had a whiff of something smelly. "I was just hangin' around."

"Uh huh. Still running south?"

"I'm here ain't I?"

"Almost," Shirley told him. She came from behind the counter to sit on a stool beside them. She was not very tall and was a little bit blocky, but she had a nice face and narrow ankles like you did not often see on a short girl. "You're getting there," she told Rusty. "You were a tired guy for awhile."

The other driver half turned and looked down the counter. He was short and muscular. His black eyes were dilated and his black hair needed cutting. His nose bent where it had been broken some time. Under the black hair his saucer eyes seemed to go all the way up to his forehead.

"More coffee."

Shirley got up and refilled the cup. Then she went to the kitchen.

"I got to go." Rusty headed for the door, then stopped. "Heard you jumped a mess down by Asheville."

Singleton considered. There were no secrets on the road. A twenty-four-hour-a-day, sixty-mile-an-hour telegraph. "It wasn't much. Don't even want to think about it."

"I guess. Man, I got to git."

"Take it easy," Singleton told him.

"That stupid truck knows this here road. Won't pull any other road, but this road." Rusty opened the door and left. Soon there was the high rushing whine of a diesel starting. Shirley came back from the kitchen and sat by Singleton. She put the coffeepot on the counter.

They listened to Rusty running through his gears. "Always

sounds nice," Singleton said. "Cool morning like this. Light not far away."

"I suppose." She reached her right hand across to rub her left arm just above the elbow. Her wrist was close in to her body and pushed her left breast upward. He figured it was conscious.

The short driver was nervous. He hopped from the stool and walked to the juke. The mechanism turned.

Leave these blues behind me, let that tandem call

The juke was turned low. The guitar was restless under the strained country voice. The record was a fraud.

"How are things?"

"Like always. Jim's on the road by now." She looked at the clock. "Be in at noon, leave out day after. We make the mortgage payment."

"You'll have that done soon."

"Sooner, if he'd drop the shack job in Sedalia."

"That's new."

"Just to you. To me it's getting pretty goddamn old."

Left a girl in Pittsburgh, cried to see me go the short driver sang with the juke. "Ever been to Pittsburgh?"

"I'll live and die in Harrodsburg."

The driver's jaw sagged. He snapped his mouth firm. "It's all the same," he told her. "All the same anyhow. Everywhere."

"What kind are you on?" Singleton tried to make it sound like a joke. You could not always tell what guys on drugs would do. Some guys carried their guns on them.

"Chicago," the driver said.

"Headed north?" Singleton looked straight ahead. Shirley stayed quiet.

"Birmingham."

The juke stopped. The restaurant was silent.

"Run ask the guy on the pumps does he have clean rags. I messed some up."

"I've got some old dish towels."

"Scoot."

She left. Singleton turned to the driver who watched her leave.

"Split tails is all the same."

The guy was in bad shape. Singleton made his voice soft. "Footballs? That stuff can kill a guy."

"Her old man's gonna kill me."

"Her?" The guy was high, okay, but he sure was low on women. Singleton wondered if the guy thought he invented it.

"The next one which is maybe in Birmingham, or the one after, or the kid in Bluefield that was the one before. Same all over."

"A long way to go, Birmingham. Seven or eight hours with the roads." He had to move him out.

The driver laughed. It was bitter with an edge of hysteria. "Don't shit me mister—as soon as I finish this joe." He slurped at the coffee then stood. "They're all the same. I'm gone." He walked across the room. As he reached the door Shirley came in. "Sure you've never been to Chicago?" He went out.

Singleton walked past her and stood watching through the window. A high, slab-sided furniture rig pulled past. A marker light was out. The van was mud-splashed. A gas rig. His own truck looked pretty there, shining and reflecting the blue island lights, solid like that rock of ages. When the furniture rig pulled into the roadway Singleton returned to the counter.

"Know him?"

"No," she said. "Furniture guys. You hardly ever see them more than once, not down this way. Indianapolis, maybe."

"Be hallucinating next. I've seen so many tore-up guys."

"Try living with one."

"It's that bad?"

"Let's sit in a booth. I know every scratch on this counter." She stood. Going away she still looked blocky. Her short hair did not give any length to her back. Singleton watched and then followed with the coffee pot. They sat in a booth where they could see through the windows. He looked at the girl. About twenty-seven. Pretty but losing it.

"You're tired."

"Sure," she said. "And a little bit sick. Up all night with guys coming in and out. Goddamn dope, smelly guys, jukebox, all the time somebody talking trucks."

"You are tired."

She smiled. Her mouth was wide. Her lips were more full in the smile. It told him something about her. He had seen it in other women, even tough ones. The smile and the look in her eyes showed that some part of her was private and nice. Somewhere in

[49]

her mind she was still thinking good. Her husband was not a trucker, he was a truck bum. She worked too hard but some part of her was free.

"Sorry for myself like a kid. Sorry for the guy that just left. Sorry for everybody, maybe, but mostly for myself."

"I'm just sorry it's bad."

She rubbed her eyes. Her dress was white work clothes and had a spot of something on one sleeve. Small hands and well cared for. There were no wrinkles on her hands but there were some around her eyes. "Look," she said, and pointed to the floor. The floor was dark brown and tan tiles laid in a checkerboard.

"Nine hundred forty-five squares." She motioned the length of the room. "Headed that way I can get maybe seventeen steps. Head across and I get eleven or twelve. Thirty by forty-two. Back of the counter."

"Take some time off."

"Is it really the same as he said. Is it really the same all over."

"It is for him."

"Maybe for me too."

"I don't know. I doubt. It's the way you look at things. For me New York is always different from Georgia."

"Can't even understand why we talk. I just know I'm lonesome and mad and tired. Sit here and guys come through; 'Toronto,' they say, 'then we dropped on down through New York.' Or they say 'Bakersfield,' or 'Billings' or 'Duluth.' " She looked up and her faced showed confusion and unhappiness. "Never been any-where. Never even seen an ocean."

"I saw one day before yesterday." He was startled. Somehow the waitresses all seemed to be a part of the road. You moved around a lot. You saw them sometimes, the way you met guys you knew. It was hard to realize that she was a part of it and still did not go. He thought of Catherine, how different she felt. Catherine was glad to stay. Worse, she insisted on staying.

"Women get cheated." He turned, ready to slide from the booth, knowing that he had to go.

"Not always. Staying ought to be all right if there's a reason."

"And there's no reason?"

"No good one. I'm going to leave."

Singleton hesitated. Once he would have thought it his place to say no. There was a time when he advised people, when he gave an opinion. Instead he reached for his notebook, then wrote the address in Indiana. He gave it to her. "Best to have a friend in court." He wondered if she knew that he did not want to lose her, even if nothing ever happened between them.

She stood, sliding from the booth, and touched his arm. A nice thing; the touch put a shot of excitement through him.

"Why?" She folded the paper.

She was young. "Sometimes you need a friend," he told her. "I got to pull Louisville and drop."

He turned, went through the doorway, found the crippled attendant and paid for the fuel. Then he climbed up and pulled. She waved at the rig through the window. It made him sad to think that she had never seen an ocean. Still, busses left town every day.

Dawn found him outside Lawrenceburg with only seventy miles to go. Ten miles beyond Lawrenceburg he connected with raw interstate for Louisville. The truck roared on the new ramp. He had the flashers going for the lane change. They threw a glisten of traffic yellow against the bottom of the mirror. With the day at his back he pushed through the gears. His truck had fifteen gears to pull eighteen wheels from two drive axles. A song of speed cried out from the great wave of its passing. He drove with care. Somewhere along the road, when his mind was right, he thought he would hear Catherine's voice.

6

WARPING by yourself was no joke even when the loom was your good friend, as this old jack certainly was. It was probably the only old one of its kind in all of North Carolina, and the man who made it must have been proud. Almost all of the old looms were counter-balance, because people in those days did not have the tools or the time to do this kind of job.

Catherine imagined him sometimes, and how it would have been. Him choosing the beautiful, tight-grained maple. The best rifle-stock maple. How he would wait, and the wood would wait, him sealing the ends and feeling it season against the time when he could start. The old people said that wood had to go through four seasons before you could put a tool to it. She guessed, knowing the loom, the smooth, hand-worn surfaces, that he had known better and had seen the wood through a great number of seasons.

He had probably been one of the Germans who arrived after the Scots-Irish. She imagined him compacted and square-fisted, at work before the fireplace through the long winters: the maple curling delicately from a small hand plane, the close-fitting joints planned and stressed so that the warp added its strength to the

[52]

wood in a sort of music of fine grains, one kind laid as closely as the other. If he was not German then he must have been a Swede. She could still feel in the loom his delicate, exact touch and the close-coupled imagination that thought of production. That is why he had gone to an underhand beater instead of an overhead. It was not the best rug loom in the world for that reason, but for fabric it was a masterpiece. For hangings and belts and yardage it was as good as any four-harness ever made.

And she imagined the woman, too, sitting beside him before the fireplace while the wind howled and called in the hollow. She would be working in the wool, in the flax, and spinning the cotton warp from the short fibers with fingers more intelligent than an ancient goddess of the hearth.

Yes, she thought of them, and while she admired and respected and even loved the man in a way, she wished it was the woman who was here to help her with a twelve-yard warp. Getting equal stress on the warp was crucial, and if Singleton were here she would show him how. She would actually pull back on the warp, leaning against it and trusting it like sailors trusted their rope. It would take her heels and body and every one of her hundred and twenty-seven pounds digging in to make it right. As it was, she had to use weights, which were impersonal.

"I remember you," she whispered to Singleton who had been gone for ten hours. "When I am with you I remember you." To her the words sounded romantic, even if they were true. The problem was that there was not all that much to remember.

"What do you do?" He had asked that on their first day together, that is, the first day they had made love. She had lain beside him feeling the movement and stretch of being open. It was one of the best times, for she felt open and intact at the same time. When he got soft and withdrew, he had gently taken his fingers and pressed her labia together. Like he was thankful. That had been the most personal thing about it.

Or maybe the best part had been the clean lines of their bodies side by side, the changing form and shape of his body as they made love. She liked the light on his gray-haired chest, the shadows across his muscles, his face. There was a turn and bend and twist and flow to sex that could be distracting sometimes because the shape of it was so beautiful. No painter could do nudes unless that painter was good at sex and loved it for itself and its shape.

He had asked that question, "What do you do?" He had asked it that first day. It had been nearly easy to answer then, but she would answer it differently now.

What did she do? Well, she resented him for one thing. If you were going to love somebody the way he said he loved her, then you should be with them. Sometimes she felt guilty about her resentment, and sometimes the resentment even flared into terrible anger, but never when he was around. She did not resent him when he was with her.

Of course, that was not what he had been asking about. He was asking about her work, as if doing was the most important thing in the world. He had stayed that night and another day and another night. She was afraid and happy, and she had been lonely in advance. She knew he was going to leave.

"I teach and weave. People buy the weaving." People from a long way off bought the weaving, because she was good at it and had been building a reputation for years. She was not going to tell him that. She survived by skill and economy, and she did not have to go tearing around the country in some truck to do it, either.

"Teach. Like kids?" He had been impressed. His eyes were blue but not light. It was a response that made her feel harmed for him. He thought himself ignorant because he had never been to college.

"There's nothing wrong with it," she said, "teaching kids. You get to travel. I teach art at three different schools."

Another time when he had been here, the third time they made love, to be exact, they had afterward dressed and walked through the pasture in front of her house. They had walked to the stream, and she had felt the presence of the land and the forest, although she thought he did not. Even then he had still been trying to figure out who she was by the work she accomplished.

"It must mean a lot, teaching kids." The furrows in his face always went deeper when he was studying on something. It was a lean face, or would be if the hair was not so short. She watched the furrows and learned to count on them later when she tried to understand him. Anger did not deepen the furrows. He never showed anger, never, but sometimes he would be quiet and the furrows would seem strained. The same old problem. She did not understand about the road, and she did not want to, either.

"Teaching means something," she told him, "but it's not the whole world." She told herself that she was not, absolutely not, going to talk about the schools in North Carolina. Or anywhere.

And why did he care about work, anyway? She was thirty-five years old, and had never really lived with a man. She had been married, but she and the man had only been together for six months. Then he was drafted. Then, like a puff of mist vanishing in the hollow, he was dead, like he had never existed. In Germany.

This time when Singleton visited they had not talked about work at all. They had talked about his brother John. There was a kind of hopelessness and sadness in Singleton's voice. She even thought she heard guilt, although he had nothing to feel guilty about. His voice had held confusion. He had not talked about work, but he seemed to be wondering about the meaning of his own work, if it meant anything.

This time he had not even stayed very long. A night and most of a day. Then gone. She slept one more night alone.

She told herself that she too had a family. She had a brother, over in Winston-Salem. She supposed that she should not resent Singleton, not this time. He had a good reason to be gone.

The problem was that she did resent him, and another problem was having to warp by yourself. It made no difference how equal your weights were, the stress was going to try to come out uneven. If he were here, helping, then the stress would be equal all the way across the warp.

7

DON'T *drive tired, no load is worth it, no schedule you set or anybody sets is worth it*

Singleton considered his brother. The tandem was a roar and whistle along the road, the stacks broadcasting a steady blur of hammers.

"Not worth it," his brother said. "I didn't build this thing making very many mistakes."

"You sure as shit made one." The wreck that caught John and Ben had looked like most of the burn wrecks you saw and which always made your stomach clench up, and made you more grieving than afraid.

"I'm tired enough," Singleton said to no one in particular. He was not staring at road, no mistake there. He felt no numbness in the lower part of his neck, but he had been driving for ten hours with only four pullovers. Only the last one had taken any time.

You could grieve for your brother like it was hard to grieve for anybody else. He had not even known John very well until he started the trucking. When that happened they got like real brothers ought to be. Talking things out, making plans and figuring for next year and the year after.

A good man. A good man. It was just crazy how bad luck hit.

[56]

By the time Singleton saw the wreck, a wrecker had pulled it out. The cab was blackened and twisted and melted down with heat; the van was smoked and burned and paint-blistered. A broken hub—but hubs hardly ever broke at speed. Maybe weight shift on the override. The terrain suggested that.

And now he was tired and breaking one of his rules. He estimated an hour to Louisville and at the wrong time for a truck to arrive in any city. Early morning traffic would clog the major routes, but before Louisville there was a rest area and he decided to lay over there for a couple of hours. His speed dropped to sixty-five. The truck was solid in the road. Singleton tried not to relax. The pulse of the drive was too comfortable.

Maybe he should just drop the load and return to Catherine. He could not. He had promised to come in.

His brother John was worse than dead, and John's wife Grace had liquidated the business. Not, he thought, because she was not competent. Women hated trucking, most of them. They hated movement, most of them; but that was changing some. Women hated the ships, but when they loved the men they sometimes pretended to understand about the ships. Catherine did not even pretend.

In his mirrors two automobiles appeared over a crest. He maintained exact lane and speed. They came fast and passed him about seventy-five feet apart.

"You dumb bastards," he told the drivers. The lead car eased to the right and broke its speed. The following car passed the lead car. Singleton backed off and waited for the foolishness to be over. After the passing car swung back into the driving lane the passed car speeded up, running behind the other at less than a hundred feet. The deserted freeway stretched in front with a view of miles. They were running at eighty.

"Don't let them trap you," his brother told him.

When he came from the east, retirement papers and steady retirement money, a guarantee after twenty years in the ships, Singleton had no notion of what he would do. He returned to his brother's farm, the farm that would have been half his if he had stayed. When he got there the land was leased. His brother was not a farmer, either.

They drove up a hard-beaten, graveled lane. In the old barn-

[57]

yard stood two trucks, a GMC tag and a twin-screw Ford. "I have eleven more on the road." His brother had been proud. "The barn is a drive-through. It takes two of them at a time. I changed the doors. We do most of our own work."

The business of trucking, Singleton learned, was done in different ways. His brother did not exactly own a freight line because he did not have the licenses. The government and the big companies and the American Trucking Association pretty well managed to put the freeze on a small operator. John Singleton leased his rigs to other companies and ran his drivers on shares. The first Sunday after he arrived Singleton saw the men head out. He understood why his brother did good business. He knew something about leading men.

The boy, Ben, seemed young to know so much. Singleton listened to him and to his plans with amusement but also with admiration. There was, it occurred to Singleton, a complicated world unlike the simplicity of the ships. Men moved through sequences of action that seemed to have little to do with the work. In fact, about half of it seemed pointless.

"Uncle Charles. We've been waiting. I'll show you dad's new Jimmy."

Ben had been so stuffed with himself and trucks. Later, talked out, he proved to be a nice enough boy. It was just that his pride and seriousness were smart-ass. Then Singleton had remembered himself when his own father bought a new tractor. His father. He thought of him sometimes, but he had not thought of that tractor in years. The whole family was conservative in almost every way. With equipment the family had always been progressive.

Later Ben had the blues. "I have to finish school. Two more years." A tall boy. Dark-haired and blue-eyed like his father and his uncle and his grandfather, brought up in the rigid pattern of rural Indiana that had not changed much in thirty years.

Our text for the day

Singleton heard a dozen voices. Voices of old men and young, passionate, indifferent, hate-filled. The congregated voices recalled many preachers and many Sundays: driving after church along white graveled roads; looking to John's crop, Isaiah's crop, Samuel's crop, and the handiwork of the many saintly named—and they sure could name them—even if the whole entire state of

[58]

Indiana had never produced anything except politicians and corn.

White houses, clean barns. Not a bad place to come from, but that was his mind fooling him; it was a terrible place to come from, but some of the things it had taught were good to know. A man learned early of work.

The men prided themselves on minding their own business. The women, some of them minded the business of everyone. The women then told their husbands all about it so the men could retain that picture of themselves as independent and generous, the nosy, greedy bastards.

He did not know how much it had changed, and he did not know whether it had messed up Ben. At least the kid was responsible, careful and hard working. He was not yet thirty, but now he was in a mess. According to Grace, Ben needed Singleton's help.

He momentarily leaned into the wheel, the way you should not do when you were tired. Dangerous to relax when you were tired. A truck would forgive you more mistakes than any car, but no machine would forgive many mistakes. He sat higher in the seat.

He did not, strictly speaking, know how much the nosy, greedy bastards had messed him up. He had lived a long time away from them. Then he came back and it seemed, sometimes, like he had never left Indiana. Grace could actually make him feel guilty for being on the road while Ben was mending. If he were there helping, she would probably make him feel guilty for not being on the road and working. He again remembered his aunt, who had raised him, and then he thought of that fat woman in that run-down truck stop.

Judgement

It was better to think of Ben and John and what he, Charles Singleton, could do to help.

The three of them, Singleton, John and Ben, had grown with the expanding industry. It was a good time for trucks, and when the new roads got in the railroads were going to be dead. The basic rigs had continued to make up the bulk of the fleet, but now they were joined by tall Whites, square-nose Autocars and stubby Macks. The rush of diesels filled the barn that had been old when the first Model A puttered beside the stalls. Now the stalls were gone.

When you're pointed home and hit seventy the bulldog turns around and starts motioning you on over his shoulder

He did not know where that one came from, did not remember that voice at all.

Then the bust had come. Wreck. Father paralyzed and mindless. Son broken and in a hospital for months.

"Better now," Grace said the last time Singleton called. "But he's worked up in his mind. I'll tell you later. Come in."

Traffic increased. Automobiles hummed by at high speed. The one thing he could not control was some damned fool running under his trailer. The drive rose with a wail. His truck ran easy. He could get a lot more speed.

"You can wreck any machine," his brother said. "You can wreck a lever. Equipment has an efficient range. Use it in that range."

A far cry from the Coast Guard. There you used the best you had in equipment and in yourself to meet emergencies, and hoped that both would hold. Civilian life was geared to avoid emergencies. That was the difference.

Still, it was a good notion. He had always taken care of equipment. He took care of the truck. It was not five years old and had been driven over four hundred thousand miles. It was good for more than twice that much. When he learned the business he had wanted his own rig. That was natural.

Some of the big ones go a million plus miles

Any time you spend over twenty thousand you get a good one

His Kenworth, with additions, was sitting right around twenty-two thousand not counting the trailer.

Cost lots more than a house, they give you twenty years to pay for a house

He had paid it out in a little over the four-year contract. The truck would last a long time and always be valuable.

The rest area was on a far hill. Singleton began to take off speed, his signals flashing as he rolled in following the truck lane. The place was nearly empty. A tractor with a flatbed going deadhead stood at the far end of the parking area. A small house-trailer hauler out of Elkhart was pulled over, the truck looking bobtail and foolish without a trailer. It was a hell of a way to make a living. Singleton had never pulled a house trailer and never wanted to. He closed down the engine and pulled off his boots to climb into the sleeper. A couple of hours would make it about right.

The cab was warm and the voices talked across his sleep. It was always this way, sleeping and driving and eating and sleeping and driving and stopping. The road was a whirl, a twist, a tangle of the seen and unseen, a cyclone of visions and signs and sometimes the signs were symbols.

Merge Left and you dropped across a hill toward San Francisco coming south from Vancouver, the city opening before you, silver and gold and green above the blue water of the bay. You checked your spot mirror, knowing the California traffic would put a sports car in the blind spot, eased back on the speed and cracked her in hard when you found a hole. Always there would be a horn and the exhaust would flutter as the rig ran against the gear in a downhill sweep toward the Golden Gate.

Slide ahead and you, with a cowboy dogging your rear, dropped some revs, whirling high in the western mountains across Rabbit Ears or Donner Pass. The road would sometimes ease, trying to drop the rig right, and it felt like the mountain had moved. It was always like that, the changing road in an unchanging pattern that could fool you. It metered. It had highs and lows, but it sang distance and looked so long that a man got fooled, got to feeling that the extraordinary was ordinary and, fooled, found that the extraordinary could kill.

Trucks use lower gears and you went over the top, the load giving it a hump on the override, and you dropped it too low because there were the ghosts of dead men down there. Tourists backed up behind you, waving in and out on the broad curves, gunning past and cutting in sharp, their faces going white as the automobiles rocketed along the outsides of curves, dancing along the narrow edge where a broadside drift meant forever.

Scales ahead and Kansas, and you, stacked up behind grain rigs and watching for police while more rigs stacked up; waiting to be weighed or checked or the drivers roughed up depending on whether it was cops, the ICC or a jackleg deputy playing the games. The fields mixed a smell of growth with the heat coming off your rig, and the air conditioner failed to keep the cab clear of steam. You crossed the scale easy if your weight was right, and some states allowed a certain percentage. If your weight was a little wrong you tried to drop a wheel, one tire, off one side.

Do you run from me

[61]

Catherine had been painting when he met her. He came over Black Mountain in the early morning and the traffic was dogging him. Her old car was parked in the middle of the pull-over. He had to run left and near the edge to get the rig completely off the road.

Painting. And he had climbed down and pulled his thermos with him because of her hair. It was long and black in the early sun, lighted by the sun which also glinted on the greens of the canvas, gloss and shine. She watched him. Not afraid.

Running, running

He forgot the schedule. Her talk was light. Friendly. You forgot about friendliness in a woman sometimes. The road. Then her talk changed.

She was tall like Naomi. Her fingers were long, slender hands; and her voice became husky, low-throated, like she would give off a moan of need. There was a suppressed violence about her. He felt that if they touched the voice would howl and sob, that fingers would tear at his back and hair, sinking the short nails beneath his skin.

Low Clearance 12'9" and you, knowing that sometimes the road crews laid a new surface which raised you inches and lowered the clearance of an overpass, you cut in the four-way and eased her down, crawling underneath with your eyes on the trailer mirror, your ears ready for the bump. There was an itch then, a running along the tense back of your neck that was physical pain. Like walking down an alley and suspecting that someone followed, stopping to look back, hoping to search the entrance. You eased her through and checked your mirrors hoping that no fool would top a rise, come skidding in and back-end you.

"Can I see you again?" Her fingers, when he asked the question, her fingers had held the charcoal so tight that the tremble she tried to conceal was accented. She wrote on paper, sketch paper, heavy, coarse, beautiful. He had not seen paper like that. Her name. Where she lived.

"Please," she said. "Yes, please call."

He had climbed up and eased it out of there wondering why he did not stay, knowing that he must not stay this time.

And upstate Michigan where the stands of poplar appear like spectres as you round a curve along the night road, where the lakes lay vast as oceans, breathless under moonlight, where pulled over you can hear the rustle of animals in the forest. And the stop outside of Reno, the free nickels for truckers, the slots whirling and whirling to occasionally dump loud clattering coins. And Albuquerque where there was dust. And Bayonne where there was noise. And laying over for three hours in Dayton so you could hear the clear song of the carillon. The road wound and turned and returned and you followed. The signs said *stop* but you waited for the *go*. The signs ran a great wheel of command, pushing you right or left, telling, suggesting, warning and threat. There was trouble in a sign that said *One Way*, and there was warning in a sign saying *Do Not Enter*.

A week later he caught a load south and rerouted to Black Mountain. They made love then and their lips were bruised and cut against their teeth.

In dreams, after that, the signs and the voices that talked across his sleep changed. Always before they had been only as demanding as the road. Lately, when he woke, ready to head into one more city and one more loading or unloading, the signs and voices were insistent and kept him from waking quickly.

They were that way when he woke outside of Louisville. He was sweating, the cab hot in the early morning sun, and he climbed down and walked around the rig a couple of times to clear his head. Two good-sized trees had been spared when the rest stop was built. He stood in the shade of one and looked out across the fields that were fading to a lighter green in the last days of summer. In these nearly flat lands there were no pockets of dark green, the way there were in the hills. Even the few gully trees looked light and tattered with wind and storm.

He climbed back up, and when he was feeling in tune with the rig, pulled onto the road which was fast and still lightly traveled. He made Louisvile in good time, and was at the consignee's address by mid morning. The consignee wasted some time giving instructions to a foreman, a laborer and three secretaries. Singleton told himself that he had seen it before. The consignee was one of those guys who did not trust anyone to understand anything. He would be a real prick to work for.

Singleton judged that the consignee was having trouble: woman, money, union, and probably a pain in the gut. The guy drove a battered construction pickup to a warehouse facility that was temporary and bad. Singleton followed. He pulled into the loading area at an old warehouse. The heat was intense. Louisville and St. Louis, the river basins lay striping the country like giant pressure cookers. Singleton climbed down.

"You got help?" The consignee rushed in the heat. The seat of his pants, even his belt, was slick with sweat. He looked like his mind was already ahead of the unloading, was already intent doing whatever it was he was going to do next.

"I'll get some." Singleton walked Main Street toward the bridge, looking for a place to buy coffee, and found none. He remembered some men standing by the bridge as he came past. He should have picked up a couple. The men were still there.

"Not a whole day's work," he told them. "It's getting late. Better than nothing."

Three men came. Two were Negroes and the third was a mix. Singleton looked at the oldest man who was black nearly to ebony. Hunched over. Old. Old. Day labor. Pension unlikely. Singleton estimated him. The man was wiry, streaks of old work cuts on his hands.

"A heavy load."

"I seen 'em before." The man grinned. The guy who was a mix said, "How do you pay?"

"With money."

"You know what I mean."

"And you know what I mean."

They arrived at the warehouse. The consignee stood impatient. He looked at the men, then at Singleton. He pointed to the old man. "That guy ought to get three bucks an hour." His finger moved to point to the other Negro, a middle-aged man who was lean, brown and with a surprisingly wrinkled face. "I don't know about him."

"He okay," the old man said.

"The other," he turned to the guy who was a mix, "gets a kick in the ass."

"Screw," Singleton told the man.

"You said you'd hire."

"Peel off."

The man left.

"He steals," the consignee said.

"And he don't work," the old man told Singleton. "He's Mex'can.

The load came off fast. The consignee helped and the old man was a bull. The other man moved quick in an effortless swing and carry. A load always came off faster than it went on. As Singleton shoved it to them they moved well. The heat was clustering like water. They went through the thirty-six-foot trailer in a little under two hours. Singleton shoved the last carton.

The old man's shirt was soaked. He was gasping and leaned against the trailer. The consignee sat on the curb. The third man tried to step in front of the old man.

"Uh, uh," the old man said and grinned. "That's the one. That's the gent we huntin'." He grabbed the last carton and moved. Singleton closed it up and turned to pay off. The consignee took the bill of lading for signature.

"Not a single bust."

"I load my own."

He signed and left. Singleton felt his own shirt. He was soaked. The two men were wet, foreheads, hair, backs of hands. Sometimes a load was good. Your muscles felt stretched and made you alive. In the heat it did not work.

"How old are you," he asked the old man. Men should not work so hard.

"More 'n I was. These trucks get longer."

"Sixty-seven, sixty-eight," said the other man. "You talkin' to a real horse, mister."

The cab was air-conditioned. It had been one of the first rigs set up that way, and now he was glad he had spent the money. He would run it for awhile and keep the window rolled down. Cool off slow. He reached for his money. "Twelve bucks," he told them. He passed them the money, hesitated and pulled out another ten. "Split that other guy's dough. The guy who owned the stuff helped. Comes to about the same for me." It was a little embarrassing.

"Anytime," the old man said.

"Next time in," he told the man. He climbed up and pulled deadhead for Indianapolis. Sometimes women like Grace worried too much, especially about their families. He was hoping Ben would be okay. If Ben was okay maybe it would be a good thing to take some time off and avoid this heat. A week with Catherine would be like having a true vacation, if the road did not catch him again before the week was out.

It might be time for Ben to get started again, if Ben was okay. He would team drive with him for a couple of rounds, just to make sure that the kid was steady.

8

WHAT Ben could not forget was how his father had lain in the ditch.

"So tall," he muttered. He leaned against the frame of the open barn door, spraddle-legged, half in and half out. His uncle was coming in. There was a chance that his uncle would make his mother feel better. For himself, he did not give a damn. For himself, he could just go on saying "so tall" like it was a bad song. The words were a holdover from the wreck and the hospital and the sedated nights in his upstairs bedroom of the old house. He looked at the house. Big. It was beginning to need paint. Maybe he would paint it, but he already knew that he would not. How could you feel so old and be so young?

The sunlight made him blink. His eyes hurt. The sun was white, like a polished rock, like a three-hundred-watt bulb held against a mirror. Beneath his shirt was a lot of sweat. The backs of his hands were dry. The sun seemed like it was trying to eat them. His hands. No callus. Baby-ass smooth. New skin, a good part of it red and always going to be red.

From the roadway, nearly a half mile off, some guy was trying for a gear. He goosed it a couple of times, missed his shift and goosed it again. The gear dropped in. Ben did not raise his eyes.

The truck was a B-67 with a Cummins. His uncle had a Jimmy in a Kenworth. A balls combination if anybody asked, but no one had asked. Engines. Besides, his uncle did not miss shifts.

"Liar," he told himself. "Everyone misses shifts." His own truck was parked in the barn. He had not run the engine for nearly two weeks. It bothered his mother, maybe it even hurt her just to hear the thing. He did not ever want to cause hurt ever again.

Off to his left and about a half mile from the house some ass was hunting. You would have to be an ass to hunt in this weather, and besides, the rabbits would not be safe just now. Some of them would be sick. A couple of mutts were weaving across the field. Behind them the guy walked carrying a shotgun. Twelve gauge, probably. Digging for rabbits you needed something heavy to defend yourself. There was a thirty-eight under his sleeper pad. Pop off one of the pups, and when the guy came after you, let him try shooting around that thirty-eight.

Stupid. He turned and walked into the darkened barn toward his truck. His anger was everywhere. There was enough of it inside that it slopped over everywhere. What was he going to be, a man-killer for rabbits?

That fitted.

In the ditch his father had looked like a damp, squeezed-out rag. It was not right. His father, big man, well built and striding confidently. Laughing. Angry. To look like a ragged bundle in a ditch.

He would like to finish the job. He could climb up in the truck and go out hunting another ditch. Easy. A quick trip against an overpass. That way he could bag three, his mother, his father and himself.

He thought of Sue in Pittsburgh. She would care about him, probably care a lot. Maybe she would not care at all.

There had been a frog. Ben shuddered. When he had half fallen and half climbed from the flipped rig, stumbling and dropping over the side of his father's truck and tearing his shoulder on a rock-hammered denting of steel, he had surprised a frog.

It was not very large. The frog leaped ahead of him as he rose, attempted to walk, and fell.

When he fell the second time his shoulder hit the jutting wheel and rolled him. He was conscious that the other wheel, the one so high above him, had stopped spinning. He was dizzy.

Then there was pain in his side, and there was pain in his right shoulder. He wondered about the pain and tried to draw away from it. The road was hot. The macadam was loose on the surface, like a man could turn it with a plow.

Somewhere there was smoke. The rig was burning. The smoke boiled high and black in the faraway sunlight that seemed not around him, seemed to have nothing to do with him except that the macadam caused pain. He did not hear anything.

It came to him that if the road was hot and the wheel dusty, he must be lying just on the edge of the macadam. He had tried to roll toward the wheel. He fell into the dirt by the wheel. His face touched the tire and he screamed. The treads seemed too hot ever to cool.

Then there was blood on the tire. It dried quick. He lay and watched the blood dry and realized that it was his. He was frightened and called for his father. His voice hurt him. It was not loud. The vibration and movement rubbed in his throat.

"So tall." He moaned it again and there was some relief in the moan. It almost beat thinking about the wreck. It was dark in the barn and he pressed his face to the cool steel of his truck. He reached up and touched a mirror. In the darkness he could barely see his reflection.

His uncle was coming in.

At least his uncle did not pity him. Right from the first, during the really bad days in the hospital, his uncle had not insulted him with pity. His mother did. And she helped herself to a little self-pity. A woman's right, maybe. Several times he had wanted to tell her why her husband was a shriveled wreck wearing diapers and drooling food from the corners of his mouth.

His friend Fonnie did not pity him either, and when Fonnie visited him in the hospital Fonnie had unloaded on him for acting like a jerk. Nobody but Fonnie could have done it that way and make it sound right. His best friend, if he needed a best friend which he did not, and he just wished all of it had not happened. He wished that he and Fonnie were back in school laughing and making out with lots of girls and digging race music. Nothing had been bad then.

He knew how her hatred would be. They had some kind of

[69]

instinct, women, and his mom could show you what hating was all about when it came to Fonnie. When Fonnie stopped coming to the hospital it wasn't hard to figure out why.

But if she hated him, her own son, then it would be all right to die. In casts in the hospital he had tried and not found the particular combination of pills that would kill him. Later, his mother required that he live. He resented it. Two or three times Sue called. He wanted to resent her also because he wanted to not love anybody or anything now.

He and his dad had come out of Lafayette on a day like many other days. It was a thing they did when business was slow and they were smart enough not to ruin those days by talking about how good they were. Usually each ran his own truck. Teaming was special.

His father had been tired from loading. They were running a conventional freight trailer instead of the usual reefer. The load was paint, glass and lumber. They were scaling heavy and the road north to connect with the interstate into Pennsylvania was two-lane. Without making a big show Ben stepped in front of his father on the driving. Not a big deal. Each understood and neither resented.

His father's truck was due to be traded. It had more than 800,000 miles and looked like new, but it was eight-and-a-half years old. It was like his father was dodging the idea of getting rid of the truck. When the business was just beginning to grow it had been his first new equipment. Now he had a fleet of twenty-two. Ben had his own. His uncle Charles had his own. On one or two occasions the entire fleet had been gathered in the barnyard at once. When that happened the barnyard was alive with a single huge voice of power. Each time it had been in winter, when roads were closed and hauls were down. The trucks stood, red and bobtail in a double line facing the roadway. He would look at them racked in, knowing that in most of them there was the same power and drive setup, but knowing that each held differences of operation. No truck was ever the same as the next one, even though they were the same make, model and specification. As for that shit box of his father's—there had been a lot of fast engineering improvement since that thing was built.

His father stretched and yawned. "Tire check?"

"While you were in the office. Paperwork done?"

"Half this job is paperwork."

He pulled from the factory warehouse. The axle was developing a slight hump in the shift between ranges. On the road the truck sat steady, the tandem of the tractor running smoothly over the warm pavement. The road was dry, the ground was wet in the fields; along the roadway the shoulders were drained and solid. The truck had a single drive axle with a tag axle. His father could catch the high side of the gears without a hump, but Ben kept finding one. On the road he ran at fifty-five until he could work into the feel of the load.

"A little more run-up, then drop," his father said.

"Can't quite find it."

"No harm. It's time to get rid of her." His father yawned. "It's used up. Feel kind of that way myself." He pulled off his boots and stored them where they would not come adrift during hard braking.

"What kind do you figure?"

His father grinned. "I've driven so much junk. Had to work with junk so long. This was my first real good one. Now I've got a couple rigs I've never pulled a load with. The best thing would be to go where we've been buying."

"Mine is good. I got a good-pullin' truck."

"We got a good deal on yours. We could get another. What I'm going to get won't cost more or do the job different. Going to get a Pete."

"West coast?"

"We'll set it up to run east. I've had Whites and T's and Macks, the whole boiling. Just something different." He started to climb into the sleeper. "These goddamn straps."

"Save guys."

"I guess. Best way is not to need 'em." He disappeared over the seat. The sleeper curtains were heavy. His voice was muffled. "Call me."

There was nothing better than that assurance. "Call me if you need me," in a tone that said his father knew he would not be needed.

There was a long, gentle curve. Ben felt the load and was satisfied with the way it was running. He smiled and thought to

[71]

himself that he had learned a good deal. He kicked the speed.

The old truck ran steady. It sure did not pull like his truck, but his truck was not even close to four years old yet and was almost paid for. When he came home from school he had started in the business. His father had not made it easy. For a while Ben drove one of his trucks on shares like the rest of the men. When his father judged him ready he sold Ben one of his trucks and went on his note. Ben paid for the truck and it made money. When it was used enough he wanted a new one. He had put up more than two hundred thousand miles in twenty months because he tried so hard.

"What kind?" he asked.

"It's your money," his dad told him. "I'll go on your note. You're doing well."

"Fit out a White."

"A lot of truck."

"Pulling reefers and all."

"It will keep you broke until you pay off. After that it makes money for a long time. What does your girl say?"

It had stopped him. He had only mentioned it to Sue. "She says whatever." It sounded lame.

"Are you conning her?"

"No sir." That part was right. He really was not conning her.

"Follow your own judgement," his dad told him.

It had taken them two weeks to trade the old truck. They sat at the kitchen table at night building it up.

"Enough transmission," his dad said. "You're spending money now. Spend enough. I've seen so many guys—big companies too—they take a little bigger engine and try to save on transmission. No wonder they have down time."

"Tires."

"Specify. I forgot to once. Now we've got them standard. When the one you're trading came in the tires cupped like mad." He reached for the spec sheet. "Go to flex clear through. Pre-heater. Raise the spring capacity. Adds a little weight but you may run into a mess. You're running civilization not west. Drop the tanks to eighty. Large radiator."

"Fifth wheel."

"We fit our own."

They took the specs back to the dealer, listened to his trade, made a counteroffer and walked out.

"Seemed fair."

"It is," his dad grinned. "But we can bush a little. He sold me the two Mustangs we run with the grain sides. On this one we can bush."

In another week they closed the deal. Without Ben quite understanding how, his father saved over a thousand dollars. His father was pleased. Driving home in the car he talked more than usual.

"At first I had to take chances. You remember some of them. Used tractors, payments due, uncertain leases. Sometimes a breakdown. We couldn't rent in those days. Always had to have one truck out of service just on standby. Always the oldest one."

"We don't rent much now."

"Don't have to. The equipment is new when we get it. We don't let it get old."

"You can always get failure."

"Sure. In the best machine. But watch them. Listen to your drivers. So many guys think a driver complains just to be bitching."

"You can trust your guys."

His father grinned. "Damn right, and screw the teamsters. Them I can't trust don't work."

It made Ben feel good, knowing that he was included.

"We're in now. People, company people, most of them know when you're doing a job. They say businessmen are hard. They are, about business. But, take a man they trust, one they see working, and they'll work with him. They even stick their necks out."

"Like how?"

"Like the Fords. 'Buy ten' they say, 'we can work them.' And the best I can get ten screws for is eighteen-two. That's a hundred eighty-two thousand dollars. What small businessman has that. So, I got a minimum. I got enough of a guarantee for the period of the note to cover the principal. The banks — banks scare easy."

"The line go to bat?"

"The president did. Said he'd stand behind it. That's what I mean. They work with you." His dad grinned. "Banks are awful

[73]

yella. You notice how when I go in wearing a shirt with grease on, you notice how them squeaky little bastards scoot around saying Sir."

They both laughed. It had been a good day.

Ben drove. Although he spoke of it to no one but Sue, he was proud that at twenty-seven he had paid for that kind of investment, had made money and was confident of his ability. He never asked himself why he preferred business. It was in the air. Everybody preferred business, except for a few jerks who were always raising hell about something. If it wasn't a white asshole in Arkansas, it was a Negro asshole in Cincinnati, and if it wasn't either one of them, it was a bunch of punks in California.

Maybe the movement was the best part of business, the action; even the heavy work of loading and unloading was an addition to the money. The money itself was different. It was not just a feeling of worth or value, or even of being able to piss some away, it was a feeling of increase during a month run at a profit. Maybe you were tired, but you had a greater amount to work with, to expand with, to hedge and juggle and figure the next move with.

He met Sue because of the road. He and a driver named Denny pulled two loads to Pittsburgh. Denny was sore because Ben had not allowed him to bring his wife. A lot of girls rode but it was not legal.

The rig ran smooth. Ben drove, glancing out front, up side roads and lanes, even among bushes, constantly aware that he might be surprised. He had never been caught, and believed he never would be caught. There was a road saying, that everybody had a ditch at least once. Claimed that the sheer weight of miles dictated a ditch somewhere. Ben was not worried. He knew how to drive a ditch.

Business was not just business. If all the people who were bitching would shape up and see it, they would have no reason to bitch. His friend Fonnie had seen it, and Fonnie was blacker than new ink. Ben grinned as he thought of Fonnie.

When the surprise came it was not in the bushes or out front. He felt it running under him. A tiny vibration. Ben dropped the speed. The vibration disappeared. He picked it back up. The vibration returned. By that time his father was climbing out of the sleeper.

"What?"

"I don't know. I was just going to pull over."

"Do that."

Ben eased his speed. As it dropped they crossed another range of vibration which dropped away as the speed went even lower. He cut on the four-way and eased the truck onto the shoulder to run out the low speed, braking carefully in taps. His father was reaching for the flag case.

"What do you think?"

"It came quick. I get it in the sixty-four to sixty-five range and caught it again around thirty-five."

"It could be drive."

"Doesn't feel like drive. Feels more like a tire."

"No bump."

"I know. Hub bumps, too." The thought was shocking. A hub. The wheels would break away. If a hub broke, the truck would be like a man with his legs shot off. Instinctively and beyond all question Ben knew that it was a hub. He felt weak with shock, the way you got after a near accident.

His father climbed down and walked along the roadway to spot the two flags at the rear of the truck. His dad looked like a man flipping a mental inventory file, checking dates, installation, maintenance data. "Might be a wheel bearing," his father said. "If it's a wheel bearing, okay. The rest checked out, uh, little less than a year ago. Front wheel bearing."

"It didn't feel like it was coming from up forward."

"It wouldn't have to."

"How about a tire?"

"You never know. A new tire will blow and take the one running next to it. Million to one shot, but you never know."

"I got a notion."

"So have I. What's yours?"

"Let me get in and kick it hard on the low side. Speed won't be up. If anything is going to bust—"

"If you're thinking hub, she'll be more likely to go in reverse. Weight shift. But I'm positive it's bearing because of the vibration."

"What's your notion?"

"Find someplace to spot the trailer and get out from under.

[75]

Then find it."

"Lose a lot of time."

His father grinned. "Son, you were just going to bust a whole damn pair of wheels off. That would have wasted a little."

Ben grinned. His father drove slowly until he found a place to spot the trailer at a service station. The vibration returned at thirty-four. When his father backed the trailer into a spot beside the station he humped it hard. Nothing broke. Ben let down the landing gear.

The service station owner took five dollars to look after the trailer. "I'm not equipped," he said. "Can't handle this. There's a garage in town."

"I know a stop." His father climbed back up and Ben followed after checking a dangling air line. The spring was beginning to collapse.

"Time to trade."

"Last year. I hung on too long because I like it."

There was no vibration at any speed. Even when his father kicked it.

"I doubt front wheel bearings."

"Why?"

"Load weight off doesn't take that much off the front axle."

"It might not take much."

"We could pull against the trailer brake."

"You sure are hot to see her come to pieces. You couldn't prove anything if you did bust something."

He decided to let his dad handle it.

When they pulled the front wheels the bearings showed wear but they were not shot. Ben argued for more time. It did not take very long to put in new bearings.

"You've taught me to do things right."

They pulled the wheels off the drive axle. The hubs looked solid. They looked over each tire. The tires looked fine.

"Are you afraid of inner separation?"

"No, they look okay. It was the hub. I had a feeling." He still had a feeling. Metal fatigue. You could get a crack that was invisible. Magna-flux would find it.

His father grinned. "If you had a feeling and hadn't checked I'd have kicked your rear end. Now you've checked. The only thing we can find is wheel bearings."

"I agree. But when we get in I'm going to replace the hubs or at least magna-flux."

"We can do that now. Cost a little more time."

"We've checked. Let it ride."

They pulled from the stop to return for the trailer. There was no vibration in any range. When they got to Pittsburgh they unloaded, put up the back haul and turned around. The truck ran smoothly all the way to Indianapolis.

And, Ben thought, that was the trouble. In the darkness of the barn the whole run of things was so solid that there were no separate parts. The main fact was that the hub had been so smooth. It tricked him. The rest of the facts seemed to cluster around that fact. By the time they returned home he had not forgotten the hub, but the truck had tried to make him a liar. The wheels turned, spinning across the miles, the distances tacked in his log, with the hub a solid center. Like it was trying to prove his fear to be the offhanded result of too little experience conducted around experienced men. He did not forget the hub, but he forgot the feeling. When they returned to the garage there was work to be done on another truck. He did not check the hub.

The accident happened on U.S. 150 above Paoli and west of Shoals, midway in the distance. They were hauling freight, grossing less than fifty thousand. The sun was high enough that headed east they did not have to worry about the glare. In the hilly terrain there was enough shadow to hide animals, people, or vehicles parked along the road. It was a normal, easy haul.

His father was driving. They crested a hill curving to the right, running at about fifty. As the trailer came over the crest there was the natural small push of override as the weight shifted to the nose and left. It was normal. Then it was not normal.

There was a vibration and a crack that was more sharp than loud. Ben heard the crack in the explosion of a tire, like a noise in the middle of a noise. Suddenly, sun, shoulder and earth rushed at them, coming in from their left. The only thing that seemed alive and in active, controlled motion was the blur of his father's hand thrown against the useless trailer brake. The momentum of the load pulled the truck into a hunch, ending in a levering rush that lay it on its side. The cab was shaken the way a dog flops dead

[77]

things in its mouth. Then there was a blow.

Ben called for his father. The third time he managed to rise—and no one ever believed that he had stood with a broken leg—that third time he had fallen far enough ahead of the cab to see his father in the ditch. His father lay motionless, small, liked a huddled bundle of rags. There was blood. The truck burned, the oil smoke black across the hills and against the sun.

A tourist stopped and pulled Ben away. He remembered the man pulling his father away from the blaze while the man's wife sat in the car and wept. When the man had done what he could do, he walked to the far side of the road and puked.

That was the last thing Ben could remember until he found himself in the hospital. That memory came to him over and over, first in the hospital, then at home, and it came to him again as he stood beside his truck as it sat in the old barn. Ben's mind was a dark funnel, like a whirlpool in a deep chasm. At the center was a cool-running treachery that suctioned the darkness of his mind and the darkness that was him and not him, the blackness of what he was and what he denied, what he wished and thought he could never be. The hub whispered and drilled at his consciousness.

Then it began to change, a glow that was at first light violet against black as the hub began to hum. The hum was a puzzled murmur like the hub was questioning the storm of which it was a center. There was an explosion. He was choking. He leaned his face hard against the cab of his truck, gasped for breath in the darkness of the old barn, tensed. There was the boom of a diesel. A sharp cracking outside. It was not far away. His uncle had arrived. Ben climbed up in his cab and hid in the sleeper. He did not want to see anyone until he got straightened out. Maybe then he could fake it.

9

WHEN Singleton arrived the sun was just past zenith. Brief shadows watered by reflected light huddled close to buildings and fences. The barnyard was empty except for a new station wagon. The old house, framed and lapped, poked out of a small grove of trees that offered little protection. The sunlight looked like red water on the roof.

He slowed the rig at the head of the drive and, with no need to estimate his swing, kicked the truck in a wide circle. He brought it alongside the automobile. The yard looked empty. It had been expanded to hold two dozen trucks.

His van was empty. He felt empty in the same way. It was a feeling that came to him sometimes at his brother's house. A coming home, but home and not home. Sometimes when he was laid over in an unfamiliar place, he wondered at the unfamiliarity of the single spot he called home. It was not like a ship. Everything known. His family, what he had left, did not understand that a ship was that way. They did not understand that sailors thought about ships as something more than tools that moved.

Two dozen rigs. On the day of the auction Singleton had pulled his truck and Ben's truck inside the barn so the buyers would not clamber over them. A good sale. Most of the trucks went as a package to one fleet; several were parceled out to individuals.

Then the letdown. He had been out for two months. In two months he had seen Catherine twice. He had also seen half of the eastern states. Seen them again. Once every ten days he called Indiana to make sure that John was still alive and Ben was holding. He did not worry about his sister-in-law. Soft but tough. Grace was a Bible name. No, a religion name.

She came from the doorway of the house and walked slowly toward the rig. Her hair was colored a deep brown and Singleton liked it that way. Grace was honest. She dyed her hair so that she would not look old. She did not dye it trying to look young.

Her legs were really good. Her shoulders were a bit heavy and slumped. She wore a housedress that had style, a dark blue dress that went well with the dark hair and blue eyes. The best thing about Grace was her smile: broad mouth, wrinkles around the eyes, hair combed back and enclosing her face to lengthen her forehead. Altogether a nice-looking woman. The worst thing about Grace was her temperament. She blew hot and cold. Easy with a man, sometimes, at other times she showed everything from resentment to anger to some kind of perverse need to be watched. But she had been a good wife for John.

When she arrived at the truck she neither waved nor spoke. She leaned against the front of the station wagon, waiting. There was a trace of smile on her lips. She was not being long-suffering. Another good thing about her.

Singleton climbed down and turned.

"I'm glad," she said, "but you look tired."

"So do you." He touched her shoulder, which was a kind of a hello, then turned to the truck and unlocked the storage compartment.

"Bring it all," she told him.

He pulled out dirty gear, work shirts smelling of sweat and spotted with grease, pants with the dust of cartons imbedded against the knees. A tangled piece of paper with the name of a dry cleaner in Duluth. White shirt. He carried at least one good shirt most of the time.

"How are things?"

"The same." Her voice was low. There was a hint of emotion in her voice, some commitment to anger or excitement or rebellion.

She was not whipped. That was another good thing about her.

"Ben okay?"

"We'll talk."

"Are you okay?"

"Better." Her voice changed. There was something like a laugh in her voice. "I put on coffee. About ready now."

"I can use it. Couple hours sleep this morning." He turned, looking out across the field. In the distance some guy was hunting. Two dogs were yipping, running a fence row. As he watched, a rabbit broke, moved out almost slow at first, its body then stretching and contracting. The dogs fell back and then jumped in pursuit. The guy lifted the shotgun and led the rabbit.

"Watch," Singleton told her. Sunlight glinted off the shotgun barrel. The rabbit was headed straight away. One dog went wide, herding it back, attempting to bring the rabbit sideways to the hunter. A sharp dog. The second dog ran the rabbit. It was too close. The hunter pointed his gun and tried to yell the dog off. His voice sounded high and thin in the distance.

The rabbit broke sideways and the second dog overran the track, leaving a clear lane of fire for seconds. The shotgun boomed. The rabbit jumped and stretched forward, contracting, stretching, jumping. The dog recovered and turned to pursue. It closed fast and the guy chanced it. There was another boom, a shock pounding across the field. The rabbit crumpled in the middle of a leap and rolled, tumbling, the hind legs flashing and for an instant hanging pointed at the sky like an animal doing a handstand. Then the rabbit disappeared in the grass and weed. There was no sound. Then there was a sound from the dog, a high yelping. The dog had taken a pellet or two around the head. Probably in the eye. It ran in a tail-down, back-end-squatting crouch, yelping pain and headed for home.

"Good for him," Grace said.

"I'm sorry I called your attention."

"I'm sorry he's got a wife." She turned and walked to the house. Singleton followed and figured the guy was an idiot to be hunting in this sun.

When they got inside she poured coffee. He did not want to see John but he did not want to tell her that. He wanted to see Ben. He sat at the modern table in the modern kitchen and waited to hear what she would say. The kitchen was the really familiar place. Not like Catherine's old kitchen with its high oven stove that stood glowing like a repeal of forty years, this kitchen was efficient and designed to handle a big work load. Often in the past they had waited here when trucks were overdue. There was always something prepared or preparing—soup, coffee. John kept good drivers, and one reason was this kitchen. No one could say that the woman had not helped.

She sat across from Singleton and pushed her hair back. She smiled.

"I really am glad. I wish you would quit." She reached across the table, placed her hand on his and held it. A kind of shock. She was trying to be concerned, but there was more to it than that. The tone of her voice. Singleton started to move his hand away and then did not. Was everybody in the whole God damned world lonely? How much did she know about herself. People lied best to themselves. How much of what she was showing did she intend to show?

"I'm not aiming to quit."

"You should. I have a plan." There was no lack of control in her voice, and it was no surprise that she had a plan. That was about right. Her voice was telling him that she had been alone for a long time. Sex, of course, but he figured that it was loneliness, first of all. That was a relief, and yet the idea of going to bed with her was like it always was with women when there might be a chance. Your mind told you that you were stupid, but your body and instincts did not know it. John's wife, for hell's sake, his wife.

"How is he?" He said it soft, telling her as well as he could that he wished he could make things better. His voice was more gentle than he had aimed for.

She stayed with the game she figured they were playing. Long range. He figured that she figured there was time, and she did not know about Catherine. She stood to pour more coffee, moving with lighter steps than he remembered. There was a girlishness about her. Where was Ben? Had she sent Ben off somewhere? No, the car was there.

The truck. Was Ben back on the road?

"How could he be," she said. "The same."

"Ben?"

"He's around someplace."

"How is he?"

She smiled. "You're repeating yourself."

"I guess. It's an honest question."

"I wish he would die." Her voice was matter-of-fact, and he was shocked for a moment until he realized that she was speaking about John. She might have been talking about the prospects of rain. At the same time her body did not match her words. Her shoulders were tensed, the set of her body like it was asking for help.

"A hard thing to say."

"A hard thing to live with. Go see for yourself."

"I'll take your word." He did not want to see his brother. It was too personal.

"You're no kid. You're not Ben. You're old enough to be honest."

How honest did she want him to be?

Singleton stood and left the kitchen. He would see his brother, but he would be damned if he would obligate himself to his brother's wife. At least he hoped that was true, but he could see himself screwing up, and that was true as well. He walked through the living room and went upstairs knowing which room it would be. When he got there he found that knowing made no difference. There was only one room that it could be.

His brother seemed to float in the smell. The smell altered the day, altered life. The smell was of medicine and alcohol and shit. It was sour with sweat and closeness and slobber. It hung like the taste of something rotten. It was rubber sheets and rubber bags to drain urine. It was thick. A shroud of smell.

His brother lay stretched full-length like a dead man. His jaw hung open like a dead man, but breath slurped in and out of his mouth in light waves like the whisper of air sucked from a just-opened tomb. The tongue moved in the open mouth. The eyes were open and blank. They stared straight ahead.

One hand lay outside the light sheet, one finger twitched and picked and pestered at the sheet. The side of his brother's head had been caved in. Brain and bone were gone from up forward.

The hand pestered the sheet. A memory lay in Singleton's mind like low fire and dull embers. The way the merchant ship had looked off Gloucester that time during the war. It wouldn't sink. It just sat there burning like a beacon for every submarine in the Atlantic. They had beat back and forth with the cutter, picking up survivors. The merchantman had been in ballast and they got most of the guys. One died of burns right on the mess deck. His fingers had plucked like that, and his head was burned black. Pieces of flesh moved and stripped away from his face at first, then he quit thrashing around and just plucked with his fingers and died.

There had been nothing they could do for that burned seaman, and there was nothing he could do for his brother.

The bad thing, and he could not deny it, was that looking at John was like looking at himself. John was younger, but in appearance they were nearly the same. John's face looked like a cartoon caricature of himself. Looked like Charles Singleton. Except that the hair was cut down nearly bald.

And Ben looked like his dad, which meant that Ben was an even younger version of Charles Singleton. No one who looked at any of them together ever missed the fact that they were related.

Big, strong features; but now John looked little. His wrists were thin. Two fingers were gone from the hand that did not move. The other three fingers looked like too many for the thin wrist. There was no meat on him and the smell was bad.

The windows were open against the severe heat, and curtains at the windows moved only a little with a breeze that was working here on the second floor. It was the one thing about the room that seemed like a compromise, like Grace was still trying to pretend that it was just another room in a normal house. The three windows were bright with sun, framed by the white curtains.

The furniture in the room was efficient. There was no night table because John did not need one nor ever would. Singleton walked to the windows and saw that when closed they would be perfectly sealed. Heavy gaskets had been mounted around the frames so that the windows would be as tight as a refrigerator door.

That would be for any day that was not summer hot.

You lost a lot of them after you believed they were saved. This room needed to be air-conditioned to make it livable, but air conditioning was out.

Pneumonia was how you lost them. Even Pat had caught

pneumonia, but Pat had been young and strong and not very busted up in his body.

Seal it tight. Keep the man too hot if that is how it went. Most likely the man did not care.

Singleton looked again at John. It struck him that John looked like a piece of furniture. He shrugged at the thought and looked at the room.

Besides the tightly sealed windows, there was tile floor. The hospital bed was sweat proof, drool proof, and it had the guard rails down because furniture did not move and John was furniture.

You could see that Grace had a problem of liquids. Water had to go in and water had to come out. He figured that defensive medicines had to be pressed against the tongue, and food, although John would need little. Then you had the fluids that came out, a changeable bag for urine, sheets for perspiration, rubberized diapers for shit, disposable cloth for saliva.

A new drain had been cut in the tile floor. The other furniture was a castered table and a large set of steel shelving that stood high off the floor. It was efficient. Maybe twice a week you could come in with a hose, shoot down the whole floor, hit it with antiseptic and you were done. Grace clearly no longer had a medical problem. It was only a problem of maintenance. You got used to the smell.

Then his brother moaned. It was a small moan, and it was one of small pleasure mixed with small pain. It sounded like a spanked child cuddling on its mother's lap after all the trouble was over and everyone was being nice again.

Singleton got out of the room fast. He shut the door rapidly and stood in the hall remembering his brother, how he had been. He and John had gotten awfully close. This was almost too hard to bear. John was worse now, and if it was hard for him as a brother, what must it be for Grace.

It had not been so bad in the hospital. Now, at home, there were no routine busy sounds to cover up the liquid noises. There was no flourescent light to make it objective.

Singleton stood for a long while, trying to get a handle on what he was feeling, and when he did get his handle he did not want it.

Would John do it for him?

[85]

A man couldn't kill. It would be easy.

Grace could not do it, or she would have. Ben certainly couldn't.

Singleton could. It, the thing, the dead man, was only a brother. He was not father or husband.

Would John do it for him? Singleton stood in the hallway, wondering over her plan, and wondering if he was crazy. For a moment it seemed to him that he had been called back to do murder—but those were his thoughts, not hers. He had just been called back.

He descended the stairs, resolving to listen more and talk less. A man like John deserved to die. A good man, a good man.

Singleton returned to the kitchen and Grace did not turn to look at him. He walked behind her and put his hands on her shoulders. He put one hand on her head, stroking her hair and then her forehead. Crazy. She reached up and held his wrist.

"You have to sleep."

"Around the clock, maybe." Her hand on his wrist excited him. All he had to do, all, was move his hand. Turn her head, even touch her lips. That was all.

"Is Ben here?" Where did that question come from, he had already asked that question.

"Outside someplace. We have to talk."

"We'll talk."

She released his wrist. "Sleep," she told him.

"Back bedroom."

"It's all made up."

He left her sitting in the kitchen with all the thoughts and trouble that belonged to her, but he left reluctantly. He did not love her, he did not want to get involved, and yet he did not want to leave. He wished that his brother would die, that the thing would die, because that thing upstairs was no longer living. He wished women were not always so important.

[86]

10

THE road ran before her like frozen oil that had somehow seeped around and down and through the hills before it became fixed. The sun turned it oily looking, and there were textures in the color that talked about the slickness of black. Here and there, where cars had pulled to the narrow shoulder and then pulled back onto the road, streaks of red dust contrasted with the oil. The shoulders held a mixture of clay and pebbles and larger gravel.

When the road was laid, no one had bothered to finish the job. The edges were crumbly and not sealed. You could not treat fabric that way. It would unravel. So would this road, probably, and the sooner the better.

Catherine drove it slow even though she wanted to go fast enough to get home by dark. The old car lugged hard, and she had been told that lugging was bad for the engine. When the ticking got too loud she shifted to second gear. She did not know anything about engines or gears and she devoutly hoped she never would. In fact, she told herself, if she ever did know anything about them then it would just prove that she was living wrong.

Singleton hated her car. Every time he saw it he reminded her of a man sneaking glances at something lewd. Then he would start making little tsks and worry noises until she thought he would sound like a Sunday school superintendent. The only real argument they had ever had started because of the car. Both of them lost, although she supposed the car had won something.

"A surprise," he said. He had climbed into his truck and come out with some small boxes filled with oily parts. "To take the play out of that wheel."

The way he said it was enough to start a fight. He was trying to give her a present but embarrassed about intruding into her affairs. No wonder what he said sounded false. Over her protests he had put the thing on blocks, worked with a couple of jacks and installed the parts. He spoke of suspensions and steering sectors and ended up wasting part of a morning and a good piece of the afternoon when they could have been making love or walking or talking. She had finally gone to the house and waited. If that was his idea of a surprise she sure as hell did not ever want to catch him on a really dull day.

The oily-looking road was enough to make you think bad thoughts, and what was worse than thinking about that kind of fight? He claimed that the road was useful. She claimed it was a hoax. They had both gotten so heated that somehow he ended up asking her to marry him. She answered that she only wanted to attend one wake in her life—when she died.

It had been a terrible day. They worked together and finally saved it, but she never wanted another day like that.

She never wanted to talk to him like that, either. She had been horrified at what she heard herself saying. After all, this was the man she loved. If he was wrong about something, that did not make him a bad man. He had been quiet. She began crying. It all meant so much and was so important, if he could only see it. She would not cry if it did not mean so much.

In the shadows were small pools of darkness where the road looked greasy and not just oily. It would be dark by the time she got home. The sun was already low on the ridges. This day was not exactly wasted, but it was a money day, which meant no production. About a once a month it was necessary to take new work as far away as Winston-Salem. No galleries sold her work, because there were no galleries. They sold from a variety of stores, furniture, antique, and to interior decorators. While in Winston she always picked up what material she would need for another month's production.

It was a long trip. The smell of the city in the vat of heat that was the city reminded her of stew left at room temperature for a week. Catherine had not seen many cities, but she knew Winston-Salem with its combination of tobacco factories and black slums, humidity and traffic. There was a good cafeteria, a terrible bus station, a memory of Moravians, and that was what she knew about Winston-Salem.

Her brother and his wife lived there, and they always seemed pleased when she visited. She did not visit often, because she did not want to wear out her welcome. Besides, she suspected that she was a recluse. Living in the country made you that way. When school started, which it would pretty soon, she would be even more reclusive. She would drive to the schools. She would do her best job. Then she would get away, fast.

It was not always more interesting to be alone, but she was timid. If a man spoke to her on the street her heart froze, no matter how nice he was trying to be. If she had more experience she would probably not be timid.

The road flowed between the hills. Before Singleton she had never thought about the road.

She was going to be lucky. The car was still running well and her time was better than she hoped. As she came down the mountain, which was always frightening, the sky was still red above the hills. She rolled into her drive, the pasture and the old house familiar and reassuring. Maybe it was not best to be alone, but it was best to be home. The air was getting chilly, the temperature would drop rapidly. While the night would not be cold it would still be a good idea to have a fire in the fireplace. She hurried to the house, put water on for tea, and carried wood and kindling. She made the tea when the water boiled. The packages of materials could be unwrapped and stored in the morning.

It was not until she carried her second armload of wood that she realized how much the drive had tired her. She felt almost exhausted, and that was frightening because it made her feel old. She had intended to get some work done this evening.

The fire she built was as flickering as her discontent. The kindling was dry and burned fast but the wood did not take. Smoke swirled like it was trying to make up its mind which direction to travel. The draft was bad.

[89]

She stood before the fireplace and felt permanently seized by fatigue and the closing night. The car was parked, a dead thing, but the valley was alive.

I feel like a field, she thought, crossed by seed, into which the wind blows alien life, burr and dandelion and maple wings. Another nice part of being alone was that you could think things to yourself and not apologize for them.

She rubbed her arms and then her belly. Was her whole life a fraud? Was she on some sexual hook because of loneliness? Singleton was long gone and would not be back for maybe a month. Living alone had not been that difficult before. Maybe she should marry him and take the chance. Even if he did not leave the road, he would probably be around more often.

"Why do you go?" She asked that on the day she refused to marry him, the day when he probably would not have asked if he had not been hurt and angry.

"To see." He tried to hide his resentment, but it did not work. He stood even straighter when he was mad, his face wrinkled deeper and beautiful with shadow. He hid his anger, but his face was questioning, too, like he tried to figure if she had a point because he did respect her. And he did respect her. It was not just the stupid kind of man-respect that you always got because you were a woman. One of the best ways he showed it was to always be careful that he was not getting in the way of her work.

His confusion was even plainer than his anger. He had a habit of rubbing the side of his face when he was trying to think things out. An easy man to like. He had offered what was most valuable to him, what he understood as the biggest demonstration of love he could give. But he had not offered to leave the road.

To see. It had been a stupid answer. She thought so at the time. Of course, she was just getting over being mad at the time.

"You mean curiosity? Not that that's bad, but only curiosity."

"More than that." He was uncomfortable and she couldn't blame him if he had to defend that proposition. "It lets me know things. I don't just live in a place understanding everything by reading the newspapers. I can't live on a few acres all my life and call myself American or Canadian or whatever."

"I'll bet you don't even vote." Maybe hurting his feelings some more made sense. He could get mad and get it all worked through his system at once. At the same time it made sense to mitigate it. "You and I," she said, "had better go for a walk. I'll take you to a place I know."

Behind the house was the forest, leaved and damp and fecund. Tall old trees stood like statements of decency, at least they always seemed that way to her. The stream ran off the mountain, and above that stream was a feeder spring. A trail, a path really, wound across the face of the mountain and led to a private place that only she knew about. She walked silently beside him, and he was not saying anything, either. When they entered onto the mountain path they had to walk single file. She went ahead of him, and as she walked she wondered if he would understand what he was going to see. The forest was a continuous sound that she heard and believed he did not hear. The stream was talking like a voice.

She told herself that she could not even expect him to understand. She had taught enough people over the years to know that most people did not handle abstract ideas very well. Even people who studied art—or maybe, she thought, especially them.

She supposed he really was trying to say something. It seemed like he was trying to explain to himself as well as to her. She turned.

"Just because you can't see a thing," she said, "doesn't mean it isn't real."

He was not sullen, and he was paying attention, but he sure wasn't talking. He followed her until they arrived at a glade. Sunlight illuminated the clearing. Grass was thick, so tall it was bent over, and it nearly obscured the few remains of timbers that had once been a cabinlike house of rough-cut boards.

She turned to him, loving him and slightly detesting herself, and still a little angry with him.

"This is my place since I was little. When the mountains were settled some man with a woman, maybe like me, and some children, they came and cut the trees and built a house because the lowland water is not always good. There's the spring. It pools, and when the man was dead and the children moved west the glade was left. I've never dug. Do you think if we dug we would find a rusty skillet, a bullet mold, the bones of the man who cut the trees?"

"It's what I mean about going," he said, "except you do it with the past."

"It's not the same." It really was not the same. You didn't have to think abstractly to drive a truck.

"You complain about the mountains being wrecked," he said. "All TVA wants is cheap coal."

"That's not the same." Now she felt angry.

"If the lakes up north freeze early, do you care? Suppose a man around here dies. You hear about it and feel sad. Read in the paper about a dead man in Des Plaines and you don't feel the same amount of sad. You can't. Here you know the same sort of things that another person knew."

So, if some bum died in Des Plaines . . . . He really was saying something, even if he was not saying it well.

The spring was a feeder. It lay to one side of the stream and trickled over mossy rocks; cold water that tasted good from cupped hands. Once, where the spring pooled she had searched the bottom with her hands and found a baby chipmunk. It had been drowned for a long time. She dropped it back into the pool. The memory made her shudder. She touched his arm. "I just want to understand it."

"I go around seeing. Name any ten towns and I'll have been in eight of them. Mention a bay, a harbor, a river and I'll have seen it and I'll remember." He paused. Some of the excitement was gone from his voice. "I don't haul coal. There's lots I don't haul."

What did that mean?

"I don't haul liquor, either. Drink, but won't haul the stuff, and I'm plenty bondable. Some of those guys make good."

Sometimes his morality was so weird that only someone possessed could understand it. She momentarily felt like she had somehow violated this place by bringing him here. Then she told herself that was not true. Men and women did not always understand each other. The man who built that house had surely not always understood his woman.

If she had more experience, if she were not shy, then all of this would not have happened in the first place. She moved to put her arms around him, trusting touch more than she trusted words. He held her, and he was not indecisive about that. He held her for a long while and she told herself that there were things she did not know that she must surely learn. She managed to save that day and he had been sorry when he had to leave.

The fire struggled for air. Catherine stood before it, wondering and discontent.

"You need air," she told the fire. "Fresh, strong air." The fire had drawn well during the storm. Now it was just holding at the combustion point.

There were plenty of men around. At least she thought that was true. If she needed a man, then why did it necessarily have to be this man?

Maybe it was not a matter of needing a man. Maybe she needed something else, and was using Singleton as a replacement for what she really needed. If that was so, then she did most dearly wish that she could figure out what she needed.

The fire was doing a little bit better. A breeze must be stirring out there, making motions of air through the valley.

She was too fatigued to work, and it was too early to go to bed. She decided to sit and watch the flames and later, when it was time to sleep, she could roll up in blankets before the fire. You could do nice things like that when you lived alone, especially if you had a fire screen.

You could do anything you wanted when you lived alone. You could sit naked before the fire if you wanted, and you could touch yourself and feel the warmth of the fire and the warmth of yourself combining. You could even make love to yourself if you wanted to, even if no one else seemed to want to make love to you.

WHEN Singleton woke it took a few moments to realize that he was at his brother's house. He did not know whether the sun in the window was morning or afternoon. Then, understanding it was morning and that he had slept for part of an afternoon and all of a night, he sat up to rub the pressure from the front of his head. He dreamed of the ships, that he had just enlisted and was assigned to his first ship; coming aboard as a seaman deuce full of aggressiveness to make up for his ignorance.

Pat was the captain and he laughed with one of the chief POs, laughing at the way Singleton could not handle a scraper, how he stumbled and barked his shins on a ladder. Laughed at all of the foolish things that rough men laugh at with a new man.

Pat's laughter hurt. He shook his head and remembered that Pat was blind and was a teacher in Ann Arbor. It was Pat, not Singleton, who came fresh aboard with a little knowledge and a lot of eagerness.

Singleton sat on the edge of the bed, remembering Pat, re-membering Naomi, Catherine, his brother, Ben and Grace. In the morning sunlight and the stuffy, oppressive room, it felt like too many people.

He sat straighter and realized he was tired, that after fourteen hours sleep he was tired like an old man. From the hall he heard footsteps, slow ones and heavy. He wondered at them until he understood that it was Grace going upstairs to look after John.

The window gave onto a view of the land. About a half mile away, and to the right a couple of points, there was a grove. Nearly every farm had one, in addition to the trees around the houses. He figured that this one would be in bad shape. It would be overgrown with scrub and brush. He remembered the grove the way it was when he was a child. The cattle, Guernseys even then, seeking the shade during the middle of the day. They had owned a dog, his family, and it was a good dog that brought the cattle home.

His father's name had been Daniel, and that was Bible too. For a moment he could almost remember his father's face, the seriousness, the tone that tried to be fair and always showed there was not quite enough respect to allow you equal presence.

From the highway came the sudden cracking of a downshift, and a guy riding hard on the gear. The morning was still. The air brakes puffed. If he had not been listening careful he would not have heard. The puffs were like small exclamations of fear. He waited, tensed. The puffs stopped and the guy revved on out, dragging for the next gear. Singleton relaxed. A close one. Maybe a tired guy or some jerk cutting in.

Don't let them trap you

"Sound advice," he told his brother. "Do you want to eat it now or later?" He was going to have to think of his brother. He would have to think of Ben and Grace. Catherine was going to have to fit in there somewhere. Altogether he was in a lousy mood and did not need any part of it. The dream had been wrong and bad.

Grace had said, "Come in, we need you." True, he had not seen Ben, but going over the previous afternoon he could not see why he was needed. She said she had a plan.

Well, maybe he had a plan. How much of that had occurred to anybody?

She had a plan and he, telling himself that he understood nothing of people, suddenly felt that he understood her. She'd be about forty-five. Still good looking. Still wanting a man and nobody could blame her for that. He was going to be elected. How would that work, even assuming that he went along, which wasn't going to happen. Her husband, his own brother, in the house. What did she want to do, send Ben back on the road so she could get laid?

He had not felt so bad for a long time, except he had felt pretty bad after the mess in the storm. He was not disrespectful, but here he was pushing people around and throwing dirty motives at them. Suddenly he was ready to start calling names, or start thinking about Grace in ways she did not deserve. Or, if she did want him to take over, did not want it in any crummy way. He would have to get his mind straight.

Hard to figure. He went over the things that were always with him, the stuff that bothered a man and made him wish he was a kid again. Nineteen, maybe, and thoroughly stupid and ignorant of the fact. You picked up all kinds of ballast. Not ballast, either. He strung kedge anchors behind him and they slowed him for the rest of his life.

First, he was not ever going to get over Naomi because he had built it in his mind to the point where it was like a different life. It *had* been different, young and free and illicit.

Second, he loved Catherine but there was none of the play or laughing or fun about it that there could be, if a man wasn't old enough to have memories. Third, to be truly honest, to be absolutely truly honest, he was not at all sure that either Shirley at the truck stop, or Grace, or some other woman, if he knew her well enough, could not get him in bed and get him obligated in spite of what he figured was right. In that part, at least, he was just as ignorant now as he had been at nineteen.

And then there was Pat. He paused. Now this was one that he was going to have to quit avoiding and really think about someday soon. He kept telling himself that he was going to go visit Pat, but he never did it. And Pat had been like his own son and they had worked together on the same ship and done a lot of good jobs.

Then there was Ben to whom he owed nothing, except that there were family connections that meant that he owed something. Then there was his brother who was not dead. His mind balked. He heard Grace coming down the steps. She was not moving so slow now, not making a plodding noise.

Yesterday she said she wished John would die. Not fifteen minutes later he wondered if he could kill John, and wondered if

John would do it for him. It was no surprise he was in a filthy mood. Some part of his mind had been thinking about murder.

Always you shocked yourself by thinking of things you could do that you never were going to do. He stood, rummaged in a stack of clean clothing, and pulled on his pants. Once you understood a thing you did not need to worry so much. He was not going to kill anyone.

He pulled on his shirt, slipped on the low shoes and went to find breakfast. There was one good thing and that was the truck. Any time the weight got too heavy you could at least be free, or at least look free. You could climb in the rig and go. No one except Ben understood that. It was a cinch that Ben would never tell, either, because Ben felt the same about his own rig parked in the barn.

Grace was in the kitchen. She looked up and smiled as he walked in. She was wearing a blouse and skirt, youthful clothing that somehow looked special. That was his mind fooling him. She always dressed nice.

"Feel better?" She already had cups on the table. He sat down and she poured coffee. It smelled fresh and strong, the way you could make coffee when you made only a few cups at a time. There was so much coffee, a part of life. Often in the stops it was rancid or flavorless, because they made large quantities and allowed it to stand. His taste was clear after fourteen hours sleep. The coffee would be worth spending some time over.

"Feel fine," he told her, and found that it really was true. He did feel much better. The thinking and the coffee did it. "Where's Ben?"

"Outside. He'll be in soon." She sat down beside him while he tasted the coffee, then she pushed a pack of cigarettes at him. The smoke and coffee were perfect. He found that he really felt very fine.

"How is he? Yesterday we didn't talk."

"Not good, at least not like he should be."

"How do you mean? When I left everything seemed to be going all right."

"It wasn't." Her voice was low and he read a note of accusation, although to tell the truth he could not really say that any was there. "Even then he was restless," she said. "Losing his temper,

[97]

talking to himself. You didn't notice."

"I think I did. But what was wrong with it? Anybody would."

"Not that way. He stays steady, smiles at you, doesn't talk much but you feel like he's listening. But you also feel like it doesn't make any difference." She went to the stove. Breakfast was going to be eggs and he felt like he could eat a lot of them.

"Give it room to breathe," Singleton told her. "After all, busted shoulder, busted ribs, leg, burns, concussion."

"He's had room." Action with her hands seemed to help her speak carefully. "Plenty. But he won't give himself any. Walks around doing jobs halfway, then quits mad. Stays alone. Won't call Sue."

It was clear to Singleton. There was no mystery. "What kind of jobs?"

"Fixing the place. Roof leak. Cleaning the barn. Goes out and fools with the truck, gets it revving and screaming out there in the barn. I wish the thing would explode."

"It won't." He finished the coffee, stood and walked to the stove to pour another cup. Impulsively he put one hand on her shoulder, partly as comfort, partly because he wanted to. She looked at him quickly, a glad smile that was acknowledgement, eagerness, expectancy. Then he dropped his hand and she continued working. You did not see that particular look very often. Not all women were capable of feeling enough to have that look. He felt his reaction like always, poured the coffee and sat down. It was like there was going to be a mess no matter what he did. After that it would probably be insulting to even say anything about Catherine. Still, it was an obligation. It was also a good way out.

"Ran mostly south this time."

"I know. When we heard from you it was always south. Can you do any good?"

"Wages."

"I think so too. We tried to never take anything that way without a guarantee." She turned from the stove. The eggs were cooked and she brought some of them. "Start on this. The other will be done in a minute."

Ham too, and not just a little bit the way you got it with a buck breakfast on the road. He was hungry. "There's another reason," he said.

She turned quickly. There was more anger in her voice than there should be. "Sure there is. There's always a girl. Do you think that's a mystery to me after all those years in this business."

It surprised him. A man was entitled to do what he wanted if he did it right. She had no line on him.

"I'm sorry," he said. It did not sound right. It sounded stupid.

"What are you sorry about." The anger was gone as quickly as it came. She served more food and sat down. "I have to call Ben. This will get cold. What are you sorry about?"

He remained silent. He was not going to be pushed into any more stupidness.

"Twenty years at sea." She was almost laughing. "Eight years on the road and you say something like that." She did not laugh. Then she placed her hand over his. "You sit here eating and uncomfortable and saying you're sorry." She stood, walked to the doorway and called Ben. Then she turned around. "He's another prude," she said, "but he rode with a girl anyway. Everyone does."

"Everyone."

"As near as I can tell." Her voice was quiet. The sadness was a light thing, something that was unhappy but distant like it was only remembered, already figured out. Which meant, he guessed, that John had had a woman too. Somehow it made her nicer, more exclusive.

"Ben's coming," she said. "And you're too old to be a prude, but most men I ever met were."

"How about women?"

"They may start off that way, but most of them end up as realists." She pushed the door open, stood for a moment and turned. The released door swung and was caught. Before Ben came in he stood for a couple of seconds, either looking over the land or looking at the truck. All Singleton could see was one hand that was white and red. Long fingers wrapped around the white door. The red spots on the hand stood out in the sunshine and made the hand look diseased.

When Ben came in he looked fair. He walked quickly across the kitchen with just the hint of a limp. Singleton kicked a chair out for him.

"She must have been a bruiser." No hello. Ben grinned and tapped him on the shoulder. He was talking about the trip.

Singleton could not see what Grace meant and he was looking. There was enthusiasm in Ben's voice. Maybe not like a year ago, but you could not expect that.

"We've had worse," Singleton told him. Grace poured coffee for Ben. He seemed shrunken and thin. There were lines around his eyes, his face pulled tight at the forehead. He had lost height. Singleton guessed that Ben was slumping an inch or two. That would make him about six feet. Ben drank, wiped his mouth with the back of his hand, saw his hand and dropped it in his lap.

"Make a buck?"

"Here and there." It was not quite like talking to a stranger. Ben was changed a lot. Before, you couldn't blame him for hiding the hand. Before, you could take this tall kid with the college education who could kick off a load with the best of them, could set him on the road with a thirty-thousand-dollar rig and a hundred-thousand-dollar load and forget him until he showed up. He was different. Hiding the hand was wrong. You did not have to be self-conscious with family.

"You look good," Singleton told him.

"Much better. Did you get north?" His girl was north.

"South and west. You take what comes." Singleton was finished eating and leaned back. "Eat before it gets cold." He looked at Grace who still stood. She was listening to Ben, watching him, and there was a look of surprise and pleasure. Ben looked bad but he was talking good. Maybe it was time he went back to work.

"Stay for awhile?" Ben was eating and talking. He hunched forward, a curve in his spine while he bent over the table. That was the way it used to be. Hurried. Too busy to eat.

"I don't know," Singleton said. "Your mom said to come in."

"Tell you why?" Ben was hurrying to finish, speaking through mouthfuls. When he was finished there would be no place to go. Habit.

"Not yet." He looked at Grace.

"I'll tell him," she said to Ben. "You finish. I'll be right back." She left the kitchen and headed for the stairway. Singleton wondered how many times a day she was obligated to climb those stairs. Did she have to get up at night. A couple of days in the house would tell him. He dreaded the days. He ought to feel sorry for John, and he did. The realness of it made you want to cry with

[100]

what you had lost, and for John. Right now he felt sorry for anyone around John.

Ben finished and went for the coffeepot. There was not much left. He split it between the two cups. Then he walked to the window and looked into the yard at Singleton's truck. A professional look.

"I have to get it washed." He did not need to apologize, didn't need to tell Ben that if you ran south you often ran dirty.

"We'll run down to the stop." Ben sounded eager. "She surged pretty hard when you pulled in." He stopped. Singleton ignored it. Ben had been around someplace just listening yesterday.

"It always has."

"We might touch it up. I've still got tools."

"We might, but she's running good."

"Lot of dust."

"I was going to let them change the filters." Singleton walked to the window. "How is she going to feel if you start messing around with trucks again?"

Ben looked at him. "Come on outside."

"Now? She'll be back in a minute."

"Any minute. It doesn't take too long up there." Ben looked at the doorway, then looked down at the floor. "We ought to talk." His voice was different. Nervous. A little wild. Singleton figured that this part was what Grace knew. He wondered how bad it could get and figured to find out.

"I'll see her first."

Ben's reaction was not worse. He was in control. He stuck his hands in his pockets, turned and looked at Singleton. The look said that he could not believe a grown man would wait for a woman to tell him what to do. When you stopped to think about it, and where it was coming from, it was pretty funny.

"You get loose," Ben said, "I'll be in the grove taking out deadwood." He went outside, hands still in his pockets, and headed across the lot to the barn. He emerged carrying an axe. It was a stupid way to clear brush. You could rent a tractor and a portable saw, set the rig up and have the whole job knocked out in a day. Maybe that was the thing to do. Get the equipment and spend a day or two working. You could tell a lot about a man by working with him. Singleton picked up the empty coffeepot, measured more coffee, and put it on the stove. Then he picked up the breakfast dishes and ran water. By the time they were soaking, Grace returned.

She looked for Ben.

"He's clearing wood," he told her.

"It won't last. He'll be in within the hour." She watched him. "Sit down. Why is it men get uncomfortable when there isn't any work?"

It was a question he had asked himself a hundred times when he was laid over, reading a book or magazine and the truck in first-class shape; the sunlight brilliant on Texas or Alabama or Michigan concrete, guys working, and him with nothing to do. On the ships there had always been something to do. On the road there were times when there was nothing, except to walk around, read or get drunk. But he had never liked to drink during the daytime and at night you were mostly driving. Some guys did both and did it pretty well, but it was a wrong way and those guys did not last many years.

He lit another cigarete. "Looks like a lot to do," he told her. "The place is running down."

"That's part of what I want to talk about." She was smiling very open now, quite friendly. For a moment she reminded him of Shirley in Harrodsburg. In spite of being older she was better looking than Shirley. There was an eagerness about her that must have something to do with her plan.

"Tell me."

"In a minute. What are you going to do while you're here?"

He was going to try to set up a steady run again instead of all this gypsying, if he could set it up for North Carolina. There was plenty coming north out of Hickory, if only you could find a steady back haul.

"I was going to scout around a little. Take a few days. Thought maybe Ben would go along."

"I don't know."

"Sure you do. Half his problem is that he's going nuts from not doing anything."

"What's the other half?"

"I don't know." He told himself that he did not even believe there was another half. Ben was bored, feeling useless, and had been out of action too long. That took any man apart.

"Promise one thing."

"Sure."

"You won't take the truck."

It was a hell of a thing to have to promise but he agreed. She did not like Ben to go and she did not want Singleton to take him. But, he thought, Grace was fair. She probably figured that he might be right.

"Tell me about the other thing," he said. "Tell me what you are planning to do."

12

GRACE wanted him to farm. Of all the crazy, perverse, jackleg schemes that any one human being could come up with, she had chosen the worst. She wanted to stop the leases when they came up for renewal, wanted him, Charles Singleton, and Ben, her own son, Ben Singleton, she had wanted them to trade off a fifth wheel for a three-point hitch.

He said no. She said think about it. He said all right.

Singleton sat at the stop with Ben and wondered if he was losing his mind. He did not say anything and Ben did not say anything. It was obvious that Ben was waiting to see what he was going to say.

He knew what he was going to say. He was going to say no. If that didn't work he was going to say, hell, no. Out of the question, but why hadn't he already said it?

He wondered if Ben had it figured out, that she was trying to start another family, sort of. There was no question that she was part of the package, there was no question of that. It wasn't like Grace. It must be like Grace. She had set it up. Singleton figured that Ben was not onto that part.

The stop was busy, which was the reason he had driven there. After the quiet of the house, and knowing that he was acting weak (why, goddamn it, why, couldn't a man just say no, and the reason was because she had run her fingers up his arm and he had been wondering what next, like a punk seaman left with someone else's shack job); after the quiet house and the tension with the woman the busy truck stop was like a refuge.

They sat at the counter drinking coffee. Singleton wished they had brought his rig instead of the station wagon. For one thing he could have a wash. For another thing automobiles scared him. You couldn't see where you were going, always had the feeling that you were running shoal water in a sardine can. He drank coffee and sat watching the ready-line. All of those trucks going someplace in a little while, and screw the railroads. They would roar out of the slots, leaving a gap that would quickly be filled with another rig. The whole country was full of trucks now. Every month there were more guys on the road. Not at all like before the war, not like after, either, when there was a lot of confusion about what was going to happen. Trucks were beautiful, most of them. He counted them out, the diversity, the difference in power, the body rigs. Chevrolet hauling new cars. You'd want to use it that way because it was not worth a shit for much else. Parked right in between two Kenworths. Machinery on one flat, reefer box on the other. Say what you want, but Kenworth.

The trucks were stacked in pretty. Whites, Diamond T's, GMC with a single axle and a furniture box, good truck for furniture, old Autocar, old Reo and where did they dig that up? Be seeing a Marmon Harrington next. Lots of Fords, all kinds of Macks. There was a whole boiling of Macks and that figured; a Peterbilt—not many of them in the east; International, Emeryville, not much difference. From the distance there was the sound of a Mack running the low side and cruising into the stop.

"61 or 67," Singleton said, proud that he could identify the truck without looking. It was the first thing he had said since they left.

"67-H," Ben told him. "Hear how she echos a little?"

"No."

"Conventional doesn't work up that double sound."

Singleton did not know whether he was amused or envious. "Are you really that good or can you see from here?"

"I like engines. Take the same engine in two different makes and it will sound different."

[105]

"Can you tell them all?"

"Pretty near." Ben was not grinning or making a big deal. Once he would have grinned. "In bed I used to listen nights. Learned them. Take a sound, remember it, and match it against something like it that came past next day."

"You were half a mile from the road."

"I can see half a mile. Another month and I'd been able to tell you what he scaled, give or take five thousand."

The rig rolled onto the lot. Ben did not look up and the tractor was a 67-H.

The stop hummed. In the restaurant three waitresses were moving quickly and quietly, quiet because they were so busy. A bad time for waitresses. Tips went down when you were busy. Guys on a schedule didn't give a damn about other people's problems.

Leave these blues behind me

The juke. He was trying to figure something out and somebody had plugged the juke. A waitress stopped in front of them with the pot. Dark-haired woman of thirty. Neat. Hair tucked under her cap, nice figure, couldn't see her legs because of the counter. Drive a man crazy, this woman business that complicated every-thing. He swore to himself that it was easier when he was fifteen and ignorant. He pushed his cup at her.

Let that tandem call

The trouble with a lot of guys was that they got fooled by the road, fooled by the expensive and beautiful trucks, thought they were some kind of special guy. They made a big deal of it, and any time that happened somebody was going to be there to write songs and take big money from the juke box. The waitress poured the coffee, took the necessary second to push it back at him, which meant that she was still trying to do the job right, and hurried on down the counter. The juke thumped in the background.

Beside him two guys running freight were slurping hard at the coffee. One was sopping bread in the leftovers of mashed potatoes and gravy. Singleton turned from the counter.

Pulled from Pittsburgh, pulled her in July

The stops helped feed the feeling of specialness. Lots of them were now setting up special dining rooms for truckers only.

Got back in November

[106]

Three steel rigs were backed up on the road waiting for the entry to clear.

Want to die

"What do you think?" he asked Ben. Three guys were trying to hustle a waitress, trying to give her a hard time, get a little reaction. Was everybody in the whole world lonely? The girl was sore but hiding it. She was only about twenty-three, a nice-looking little girl. Maybe she was used to it.

Truck gypsy blues, make your bad news

"What kind of question is that?" Ben picked up his coffee.

Chasin' that lonesome road

Ben was acting like a sullen kid.

"Let's get out of here," Singleton told him. He stood, tossed two quarters on the counter and headed for the door. Ben was following. Before Singleton could make it he was pulled over by a guy. A guy from someplace; where had it been? He was one of those older, friendly types, one of those guys who were always sunburned and never tanned. Wisconsin? Nevada? No. Illinois? Singleton could not remember. It had been the northern route. Someplace they had dropped a few bucks in a pinball one night and drank a couple of beers. He remembered. The guy was all talk. Pulled house trailers with an old Stude and talked about places he'd never been.

"Where you headed?" The guy was set to waste an hour of someone's time.

"Came down for a part," Singleton lied. "You still on ball hitch?"

"Yeah, but a new truck. If you got a minute."

"We're running behind now." He slapped the guy on the shoulder and grinned. Ben waited.

"Take just a minute."

Ben pushed by and out the doorway.

"Next time," Singleton told him. "We got to go." He stepped through the doorway after Ben.

"Keep it between the fence posts," the guy yelled.

Singleton waved his hand backward, going away. A guy he didn't need.

They walked to the side of the building, crossed the lot and found the car where they had self-consciously hidden it. Not arriving in a truck was too much like dropping in as a tourist. They walked alongside a furniture rig. The padlocks were open. The guy must have a pickup or a drop before going out.

"Cincinnati," Ben said. "Place called the Coffeepot or Coffee Cup or something. All the furniture guys go there."

"I've never been."

"I went once. There were lots of girls. Fella was laying over waiting for a load. Nearly empty. He opened the van and made beds of furniture pads. The girls were selling it right there on the lot."

"Yeah." It did not sound like Ben. It sounded rough. Always before Ben had not been rough. A tough guy, a tough mouth, but Singleton doubted that he meant it. Ben had been raised too strict. Singleton forced a grin. "You been laid up too long."

"The truth." Ben's voice was lower. They were past the ready line and headed toward the station wagon. "Where do you want to go?"

It was a good question. Singleton did not know where he wanted to go, except that like Ben, he did not want to go back to the house until absolutely necessary. The woman was there and she was a fine woman and there was no doubt about that. There was also no doubt that she was trying to kill both of them in her woman way; a way that she understood as being helpful and not killing at all. Twenty years around the business and she still believed that you could settle in and run a farm.

"Run to Louisville to shop the trade." He said it because he did not know where else to go. He did not want to stay in Indianapolis because they would end up home too soon. Louisville was only a couple of hours.

"We can get loads here."

"I know."

"We can go get your rig and go right over to Smitty's and head for New York right now. Smitty's always good for a load."

"Cheap."

"I got to admit, old Smitty is cheap." Ben grinned. "Right now I'd turn it for expenses." He opened the car door, slid behind the wheel and dragged the keys from his shirt pocket. Singleton climbed in. "I like it that you're back," Ben said. "For awhile I was just sitting."

"You know what she wants?"

[108]

"Yep."

"Then let's go to Louisville."

"It's pretty late in the day but what the hell." Ben had a lightness in his voice, a kind of eagerness like he used to have when he was running north and getting by to see Sue. His hands on the wheel were red-splotched and looked like picture hands, painted hands like bad movie posters. He was not thinking of his hands now. The fingers curled correctly. They were eased onto the wheel and looked sure and firm. He started the engine. It was a new car. There had been a lot of money from the sale of the fleet. Ben eased from the lot, made a turn, and connected with the brand new four-lane.

It felt strange to be riding, and in a car. Ben cleared the twister, entered the road and sapped it hard. The station wagon sat down momentarily and Singleton was pushed back in his seat. At seventy-five Ben leveled it off and they were solid in the road. For a car.

The land was brown and the trees were changing in the groves. Before long, autumn would be real strong. Then it would be winter. Then it would be a good idea to hang south even if the money was bad. Singleton looked at the brown fields and thought of ice. There had been icebreaking in the Coast Guard during many winters. Usually it was in the rivers and usually it was the Penobscot River in Maine.

"I remember a day," he told Ben, "day something like this except it had about four feet of snow and maybe eight inches of blue ice. We were in a river, the Penobscot, and the sun was hot like now. Middle of winter and the sun was hot."

"Gets like that in Pennsylvania, sometimes." Ben was closing a line of three rigs, coasting up to them, closing at the right speed and with good control. He made his signal, went around, and slanted back in. His form was still good, but somehow the edge was off.

"It's nice," Singleton told him. "You go up the mouth of the river a mile. All salt ice. White and pretty slushy. Then you get into the hard stuff. Hit into it, start a crack and then follow the crack up. Crack runs maybe a quarter mile up the river ahead of you."

"Yeah, I wish sometimes I'd done stuff like that. A lot of time in school, few years on the road, little National Guard time but we never got activated to Korea."

Singleton leaned back. No one was going to understand if they had not been there.

You hit the crack, following it up the river and the icebreaker bow would ride up on the ice. Then the cutter, still kicking ahead slow, would wallow and start pushing the ice down. There would be shattering and splashing on each side, the crack would run further, and you backed her down and hit into it again. You did not get much each time. A mile or two aft, the coastal tankers you were making a way for would lay back, moving in slow to keep it from freezing again. On the mountains surrounding the river the pine trees would be black against the white snow, and you would moor someplace and walk the ice. Sometimes it would happen near a small town or store and then guys would wade through the huge drifts and complain. Every winter someone said that they ought to make at least a couple pairs of snowshoes. Every winter no one did.

That day, the pretty, beautiful day, the crack had run in straight lines. It glistened along the edges. At noon everyone, including the captain who was a warrant officer on the hundred-ten footer, laid aft to the fantail and took off their shirts. They loafed in the sun. From a nearby air base an occasional fighter came over, roaring and silver and full of noise, the noise kicking up and down the ice-filled river and dying with light reverberations among the black trees on the mountainsides. He had broken ice plenty of times, but there had only been one day like that; and there was never going to be another day like that because the truth was that if he ever did get back on a ship it was going to be as a tourist.

"Why don't you kick this thing?" His voice was too loud.

Ben looked over. "I'm above seventy, but she's pretty new. Could fuck the engine."

"Tell the truth I was thinking about something else. Forget it."

As a tourist, and even if he had gone ahead and taken the commission and stayed in a full thirty years there might not have been another day like that. Maybe he should run north. Certainly he should run north.

It was tough to be a rider. There was nothing to do, and it made him nervous. Grace made him nervous. Catherine made him nervous, and he had wanted to marry her and maybe still did.

Women made him nervous.

"What do you hear from your girl?" He already knew that things were messed up there. Why was he bugging Ben.

"Nothing." The hands on the wheel grasped a little tighter. The red did not get redder. It probably could not.

Once at sea three trainers had gone down. Out of fuel. Miscalculation. They got three guys of the six, would have gotten four, but the fourth had been trapped in the sinking wreckage. Besides, his instructor said that he thought the guy was dead anyway. They picked up two of the guys just a little after it happened. One of them was burned. One of the old Grummans took him off while they were still looking for the other one, and then the Grumman hooked a swell with its wing and tucked it in. They got the crew of the Grumman but they did not get the guy who was burned. It was like the guy had no luck, but Singleton had always liked the planes, and even liked the noise they made cracking a straight line over the hills. Jet planes now, of course, and maybe it was just that he was old-fashioned but they did not seem personal like the others were.

"You could have me or your mom call. We could straighten it out."

"Maybe, just maybe, I don't want it fixed up."

"I didn't know. I think you've been shut up for too long to know yourself."

"Been living at home for a year. We going to lay over?"

"How about one night?"

"Then," Ben said, "you scout around as much as you want. For myself, I am not going to farm and I am going to look up a friend—my very best friend—who runs a high-class whorehouse. And I am going to get stinking, almighty drunk." He kicked the accelerator. The engine began flattening out at at eighty. "Chrysler makes station wagons," Ben said, "so why'n the world did Mom buy a fucking Buick?" There was real misery in his voice that clearly had nothing to do with automobiles.

"And a Farmall," Singleton told him. "She wants to buy a tractor and get us to make scratches in a field."

"Don't want to talk about it, not yet." Ben drove, and when they crossed the bridge into Louisville he stopped at a package store. He returned to the car with a half-dozen bottles of beer.

[111]

THEY had been unable to discuss the Problem in Indianapolis. They had not been able to talk about it on the road, and now they sat in Louisville's Cherokee Park, watching kids play on slides, dabble in the water from Hogan's fountain, and bicycle into each other. Singleton slugged the first beer fast and turned to find that Ben had already finished his. Ben popped two more and passed one.

"You never drank much."

"Never had time."

Singleton figured that he could leave Ben and Grace to their own affairs. That would relieve him of them and the other way around. He wished he could do it, but they were the only family he had left, them and Pat. But Pat wrote at least every Christmas and claimed to be making it fine.

If he could persuade Ben to stay off the road then things could continue the way they were. Things had not been all that good, but nothing was as bad as letting Grace get a hook into them.

"How much money you got?"

"Hundred ten, twenty bucks. You need some?" Ben was surprised.

"No. I mean how much can you get hold of if I get an idea?"

"Let me figure." Ben sat back in the seat, staring first down a long, partly wooded hill, then up into a tree. The tree was changing, the leaves yellow, and the grass was brown with a little reviving green on the hillside. It would be one of the last really hot days.

"Seven thousand in the bank. Easy to borrow out eight on the rig. A friend of mine will probably go five more just because he trusts me. Say twenty thousand."

"That's a pretty good friend." Twenty thousand was about what he could come up with himself. It was looking good.

"We went to different schools together."

"What does that mean." Singleton reacted to the sarcasm in Ben's voice.

"He's a spade. How was a spade going to get into the uni-fucking-versity of Louisville?"

For a moment Singleton was shocked. The hatred in Ben's voice was like cracked ice, harsh and sharp and cold. He thought quick of Naomi, pushed it away, but the color came back and then he found himself the way he did more and more often lately when he ran into this race business. He could not help it if Negroes had been fucked over. He had not fucked them over, and he did not need some boneheaded college kid preaching to him. For a minute all he could think of was hands, the hundreds of hands that had moved through and around his life, the gnarled and busted hands that helped him kick hundreds of loads. The white hands and the black hands.

He wanted to tell Ben what Ben should already know: that you could not live the way the home-folks did, going all over and mixing in with people; you could not live that way and be hateful. Hateful was for the old, the people like his father and his aunt who had never left the farm. How to tell it? The hell with it, you couldn't tell it. Change the subject.

"I can match twenty thousand. What about your mom?"

Ben wasn't hating him. Ben had just been making some kind of point, because the minute he asked, Ben started thinking about something else. He sat up from the slump, swallowed the rest of the beer and opened another. "Don't count on nothing unless you've got a helluva plan. Over eighty thousand after they sold the fleet and cleared the debts. More than that now if her attorney's any good."

"I didn't think it would be that much."

"It was a good business. I don't want to talk about it." Ben started the engine. He gulped at the beer, lit a cigarette, and drained the bottle. Then he flipped it into the back seat. "Get outta here. Go get a room."

"Stop in Indiana."

"Hell no. Motel room. Don't like to go around the stops drunk."

"You really meant it." Singleton had not counted on Ben really wanting to get smashed. Grace was not going to like it. It was not right, take a kid out after a year and get him loaded.

"Told your mom I'd keep you out of trouble." He tried to make it sound like a joke.

Ben turned. "I am almost thirty years old. For the last year I've got to — got to talk to nobody, see nobody, losing my connections — not talking to anybody but my mom. Now lay off my ass."

"Hittin' you already?" He would have to go along. If Grace was right then Ben might not be too dependable out there.

"Course. We're not moving around. Go someplace and park this junk."

Down time called for a different pace. This was down time. He had not been drinking since he met Catherine. Sometimes it helped. "Let's go."

Ben eased from the pull-over to run the long, downhill winding road from the park. In the afternoon sunlight, slanting shadows obscured the roadway. Ben was automatically taking account of them. Singleton thought of booze and the road.

Most wrecks came from inattention. Most fatal wrecks happened at intersections, and that was where your attention had to be best. Drunks had wrecks because they were inattentive in the first place and the booze reinforced their habit patterns. No one could ever call himself a professional driver if he got surprised on the road.

"We going downtown?" He did not know Louisville.

"Going out by the U. There's a place just south to bed down." Ben made a turn onto Eastern Parkway and was caught by a light at Bardstown Road.

"Left is Bardstown — old folks at home, Stephen frigging

[114]

Foster—right's to Indiana, straight ahead to Knox. All the gold in the world." It was a thing you did to orient another guy. Automatic.

A half mile down the parkway Ben pulled over, got out and came back with two quarts of beer. He passed one and opened one, wrapping it in the brown sack and slugging twice before he pulled back into traffic. Singleton checked his watch. A few minutes after five. He figured Ben would pass out or drown by nine o'clock.

All the drinking he'd done for the last eight years had been for the wrong reason. It was not like making it ashore with a couple of other senior POs from the cutters. They would leave for the weekend on noon Friday. Singleton and Hannah, who was also a chief bosun mate from the buoy snatcher across the pier; and maybe Watts who was chief engineman on Singleton's ship; checking out ten minutes after the old man left, and the old man always left early on Friday so they could check out; the three of them with money and self-respect and a thirst.

Hannah, who was short and too runty for a bosun mate, but who was better with the buoys than any other man Singleton had ever known, would tip his hat seriously to the other two. He would straighten his tie, solemnly inspect them and reprimand them for evil thoughts. He would make them promise to remain sober, make them promise not to get him drunk; a long read-out about transgressions of the flesh. Then Hannah would flip the finger in the general direction of the buoy deck.

They would walk, laughing from the pier past the small boat moorings at South Portland, past the weed-smelling, kelp-smelling, red-lead-smelling, dead-barnacle-stinking and rust-flaking buoys in various stages of repair; past the lighted bells, the lighted whistles, leaning at a sixty-degree angle on their tubby bottoms. The decay of barnacles, the hot sun—why did he always remember the sun? Portland, Maine. Your memory would naturally lean heavy toward the sun.

Climb into a car and go across the million-dollar bridge, all three of them serious now, loving it now in anticipation. Up the brick streets, cruising, then to the waterfront, hungry for the long afternoon and the long night. Hannah kidding Watts about his shack job. Watts insisting that at least old Watts did not need to

[115]

make it with no whore. Hannah saying that all women were whores at heart, and he had not understood that until he married a nice girl; which he hadn't seen her for years, that's good.

Singleton thinking of the women, seeing them in the beer joints and sometimes later in bed. Kids mostly. From upstate where the saying went that a virgin was a girl under twelve who could run faster than her brother. Singleton glad for the beer, for the first twisting and beautiful feel of it in his head; and it made all women beautiful. He stayed away from the kids. He saw a woman who worked in the library. Her name was Martha and they were careful to be independent. They told each other that the other was truly, truly free, and she obligated him to read the books she brought but she never asked whether he actually did read them or not. It was best because no one knew about it and because of the freedom. When he left Portland she had cried and he felt bad.

He opened his beer, drank and turned to Ben. "Sometimes I think I should of taken a commission and been an old sailor."

"It would beat hell out of this traffic." They were hauled down by a light, long lines of automobiles rising on the hill ahead of them. Cemetery to the right, a smelly creek running to bisect the road beneath a heavy concrete bridge.

Once Hannah had caught the clap from a woman named Prudence, which was pretty funny. Even Hannah laughed, but he did not laugh much. Later on he stopped going to town and spent the evenings boozing in a joint in South Portland with the fishermen. Funny to think of Hannah. Be retired, probably. From Ohio. A lot of good sailors came from inland. Maybe went back to Ohio.

"You should go back to school." It was a good idea. Did he have to drink beer before he had good ideas?

"For why?"

"Why not? You're an engineer. Learn design. Make a lot of money designing things."

"I already can." Ben turned left, was halted by more traffic, then changed a lane when there was a break. "I got the principles. You don't need more classroom if you've got the principles."

"What can you design?" He had not thought of this.

"Anything. Automatic transmission for a truck."

"It won't work. They tried it." It would not even work on a pickup very well, local freight pickup, not an old lady's truck.

[116]

"They did it wrong," Ben said. "You watch, some smart guy will do it pretty soon. Minimum power loss, better gear selection than a lot of guys can figure with a clutch."

"It won't sell. Guys are never going to give up bustin' gears."

"That's what I think, too. Why I never did it." Ben took a right after passing beneath two viaducts. "Motel's out here."

It might be possible to start a design company. Ben could run it. Singleton could stay on the road. Plenty of competition, but maybe Ben could do what he said.

They found the motel, got a big room against the price of two small ones, and locked the car.

"Maybe I'd better swallow the key." Ben was grinning. He moved fast, trying to get even with the beer.

Singleton tore the paper from a glass and poured his beer. "Get something to eat pretty soon."

"Sure, make the evening last longer." Ben headed for the bath-room and the shower. He turned on the water, then started throwing his clothes through the doorway. In another minute he gave a yelp as the cold water hit him. It would be a relief when the weather broke.

In Maine you never wished that. In Maine, toward the middle or back of September, the first northeaster would start to blow. Then it was winter. And it stayed winter until April, and some-times May. In Maine the summer was precious and it lasted short. The days were not short, but they seemed that way. Once he had taken Martha to the beach. Tall woman, older than him, but in a lot of ways as graceful as a girl. They waded like kids and felt the killing chill of the North Atlantic which reached all the way from Greenland. Funny to think of Martha now, because it had been a long time and it had been no obligation.

She sure had been a serious person. Even with the sex she was serious, nearly studied, and it was obvious that she could do without the sex, just as obvious as the fact that he could not. Somehow it made him feel compromised, although he knew that she didn't mean that to happen.

Once they stood in five-below weather across from the library and listened to a Salvation Army band. It was impressive, a band playing in that weather. Martha said she was a kind of shirt-tail Baptist turned atheist because that was the only thing that made sense. But they both admired the tenacity of people who would play music at five below zero.

He filled his glass. Three bottles and a half quart of beer. Feeling it already. Maybe he should route north for awhile, run some of the old places. A man got out of touch.

Do you run from me

He drank half the beer in one swallow, stood and started pulling off his shirt. His armpits smelled sour with sweat. A shower, a steak, and maybe some of it would be like old times.

THE joint was three miles from the Downs but it was horsy and julepy, southern tradition in the center of a seedy, middle-class, middle-west town. A concrete nigger stood at the curb holding a ring where you could tie your horse if you had one. The bartender wore a white shirt, a black string tie, and the air conditioner worked.

Down time. Down time was different, the pace slower; and if a man took time to appreciate it, savor the slow-flowing luxury of it, then down time could take a lot of weight from the hours and days and miles. The miles already behind you could seem easy, and you did not have to think about the miles, the time, the tick-tocking ribbon of asphalt joints across the concrete highways out there waiting.

They sat in a booth near the door and drank the first cold ones of the evening while watching three impassioned pinballers dickering with flashing, promising, tilting machines.

"Knew a fella once," Ben turned from watching the pinballers. "Drove furniture in an old five-over Ford that was run to death. Used to route Reno every time he caught one west, get a five-hundred-buck advance, drop it on the way through."

"Never liked gambling." Singleton was drinking slow. If you

drank too fast after eating, your gut bloated.

"Neither did he. That's the point, or I think it is. Went through every time, got cleaned every time, but always figured there'd come a day when he walked out with the price of a new rig."

"I hope he don't hold his breath."

"I guess." Ben signalled the waitress for another round. The girl came, a short, unpretty girl who was making her tips by being quick and friendly. Ben watched her walk away then turned back to the beer. "What do you want to do?"

"It's early."

"It's late. I'm a year behind."

"Whatever." Singleton sat wondering about Ben. He had some patterns that were pretty well developed. For one thing, you almost never saw his hands. Unless he was actually picking up something.

"We hit Fonnie's later on."

"Who?"

"The guy who'll lend me money, the spade guy who is also rich because he runs a classy place."

"Sounds like a girl."

"Short for Alfonso. You ever have a real best friend, your own age I mean." Ben pulled it back so that it would not sound insulting.

He thought of Pat. He had no answer.

"He's a musician, too, but that's not why my mom hates his ass. He's not what she would call a good influence."

How well did you ever know a guy? It was like making liberty with a married guy when you were someplace other than your homeport. The married guys went ashore then. The single guys did not much care. Their connections were back home. He had taken a lot of duty over the years so married guys could have a little adventure. Usually the next day they would be hung over and quiet.

The hum of conversation droned, buzzed, hovered above the clinks of glasses, was separate from the silently moving, quick-eyed bartender. A hiss from the neon beer sign in the window mingled with the rushing sound of the air conditioner. Blue lights and red lights and gold lights twisted behind the bar and on the wall from advertising signs. The clock was a green neon glow.

The door opened and three girls came in. They were well dressed, manicured, and their hair was meticulously styled. They walked to the back of the long room, attempted to sweep past the front booths, and the attempt was self-conscious and pathetic. Ben watched them.

"Lots of secretaries, office people out this way."

Two couples were in the joint. There were a dozen men along the bar. Singleton leaned back, amused, and watched the strings start feeding out.

At the head of the L-shaped bar and beside the pinballs a man stood, walked to the head, and returned. When he took his seat it was changed. He had moved two seats around the ell and could now look the length of the long room, at the end of which the girls pretended indifference. He was an older guy with a belly like a small balloon. Thin gray hair and stubby legs. He had working hands.

The waitress brushed twice at a hanging strand of hair, stopped to re-pin it, smoothed her skirt and walked to the booth. The girls ordered, took their time, gassed with the waitress who knew them, then settled back to light cigarettes and wolf at the smoke. The most striking girl was tall, narrow-hipped and had blond hair rolled high. The other two were pretty in a quiet way, slender girls with dark hair ornamentally waved to their shoulders, light summer dresses, and crossed legs so that ankles and the smooth, stockinged line of calf showed from the sides of the booth. They were in familiar territory.

A dollar player turned from his pinball, plugged the juke, then shrugged and got a roll of nickels from the bartender. Two booths away a couple stood to leave, the man deadpan, the woman talking with animation. The man turned back to the table, scoffed the last of his beer, looked to the rear as he turned and the couple left.

The juke remembered The Red River Valley.

Like marionettes the men along the bar adjusted themselves. The bar mirror was well polished, the one required-to-be-polished item of any bar's equipment. The men moved on the revolving stools by fractions. Here a quarter-turn, there a deliberate swiveling to face down the bar.

The second couple began an argument. The subject was

baseball but the argument was heated. The waitress brought the girls their drinks.

The girls chatted again, paid, and the waitress left. The juke had now gotten itself locked in Folsom Prison.

The air conditioner throbbed. The neon buzzed. Singleton thought that the important part was that no one was talking. The men hunched over their beer. Except for the juke and the rattle of glasses from behind the bar there was no sound except the flutter of the pinballs.

"When I was a kid," he told Ben who was watching the girls, "I used to go to a stag bar. Have a lot of fun at a stag bar."

"I never been."

"Lot of fun." In a stag bar guys talked louder and more confident. There were not very many stag bars left.

The juke came in with a rumble, that punk kid, old hip-slinging cracker Heartbreak Hotel.

"That cuts it. Let's move on."

"Race music." Ben stood up. "Hear lots of it. Nothing wrong with it."

"Don't know anything about it, don't want to know."

"Sound like my mom." Ben finished his beer and they left, pushing through the doorway into the hot-feeling air after the coolness of the air conditioning. "Nothing but trouble," Ben said. He had had two beers, slowing down on the drinking, slowing down on conversation.

"I think so too. He's going to swivel that ass until somebody kicks it up between his shoulders."

"I mean the girls."

They walked slow and Singleton felt pretty good. The evening coolness was beginning to take the heat from the sidewalk. Small drifts of leaves were raked into gutters and he did not feel the beer yet because he was drinking slow. Ought to call Catherine. Ought to figure out whether it was right or wrong to run north in winter.

They hit two more joints that were sullen and quiet and dull so that they left each after one beer. In the next one there was a little action, a light spirit to the place that Singleton always needed to get a night of drinking started. Two soldiers from Knox were trying to pick up a couple of girls. The soldiers were kids but the girls were not. At a back table a group of older people were celebrating

[122]

a birthday. The bartender was quick, joking on the run, apparently enjoying himself. It was a valuable talent in a bartender. After another beer Singleton switched to Scotch. You could only drink so much beer.

Ben sat watching the GIs and tapping his foot to the juke. He said nothing. Singleton began to feel better. At some other time, in some other life altogether, he would have been willing to start something with the girls just to see how it turned out. It occcurred to him that he had not been in a fight in years. Was that right? Was that the same thing as running south? He knew what Ben was thinking. He thought with amusement and affection of that younger Charles Singleton who would have tried to make it with some other guy's pickup.

Ben turned, looked at Singleton like he was judging the chances, shrugged and gulped the rest of his beer.

"The hell outta here."

"Don't let me hold you back." It was insulting, being looked at that way. It would almost be worth getting whipped not to be looked at that way. Singleton left. When he cleared the door Ben was with him. Neither of them was talking.

They worked a couple more joints. Ben picked up the pace of his drinking. It was like he was trying to flood himself with beer. As he drank he continued to move.

For a while Singleton tried to gear down. Then the whiskey began to settle in and he moved with the evening. Ben spoke less and less. He drank in an obvious attempt to get walleyed.

They hit more places, places that were silent and brooding, places filled with old-timers, places nearly deserted. In a couple of the joints there were women obviously waiting to meet truck drivers or sailors or insurance salesmen. In those places Ben grumbled obscenities over his beer. When they ran out of joints they called a cab.

The cab took them back to the south end where they sat at yet another bar and argued with the taxi driver they had invited in for a drink. The taxi driver was a small, serious man, who believed that Findlay, Ohio, was the prettiest town on earth because he came from there. Before he was finished he nearly had them convinced. They had both run Findlay at one time or another, and remembered it green and quiet with a lake and old brick buildings that were very nostalgic, very romantic, really, in the smoky-crowded-sweat-smelling bar with the head that stank of disinfectant, sour beer, vomit, and which had floors slick from guys deliberately pissing on the wall.

For a while after the cabby left they talked about Findlay. It was a little past eleven and Singleton was feeling pretty drunk.

He had been high. Now he was coming down. It was no use to prime the high—the down would continue. The only way to avoid the down was to do something, get your attention focused. It was dull in the bar.

"Let's shove."

Ben stared wisely at him, turned to look at the clock, turned back and continued to stare.

"Le's go." He could not quite get the slur from his voice.

"Go Fonnie's." Ben swiveled, stood and headed for the door. He was not steady. Once on the street Singleton felt better. The fresh air hit the whiskey and made him light-headed. For a minute he felt like he was walking in front of himself, then his head caught up, his shoulders squared, and the booze was no longer a pressure but a lift.

He walked beside Ben and wondered how far it was. After several blocks he found that it was going to be quite a walk. He was glad. The walking and air would allow him to catch up. He told himself that he was about halfway tight, knowing that he was more than halfway, telling himself that the drunkest guy in the world never admitted to more than halfway.

The old caution suddenly hit him. Drunk in a strange town. Money in his pockets. The caution caught him crossing a street, stepping into the street with a green light and halfway across before he realized that he had not looked.

"Where we goin'?" His voice was too thick. He did not like himself. Ben did not answer.

The caution was at the back of his neck. He turned, found no one, and turned to catch up with Ben. They were on a side street now, passing beside the large warehouse of an auction company.

"Shurshill Down," Ben said, pointing toward the end of the block. "Biggest race track inna worl'."

It was not, but there was no reason to argue. It was a big race track. As they approached, the stables became individual in the darkness. Flaring blue lights flooded the roofs, dispelling shadow and casting other shadows. Beyond the stables horse vans were racked in, ten or twelve of them, and a couple of single-axle Jimmies.

Get to swaying and they'll throw you over, way to break it up is snap the wheel hard agin the sway, bang 'em inta each other

But that guy had been hauling cattle. Were horses the same? But you didn't pack race horses, at least he figured you didn't. The trailers were low and streamlined. Pull them fast.

Ben turned into an alley, walked a few feet in the darkness, and pissed against a fence. He came back and they continued around the Downs. Then Ben turned left and headed south. It was a cross-country hike. There were no taxis in sight. Singleton kept looking for a sign, neon that would tell him they had arrived at a place where he could nurse one more drink, call a cab, and they could return to the motel. As a drunk it was a bust.

Ben entered a street of small houses that was parked up with old cars and beat-up trucks. Past a moving company, a couple of single-axle Trailways and a North Carolina job parked against the loading door. Past a couple of warehouses. Then Ben turned into a lighted alley and walked toward a small warehouse a half block distant. Cars were parked in the alley. New ones. They were shiny beneath the lights, a contradiction to the junk that had been parked in the street; Cads and Olds and Packards.

Ben stopped and looked at the automobiles. His lips were moving. He was counting.

"Friday night, good old Friday night." He was humming, and besides, it was Saturday. He turned, staggered, caught himself. He began humming louder.

"I will be damn, damn if I won't. You have led me to a whorehouse."

"My old frater-ery," Ben said seriously.

"Let's go back," Singleton said. Ben kept walking. Singleton hurried to catch up. He grabbed Ben's sleeve. He felt himself sobering. "I'm sober," he said.

Ben pulled away, turned. "Okay."

"Then let's go."

"I'm okay, okay, okay. You sober, you can't come. Franterity rules . . . ." His eyes widened. "You sober?"

[125]

"Yeah."

"I am sorry for you. For you. You sober, kid. Out with you, kid."

Singleton grabbed his arm. "I'm tired. Let's leave."

"You go." Ben pulled too hard, took three steps sideways, and recovered as he realized he was not being held. He grinned, standing not far from the circle of a shaded light on the side of the building. "I'm okay." He was singing. He was singing, singing. He slapped himself on the face with one hand. "Still feel it."

Singing. He held his hand up in front of his face to show how steady it was. He looked at his hand. Dropped it. "Fuckit," he said, "just lea' me alone." He turned and continued down the alley.

Singleton followed. He wondered how drunk a man could get on beer. He was surprised that anyone could get pushed over on beer. The whiskey feel was lighter now, like the whiskey you drank two shots of after twelve hours driving that you logged as ten, when you showered and then belted the whiskey to get you clean of the road.

A whorehouse.

"You got to go home sometime." He was yelling at Ben. "You got to go home." He ran after Ben. He was shocked by the sound of his yelling in the empty alley. He caught Ben's arm.

"You got to go home sometime, kid."

Ben wavered. "You're drunk," he told Singleton. "You say you're drunk."

"Why?"

"I'm sober," Ben said. "Sober and goin' to a whorehouse and if you ain't drunk I'll get a rock and kill ya."

He wondered if he should lay Ben out. It was a bad idea. There were no cabs. He would have to leave him to find a phone.

"I'm sorry," he told Ben. "You haven't been anywhere in a year."

"It's sad. It's so sad, it's sad." Ben had already forgotten. He was humming. "No place ina year, no one ina year."

The door looked solid but when it opened it was flimsy. Which meant that there were other doors beyond it or that the management was without fear. The door opened outward when Ben knocked. A heavy, wrestler-bodied man came out and shoved his hand against Ben's chest. Ben fell back against Singleton, staggered, regained his balance, blinked twice and walked back to the door. The man waited.

"C'mon," said Singleton. "Let's go."

"Fu-kin-min-it." Ben enunciated the syllables carefully. "Who you?"

"Who're you?" The wrestler's voice was low and tough. He was dressed in dark pants, no tie, sport shirt.

"Use to come here, I guess," Singleton said. "Tell us to go so I can get him outta this."

"Just a minute." The wrestler turned back and there was a click, a phone lifted. The wrestler muttered, then he turned to the doorway. "Name."

"Singleton," said Ben.

"Singleton," the man said into the phone. He looked back at Singleton.

"You?"

"Singleton," said Singleton.

"Then who the fuck is he?"

"Singleton," said Singleton. "He's Ben, 'm Charles."

"Pretty drunk" the guy said into the phone. "No, just pretty drunk. Fact is, the young one's knocked on his ass." The wrestler waited, patient, not giving a damn while someone made up his mind. Then the wrestler turned to them and he wasn't belligerent at all.

"Tough shit," he said. "Get some sleep. Come back tomorrow night."

Singleton thought the guy was handling it pretty well, despite feeling that he would like to tear the bastard's head off. Then the bad feeling went past. They were being kicked out not because of him but because of Ben.

He turned and Ben was standing there and before he drooped it was like he was almost sober for a second. For a second he thought Ben was going for the wrestler.

"Can you get us a cab?" Singleton asked the guy.

"Ten-buck cab," the guy said. "Take a couple of minutes."

"Sure."

Something was bad, bad wrong with Ben. He looked like he had just been told he had cancer. He looked all ashamed and withdrawn and you could feel his pain even under the mushy look.

[127]

"Get him over by that lamppost," the wrestler said. "Cab be here in a minute."

Ben looked awful sick.

"Before he gets to puking," the wrestler said apologetically. "When he wakes up tell him Fonnie's really honest to god sorry. It's just that Fonnie's got a bunch of big people up there tonight. Real important business."

They must have been awful good friends at one time or another. Ben wouldn't look so sick otherwise. Singleton caught him by the arm and it was like leading a survivor, like directing a wounded man to a place where he could lie down.

Ben started puking about the time the cab showed up, and they had to wait for that. When the cab got them to the motel Ben had to go through it again before he got to the room. Once inside, Singleton managed to get him out of he sour-smelling clothes and into bed. First thing in the morning he would have to get Ben something else to wear. He pitched the dirty clothes in the bathtub and ran cold water. That made them smell not so bad, and the air conditioner helped a little.

15

THE morning began with autumn mist that covered the tops of the hills, concentrated along the bed of the stream, and blocked the view beyond the road.

On such mornings the life of the valley moved in different patterns. Birds made short whirring flights, and deer became bold. You might suddenly chance on a standing deer, or see a long-legged figure easing back along the perimeter of sight so it seemed a suggestion of life rather than life itself. On these mornings the spring was muffled, yet strangely more distinct as the different sounds were like the enclosing background wool in a tapestry; and always on these mornings, there was an impression of secret motions, of arrests and indecision, of mating and dashing and stopping to whirl for another direction. An impression then of life, or an impressionist mental sketch that in the mists became life itself.

And on these mornings, because such mornings came most often in early spring or late fall, there was bone cold that made sluggish the movement of snakes; that huddled mice beneath the wood pile and silenced the crowing of roosters as the birds flocked together, low clucking in the damp grass, scratching to uncover the hints of moisture in the dust along the road. The trees were distinct, especially the conifers, and close observation showed a film of mist on every needle, an amazing reflective capacity if the sun should arrive before the wind. When that happened—and it often did—a tree would suddenly burst into a luminous green-and-silver exclamation shouting life and deep roots and water and sun. The earth, the soil of the valley that had been crumbled for the millions of years that the mountains had stood, the earth seemed translated then, and it was at such times that a hill farmer would stop, would stoop to pick a rock from the field cleared for shotgun corn, and feel that he almost understood something—but he did not know what—and that the feeling did not last.

On such mornings the old women of the hills muttered to themselves, and instead of their work, instead of chicken feeding, gardening, picking the last of the greens, canning or washing, they remembered the hot words of their preachers and for moments before entering into that day, fingered the cold covers of ragged Bibles and hoped that God really was love, although it was an idea for which they had only The Word and no particular explanation.

Catherine woke and she was thirty-five years old and had only slept with two men. The sunlight had not arrived and the room was chilly, but the blanket she had wrapped herself in made her feel seedy and trapped and enclosed. The fire was burned down. She moved and the blanket seemed like a hand holding her down. For a moment she thought that she had waked to discover that she was raving mad.

She didn't care, didn't care, didn't care. Thirty-five years old and still waking to find herself alone. She would become a lesbian, a nymphomaniac; she would breed horses and learn to swear. If he loved her, why wasn't he with her?

She dressed before a mirror. Her breasts sagged and that was pretty funny because they were not big enough to sag. She pressed them upward with her hands, and she watched her reflection. You could translate those shapes, human shapes, natural shapes. You could if you were an artist and not just a weaver.

She looked for wrinkles around her eyes and found them. She looked for wrinkles at the fore part of her shoulders and neck, and found them. They were such little wrinkles, not any bigger than the Grand Canyon—it was not fair that an active woman should have such things. She dressed in her oldest and ugliest work clothes, slipped on rubber-soled shoes and went to the kitchen where she put coffee to boil. As she passed her working area the loom seemed no more than a deserted web. She could not see, the way you had to see; and the colors of the stuff on the loom looked no more important than the colors in a mail-order catalog.

And if he loved her why was he the hell and gone off in stupid Oshkosh or somewhere. The day was terrible. It was depressing. There was death in it. If she went into the forest the mold would be talking death around the roots of every tree.

Plus she was a failure. She was the world's worst painter, and even if she could weave that meant nothing. She was a phony who taught art and could not paint. She could not paint spots on a barn.

That made her feel just great. She would become a lesbian painter and move to New York and take a barn with her, and paint spots. The coffee boiled and the telephone rang at the same time. She stood and told herself that it was a big day when two things happened at once. She poured coffee and carried it to the phone. Singleton called every few days. He was due to call.

It was not Singleton. It was a friend in Asheville who invited her to dinner to meet an eligible man. A fine, upstanding, business-type man on his way up the celebrated ladder; who her friend could do nothing about because her friend was comfortably married. It happened three or four times a year. People tried to mate her to minor figures in business, arts, entertainment—like the headings in *Time* magazine.

She had done so well before she met Singleton. Maybe she had not been absolutely happy, but she had not been angry and lonesome and resentful.

There were wrinkles. Singleton had not called. She did not care enough to be excited, although she tried to sound excited and said yes. Yes, she would be there on Monday night and, what was it? Saturday already? And how did the week slip past so soon?

And her friend explained that her husband fished on weekends and Catherine said she understood. She would be there Monday. It took half an hour and her coffee was cold.

She returned to the table and realized that she had to get out. She was in no mood to approach the valley. It lay in the beautiful and quiet part of her mind that, since Singleton, was coming forward very seldom. She had not worked even halfway well in weeks. There was nothing.

It was simple. He said he loved her. He liked to make love to her. He did not need her as much as he needed to be away. She ran her hands across her belly. With that kind of arrangement it would be more profitable to take herself, take this body, and rent it out—a way of meeting new and interesting people. There was cash in her purse. She could pack, spend two or three days in Asheville. The trouble was that when you went to Asheville you were in Asheville.

She had to get out. She should never have gone to bed with him in the first place, never tried to love him, not if it was going to make her feel this bad.

For long moments as she sat in the familiar kitchen, the room no longer seemed friendly or even particularly safe. It was like an old room furnished with junk; and the fading windmill wallpaper, the colorful tablecloth and dresser scarves made from remnants looked like remnants; and the old side-arm bookcase which had belonged to her father looked like it belonged in the lobby of a poorhouse.

Except for the years at college, and the six months with her husband, she had lived here all her life. It had always been safe here, and if her mother and father and grandparents were dead, they had never really gone.

You worked hard, you worked long, you established at least a decent professional reputation, and then one day you raised your eyes and looked around and you were thirty-five and living in an ugly, dangerous place. Where had the years gone? What had happened?

She had to get out.

Maybe Singleton had been trying to tell her something important after all. It could feel no more dangerous out there on that road than it felt right now, here, in this house.

She would not go to Asheville for the weekend. She would go somewhere new and far away and drive back to Asheville on Monday. Maybe something would happen that she could learn from. She would not understand Singleton, but she might learn just how truly wrong he was. She hoped she would not run her car off a mountain.

She stood and headed for a closet before she could change her mind. She pulled out an old suitcase and packed, thinking that anger was a terrifying and dangerous thing, but she did not try to dismiss her anger. The suitcase was large. There was plenty of space for clothing and toothbrush and hairbrush. It was awful, maybe, what she was thinking. She felt guilty as she thought it, and then anger returned. She opened the drawer in which she kept her diaphragm. She packed it, embarrassed, a little shamed, but with the indignant knowledge that she was engaged in a defiant act. Taking the thing along was a way of telling him to start taking better care of his own.

That car out there in the drive was going to get another chance to kill her or cause some kind of trouble.

When she was ready to leave she sat for a few moments in front of the cold fireplace. Its smoked, fieldstone face was as immutable and indifferent as ancient and enduring ruins, totally uncaring of its purpose of fire and heat. For a moment understanding mixed with fear in her mind, but the understanding went away and the fear remained.

She sat silent and still angry. Perhaps she should wait for another hour, get rid of her anger. The suitcase was packed and waiting. If he loved her, why wasn't he with her? She drank one more cup of lukewarm coffee and she hoped the phone would ring, but it did not.

16

SINGLETON drove. It had been a hell of a night, a terrible morning, and the afternoon was not looking great. They were never going to be allowed back in that motel, not that it made any difference, except that it always made a difference when you were wrong and there was nothing you could do about it.

Ben was still in bad shape. He was beery-smelling, even after two showers and new clothes. He was quiet, sullen, and he was acting like all of this was Singleton's fault.

Probably unfair to think that. Ben was not blaming him, but Ben was acting like a kid who was busy blaming the whole sorry world that had conspired to make him stub his toe. A bad drunk was a bad drunk. Wasn't Ben old enough to understand that? Neither of them spoke until they were beyond Jeffersonville and clear of local traffic. It had not been quite twenty-six hours since they left Grace. It seemed like a month.

They had still not discussed alternatives to Grace's plan and if they did not have a good alternative Singleton knew her well enough to know what would happen next. She would proceed against their objections, get a situation built up that she could not handle, and they would be the shitheads who were guilty if they did not fall in line and pull her out. Yep. He could see it now, and truth to tell, it *was* now if they did not get something figured.

Nothing was real except the road. The road would never fool you, or deny you, or trick you as long as you knew the rules and played them with complete accuracy. There were no mysteries, although sometimes there were surprises, not inattention surprises, but mechanical or emotional; and some men lived all their lives without being tested to see if they could handle an emergency. It was the same way at sea.

Driving a car imposed strict observation of some of the rules and eased others. He did not like to drive cars, although up to the time he had nearly lost Pat, he had liked to run small boats. Ben was about the same age that Pat had been when the trouble happened. Not a good thing to be thinking.

"Why don't you climb in back? Knock down the seats and stretch out for awhile."

Ben made a low noise in the back of his throat, not a sick noise, but a low, burbling snarl. He rubbed his eyes with the back of his hand. "I'm okay." His voice was flat.

"Want to talk?"

"No."

"Later?"

"Ask me later."

Down the road a car was pulled onto the shoulder. Singleton automatically signaled left, drifted a lane and came off the gas to coast by. It was only a flat tire and a guy was changing it. If the guy had driven another hundred yards he would have been on the face of a slight rise in the road. It would have doubled the distance from which other drivers could see him. He had saved a fifteen-dollar tire and taken the chance of getting killed by some looking-down-the-road-as-usual farmer.

They had to get one thing straightened out before seeing Grace. Grace was not like Catherine. Catherine might say that she wanted you off the road, but she would never set you up. Grace was setting them up. Not that he especially blamed her, and not that he couldn't personally get out of it. Grace was not operating all that different from most women. Catherine wasn't most women but Grace sort of was.

Naomi. Maybe he was entering a second childhood. Here it was, twenty-five years and innumerable pieces of ass later, and it was still causing trouble. He turned on the radio. Shit-kicking music. He turned the radio off.

Maybe he was in love with two women. Maybe he was walking around with an Indiana corncob up his ass.

It was a fast road and he took it fast. In an hour they were more than halfway, and for an hour he tumbled it back and forth in his mind trying to figure how to act. It was like you always owed everybody everything and had no room for yourself.

Ben sat without moving, his hands dropped between his legs, clamped in there so that they were out of sight. Occasionally he took a deep breath, but he was giving nothing away and was making no sign that he needed anything that Singleton could give. Maybe he felt like a prisoner being returned to jail. When they were twenty miles out, Singleton could no longer stand the mess.

"What are you going to do?"

"Pull in at the stop." Ben's voice was still toneless.

"We have to stop fooling around. We can talk at the stop, but we'd better start talking now."

"What's to talk about."

He wondered how Grace could have stood having the kid around for a year, because he was a sullen, angry kid—and not even a kid. "You have to make some kind of move. You can't sit forever."

The first expression he had seen on Ben's face in three hours was a twisting of absolute hatred. "Sitting."

"We can start a design company," Singleton said quickly. "You said you could. What's wrong with that?"

"You don't see a goddamn thing, do you?" Ben's face was white, tense, and his mouth was set against his rage. "Design or road or farm don't mean nothing. You come rolling in like a hero and the best you can come up with is start a business, keep your hands busy." He raised his hands to look at them. "Well, fuck you, mister."

"I didn't wreck you."

"I did. Now lay off my ass." As he yelled it he froze. He sat straight, not turning away, not turning toward Singleton. His hands were tucked away again and he sat motionless. Color was coming back. His face was red. There was a tremble starting around the tight line of his mouth. Singleton drove and caught looks at him with short sideways glances, and he did not know what to say. It was too big. He thought that Ben was going to start breaking up, maybe start crying, and he was embarrassed in front of that.

"Your dad was driving. Wasn't he?"

Ben said nothing. His tremble was getting worse. Singleton was willing to bet that it was also in his hands. No one had questioned Ben's story. No one had doubted that John was driving. When he saw the wreck after it was pulled off there had been a broken hub, but if a hub had been the cause—as it almost certainly was the cause—then it did not make any difference who was driving. Of course, the hub could have broken from the force of the wreck.

"You'd better level. You can't live holding something like that. Who was driving?" The logs were burned with the truck. There was no way to tell who was signed onto them. Maybe the kid had been lying all along.

Ben made a motion with his mouth like he was trying to speak. He sucked hard at breath, worked his mouth and nothing happened. Behind them a train of three cars was overtaking and traveling close. Singleton maintained speed as the cars came around. One of them was jogging on bedspring suspension and bad shocks. As it passed, Singleton eased off and allowed it to get around quick. Eighty miles an hour and not a shock absorber left. It was like a two-and-a-half-ton grenade.

"Break up if you've got to, but sooner or later you'll have to tell. Get it over."

It occurred to Singleton that Ben might be crazy. They were doing seventy, and it would take one snatch at the wheel from a crazy man. He dropped the speed to cruise at fifty, but prepared to sap it if anything closed erratically from the rear. Was it better to push it out of him or let him take his time? He had already had a year. Push.

"Were you driving?" He suddenly did not trust Ben. You did not make that kind of mistake. If it was not a hub, and if Ben had made that kind of mistake on a lousy sixty-mile-an-hour road, then he could never be trusted again. One thing not to know what you would do until the time came, but it was entirely different if the time had come and it was handled wrong. Ben did not answer. He had his eyes closed.

"You did it," Singleton told him. "You really did, didn't you. Didn't you?"

The reaction when it finally came was a relief because it made him cold. Ben raised both shoulders, tipped forward in the seat, grabbed at his face, sobbing and rolling to the right against the car door. He huddled against the door like a small child, crouched around himself, his shoulders and body pushed back and forth by the sobbing. It was a choking, panting sound and it was filled with horror and remorse.

Singleton told himself that he should care, that he should say something; and he found that he did not care. The sympathy he had almost felt was wrong. He was cold. For the first time he could remember, ever, he felt cruel. He did not want to say anything, and he knew that the silence was the harshest thing he could do. He wanted it that way.

He watched Ben and kicked the speed back up and looked forward to the stop and coffee. When they got there Ben would have to let go of the whole story. Then, if there was anything in the story that could be bent to make it right, maybe he could make his mind okay and help.

He pulled in to the stop. "Be right back." When he went for the coffee he walked three paces and stopped. He really did not trust Ben. He walked back to the car and lifted the keys knowing how cruel it was, watching Ben still crumpled in the corner. Ben's face was hidden, but when Singleton pulled the keys Ben looked at him. The face was blank, the eyes dull, the mouth passive. He looked nearly like an idiot. After coffee and a smoke Singleton figured that Ben might be able to talk.

The restaurant was crowded. It took ten minutes to get the coffee in paper cups. It took another minute or two at the cash register. He cleared the door, walked past the first rig pulled in beside the building, and went to the rear where he had parked. The car was gone.

Later he would tell himself, tell Grace, that it could not have been more than ten minutes at most. On the road, hunting through cities, busting against crosstown traffic, he would explain to himself that for anything like that to have happened in such a small amount of time was ridiculous. Damned near impossible, but Ben had jumped the ignition and was gone.

And then Grace's voice, the tears that helped nothing.

"Find him."

It would sound in his ears across Kansas, into Duluth, Pittsburgh, Columbus, through fifty towns because Ben knew the secret that Singleton knew, that few people knew unless they were pilots or showmen or migrant workers. The road was easy. As he stood in the place where the car should be, his knowledge was clear and awful.

He stood knowing that it was not more than fifty hours to anywhere. Miles meant nothing. Miles were as meaningless to the going as horsepower. Miles were a measure to keep people at home. It was the hours that counted, all the hours of a life, and the road was only a tangled string, twisted and knotted and serving one function; and that function was to go.

If he had not lifted the keys Ben might not have thought of going. He stood blinking, wondering, the light bright on the parking area and brilliant against the parked equipment. He twisted the useless ring of keys around one finger, little metallic clinks popping against the flat of his sweaty hand. Then he turned back to the restaurant, dropping the cups of coffee on the asphalt, and searched in his pocket for change to call a cab. He thought he might stumble, might fall on the asphalt right there among the rigs, and he walked along the ready-line and braced against the vans with one hand.

It was happening again. He could feel it happening. He was responsible and if something like the same thing happened again—because he did not think of Ben the way he had thought of Pat, but Ben had been just as much in his keeping. His mind, while he was waiting for some dumb bastard to get off the phone, while he was dialing for the cab, while he was waiting for the cab, kept reeling it back to him, and always before he had not allowed his mind to do that; kept reeling it back like he was explaining to someone, Pat's father, maybe, or to a judge, and finally explaining to Pat.

"Just a kid, Pat Donner, twenty-seven. Downeast kid that you give a pair of boots and some homemade mittens and he'd go out if it was blowing the hinges off of hell.

" 'Blowing, Chief,' he'd say. Face broad, eyes set in, squinched up when he grinned. Frenchy, maybe some Indian in there too.

"Seen him stand in the wind 'til it knocked him down. Storm blow steady northeast all day, harbor running like the ocean and Pat standing with his face to the breeze. Temp down. Him standing the bow or on the end of the pier, 'Gettin' a little air.' Just a kid, but he'd been at sea ten years. Loved weather, didn't trust it but didn't believe it could hurt him either; and neither did I, except it was like it could get me along toward the end."

Singleton braced himself against the side of a trailer.

"The harbor used to be more important than Boston in the old days. Shallow in spots, cliffs not far from the channel. Over on the backside is a lot of islands. We figured the islands would break the storm some. Lot of flooding to the south, hundreds of small craft ashore and a trawler missing.

"We were in South Portland moored above the small boats. We lashed the cutter down, lifeboat doubled up, hawser stowed. Pat worked some of the guys, and I worked the others. He reported secure and I took his word and I was right. That cutter didn't have a thing come adrift. I came on, carried aboard, before they took me to the hospital. She was still lying doubled up on the mooring and neat like she was going to be inspected. Half my work, half Pat's."

Singleton rubbed his eyes, confused. He was waiting for something. The cab. How long was it going to take for the cab to get there?

"He loved weather. Seen him rig a life line with a sea breaking over the fantail, then come off that deck with ice in his hair and laughing because the line was rigged. There he was fretting. I allowed I'd as leave ride the storm out against the dock.

"'That's old man's talk,' he told me. 'With trouble you're the first one there.' "

"I had that reputation."

He realized that he was dazed, talking to himself, talking to Ben; and behind his voice there seemed a thousand troubled voices. He was in the grip of a memory in this place a thousand miles from any ocean, more real than the asphalt and steel and roaring engines. Singleton pushed the remembering and it gave a little, enough to keep him from talking. But he could still feel the tossing, the thrown spume, the crashing water.

The base had called, asking them to stand by. A few minutes later a call had come back asking them to check the small-boat mooring. An engineman from the base joined them. The cutter was on repair status and would not go out. Pat sat laughing and drinking coffee on the mess deck. His black hair was tumbled and thick on his neck, the way you grew it in Maine coming into winter.

Somehow he was standing on asphalt, waiting for the cab. Two drivers pushed by him, laughing, while a fouled freight rig choked across the lot blowing black smoke. A carload of work guys roared by on the road and in the sunshine there was the high-sailing arc and shatter of a beer bottle against a post at the corner of the lot.

Don't let them catch you

"What happened is the base called. Wanted a detail to check the small boats. Civilian force was busy with the buoys. The base guys were helping. Buoy rolling loose can cause a mess. There was a second class bosun up there. Their chief was on leave.

"I took Pat and a kid engineman. We knew those small boats might be needed. We checked the mooring and walked to the Base to report. Hung around the radio room watching the yeoman with the watch—never did have a radioman at that base. He had receivers on seventy and ninety-four, phones ringing, the TWX starting up, guys popping in with questions, a regular go-round. And that yeoman so quick and cool. Moved from one thing to another regular, seemed to get everything done at least just in time.

"'How far?' says Pat.

"'Less than an hour,' the guy tells us. 'Ought to be right in the middle of it in fifty minutes.'

"We went back down to the moorings. Pat was like a kid. Across the harbor the weather cutters had everything on the line. Pat was sure we were going to go out.

"I doubted it. I'd seen a couple of those storms. That harbor was going to turn to dirt."

Singleton really had doubted it. He raised his head. Now it was not wind he was hearing, it was the rush of a starting diesel. He shook his head to clear it, looked at the sky, at the restaurant, across the road toward fields.

It hit quick like a white squall, but it was not over quick like a squall. He could remember the first shock, could remember climbing the ladder to the bridge behind an excited Pat, the ladder already surging beneath his feet as the cutter knocked against the pier. It was like the storm was trying to scoop Casco Bay and fling it on land. The wind picked water from the tops of swells and threw it, spray and solid, against their ship, against buildings, against the base itself which was hazy with the shatter of blown water. The harbor was a mess. Boats dragging. He was turning from the bridge to go below when the phone on shore-connection rang. He was so certain they would not go out that he continued on down the ladder.

By the time he was back on the mess deck he heard his name on the PA. Pat came bumping down the ladder.

"What?" He had not believed it.

"Boat adrift," Pat was yelling. Even on the mess deck with all the hatches dogged the wind was moaning, crying about the vessel which thumped against its fenders, hit the pier, rocked and nosed down to come back with the splat, sigh and wash of break-ing water. The kid engineman from the base looked scared. He was not as old as Pat and he spoke with a western accent. Single-ton did not trust him.

He did not believe it even when Pat said they were going because a four-striper on one of the weather cutters said a small yacht was being blown down on him. It was a three-hundred-eleven-foot cutter, for God's sake.

The four-striper was just the kind of prick who would spend another ship's men to protect his own ass. At least Pat should not be glad.

"Which one do we take?"

"The thirty-eight."

"What about the thirty-six?" The thirty-six was safe as a church. It would right itself if it rolled, assuming a man could hang on. The thirty-eight was a tough harbor boat, but it was not a surf boat.

"The guy from the base has got it."

There would be two boats out. The second class from the base. Singleton tried to remember what he knew about the guy.

Pat tumbled back with gear, the deck heaving like they were a hundred miles offshore. There was a blow against the cutter so that it staggered against the pier the way it staggered running into a sea that put green water against the bridge. The cutter actually heeled right there at the pier, and the wind began to scream. They looked at each other. They believed the storm was blowing as tough as it would get, and now it had increased. The cutter was small but tough. It was actually being beaten while moored. Singleton took a deep breath and pushed through a hatch and into the storm.

He had heard wind moan. He had heard it howl. He knew the whistle of wind, the thumping noises, but he had never until now heard it scream. As they pressed hard to get through the hatch the wind knocked him flat. He fell into the lee of the solid rail, pulled himself up just in time to be bowled over again by the falling engineman, and lay for a moment beneath the kid and listened to the scream of the wind. When he untangled himself, Pat was braced above them. It looked like the little prick was laughing. His mouth was blown flat with the wind, but it sure looked like he was laughing. The scream sounded animal, like it was hunting.

The gangway levered back and forth. They made it by swimming and then crawling into the wind. They clung to the steel lines of the gangway, got across, and swam, halfway crawled up the pier.

The wind pushed their faces flat. It compressed their brows and nearly closed their eyes. At any minute Singleton expected to be killed by something carried in the wind. It was like swimming against an impossible current with someone shooting at you. An iron bolt was being tumbled down the pier. A bolt. It hit his boot and he watched it as it nudged by. They reached the lee of the buoy building, and as they reached it the wind increased. It was impossible. Not this close to the coast. This was typhoon wind, deep-sea wind, this was wind that hammered ships beneath the surface, skidding them under.

"How hard?" he yelled at Pat. Pat was right beside him. The wind screamed around the corners of the building and nearly drowned his voice.

"A hundred and—I don't know chummy, don't *know* chief." Pat's voice was faint like an echo from the other side of an enormous gulf of wind. There was an edge of fear in Pat's eyes. Singleton did not believe he would ever see that.

[143]

"Let's go," Pat yelled.

Singleton considered. If they tried to return to the ship the wind would knock one or more of them into the water, tumble them off the pier to be found later on the mudflats. If they stayed in the lee the building might rip down. He felt like he had his back to a cannon. The best thing to do would be to run the boats to the lee of the cutter and ride it out there. He turned to the engine-man, smacked him on the shoulder, and crawled low toward the ladder and down to the small-boat mooring.

At the mooring it was easier. The dock cut the wind. The boats tossed heavily. They banged against each other. Nothing was normal. Nothing. This was steel-wrenching wind, the kind that at sea built waves that carried away railings and steel lockers and hatch covers.

The thirty-six was fifty feet out with its engine running high. They were tossing bad, but it was not dangerous in the sheltered water. Singleton jumped on the boat, headed forward, and Pat began to check the towline. He still thought they were going out. From aft came muffled sounds. Then the engine was running high and smooth and he had power. Pat cast off while Singleton tried the little squawk box radio to talk to the other boat. It was no good. At fifty feet the storm should not be able to break up reception.

Singleton gunned the boat to come alongside. As he gunned it, the other boat moved out, sliding down the side of the pier, past the cutter and into the harbor. As it hit the full force of the wind it lifted, staggered and rolled hard. Singleton cursed. The damned fool was going to try it. He eased ahead expecting the other boat would make a turn and come back. He also knew that if it did not turn he would have to follow. You could not abandon even a fool to that wind. He tried the radio again. No answer. He smacked the transmitter with the heel of his hand. Maybe it was not putting out.

"Can we make it?" Pat was beside him and yelling.

"Don't know." He had never handled a thirty-eight before. Maybe they were better than he thought. "Try to raise them," he yelled and pointed at the radio. They were abreast of the cutter. In another minute he would have both hands full with the dinky helm.

In the moments before he cleared the cutter he was afraid in a way that hardly ever happened. This fear was a premonition, like the fear you got in shoal water when the rocks were alive and eager and thrusting at the hull. The wind seemed supernatural. He watched the bow of the cutter as he slid by, the black paint bubbly in a couple of places where rust was working underneath, the white WYT designation yellowing. It was really only a harbor tug, only a hundred-ten feet but the steel hull looked safe and permanent.

He cleared the cutter and they were smashed down by the wind, the boat forced down like a gigantic hand was trying to thrust it under. The prop took hold and they moved. On the first roll they were picked up and shoveled from a swell to be kicked hard by a second swell. The gunwale went under. He was positive she would not live five minutes. The thirty-eight came staggering from beneath the weight of water. She seemed to have no more buoyancy than an old log.

The water was not the real enemy. Singleton goosed it hard, put her stern to wind, and they began to ride. Picket boats had been through godawful weather. He hoped she was more watertight than he thought. If the engine killed there was no chance.

Two points to starboard and a hundred yards off, the lifeboat was laboring across the wind. The lifeboat had a freeboard designed to handle wind. It was all curved surfaces. The picket was like a box. Its only advantage was a closed house. You could stay dry until you drowned. There was only one way to follow the lifeboat, to sideslip at speed, make a turn if he overshot, then sideslip back bow to wind. It took longer, but it was the only thing he could do. Visibility was shot. He was not taking water forward, the way he would be coming back, but tops of swells were being blown off all around him. It was like being in a heavy fog bank.

Pat was yammering into the radio. His voice was high-pitched but controlled, but just barely, and his voice was not quite as murky as the visibility. Then the yeoman at the base broke in calling the lifeboat. The voice was cool, imperturbable, in complete control. While he admitted that that was exactly what they needed, Singleton found himself hating the voice, hating the guy who was sitting in a warm office and radio room out of the storm. At least their box was receiving. It was the base's opinion that the winds were going to moderate fast. And fuck that old man too, a lousy lieutenant who, the only time he had ever handled a ship, had run into half of Portland, Maine. A shore-base jock.

He sideslipped her, coming across at about a forty-five-degree angle. The bow buried then shrugged it off as he skidded back stern to wind. It could probably be done.

He beat his way across the harbor to lengthen the distance between himself and the lifeboat, but it at least closed the width gap. After the turn it would be easier to close upwind. He had gained enough advantage to close the two boats by the time he covered the distance. He was so occupied he had forgotten the yacht.

"Where's the tow?"

Pat pointed through the spray. A mile to starboard. It was dragging anchor and that was keeping it head to wind. Otherwise it would surely have capsized by now. The lifeboat would reach it first.

He got ready for the turn. When there was a letup, a slight one that he told himself he was probably imagining, he kicked it hard, threw the wheel down and the boat spun, pushed crazy sideways by the wind, skidding, falling off and throwing them hard. There was green water against the flimsy wooden hatch. It was pouring into the compartment. The horizon was lying in front of him like a perfectly vertical line. He had lost her. He was sure he had lost her. The engine was singing, the prop in and out of the water, and then slowly she began to come around. A wave smashed the bow down, lifted the stern, and then it helped them around. The boat righted and they were facing into the wind.

He felt sick. Pat had tumbled against him. Now he jumped up, white-faced. From the stern came a muffled yell on the voice tube. The engineman was okay. Pat relaxed and some of his color came back.

"Close." There was a big scrape on Pat's broad forehead where he had banged against the wheel. Singleton could not see anything and had to throttle back. They were taking green water.

It took them a half-hour to arrive at the scene. When he arrived the lifeboat had a line aboard, holding the yacht head to wind, but it was not making way. The yacht rode low. He gunned alongside, the wind forcing him down, cutting away, trying to force him off.

In the half an hour, it seemed like the wind had dropped but the water was higher. They were still riding hard but it was not the crazy, twisting, skidding feeling that came from being right on the edge of control.

Pat went aft to rig the tow. He would have to board. Singleton figured that his hull was pretty good. He pulled ahead to allow the wind to drift him down. He would kick it after Pat jumped. It worked well. Pat boarded, slipped in the wind and fell. He hung on, made his line fast, and then Singleton backed and drifted it again. Pat made the second jump. He did not look good.

"Seaman aboard the tow," he said. "From the lifeboat. She's pretty tight. Just tow her in."

"It was never a menace."

"That dog-shit son of a bitch," Pat yelled. "That ass-licking four-striping dong-pounder." It was not swearing. It was description.

The wind was dropping to the point where it would soon be no worse than a bad storm. The two boats were towing in tandem and making way. It was not until they nearly had it in, nearly had it secure and drinking coffee on the mess deck, talking—telling each other that it was the worst they had ever seen—that the trouble happened. It happened so quick and it was so simple that he could not believe it. He stood at the suddenly useless wheel shocked into stillness.

The engine died, hit again, died and stayed dead. Before the engineman could work his way from the stern to tell him that they were out of fuel, the boat was already broadside and trying to go.

Out of fuel. Whose responsibility? A civilian, the punk engineman, the guy on leave? Finally it was his because he had checked those boats and reported them ready. Green water slapped and flowed against the port side. They were spun broadside, wallowing, falling, rolling.

They were broaching. The horizon jumped sideways like the needle on an erratic gauge. He turned and headed aft. If the line was not cast off they might pull everybody under. They were coming stern to. The lifeboat had continued to tow and they swung aft of the tow. They were being pulled around and were taking water in the engine compartment as it broke over the stern. It was a crazy pattern, the lifeboat headed one direction, them headed another, and the yacht half-swamped and canted in the center. It was then that the bosun mate on the lifeboat dropped his tow.

Later, trying to figure it out, he could never decide whether the bosun mate had been right. The storm steadily blew itself out over the next hour. They might have been able to ride that way for an hour. On the other hand, the bosun mate could not have known that at the time. He had two dead boats to contend with, a fritzed radio, a man on one boat and three men on the other. The rule of life and property always said that life came first, but if that was true why the fuck were they there in the first place?

As the yacht broached to, the lifeboat closed and collected its man. Then it headed toward them, had almost got to them to pass a line, when a combination of swells put them over. The swells were no bigger than those they had been fighting, but the distance between them was just right to kick him, kick him again, and then secure the job. The last thing he remembered was the gut-emptying, going-on-over roll and the cold water closing on him. When he returned to the cutter, and later to the hospital, he was too dazed to remember much else.

And it was not until he got to the hospital that he learned that the lifeboat had picked up all three of them. He only remembered being brought back to the cutter, then remembered being taken somewhere. He remembered no ambulances. It was at the hospital that the first and worse memory came. He found out that Pat had been hit hard when they rolled. He was torn up. He would be blind for the rest of his life; and if there were other things to love it might be that Pat would find them, but the permanent, all-time cure had been put on Pat's love for weather.

HER memory was like a wound that might never heal, a part of the colors of her work. The memory knew not only the many colors of blood, but the textures of blood and the particles and lymphs that lay white and yellow and granular in blood. It was not going to stop affecting her work until she understood the singular awfulness of the memory.

It all began with the most horror and violence she had ever seen or known. Even now, when three times a week she drove to teach at a school, the memory was as sharp as shattering glass. It was red, silver, enameled like teeth. It was sunlight turned cold with the colors and forms and pale shadows that only a painter could know.

When she drove to the schools—jealous now of the time she gave to them—she no longer tried to fight her car. She tried to get it to move with a relationship to the road that made sense of the lines and weights and shapes involved. She did not want to be a good driver. She did not want to drive at all, but if she had to drive then she must do it without mistakes.

The wreck she had seen told her that a crazy world lay all around her and the insanity of that world opposed everything she had ever learned. Steel was as malleable as clay, and the madness building around her was wanton, unapologetic, gleeful as demons. The modern world was running those wide roads everywhere. It was making people violent.

When she left home on that day of anger, after waking beside a cold fireplace, the sun had been over the ridge and into the forest. The chill of the mist, and the portents of age and dying that came with the mist, were disappearing. The stands of pine seemed to be exploding with light. Catherine knew that she was irrationally angry because Singleton was not with her. At least that seemed the reason for her anger.

Always, when it had been cold the night before, her car choked and bumped along. At the bottom of the drive that ran across the pasture she stopped before entering the road. The car stalled. It did not want to start again, at least not right away. She sat in the car and waited. She looked at the stream, at the surrounding mountainsides, and she rolled down the window to listen to the sounds of the day. From somewhere off the side of the mountain came the high wail of an engine. Catherine wondered if she was as angry as she was pretending she was. It seemed to her that life was going to charge her for not being able to live alone.

Her suitcase lay on the front seat beside her. It smelled old, musty, and it seemed even stranger than the idea of traveling. She had no road maps or much knowledge of routes.

Another engine sounded from far off above the hills where a light plane buzzed like a blowfly. The road she was going to travel climbed up and around the mountain, still winding upward where it disappeared on the other side. She put her foot back on the starter. This time the engine began coughing. Then it started to run pretty well.

If he loved her, then why wasn't he with her?

She told herself that she really had to get out. She understood that she really was angry. This anger was not pretense.

Driving demanded a lot of your attention, but after you had gone a few miles you kind of got used to it. When that happened it was possible to look around, see some of the countryside. The hills were quiet, and mist cascaded above the tops, slow-rolling toward the valleys. The movement was there, even if you could not see it because you were driving forty miles an hour.

She filled the gas tank at a roadside station. The attendant raised the hood, checked the oil, and checked the tires. He tried to sell her a new tire. She was not fooled by that. The crack in the side of one tire was so small that she had never even noticed it before. The attendant was a gray-haired, farmerish-looking man who walked with a slight limp. The filling station was small. Its front was covered with sheet-metal advertisements for soft drinks. It had a grocery attached. When she paid for the gasoline the attendant gave her a free water glass. She did not need some junk water glass. She tossed it on the seat beside the suitcase. She pulled away, and before Asheville a sign pointed to a road she had never been on. If the sign did not lie, Atlanta lay at the other end of that road.

She pretended to herself that this was just another country road like the ordinary roads she had traveled all her life. Some roads were busier than others. Some times of day were bad for driving. She had learned, teaching at high schools, to wait after school until the students were gone. High school students drove like maniacs.

On this two-lane road, which she later figured out was a main route, everyone was driving like high school students. Traffic began to howl and weave around her, sporadic bursts of fast-moving cars and trucks. The traffic burst over the tops of hills, running downward toward her like many-colored cars on a roller coaster. This main road was different from the Winston-Salem road. There were not as many big trucks on the Winston road. It was the trucks that were most frightening. She would hear them roar, and she would suddenly be conscious that one of them was passing. When that happened she put on the brakes so it could get around fast.

She clung with both hands at the top of the steering wheel. Her car ran sideways each time a truck passed. Singleton drove a truck like that. She told herself that she had been trying to love a sadist. Either that, or Singleton was criminally insane.

Eight hours later, and completely exhausted from tension and fear, she was lost in the slums of Atlanta. The ramshackle old houses and buildings where Negroes sat on porches or on curbs outside of corner bars seemed almost sane. The brick streets, the cobblestone alleys filled with stink and the trash in the gutters were at least sensible. Movement was slow. People lived here.

[151]

They did not go blazing around like they were crazy.

She did not know anything about Negroes. When you lived in the hills you never saw them. You did not know how to act. The world was changing. *Time* magazine told her that, but the world did not understand that through large parts of the south there were people who had never even seen a black person. Of course those people lived way back in the hills. Catherine drove until she saw a man and woman and two children before she stopped to ask directions. The man backed away, and the woman told her to go "that-a-way." Neither of them would say anything more. The children stood and stared, wide-eyed. They looked frightened.

It took an hour to drive through the hot-smelling, rotten-smelling slums. It took another hour to find a hotel. When you were a woman traveling alone you had to stay at the very best hotel. Even then the desk clerk seemed ready to give a lecture. The hotel lobby was large, with cut-glass chandeliers, plush red carpet and old walnut and cherry furnishings. The desk clerk wore a suit, and he had a simpery, pinched little face. His pursed mouth showed that he disapproved of her, but his eyes had the ugly look of a man who was trying to see beneath your clothes. He did not actually tell her that this was a respectable hotel, and that she could not bring her customers to her room, but his mouth and eyes conveyed filth more nasty than the filth of the slums.

The desk clerk called for an old Negro man to carry her suitcase, although it was not necessary. When they arrived at her room, she tipped him and he nearly ran away.

The room was not bad. It was small and modest for such a fancy hotel, but at least it was private. At least you did not have the howl of traffic and the dirt of slums and filthy minds. She unpacked, bathed, changed clothes, and sat on the edge of the bed. Catherine told herself that she was learning something, if she could only figure out what it was.

The road was where you packed up your anger, or your trouble, the same way you packed a suitcase. You threw your anger or troubles onto the seat beside you, and then you did not have them any more.

Until you arrived at your destination. Then, just like a suitcase, you unpacked them. They were the same old troubles. You had the same old anger.

There was one advantage. You had no responsibilities. When you were in a strange hotel room in a strange city there was nothing you could do about anything. Singleton had surely called by now. She had not been home. Yes, he had surely called. She tried to feel guilty and found that she could not. That made her a little less angry.

Catherine ate dinner in the hotel restaurant. She hated to do it because of the expense, and she only made the decision after stepping from the hotel and into Atlanta's streets. This city was different. It was no hotter than Winston, but it felt hotter. The feeling was not just natural heat. This was the heat of violence. Catherine had often felt timid on Winston's streets, but she had never been so afraid that she could not walk in them. Atlanta terrified her.

She was treated courteously in the restaurant, and that helped. She took time with the meal because there would be nothing to do when it was over. She told herself that if this was the kind of life that Singleton lived, then he was crazy. He might be a good man, even a kind man, but he was *crazy*. It would be better to find another man. Someone sane. Then she remembered the diaphragm she had packed in her suitcase. She felt guilty, embarrassed. Suppose she were run over and taken to a hospital. Suppose someone like that desk clerk opened that suitcase. Just thinking such thoughts was enough to ruin dinner. When she finished she went to her room and was tempted to throw the thing away.

Catherine sat on the edge of the bed and was miserable. She was exhausted. In all of her years of isolation she had never felt so vulnerable and alone. Her valley had never seemed this deserted, although sometimes in the valley you did not see three cars go past in twenty-four hours. Her anger nearly matched her fatigue and misery, but she tried to ignore it. If you were too angry then you probably could not sleep, and although it was still early evening there was nothing left to do but sleep.

The accident happened in a chilly dawn on a wide road that ran on a high embankment. The embankment ran through fields.

On Sunday morning Catherine waked before dawn to find herself only a little less exhausted and slightly less miserable. Her venture onto the road, her need to get out, to flee—well that

[153]

venture was a failure. She had known it would be, but she had not expected it to be so grim. It was still dark when she left the hotel. It seemed stupid to be driving around out there in the dark. At the same time, it was stupid to sit wide awake in a hotel room listening to hillbillies on the radio; and it was a choice of either hillbillies or ugly-mouthed radio preachers.

If she left early she could be in Asheville early. She could get a hotel room, attend her friend's party that night.

The next day she could go home. Home had never before seemed quite so decent, quite so safe.

When she checked out there was a different desk clerk. This one was tall and skinny. He wore a suit, and he had one of those streamlined haircuts that was supposed to make you into a success. He looked at her like she was a tart who had just finished work. Catherine told herself that the clerks in this place were just indifferent pieces of hotel trash, but they certainly knew how to give you a wonderful start on the day.

One thing about starting early was that the streets were deserted. You could drive through them without worrying about whether somebody was going to come around a corner and wreck you. The suitcase on the seat beside her smelled a little less musty. The water glass had tumbled from the seat. It rolled around on the floor of the car. For the first time since she left home she felt moderately safe. The darkened storefronts, the streetlights, and the quiet streets were certainly not like her valley. They were, she supposed, peaceful to city people in the same way that her valley was to her.

Sunrise found her north of Atlanta on a broad stretch of divided highway. Her car was running well. It was going faster than it had ever gone before, because it was going sixty. If you went that fast you could get to Asheville far sooner than you had hoped.

From out of nowhere, absolutely nowhere, a car appeared beside her. It zoomed by so fast that she was scarcely conscious of it until she was looking at it running ahead of her and growing smaller. It seemed no more than a minute before it disappeared over a far rise in the land. It was like a streak along the road, and the two-toned black-and-white shape cast a long, streaking shadow sideways in the dawn.

The sun was coming up red over the land. Mist lay across the fields, lighter gray than the Carolina mist, no blue tones in this mist. The fields had been cropped. They lay darkly beneath the mist and the red sunlight. Some of the fields were enclosed with modern fencing, others had old, wooden-rail fencing. It was easy to watch the land because you did not have to worry about cars coming toward you. There was a broad, gully-like strip between the roads. The cars coming from the other direction were on the far side of that strip. Since entering the road she had seen only three cars and one or two trucks.

The sun rose rapidly, which was different from the way it rose back home. In the hills the sun seemed to be a partner with the slow-rolling blue mist of the mountains. The sun would rise, but it would be unveiled, emerging, like form that lay in a design and gradually appeared on a loom. Here the sun just seemed to pop right up and start to attack the mist that lay over the fields.

Her car was running quite smoothly, steady and cooperating for once. She was still going faster than she had ever driven before, but the wide highway and the rolling, mist-covered land caused her to feel that she traveled slowly. It was almost like floating, like being in one of those old-fashioned balloons drifting before a light wind.

Another car passed. She had not even realized another car was around. The feeling of slowness disappeared as she fought her wheel and kept her own car on the road. The land was still slow, timeless, but the road in front was rushing at her. Her car kept wanting to swerve, like one of its wheels had suddenly become heavy.

Ahead of her the car that had just passed suddenly seemed to be acting wrong. It acted like something had broken. Her own car was wiggling its steering wheel, and she was hanging onto the wheel and did not know what else to do. The car ahead of her was red and white. It looked new, but it looked like it was trying to do a trick. Its back end seemed to be lifting, especially the back part on the right side. The back end seemed to lift as slowly as her stunned thoughts. Her own steering wheel was trying to turn right, and she hung onto it while the red-and-white car ahead of her lifted right up in the air and did a half circle to the left. It looked like the back end was trying to trade directions with the front end, like a dog chasing its tail. Then the car seemed to give a little skip like a machine that was happy and trying to dance. As it skipped, a short puff of dust exploded against the road and then the car bounced, rolled over and over and over, right down the highway in front of her. It hit three times, and each time there was a cloud of dust that exploded. The car seemed to be shedding half the dust in the county. She knew, as she fought her wheel, that dirt was being knocked loose from beneath the car. She knew, fighting her wheel, that all of this was happening desperately fast, but it did not seem fast. It seemed timeless.

The sunlight lay directly across the road and a sparkling shatter of glass, like a giant handful of ice, scattered and twinkled down the road. It was like the road was glazed with the brilliant red and ice splinters of glass in sunlight. Catherine was so automatic, so without directed will, that she did not know what she was doing. It seemed that she watched the sprays of red and ice shatter for minutes. It seemed that the pounding clouds of dust were going to explode forever. Then the red-and-white car bounced on its front end, kind of slantwise, like it was trying to do a headstand. Then it fell right into the gullylike strip between the roads.

Catherine had been hitting her brake, but it felt like her car speeded up. It was getting harder to steer. Her car was either skidding on the shatters of glass, or her brakes did not work. She kicked desperately with her foot, felt something roll away, and kicked again. Her brakes began to work, but as they worked her car was even harder to steer. It began to twist sideways, and then it began to thump. She let up on the brake. She hit the brake. The wheel thumped and twisted. The broken water glass that had wedged beneath the brake pedal cut a long, deep slash in her leg just above the ankle. Her car stopped. It was kitty-corner, halfway on the road, halfway off. The suitcase had flown off the seat, bounced at her like it was attacking as the car turned. Now it wedged against her leg trying to push her foot off the brake. She sat, fighting to hold her foot on the brake and trying to push at the suitcase with one hand. The suitcase was like a dog that had its teeth set into something. It would not move. She was terrified. The thing seemed alive and determined. Then she realized that she was already stopped. Her leg was jerking, and when she took her foot off the brake her leg jerked even harder. The suitcase fell toward her foot, chasing her. She fought to get away from the thing.

It was not safe in the car. Not safe. She fumbled for the door handle, shoved on it. Nothing happened. Then she remembered to pull on it. The door fell open and she nearly fell out. She got outside, stood, crouching, ready to run as she looked back to see if the suitcase was following. When it did not, she stood and began to sob.

The road at her feet was washed with sunlight. It was pink and white gleaming all around her. A tiny sliver of glass lay beside her foot, edged by the sun so it looked like a little diamond, hypnotic, like you could read all of the past and all of the future in it. She stood benumbed, in a trance.

An engine suddenly started crack-crack-cracking the way Singleton's engine sounded when he came off the mountain. The cracking came from far off, way up ahead, and it cracked-cracked-cracked until she thought it would split her brain. Its cracking diminished, and there was a sound like pebbles being sprayed before a broom.

She stood and stared at the washed white-and-pink road, and at the brilliantly lighted piece of glass. It was right between her feet almost, and she kept looking at it. She was only abstractly bothered when a splash of red ran over the side of her shoe and spread beside the glass. It was not intrusion but contrast. It was surreal and the sparkle was hypnotic. Together, the red splash and the sparkling glass would know the past, the future.

A shadow was moving toward her, fast. The rapid shadow seemed to be attacking. It shaded the sliver of glass. It made her sad. It made her a little angry. It was like someone had promised you something, and then gone back on the promise. Something was tugging at her.

"You okay?" The voice was harsh. Hands were lifting her hands, then letting them drop. "Turn this way." She did not turn, but she was being turned. "Turn that way." She was being turned in the opposite direction. "Gimmie a look." Her leg was being lifted. A hand was actually around her leg. She momentarily panicked. She was being assaulted. "It won't kill you," the voice said. "C'mon, you can walk." It was a man. A man had hold of her hand.

He was pulling her. She resisted.

"You are standing in the middle of the motherfucking road," the voice said. The enunciation was clear, defined, careful. The voice sounded like it was making itself go slow because it was in such a hurry. "C'mon." The man jerked on her hand. She stumbled after him. She seemed to be running downhill, through autumn grass that was tall but beaten down from storms. When the man stopped pulling on her she stopped, confused. She realized that she was in the gullylike strip between the roads. Not far away the red-and-white car lay leaned over against one side of the embankment. Its wheels were in the air. The grass beside her foot was turning red, like it was being painted.

"Dearest Jesus, Jesus dear," the man said, "I ain't got no help." He touched Catherine's shoulder, like he was trying to jog a sleeping person to wakefulness. "All I got is you," he said. His voice was sad, urgent, and it seemed filled with fear.

She was bleeding. She understood it now. She leaned over to look at the cut, and knew as she looked that it was a bad, bad cut.

"Maybe somebody will come along," the man said. "Right now, you come." He jerked at her hand. This time she seemed to have some control. She was able to follow him without being led.

The red-and-white car lay leaning against the slope, three of its wheels pointing straight up. The wheel on the left front side dangled sideways like it was attached to the car by strings. She started to follow the man as he approached it, and she tried not to look at her leg. The upside-down car was a cloudy network of shatters and cracks and webs. The windshields were like stars that had red centers. The man was carrying something red. He turned back to her, pushed her backward, but the push was gentle. This time she was able to see him as a real form. He was no longer just a force that pushed or pulled on her. He was blond-haired, but his lips were thick and his nose was broad. His hands were trembling, but they were busy with the thing he carried.

"Can you hear me? You understand me?" His voice was methodical, but it was forced, like he was trying to keep from rushing. She nodded, at first unable to speak. Then she tried to speak. "I can."

"Loving Lord," he said, "I got to crawl inta that piece of shit." He was bent over, looking into the car. He turned back to Catherine.

"Take this." The fire extinguisher he gave her was heavier than it looked. She nearly dropped it. He moved her backward, about eight feet from the car.

"You know how to work that?"

"No."

"Like this." He took it from her hands. "Hold it thisaway. When you press this—" He pressed a lever and a roaring cloud of mist came from the extinguisher. It was only a short roar for such a large cloud. It stopped almost immediately. He passed the extinguisher back to her.

"I'm going into that wrecked car." His voice was trembling, but he sounded like he was thinking about his voice and his words. He sounded like he was teaching a child the ABCs. "If that wrecked car begins to burn you shoot this extinguisher right at me as I'm coming out."

"Shoot?"

"If you see fire, any fire, just the least little bit of fire, *spray* this extinguisher right at me."

She nodded, held the extinguisher.

"You understand? Do you really understand?"

"I'm bleeding."

"It's not bad, not *that* bad."

She nodded. "I understand."

The car leaned against the bank so that its upside-down door was slightly canted toward the bank, bent and partly open. The man pulled at the door, strained, and the car moved. It settled more firmly against the bank. The door wrenched and squeaked and squawked, but it began to open. The man reached inside.

"Oh you motherfucker," the man said, "Oh you sonovabitch." His voice trembled with fear, but she heard more than fear in his voice. He sounded like he was weeping. From where Catherine stood she could see a red-and-blue bulk. It seemed to be wrapped around the steering wheel, like a cloak thrown over the wheel to hide the upside-down, silly and useless-looking thing. Then she realized she was looking at a blue suit that was soaked in places.

"You still out there?"

"Yes."

"I got one still alive, but I got to get this thing out first." The man's voice was choking, trembling, and it spoke in short sobs of breath. The man's back was braced against the car, his body was mostly inside the car. He seemed to be lying right on top of the blue suit, manipulating something in the car. "Gotta work him loose, he's tangled." Then he backed away and stood for a moment beside the open door before he once more leaned down. In the second or two that it took him to stand, then lean again, he glanced at Catherine. His side was wet, black-wet and slick-looking. His eyes were tense and his face was wet with tears and red with blood. Water washed right through a smear of blood on his nose and cheek, the tears making a clear line that ran onto his thick lips. "You goddamn bastard," he said as he leaned down, "get the fuck outta there." He pulled hard, leaning into the pull like he was tying down the warp on a loom. His heels were braced, and for a moment he seemed in despair when nothing moved. Then he began to move slowly backward. A body appeared over the slightly canting angle of the doorway. The body was loose, floppy, not human, somehow too long, like it was stretched without enough bones to hold it together. It flopped onto the ground.

The man pulled the body across the long, beaten grass until it was a few feet from the car. Then he turned and nearly dived back into the car. From the road came the fluttering, crack-crack-cracking of an engine.

"Thank Jesus," the man said from inside the car. His voice sounded prayerful, but muffled.

There was a wedding ring on the left hand that lay flat on the grass. The hand was incongruous with the outstretched arm, turned impossibly in relation to the arm. The hand looked firm, solid, and was strong and perfectly formed. There was no blood on the hand. The wedding ring gleamed in the sunlight, dull-gleaming, rich-gleaming, gold. Catherine watched the hand. It seemed wrong that the hand was not moving, not helping. This was terrible, terrible. The hand lay motionless like it did not care if someone else was afraid and crying and working.

"Go ahead," another voice said. "Get rid of it, but hang onto that extinguisher." A second shadow was beside her. She realized that she was leaned over, vomiting, and holding the extinguisher like it was a tree planted firm in a forest.

"What've we got, buddy?" the voice said. While he was saying it, the second man was kneeling beside the outstretched hand.

"Don't worry about the guy," the muffled voice said. "He's a goner. Get over here."

The puddle of vomit smelled sour. She backed away from it, then remembered that she was supposed to stand still. She made herself stand beside the vomit. She held the extinguisher in one hand and wiped her mouth with the other. She wanted to spit the taste from her mouth and was afraid to spit for fear she would be sick again. She looked down at her leg. It was still bleeding but not as bad. Blood mixed with the sour-smelling stuff. Her shoes were soaked.

"Lift her thisaway."

"Don't twist."

"How the fuck you gonna do it without twistin'?"

"Feel the back, first, feel the back."

"It's okay. I think it is."

The great painters knew this. They knew the anguished quality of facelessness. They knew the violence and pain behind the mechanical task. They knew the horror and sorrow and loss. Rembrandt could paint an anatomy lesson. His painting could make you weep, could make you shrink into your soul, could make you vomit.

The three faces, two alive above working hands, one alive, apparently—or the other two would not be so tense, the hands not so hard working—the three faces—Catherine looked at the woman as the men knelt above her. She watched the men's hands.

It seemed all right now if she sat the fire extinguisher down. It was all right to sit, right here in the sun-warmed, strangely and brilliantly illuminated autumn grass, and it was all right to weep. The car was red, red, red, and the sunlight sparkled from a diamond on the woman's hand as one of the men raised her left arm.

Catherine never did go to her friend's party, but she somehow did make it home on Monday. She spent Sunday morning in a hospital and Sunday afternoon getting her car from a towing lot where the attendant showed no sympathy and she asked for none. He charged her twenty dollars for towing and storage. A service-station attendant installed a new tire on the right front wheel. Catherine spent Sunday night in the same hotel she had checked out of so early on Sunday morning. This time she had a dozen stitches in her leg, and she did not put up with any nonsense from the filthy-minded hotel clerk. She was prepared to take fast, decisive issue with the smallest slighting look or remark. She was nearly disappointed because the man somehow felt the difference and remained courteous.

Alone in that hotel room in a city where fears crawled the night, she undressed and wished vaguely that someone were with her. That someone did not even have a face. She moved her hands about herself, became mildly aroused, and brought herself to a single indifferent orgasm. Sex was apparently not the problem, although sex had something to do with it.

She tried to sleep, but form and color and thought shoved sleep aside. It had been years since she had really *seen* in the way she was seeing now. The colors and shapes appeared in clear, firm relationships, like they already were completed on canvas. They were not impressionistic, but abstract; but as abstractions they contained representational forms. They were not a little of each, but both in brilliant interdependence. Her mind was rewarding her with sight at the same time it was preparing to punish her. Her mind was going to make her look at something cruel, because she had viewed such indifferent, out-of-nowhere cruelty. That woman in the car had died. The two men had been unable to save her.

To look at more cruelty was a pitiless, merciless thing to have to do.

She sat naked, on the edge of the bed, and wondered if she was once more going to be sick. The sickness was not just in her mind and belly, it seemed spread through her entire being, staining her. It was the sickness of history, of her history.

Were you wrong to seek peace when there was no peace? When the world took your young husband, your boy husband, and shot him dead in Germany, was it wrong to try to find a place to hide in a world with no hiding places? His death was real now because she had seen death. All death was real.

She told herself that she had become those things she hated most; and she had not even known that it was happening. She was every cliché ever devised about women. She was the woman driver, the old maid schoolteacher, the hobbyist with paint. She was a set of female glands that ran through life and shaped the world according to glandular notions of love. She was a paper doll who brandished a diaphragm to proclaim her independence and to threaten the man she loved.

Her belly clenched, seemed like a pump. She stood, walked rapidly to the bathroom, and choked sour stuff into the toilet. She rinsed her mouth with water, spat, then sat on the edge of the tub and waited for more. There was bound to be a lot more if you were vomiting history.

She told herself that she was still in shock. She was genuinely sick, genuinely weak. The tiled floor was cool against her bare feet. She looked at her feet, at her bandaged leg.

A cold war was only a hot war waiting to happen. Was it wrong, when the lines of love and peace and war and culture knotted like a diagram of frenzy? Was it wrong to love the clean-lined truth of an old loom? Was it wrong to find the truth of the stuff: the wool, flax, cotton?

She once more told herself that she was weak and sick. The problem was that she did not feel weak or sick. She was angry, but this time the anger was different. It was a fury that might strike itself in its need to make order, but it was a fury that would strike. She stood, leaned over the toilet, and gagged herself. When nothing came she gagged herself again. Get rid of it, rid of it, all of it. Get clean. Clean yourself.

After fifteen minutes she was weak. She returned to the bed and sat thinking.

She was *not*, absolutely *not*, a cliché. Not just a cliché. She had worked too many years. She had paid for the work with mistakes made in the work. She had spent hours and hours and hours in making mistakes, correcting them, learning from them. In the entire nation there could be few weavers who were better.

Too many years of work, and she was not going to dismiss those years or disrespect them. If life threw new facts at you, maybe those facts changed life. Those years would never work the same way again, but she would not, could not, disrespect them.

She felt better and lay back on the bed, knowing later that she actually did sleep. It was not troubled sleep, but it was not deep sleep. It was like her subconscious was rediscovering color and form. It was like her subconscious was summing all experience, making her move toward old canyons of belief and innocence and hope. Life trapped you. It made you so concerned with your ego that you could not *see*. Her subconscious was telling her that she had forgotten what a great privilege it was to be an artist.

Sometime during the night she was overtaken by specific memory. Memories came of teachers who had been passive or excited or firm. Her college had been just another college, but a few of the teachers were fine. Exciting words. Words long forgotten, but they had made exquisite sense at the time.

"Painters were producing fine work long before anyone used the terms color, line and form. Great stories were told before written language." She remembered him, small, balding, and walking a high-strung anguish of words that at the time had been embarrassing.

"To be true, it is. Only to be true. Is clumsy, fine. You will learn. Is a lie, kill yourself."

Catherine woke early in the morning, checked out early and this time drove with care. She passed through Asheville a little after noon. When she arrived home the valley seemed different. The work was different. She was not uncomfortable with either, because of her new understanding. She was no longer angry or lonely or afraid because of her understanding. People were born, they reproduced and died. Between those lines were where they struggled, where they either did or did not *do*. And if they did not do and if they died, they had wasted it all. Form, love, life.

18

SHE loved him. That was one big discovery. Working in September and into winter, daily pushing the production to meet the coming Christmas trade, the shuttle like an eager-running bridge between her hands, she thought of him. The beater packed the weave with the in-drawing, velvetly enclosing thump she loved so well, and which this fall sounded like a voice explaining the authority and beauty of the craft, the truth of wool, and the endorsing presence of thousands of years of weavers dealing in a basic stuff of life.

She loved him. Singleton was not artificial, ruthless, unkind. Sometimes he was even gentle. If he had a different ethic at least that ethic was honest.

And September itself was the best month ever. The pears and wild apple and quince began to crop. The blackberry feathered and silvered and drooped, while further east toward Winston, tobacco began to appear like great sheaves of golden flowers in the drying sheds and barns. The valley was enclosed and brushed green with mist.

Twelve-hour days, fourteen hours. She painted in the mornings when the eye was clear and when color was mysterious. The valley was alive with ancient voices. The fog-shrouded mornings called to them and they called back. She was still not a good painter, but she was going to be.

Singleton called regularly through September and in the first week of October he came to see her for a night and a day and part of another night. His phone calls were not encouraging. They came from places too far apart, and while she knew nothing of the road she knew that he tried to work sectors of the country. She imagined him crossing over colors, like on a map; the truck popping and cracking across the red and green and blue shapes on a map. Too much distance in too few days meant more driving and less loading.

He came off the mountain and the truck cracked through the valley, now colored in red and brown and gold. The greens, here in October, were bled thin and were decapitated by frost. She told herself that she really did not feel the cold and it seemed true. Her month of hard work had not made her warm, but it made her tough. She seemed to be learning art all over again, for much of what she knew no longer worked.

When Singleton backed the truck it was as slow as always. He went through the pulling up, the backing, and the work in the cab. Each time the truck was parked in her drive it was pointed toward the road and ready to go. She supposed there was a reason. The one good thing about the truck was its slow progression of shifting angles and planes as he backed.

The truck seemed even slower than usual. He was probably tired.

The truck hissed to a stop and she walked forward. He looked out at her, smiled and seemed to be working fast. In the fading afternoon the furrows in his face were shadowed, and the red sun that hung just above the ridge turned the truck cab into a frame of embering light. Then he climbed down.

"You look different." His voice was withdrawing. It was necessary for somebody to do something.

"I am different." She took his hand. She reached toward him, and actually, really, but softly, took the other hand. "I'm glad you're here."

"Is something wrong?" He was so serious, even while his voice was filled with apology.

"Everything is right." She tugged at his hand. "Walk with me.

[166]

I'll tell you soon. You look so tired. Let's go to the house."

He protested. He had slept.

Of course he had. That was not the point. This man. What did he know that he could teach her? Once, almost shy, he had mentioned a million miles of road.

The kitchen was warm when they entered the house. She hurried to the living room and knelt to start kindling in the fireplace. It caught and drew well.

Always before he had talked. Always before he had kissed her right away and they had laughed and been excited. He did not kiss her, but when she knelt to light the fire he touched her shoulder.

It seemed like they were in pantomime, or walking silent through the mechanical parts of a play that they might someday stage.

—Enter stage right. Man sits. Woman lights fire. Man reaches forward. Woman smiles. Stands. Exits right to reappear with coffee on tray (timidity, restraint, fatigue). Woman reacts and silently pours coffee—

Except that silence was no good.

"What's the matter?" He could not drink the coffee because she moved behind him, her fingers stronger now it seemed, and touched and rubbed and massaged his shoulders. They were tense, like hers got sometimes when she was emotional. She did not think the tension came from driving.

"Nothing," he said. Then lower. "A couple of things that can't be helped, not now."

The fire was burning well, brightly, and with a nearly ambitious-sounding snap and pop from the dry wood. It cast shadows. She half turned to see the both of them silhouetted dark against the far wall where her loom stood covered with a cloth over its hand-rubbed frame; shrouded and cloaked like a memory. The silhouette looked like a nineteenth-century photograph, a man sitting, a woman standing behind him; and she did not recognize him and she did not recognize herself.

She watched as he talked. If his hair was longer he would seem even taller. His shoulders were not relaxing. They felt thinner than they should, but he was not thin. As she stood behind him she moved sideways until she saw a quarter profile. There was a smudge of dirt high on one cheek. Maybe he had changed clothes in a restroom somewhere that did not have a mirror. Lower down was a small scratch that was nearly healed. He was always scratched or bruised someplace, and he always dismissed it as a matter of course. His job.

She already knew about Grace and John and Ben, but she did not interrupt. He seemed to be looking for some kind of continuity so she could understand how terrible and important his story was. Gradually she understood part of it. Something had happened to Ben. Singleton was running the roads, searching for Ben.

What she did not understand was the fatalistic sense behind his words. He seemed to feel that his story meant destruction. They were done. He did not actually say that, but she felt his pain and she felt his guilt. He seemed to be saying that she could not love him because he did not deserve it.

But the story, even if she only halfway understood it, was not good enough. There was something else. Either he was lying or was reserving some part of the situation to himself. Yet. Yet, she knew him to be honorable.

She had to do something, and it had to be right now, and it had to be the right thing to do.

Be honest, she guessed.

"First," she said, "I love you, and I want you to make love with me now, and every time you come here. Remember. That's first."

He reacted by seeming a little less ashamed, a little less uncomfortable. For one thing he actually turned his head and looked at her instead of staring into the fire. His eyes were deeper seeming than she remembered. They were not filled with pain, but pain was invisible behind them like gesso on canvas.

"Second," she said, "Ben seems to have done this to himself, and yet I feel your pain. I think you have not told me the whole story." Then she paused, faintly a voice, hers, and it trembled. "Is there someone else, somebody else?" She had not meant to say that, oh, she should not have said that, it was wrong to say that.

He sat motionless. The fire colored his face, shadowed it, sculpted it and turned it into a masterpiece of grief; and, may every god and goddess who ever lived help her, she was watching the shape of grief and taking notes in her mind. She was cataloging the colors and shadows of grief. How the light fell, and the form of it.

"Yes," he said. "Not how you think. Not a woman, but there is — was — someone else."

She had never heard his voice so low, so indrawn, so harmed. She reached toward him, touched his arm.

"Please tell me because I love you." It did not make much sense, but emotionally it seemed right.

He had never before told the story, maybe even to himself. He could not have told that story and still be so clumsy in the telling now. She knew nothing about the sea. She knew less about the sea then she knew about roads, but somewhere in his tale she began to believe she understood.

He was not actually saying that Pat was his son but it was obvious. For a moment she wondered if Pat was actually his natural son, then estimated what kind of years must be involved and thought that it was unlikely. She was shocked. Shocked. This man lived as deeply in himself as she did in herself. She had never suspected. She knew he was not superficial, but she had never expected this inwardness, this depth.

She did not know what to say. With his clumsy telling she thought that Pat was dead. Then she understood that Pat was alive but blind, and that Singleton blamed himself for all of it. Too much was coming out too fast and it was not coherent. She could see that the key was with what was happening to Ben. He thought he had fumbled the same way with Ben. That must be. She could not see how it could be anything else.

"What will you do when you find Ben?"

"I'll have to wait to see what happens."

That was no good. She had already tried that way of living, and that was no good. "Do you know what happens when you wait to see what happens? Either nothing happens, or something bad."

"I don't understand that."

"You are best off armed with options."

"Yes."

"You are a good man," she said. "I couldn't love you if you were not a decent and honorable man."

That really might have been the wrong thing to say. He looked nearly afraid. Then he seemed to gather himself around some resolve. "All this stuff has bothered me too much and too long. I didn't mean to come here like a wet blanket." He reached to touch her arm and he was smiling out of the resolve and it looked like he had himself convinced. She remembered her own pretending, or lying, or whatever it had been; but now, she really loved him.

"I'm sure there is more than that to say." She could not allow him to close the conversation when nothing was resolved. She felt urgent and afraid. It was all going to be said, his story, and it was going to get away from them and they would have done nothing. The distance would not be closed.

"I don't know what else there is to say."

"Ask yourself what you want. Say what you want."

It was not working. He could not understand that.

"Something has happened," she said.

"What?" He seemed wary.

"My story is good. It's also bad, but it's good."

Her words were more than she planned. Somehow she was inside the words, listening to her own monologue about the meaning of the wreck she had seen; of how the hideous was truly, truly hideous, but how it could make beauty and get through loneliness. How that which was hideous helped you turn from past to present, so that you could give sensible form in a world filled with harm. Her agitation seemed to mesh right in with the words, then get behind them so that the words became independent. They formed their own reality in the air. Once or twice she had felt something like this while teaching, but never so much. When she finished he stared at the fire.

"I don't understand."

Impossible. He had to understand. She looked at the weathered face, the scarred hands, the long figure slouched in the chair giving the impression of a child who has come to a costume party in his best clothes. She had made it real. Why was he miserable?

"How can you not understand?"

"I don't." He looked helpless along with the misery.

He was not stupid. She could not have loved him if he was stupid. He could make her feel helplessly ignorant with his knowledge, or with his offhanded comments that went to the crux of seemingly complex matters reported in the papers. He was even theoretical. Once he had explained the working of her entire car, got caught with enthusiasm and in a long digression explained not just the process but the actual chemistry of fire. In the woods he often surprised her with his intuitions about trees and geologic particularity. He was not stupid. Was he choosing to misunderstand?

"It's simple." She felt like wailing.

"Part of it sure is." His face was apologetic. It once more looked almost guilty, like he had a part of the responsibility for the accident that had happened. "The suspensions are no good. They're either fixed-axle on bedspring, or spring on fork. You saw a spring on fork. Sometimes they explode at speed."

Two people had died. There he sat, talking about suspensions. She wanted to slap him. Then she realized that he really was trying to explain something.

"Now I don't understand you," she said.

"You do the best you can when something happens, but you can't do anything beforehand. You can't keep it from happening." Beneath the helplessness in his voice, there was subdued anger. "Those guys that helped, they did their best. They didn't set the speed limits, and they didn't design the suspensions." His anger seemed to come from frustration, or feelings of futility that were not unusual or new.

"I know that," she said softly. "At least I do now. I wasn't blaming."

"As for the other, it probably is simple. It's just that I never read about that stuff. I don't know what you're talking about in the first place."

She was relieved. She was simply out of his frame of reference. Now his face was all apologetic for not being educated. When words failed, she thought, but words had not failed yet. She sat on the arm of the chair and nearly made the mistake of petting him.

"It isn't fair. I start telling you the middle and end of a story when you don't know the beginning." She had been secluded for so long, and he had been anything but secluded for all of his life. At least she thought that was true.

"It begins with this place, with this valley, and all of the years of work. I got the place and the valley all mixed up with the work." There must be some way to explain. His truck. Maybe someone

[171]

could feel that way about a truck.

"You live in your truck a lot."

"Yes."

"This might sound silly. Do you ever feel like you are a part of it?"

"All the time."

"Now listen and think about it. Does it ever seem that you are not just part but all of it. Does it ever seem like you are the truck?"

He stiffened. "No."

"But if you did then you would know what I mean about the valley and the love and the work."

It was not working. He was still distant. She needed him close. Put it in the very most simple terms.

"What it means is the easiest and most simple thing in the world. I was not ready before, but if you still want to be married I am ready now."

His smile was gentle. He actually looked glad. At the same time he was not exactly doing handstands.

"I can understand that."

"No you don't, but it's the best I can explain." He did not understand, did not. He understood that she wanted a husband who made money and came home and shared a bed. He understood words like security and fidelity and divorce and alimony. Worse, he was not agreeing. Not only did he not want to marry her for the wrong reasons—and it would be hard enough to think of marriage like that—but he did not even seem to want to marry her at all. It was terrible. Terrible. What had gone wrong?

"I'm sorry," she said. "You wanted to once."

He turned, still sitting in the chair as she sat on the overstuffed arm. He seemed finally, almost, impulsive. "You surprised me. It's just the trouble. I'll be gone so much. We should have been married long ago."

It sounded all right, which meant that he must be lying to himself pretty good. Which meant that at least that side of his ambivalence was sound.

Words had failed. She sat beside him, feeling nearly as miserable as he must be feeling. Words were symbols, and no matter how carefully you arranged them, no matter your careful intonations, words could betray the heart. Painting was not that way. With

[172]

paint you could be full and truthful.

The old shyness rushed at her like some animal roaring from its den. At a time when she needed to be brave the shyness was trying to chase her courage away.

What did women do? Experienced women? There must be a dozen-million ways to talk to someone you loved, if you were bold enough. Life charged you for being bold, life asked a price, but the price was probably even higher if you were shy.

She turned to him and placed her arm gently, but a little too quickly, around his neck. She moved his head so that his cheek lay against the thin cloth that covered her breasts. He liked her breasts a lot, she knew he did; and one thing about not being big was that you did not have to go around all strapped up. Slowly, and more like a teenaged girl than a seductress, she began to loose the buttons on her shirt. It was a little embarrassing.

At least he was no longer apologetic. He was touching her slowly, softly, his breath warm against her chest. The light from the fireplace highlighted what she could see of his face, and it cast light and color into his hair. The gentleness seemed firm, not shy, and her own response this time was not rapid. For the first time, ever, it was like her body was taking its time and feeling for the possibility that lay in all of its many, many senses. She did not care if he understood marriage, or not, as long as his misunderstanding did not get in the way of this.

Lying beside him, later, as the last light faded and the surrounding forest became dark, she still did not care. Through the window of the darkened room she could see a corner of the high trailer of his truck. It was like a building block dropped by a giant's child. He lay beside her in the darkness, caressing her hair and the back of one of her hands. He was silent, but he was close.

"I have to fix dinner." The truck bulked out there. At this time of year the sounds of the forest were muted. Animals ran lower to the ground, the natural cover diminished because of the falling leaves. Most of the sounds you heard were caused by wind and the stream.

"Rather stay here." His voice sounded as if he were dreaming. He sounded like he was not talking about dinner, but talking some kind of denial of that truck out there. In the darkness he looked almost critical of the truck, and his voice was soft with thanks and gentleness and fatigue. He looked through the window, at the truck. Then he half raised on one elbow, peering through the window at the dark shape, like he was puzzled.

The van was a little high on one side, the surface of the drive slanting off toward the downhill pasture, but not enough to unsettle even a poor load. The road was dark, winding away beyond the pasture and across the mountain, but when the moon rose it would be like a silver, mist-touched line pointing here, there, to New York or Chicago or Tallahassee or St. Paul. Like a silver, mist-touched line that as the night deepened would dull down with the growing ground mist from the cold, but still wet forest. The road would be misted and slow, so that you ran the low places with your heart a little anxious, your eyes alert for the quick movement of an animal in the mist. In the high places, if they lasted long enough, some of the songs and the stillness that you got sometimes when you were dreaming might be there. The van would follow the songs and the stillness, faithful on the curving line of the road and faithful to the straight-forward drag of a perfectly centered pin held in the fifth wheel.

The van, outside the window, disappeared deeper and deeper into darkness as Catherine told him to just lie there, rest, and she would call him for dinner. The van was closed up, silent, waiting; and through the doors of that van it seemed for a moment that he could remember every carton of freight that he had ever shoved. He was drowsy, warm, and fearful of sleep. If he slept he was afraid she could not wake him. It seemed, right now, that with her love and her presence some of the songs and stillness were hovering right at his ear. He tried to raise himself up, swing his feet off the edge of the bed, and get moving. Then he told himself it would make no difference if he rested for a couple of minutes, but no more. The songs and stillness seemed to grow.

Sunlight woke him. What he had feared had happened: he had slept through the night. From the kitchen he could hear Catherine's movements. She was half singing and half humming, the small song mixed with the hums; and the smell of fresh coffee was as clear in his mouth and nose as the sunlight was in his eyes. She was happy and he was embarrassed. He bailed out of bed quick, dressed, and felt himself almost apologetically sneaking into the kitchen. She met him halfway, with a cup of coffee in her hand.

"I'm sorry."

"I'm not," she told him. "I love it. And you." She was happy. Happy. She was moving like a young girl. She looked like a young girl. Her long hair was braided, the braid coiled and pinned high the way she wore it in the forest. She actually shooed him toward the john like he was a flock of chickens. Then, when he had gone through his kit for a toothbrush and a razor, when he was clean and capable, she shooed him again. Right out onto the back porch, where, while she fixed breakfast, it became clear that she had plans for the day. Since he had no plans in particular, he asked no questions, even when she gave him the answer.

Singleton sat on the back steps, fooling around with an old axe. He remembered the night before, their talk, and he felt confused. He remembered the lovemaking and felt a little bit better. He hefted the axe and looked at the chipped blade.

An axe was a nice tool. He had forgotten just how nice an axe could be.

He sat on the back steps, the axe handle under his right leg with the head cocked slightly back toward him and resting against his knee. The rounded blade was dull. He began to take a good deal of pleasure finding the satin shine of high-tempered steel beneath the coat of black crud and speckled rust. The blade was really round. It must have belonged to Catherine's father; and it felt like a clean thing to do, filing and sharpening what must be a forty-year-old tool. A blade this round meant that some woman or kid or dumbass had put it on a grindstone at one time or another.

He picked it up, cocked it under his left leg and found that you could not get the pressure on the file that you needed. He put the handle under him and sat on it, filing between his legs. Still a little clumsy, but it worked. There were small bites taken from the blade. It would take a lot of filing. It was easier if you held the head tight under your right knee.

Catherine was in the kitchen and he figured she was happy. It seemed like she was. Occasionally he heard a small flurry of sound along with more song and hums. They were going to gather wood, directly. He drank more of the coffee beside him and wrinkled his

[175]

nose. She had bought some with chicory—which if you could just smell the stuff and not have to taste it—he lit a cigarette. Everything would be all right. Probably. The day was going to be chilly in spite of the sunshine. Small filings like tiny silver pebbles lay on his left hand.

He had not done good the day before, and he had worked to make it right. At least he had meant to. The trouble was that if he made it right then maybe he would not like that result, either. He had fucked up bad by telling her all of that stuff about Pat. Like he was a kid who could not handle problems, laying problems on her that they did not need between them.

Then she had surprised him. At first he thought that living alone was making her crazy, because she was talking with more excitement and mysteriousness than usual. Then he understood that something important really had happened, at least it was important to her. Well, it had been her first time out there. First times were bad.

It was confusing. He should not have come. Either that, or he should not leave.

No. He should not have come. He should have stayed out there and run Ben down fast instead of fooling around. He would not have come, except that about half the time, these days, she was not at home when he called. Of course, lots of times she worked outside.

Just plain confusing. It was like there were two different worlds. If you could get it separated you could live good in both of them. There was the world of trucks and the movement and excitement of action, and there were women. What man, if he was any kind of man, was not interested in strength, or in things like spending money, a lot of money, to make something happen and then see it happen. What man, to be honest, what man living who had any class would not be interested in a woman who wanted him, as long as she did not want to own him.

The other world wasn't easy to describe, and he figured that the axe coming clean and sharp was like a sign of that world. It was a big anticipation to know that he would take the sharpened axe to the woods and feel its sure bite. She had a clearing up there where someone built a house once. He looked at the tiny pebbles of steel on the back of his hand and believed he understood why the

[176]

clearing was important. Women felt that way.

He had to admit that he felt that way sometimes. It would be good to sit before a fire burning wood that you had cut. It would be good to reconstruct the outbuilding, sagging now, the heavy timbers partly milled and partly hand hewn. That suggested that there had been an even older building there once, and someone had used part of the timbers.

Maybe that was the trouble—the clearing, these outbuildings. A man could walk out on a cold morning feeling strong and with work to do. He could reconstruct, make changes, rebuild, and then sooner or later that man was going to die and his work would end up as another clearing in the forest. Either that or under a bulldozer when some other man with new ideas wanted a road. In the Guard it had not been like that. What you did in the Guard disappeared right after it happened. You saved someone and it was over, but in a way that he could never explain, it was not over in the same way as her clearing.

Coming from a house like this on a cold morning and working at building, you would be coming from the closeness of another person. They would finally not surprise you. It would be easy and comfortable. He paused, his mind refusing it. The whole idea of comfort was like trying to be old.

When they made love last night Catherine was different. It made him different, and during the lovemaking and for awhile afterward he felt nothing about anyone but Catherine. The thought of Naomi flickered past with no special feelings. Then he started thinking about difference.

You got different when you learned new things, and one of the ways you learned about sex was to have it. He had held her close, quickly, sharp feelings of loss and hurt chasing him. He could not know her. She could not know him. Then he had been ashamed of himself for thinking such a thing.

He had not done well, thinking that, along with telling about Pat. He was almost acting crazy. She had learned other things, and she was educated. She had scared the hell out of him telling about things she learned that he did not quite understand.

She acted like he was more important. She acted like sex was not as important as before. No, she went at it like they were more together, like it was not enough to just do things to each other.

More open, or something. More natural.

They were doing one hell of a lot better in bed than they were doing at talking with each other. It made him nervous. To be truthful, to be absolutely honest, it made him afraid.

The door opened. He turned.

"How is it coming?" She was beautiful. Educated. He had never wondered before, but he had to wonder now what someone like her saw in him. She looked even younger than before. Her hair in that heavy braid looked so nice.

If only he had not fucked up and told her about Pat.

"Breakfast in just a minute."

"I'll be right in."

He could marry this woman. He wanted to, but you were always responsible. He wanted to. But he did not want to become a clearing in the forest.

An axe and a truck were both tools and under the right circumstances both were exact and simple.

He stood to rub his back.

Try kerosene

Huh

For backache, that's your kidneys grabbing you, a doctor told me, you take a teaspoon of kerosene and a little brown sugar once a day, clears it right up

He remembered that one. A bullshit guy at the stop just over the bridge in Chicago.

He heard her in the kitchen. He hefted the axe. They would eat breakfast and then walk in the woods. He knew before they started that he would be working the hard deadwood, not the easy worked stuff.

The problem was that he halfway said he would marry her as soon as he found Ben. The problem was that he wanted to. He had no notion of how the rest of the day would go, except he was going to try hard to make it good. She deserved that, even if they were not talking good to each other. And later, come about midnight, he could climb up and ease that load of junk on over to Hickory.

19

OCTOBER, October, October. He rode it out, caught a load of cabinets from Hickory on straight freight to Cleveland which was a loser. Ratted around the east coast for awhile, running south to north to north to south. Time seemed in suspension. A dreamlike quality hit him, almost like he was driving shift with John—like they had sometimes, him driving, John driving, them unloading. Drive to sleep and work to drive. Shove paint and case goods, hardware, equipment. Maybe it was Tuesday and before he really understood it was Tuesday again.

The road whirled past. The coffee cups, the sweat, the standing in front of the pumps checking the rigs of other men and proud of his own rig, all of those things were like a dream.

He watched waitresses, estimating them kindly, and if a girl or woman looked at him in a way that asked for attention Singleton would feel a sudden desire and then relax. Sometimes when that happened he would call Catherine, the calls placed from along the road, the words fumbling beneath the scream of a diesel or the beat of a juke. On those times when she was home he could hear the love in her voice, but he could hear a lot of excitement too and he did not want to think about that.

He had the truck. He had the road. He had the work and the

song of the drive. It was like being immersed in a love affair, and maybe it was going to end some day, but it was not ending yet.

In November he ran the books and found that he had lost money. He got drunk in Philadelphia, sobered up for a day and a half, and settled down to business. He had not found Ben. He dickered, played between a company and a broker and caught a fat split for L.A. and Oakland, figuring to top off the split in L.A.

The roads were already beginning to tough it. Snow on the northern route, snow in Kansas which was okay, but snow above Denver. He passed up the central route and ran south doing the doctoring on the log that would make him look legal.

He had a mild decision. He could run good road, drop south and cross below, but within running distance of Asheville. The seriousness of the last weeks bothered him.

He ran it south, and the truck hummed and sang and moved like a picture of flight across the rusty southeast; and he was a part of the picture and his mind gave him other parts, his memory calling back and back and back, reeling the road to him until he found himself again in the dream; feeling, hurting, pleased by it too; his mind feeding him Traverse City where there was a little zoo with a funny bear, and a museum cluttered with thousands of uncatalogued valuables and junk, tossed together like a pawn-shop after a windstorm; and Salt Lake where rusting beer cans surrounded the shrinking waters, and outside of Salt Lake where there had been a distant thunderstorm so violent that he thought it was artillery on maneuver, the glow cracking and fading beyond the horizon, so far you could not see the strokes beyond the falling away of the land; only the dawn-red and quickly dying color; the immensity of sound that was a roar over the crack of the exhaust.

And the ice-blonde, ice-blood waitress with south in her voice who worked the first stop north into Georgia, the Georgia heat, the slow-drawling, oppressive and quick-tempered heat that killed if you moved too fast; and the claim-jumping deputy in Delaware who took him to a truck stop and held his own court with a charge of ten miles over the limit and a twenty-seven dollar fine—and then slapped him on the shoulder and paid for the coffee; and the claim-jumping deputy who did the same thing outside Corpus Christi, but this time the charge was a log book behind, the fine thirty-five dollars, and the guy did not pay for the coffee.

Or for that matter, San Jose and the hot, tiny cubelike houses, long payment along Spanish-named streets with orange trees; and the capitol of Iowa with more than twenty kinds of matched marble and golden domes; and the bar in Columbus, Montana, with rows and rows of mounted animals and other animals in glass cases staring glassy-eyed at the drunks; and the new, almost sculptured filling station in Denver, and the cool-smelling, hot-smelling streets of Denver which ran side by side, and how you rolled in level from Kansas and cleared the town and climbed straight up; and the musky, magnolia-smelling, slum-stinking black murmur of the bad side of Winston; and Harlan where they had a dynamite warehouse in the exact center of town, and where they had shot five sheriffs in six weeks, or was it six in five weeks; and Harlem where he went to see and left afraid, the rot-stinking, house-stinking, over-perfume of Harlem, and how some of the black women beckoned, but not at him; and the pines outside of Sault Ste. Marie like towers with shanties built beneath them, pine-smelling cathedral tops with bases in castoff humans and their cold shacks.

And crossroads Arkansas where asshole Faubus was making such a stink, and you walked to any restaurant (because there were no stops) wondering should you be packing your gun; the silent men dust-squatting, looking, looking, not talking, and you not fool enough to kid the waitress. And the cypress. Lake leaf, limb falling where there was wet in Mississippi, the black avoidance and sharp looks when you said "Negro"; and the bank in Yazoo which would not cash the shipper's check for a yankee until "they called ol' Billy to make certain sure"; and Lubbock where there was a good stop; and Washington, D.C., where there wasn't; and St. Louis with hell-for-leather traffic and the peace arch facing the red-brick squalor of East St. Louis; and Detroit, and what could you remember about Detroit that was not dirty rain over dirty pavement, except when it snowed and the snow was dirty before it hit?

But across the border was Windsor and that was farms and a guy who pumped fuel and said "splendid" and "ripping" and maybe it

[181]

was an act; and the guy standing dumb outside Centralia watching his wife's head framed by a hole in the windshield, throat blood throbbing, and the guy whispering over and over and over and over and over "sorry, I'm sorry, so sorry, I'm sorry, so sorry, sorry, so sorry" and the dead black bull, truck-tossed outside Spotsylvania, truck ditched, driver stunned, and a load of live chickens roosting in the early morning trees and sprinkled around the autumn land like red-and-white bits of rag, the farmer yelling because the driver had not cut old Blackie's throat so at least they coulda used the meat.

It came and went and came again, the smile of a woman, the wave of a child from the back of a passing station wagon, the jarring crunch of a small animal under the tandem, and the high, thin whisper of the wind that moved like a spirit through the Rockies. Before he knew it he was in L.A., wasted two days topping the load, dragged it into Oakland and found that the net was a little over a thousand bucks. It helped make up for October.

California started to hurt him. He felt it deep, the certain blue sky, the yellow-and-brown hills, the eucalyptus-smelling wind. He laid over for three days, caught a ride across the Bay Bridge and walked in San Francisco. A stranger among strangers, but it was different there. His legs were uncertain on the high hills but his mind reached toward the city, trying to digest the fact of Chinese and Italian, of Russian and Scandinavian and Negro and Jew and Japanese and French. It made the other seem remote; and even if he knew that she was not more than ninety hours away she seemed further, for in miles the distance was almost three thousand.

It was like something was drawing him north, and he waited over a fourth day to catch a load for Vancouver. It was with that shipper that he first heard of Ben, and it was also with that shipper that he was tempted to lease. You could not fake licenses and bills of lading forever. You could run the registration tricks, but sooner or later you would get tagged. It would be good to stay on the coast running north. It would be good not to know, not to have to figure out what had gone wrong with them in October, but he did not lease because sooner or later he would have to talk to her. He did not know whether it was him or her or them.

Still, he spent all of November on the coast, and that first northern trip routed him through Oregon. He fooled around, drifting, and November which had started good netted only average. It was an attempt to get back east to his connections that put him on the road where he would find Ben; and, finding Ben, would discover that the restless voices were not stilled, that the road still required something from him.

20

GOT inta Boston and they said use union help. I said they could blow it out their ass and hired a coupla wops. Di'n't speak any English but they sure could push a load. That night three punks showed up. Goin' to cut my tires, knives as long as your prick and I climbed in the cab and pulled old Betsy. Let one off between a guy's legs.

That did it, huh?

That did it, you bet. A cop arrested me for discharging a firearm in the city and when I got back my tires was cut.

Singleton sat in his truck trying to ignore the last five minutes of his fiftieth birthday by reading his mail. He felt the cold seeping in and down the back of his neck from the curtained sleeper. Off to one corner of the lot the snow had been plowed into a huge bank that would not melt until spring, snow compacted and icy with the dirt and grease of trailers, or road crap picked up and then steamed off. A full-sized rig could pick up three hundred pounds of dirt. Dirt could actually scale you overweight. Add ice, a thousand pounds maybe, and you would be thinking you were legal until you got pulled over and busted the scale.

He slurped at coffee from a thermos and thumbed his mail. Grace had forwarded it twice, and it finally caught him here at the big stop outside of Bismarck. The temperature was close to zero which helped make it a good night. Beyond the lights of the stop it would be shine and crystal, the land lying bare and gleaming; looking smooth and solid, like you could turn the rig off the road and cruise like a skater over ice.

Lately ideas like that had been coming to him. Lately, when his hands were raw in the thick gloves, swollen and hurting when he warmed them under the cold-water tap in some john his mind would want to stray. Want him to wander off the road to a quiet road, a smooth, easy-feeling road where there was no schedule or delivery dates. He had been on some roads like that. Usually they were through national forests or back routes to small towns where there was a single manufacturing plant. In the last few years those roads had been drying up.

It was not his age. Repeat. Not his age. He had felt this way before when it was 1943 and everybody was dying in January. When the sea lanes of the east coast were scattered with flotsam, and bodies sunk fast unless they were in life jackets. When that happened the bodies bobbed around for days until the basking sharks took care of them. Not his age. Repeat. A man just got tired. In those days the convoys had gotten the shit shot out of them. Search and Rescue had no longer seemed heroic or good. It was a wet, dirty job and you were almost always too late.

Most of the mail was routine. No trouble to pay the bills, he was making pretty good. The trouble seemed to be in getting the bills. He did not want to ask Grace to handle his book work.

He did not want to ask Grace for anything until after he found Ben. That was going to be tonight.

The cab was cold but he waited to put the truck back on the line. It was the feeling that once the engine was running you had to move. He did not want to drive but now it was necessary. He ran it over in his mind. Brake check complete, and in winter there was almost nothing more important than making sure your brakes would work. Condensation in the lines could freeze and knock them out. Most guys kept some kind of antifreeze in their lines.

He had come to this stop thinking he would plug in to the heaters alongside the building. They would keep the engine block warm, keep the truck's heater going, and then he would have slept for a few hours. No chance for that now.

Four checks, a couple of bills, some advertising, a letter from Grace and another letter postmarked Oregon. He did not know anyone in Oregon and opened it with curiosity. It was from Shirley who had lived outside Harrodsburg, and he wondered how she had gotten so far away. He was only a little nostalgic, thinking of her, and was surprised she had gotten up the nerve to get out.

It was wet, she wrote, and she hated it and did not believe that it was ever not wet. The people were crazy as hell, the traffic was crazy, and she was willing to bet that even the animals and birds were crazy because of the company they had to keep. It was a pessimistic letter and short. She was working in a restaurant. Thought maybe she would move in with some relations in a small town. There was an address and a p.s. saying that she had finally seen an ocean. He knew that for her it was a real triumph. He also knew that she would not have written if she was not lonesome.

He flipped the letter into the glove box, feeling sorry for all the losers in the world, and turned to the letter from Grace. The night was quiet, but he could hear the muffled racket from behind the doors of the tightly sealed shop, the high wail of a grinder on steel; and even further off there was the sound of a tandem spinning where some guy had caught a spot of ice.

Grace's letter was even shorter. John was alive, she was pretty well, and there was no news of Ben, love Grace. She always signed them love, but he knew it was a fraud. Knew it now, although he had not thought so before. He also knew that Ben might not go back even when he was found. That would be tough for her to take.

The cold was sharp. He wound the engine up and let the heater run while he felt tired and looked at the handful of mail. It was not much. Hard to believe that was all the mail you rated after two months. Ought to write to Pat. It had been awhile. Ben was not far off. He might overtake him before Minneapolis, but to do it he would have to overdrive him, stay at the wheel a long time. He had already been driving seven hours and kicked up a load before that. Play the radio and maybe learn something. Anything was better than just driving around catching loads and chasing a punk kid.

He was fifty years old. He had been telling himself that for nearly a year and now it was true. Fifty years old in Bismarck,

North Dakota, with a half-loaded rig on a run that would about break even. There would be plenty going out of Minneapolis. You never had trouble catching a load in Minneapolis.

But now he was fifty years old. He checked his watch. He was fifty years and fifteen minutes. Time kept moving, although lately it had been hard to gauge. Lately time had been a continuous line of half-felt, partly seen impressions. He was too old and too tired and it was fifteen, no sixteen minutes now past midnight. Singleton shoved it in gear and pulled from the stop, easing it across the never quite unslick lot to the almost always slick roadway. He hoped there would be no more snow. It was one of the worst jobs in the world to mount chains.

It was good in the snow sometimes. Only in the snow was there a surrounding quiet, and it was in the quiet that you could hear all of the tiny, subtle sounds that your ears lived with every day but did not identify. The snow muffled the hum of the tandem, cloaked the roaring blur of the engine, and it was sometimes like the engine noises seemed to separate so that the engine was a rush of air, a forced flowing of diesel, a measured, almost leisurely movement of oiled pistons and the low and steady churn of the crank. It was in the snow that your ears picked up the individual hums of the defrosting fans, the slight squeak in the seat that had cost over two hundred dollars and would adjust to your weight. The whisper of air that he had never been able to find, indicating a small leak in the truck, the rustle and slide of a roll of paper and ball pens adrift in the map box, the tiny rattle in the doghouse. It was all a part, and the part he liked best was the ticking of the flashers when he signaled, the long narrow bands of red and yellow casting against the snow or illuminating the corners of the cab.

On nights in the snow it sometimes seemed like you were not moving at all. Looking in your mirrors you would see the small markers glowing dimly through the shower of snow that the rig threw high on each side, swirling and sparkling, obscuring the view to the rear so that a man had to be more attentive about overtaking traffic.

When everything was right: when the snow was powder, the cab warm and the load solid; when the road was flat like it was now and straight; the long wide lanes walking into the night ahead of

[187]

the lights; the banks of snow along the road like long silver pillows; then the driving was like slow movement through a passive dream. Practically, also, it was slow because you got between forty and fifty-five. Powder was pretty dependable, but no snow was really dependable.

He rolled it out, resenting the sound of the engine as he dragged for gears. Then the rig settled and he had it solid, safe, an easy go through the rest of North Dakota and through most of Minnesota. It was only about four-hundred-fifty miles. He would arrive in Minneapolis and he would be fifty years and ten or eleven hours old. The snow would take the extra time, would carve a couple extra hours from his life.

Singleton shook his head. It was time to stop thinking about it, time to quit worrying it, because he had worried it long enough.

It was just this, and this was the whole problem. When a man got to be fifty it seemed like he should have something, and for two months Singleton had been trying to figure out what he had. He resented the need for an answer, and yet, by God, there it was. At fifty a man should stand for something, should be able to show fifty years of—accomplishment, he supposed.

Hauls were down. Even here, on the heavily traveled northern route, the trucking was slow. A lot of guys laid over. A lot of companies were riding out the weather. Automobiles were always scarce at night, but on this night in the powder there were no automobiles and the few trucks were dragging it easy. He settled in, feeling not so tired now, warm and comfortable as the rig cruised the air-freezing, crystal coldness of midnight in Dakota. If it were not for loading and unloading; if, actually, it were not for the fact of having to stop at all; if a man could just drive on and on, measuring his skill and feel for the road against hundreds of thousands of miles, not stopping for fuel, not stopping.

He knew why Ben was going. Back at the Indiana truck stop when he was still wandering in his mind about Pat—and he admitted, he had been wandering—he knew right from the first why Ben had jumped the ignition and left. Ben was going because as long as a man was going, was doing, was actually on the move, then that man did not have to face up to anything. Singleton had known it for a long time without knowing that he knew it. When Ben left he faced up to himself, and now many things seemed to

[188]

no longer make a difference. It seemed that the ironic part of him could have knowledge that should be harmful and was not, because that knowledge excepted him from the rules that he went ahead and followed but now figured were bullshit. Except, of course, the rules of the road.

Ben was going not because he had been stopped too long, but mostly because stopping was the time when the mental rent came down.

Do you run from me

He did not want to think of her now and pushed the voice away. Later, maybe, he would think of her, would go over all of it and see what had changed and why, like he had gone over it a dozen times. Catherine was different, he was; they were different.

But Ben was just up the road. The fifth of December, now. Ben was gone three months and Singleton was fifty years old. Truckers were the worst gossips in the world and that sometimes helped. An hour before, Ben had fueled and complained about the service. Then he complained that he would be in Minneapolis too early to unload and too late to sleep. The guy on the pumps took out his resentment against Ben by telling a couple of guys what a bad mouth he was. Probably true, but it was also true that the guy on the pumps was lazy.

There was only one place in Minneapolis where any of them had ever stopped. He would find Ben there.

When Ben started to run, way back last fall, Singleton had taken the taxi back to the house. As the taxi rolled in he first saw the station wagon, and for a moment believed it was going to be all right. He thought that Ben had only stranded him and returned home. The doorway of the barn was open. Ben's truck was gone. Singleton paid the driver, then turned to the house to find Grace. She did not come out from the house. He found her in the kitchen, looking old and tired. When he said hello in a shamed voice she did not answer. As he explained what had happened and what Ben said her face got better.

"It had to be something more than getting hurt." She looked at him for the first time since he entered. Her face got better every moment, the lines disappearing, and her eyes showed life and resolution. He thought that Grace must be as tough as harness, the most resilient person he had ever known.

She took his hand. "It's a long way from what I hoped," she said. "Find him. We still have to find him."

They did as much as they could right away. It was Sunday. Offices were closed, but they called the homes of company men who knew Ben. They called the home of the bank president and Grace tried to tie up Ben's money, which did not work. Grace called Sue, and Singleton filed a missing persons. The police explained that a man was free to leave his mother. In fact, he was even free to run away from his uncle as long as he was legally sane. They made Singleton feel like the idiot he knew he was.

There had been a good many miles since then, and now here he was bucking the northern route in the middle of heavy snow, and he was tired, and he was sick of the whole damned thing to tell the truth.

He figured that it was getting colder, more than ten below. No doubt. The snowbanks were silvering under the lights, laying far out ahead of him beneath moonlight and gleaming a lighter, different silver. There would be time to stop in Fargo. A man had to walk around a little, talk to someone a little, or the road that he wanted to keep driving and never have to stop would get him. Tired was a condition that dictated mistakes, and one of the tricks was to break up the routine every so often. Half the stops that truckers made were not because they needed the coffee or even the talk. They just needed something different to break up the mind-numbing of the road that caught you when fatigue really hit. There were a lot of tricks and, he figured, before this was over he would be using most of them.

He checked the tach and saw that he was losing speed, checking it automatically against the speedometer. When you started dropping revs it was a sure sign of fatigue. He had driven open road for sometimes a hundred miles and never dropped fifty revs. He goosed it back up, wrapped his hands back over the wrapping of the wheel which he had corded one time when they were snowed in at the farm. He had taken pride in the cording. It was the same kind of job you did on a ship. The ships, which had once seemed such an immediate part of his memory were receding now. After a couple months and a lot of work—a lot of figuring too—the ships were a part of an almost forgotten world.

It was like his mind had been laying ghosts, because now when they came at him he would think of them instead of pushing them aside. Sometimes they came back, but they came back weaker each time and some of them did not come back at all.

One night he remembered his father. Heard his father say, "Make us proud." It was what he had told Singleton on the day Singleton left home, not knowing what he would do, surprised later on when he enlisted.

He thought about the old man with anger. It was easy for him to say make us proud. A man who had never taken any chance. His father farmed all his life, had probably never been outside of Indiana. His father had been a deacon, a conventional man who never took any chance, *any* chance on anything but the weather. And God was responsible for the weather, so even when there was a crop failure it had been beyond the will of man. God was his father's crop, the one that could be held liable for depression and all other economics, or for the anxieties of looking into the sky like you could pull rain out of it with your eyes. That was not taking any chance. His father's answer, and his aunt's, was to pray, have faith and be humble. That, right there, Singleton told himself, that was the reason why the old man had been about as humble as an axehead, had been a hard-nosed, stiff-necked, no-running-room-allowed, puritan bastard. Having never taken a chance it was easy for him to advise other people to make him proud.

"Yes sir," Singleton had said at the time. He had been nervous and afraid, homesick even before leaving, and at nineteen had never been anywhere except Indianapolis.

"Yes sir," he had said, but, he thought, thinking about it firmly, that if he had it to do over again he would tell the old man to go fuck himself.

That was one ghost laid.

He had been lucky. He got himself a cutter and got into the Guard and entrenched before the Depression arrived. Otherwise he might have had to come back home. John had stayed. He never did understand that, and he never would. Maybe John just didn't have the choice of leaving, and then, of course, he and Grace got married right out of high school.

Sometimes it seemed to Singleton that he could almost remember his mother, but he never did. She died just after John was born. Infection.

He had gotten rid of his aunt's voice the same way he had with the old man. He told her to go fuck herself, and grinned every time he said it.

What did they expect? What had they ever expected? After all, they were country people who had never been out of the country. They had never seen an ocean, either, had never seen trouble or emergencies; not emergencies where you had to weigh the value of definitely losing someone who was surely dying to take a chance getting a line on someone else who might live.

In a way Catherine had been like that, but no more. He was going to think of Catherine pretty soon, think about her when the fatigue really hit. Sometimes when the fatigue was just right it was like your mind solved things and understood things that would not get answered when you were totally alert.

The snow fences were drifted heavily like bulwarks raised across the flat land. A half mile up the road another rig showed its lights faintly in the shower of snow raised by its passing. Singleton had been following the guy, laying back, not dogging. The rig was running at fifty, which was fast enough for conditions. It could be passed if necessary, and Singleton might have done so if the passing had been entirely up to him. Occasionally the guy was weaving, but the powder was firm enough that at fifty he should not be doing it. Unless the freight had been loaded by someone else. Sometimes guys caught a load that a jerk warehouseman had put heavy to the rear. When that happened you pulled the trailer feeling like a dog with a ten-pound wart on its tail. There was no control. The bulk of the weight should be forward in the trailer nose, and it could have been on a night like this. Even if you overloaded an axle no scales would be open.

The only other reason for the guy to be weaving was that he was tired or drunk. It was a wide highway, but no highway was wide enough to be passing a drunk when there was snow, not at speeds above fifty when the widths of the lanes were reduced by the pillows.

Singleton rolled the window halfway down to allow the truck to fill with cold air. It was too warm in the cab, the road too straight and flat. He checked his gauges, engine temp, transmission temp and the temp in the axles. Normal. The tach sat like it was riveted. Brake pressure level. Snow dusted against the windshields, still settling from the rig ahead. No wind. No clouds. No action of any kind. It was at times like this that a man was most alone, and he was most alone because during these times he was also closer to sleep, to the engine-lulling, snow-fence-piling serenity of non-action which told you the lie that there was no such thing as danger.

The cold air filled the cab like it was rushing into a vacuum. It was like being whipped across the face with a willow switch. Singleton tensed his shoulders and neck. His eyes watered. He left the window open for one mile by the clock then rolled it closed and shook his head. The rig ahead was fuzzy and he wiped tears, realized that he had a death grip on the wheel, and loosened his hands. They were sore in the knuckles and opened slow, like hands with arthritis. He leaned on the dished wheel with his forearms and wiggled the fingers, making them hurt, making them deny the stiffness. They had always been good hands, strong, and the wrists were heavy and capable. Once in a fight he had knocked a man cold with his wrist, missing a from-the-floor backhand to catch him by surprise. But that had been in a bar off Scollay Square twenty-five years ago, and now there was not even going to be a Scollay Square of a sort to attract young sailors. Besides, the woman had been a tramp.

Don't drive tired

"Don't live any longer," he told John's voice. "Keep your self-respect." There were pills taped back in beside the doghouse. He had never needed them yet, was nearly superstitious about the stuff. He had picked them up at a stop, the pills so cheap that he also bought some of the expensive ones, small brown ovals that looked like footballs and were called footballs. He carried them like he carried the flares, the gun, the chains, the fire extinguisher; and he checked them in the same way. Tools, but the flares and the fire extinguisher were required by law.

The guy in the rig ahead was definitely in trouble. It was more and more obvious that his trouble was not his load. The dim markers snapped sideways twice, the guy caught it the second time and leveled out. Singleton watched the gap between them. The guy had not cut speed.

When he left Grace to look for Ben he took a load from Louisville to New York. It had taken a long time because he stopped at likely places to inquire about Ben, and to leave notes that said:

"Dear Ben, we do not know what you think you did, but nothing can be so bad that you have to leave. Please call. Mom and Charles."

To the notes he had added, "I've got something to tell you." In hindsight it was pretty stupid, but that was in hindsight.

From New York he had waited for a load to Chicago and checked the main stops. He made Pittsburgh where Sue did not answer her phone and where he could not take any more delay. In Chicago he fished two days for a load south and pulled a bad split for Evansville-Cincinnati. In Cincinnati he passed a fat one, a line haul to Denver, in favor of a shipment of distressed cabinet fixtures on return to a plant in Hickory. It was chancy business and made him nervous. Most of the loads were coming through brokers, and while most brokers were not thieves plenty were slow pay. Most of them would shave you a little. He regretted the Denver load because he knew the shipper and it would have been anyway a thousand gross. Instead, he went to North Carolina because Catherine had not been answering her phone.

By the time he was two weeks out he had found no trace of Ben. He had not expected to, that soon. When you wanted a guy you could get him, but it always took a while. He had not even been trying hard, but had relied on the notes. Ben would have connected with at least one of them after two weeks. In his every-other-day call to Grace he found only her worry and no results. Later he stopped calling.

The guy was going to jackknife that sonovabitch sure. The whole rig walked left, nibbled at the edge of the snow pillow, somehow managed to stay alive and began to drift back. And the guy was still not cutting speed.

There were, by God, ethics and ethics. If the guy did not turn off at the next stop Singleton decided to turn off himself, call the

[194]

state police and have him taken down. It was rotten; in a way it was unprofessional, but maybe in the best way of all it was real professional—if the guy even made it to the next stop. How in the hell drunk or tired did a man have to be to run off a main route in North Dakota? Singleton automatically checked his mirrors. Through his own snow cloud were lights but they were far off. His markers were almost obscured. The film snow had hit the markers, been melted by the small warmth that would come through the glass in spite of the cold, and the melt had become frozen build-up in the corners. His rig must be almost invisible except for the snow cloud rising in the clear night.

When he called Catherine, before pulling Hickory, she had finally been home. She had been gone for a long while. He did not want to interfere in her business, but it was unlike her. Then she said that she had gone to Atlanta, and she had something to tell him, later. When he arrived, then she would tell him. She sounded sad and she also sounded excited. You could not tell over the phone exactly what a person was really feeling.

He was surprised by the warmth in her voice. It was different. Before, it had been an intimate warmth, an excitement when she heard that he was coming to see her. This time it held sadness, but it was also singular. It was more like a loving, and, he supposed, wifelike warmth. He was not sure he liked the change although while talking to her he had responded out of the happy and secure feelings her voice prompted. Of course, he was still low about Ben. Maybe she had heard some of that even if he tried to hide it. When he hung up he was puzzled. That was three months ago. He was still puzzled.

The problems were that he was in love with a memory of Naomi, and he was in love with Catherine who was real, but who was not much like the memory. That could be lived with. Maybe as you got older some of the thrill and exhilaration of loving another person got lost.

He and Catherine were never going to be in love the right way for as long as he stayed on the road, or until she got over her notions about the road.

And if he didn't have the road, what did he have? He had been alone most of his life, except that a ship was a kind of home. Now

[195]

he did not want to leave the road just to live with her, but it was like if he did not live with her he could not bear to stay on the road.

If it had not been him he would have laughed. Imagine being fucked up at fifty the way kids got all messed up at twenty. Still, there was something he couldn't explain and he did not see how he could quit before he got it explained.

Take the engine, for instance. Right now the engine was like a brain with small worries as it chased some drunk in a freight rig across North Dakota. Sometimes the engine seemed as simple as an electric wire, the lube splashing everything, the crank balance not even thought of, the fuel flow like a breeze through a wind tunnel. At other times the best-regulated engine would feel like it was in a bad mood. It would be like a man getting everything done one second before the job became a catastrophe. Guys said that it was atmospheric pressure, and even those few who wanted to talk about it were always cold and objective. It always ended with atmospheric pressure. He did not believe that, but he did not want to believe what he felt about the engine, either.

And he was fifty and didn't have it figured out, and he hated to think of it. He was fifteen years older than Catherine. What in the hell was he doing? In ten, fifteen years he'd be dead. He did not kid himself, a man who lived hard died early; but he did not, strictly speaking, believe that, either.

How long could you go on chasing road? You could chase road as long as you could keep your licenses. After that you could still run intrastate. He shook his head.

Once, following an urge to figure it shortly after they met, he sat in a stop in Dallas-Fort Worth and figured the miles. He figured road miles and estimated sea miles. Rand McNally claimed that it was about nine hundred miles from Boston to Asheville, from the Coast Guard to Catherine, but his figures were different. His figures showed a little over one-and-three-quarters million miles. Catherine was not going to understand that. Practically no woman was going to understand that, but Catherine least of all.

During that time he had wanted to develop it, wanted to tell her of torpedoed ships, of the quick, gut-wrenching, teeth-cracking runs past the lightships, and the lightships were not attacked because the enemy used them too, kicking it hard into a northeast swell toward a flame that looked like a candle on the horizon. The frozen men, fuel-smelling, broken, frightened, bleeding, and sometimes insane that they pulled aboard; lives saved for once only maybe to be traded later on the outskirts of another convoy in some other frozen part of the north Atlantic; and always, always, the cold, nudging fear on your neck knowing that if the sub surfaced and began to shell that you were the same as weaponless.

He spent twenty years on search and rescue and he had not done it for the pay, the occasional comfort, or even the assurance that came from knowing that security was an idea for men who wore business suits.

On the road it was different. On the road you were ready, but on the road you were mostly just confined to being honest. It was honest to haul things that people needed but you did not give much that was personal. Aided at wrecks sometimes. Maybe the best thing to do was return to the coast, spend his money for a trawler, and fish. That was honest.

Now he had two

The following lights were closing. It was this goddamned snow-pillow, drift-fence, ass-freezing Dakota that got you lulled into other times and places, got you to thinking and thinking. Warmth and trouble and love, when the truth was that it must be ten below or better out there, and he was riding forty thousand at fifty miles an hour in snow, boxed by suicidal maniacs. The road was bad. Maybe only maniacs were out.

The rig behind him was closing fast. It was like the guy had suddenly come from a loafing pace, checked his time and was coming on hard to make up. This was the northern route, for God's sake. You did not meet one cowboy in a hundred on the northern route and now he was boxed between two of them. Ahead the other freight seemed steady. Maybe the side trip back there had sobered him.

Singleton watched the closing rig. At two hundred yards it suddenly lit up, the four-way cut in, then kicked to a passing signal. The under-bumper lights flipped on and the guy danced three times on high beam, then flipped his spotlight, which nobody ever did, *ever*, and threw the beam down the road but left of Singleton's mirrors.

It had to be an emergency. No man would dare do that unless he had an emergency, because someone would catch him and kill him sure. Singleton flipped on his four-way, eased as far right as he dared and started to coast out his speed. He was running just under thirty when the guy passed, and he was busy fighting the road, the truck, trying to avoid the snow pillow in the passing. The guy signaled with his markers as he passed, but what did that mean? Besides, after getting his own rig solid and dragging carefully for gears, building it slow to avoid a dance with his drive axles, there was the mess ahead to watch.

It developed fast, but it seemed like he was watching it in slow motion. As the overtaking truck closed, the driver went through the same dance with the lights. The lead rig swung to the middle. It was going to be bad, and there was not a hell of a lot that Singleton could do. He cut his headlights, still dragging for speed, but not so much. His mirrors showed nothing behind him.

The lead driver was waking up. He began drifting right and there was a flash of brake lights as he tapped his trailer brake. Singleton found himself closing too fast. He leveled it off, hoping that the situation would be okay after all. The passing rig was almost clear when the other guy suddenly lost control.

His trailer sidestepped left, he jogged the wheel, caught it, was too close in to the other rig, blew his nerve and stuck his foot on the brake. The lights flashed, died, the trailer diddled off to the right and the guy caught it again; but this time he was caught in a slow right drift that if he tried to drive out of would jackknife him deader than hell. In a way it was the best driving Singleton had ever seen a crazy man do. The guy must have goosed it just enough. He entered the snow pillow at a gentle slant, ran fifty yards through it riding the trailer brake, and ended with the tractor still on the roadside and the trailer cocked halfway into the ditch, propped up maybe by the snow. How the guy had ever kept it from broadslamming was a miracle. For an idiot it had been fine driving. Singleton rolled easy, watched the guy with the emergency continue on up the road, and pulled in ahead of the ditched rig; a man was a fool to pull in behind a wreck.

He turned his headlights on and off to show the guy with the emergency that he was stopped. The rig kept going away. Later he was going to check that driver out. It was a company rig. It would be possible to get him through the company. Singleton expected to see him at the next stop.

His markers were amber on the road, as the white-and-bluish-tinged lanes faded away when he cut the lights. By the time he had his jacket on some of his night vision was working. The roadway looked silver in the darkness. The amber glow beside and in front of the cab looked warm on the snow.

He checked his mirrors. Behind him the other truck was nearly invisible behind the huge bank of snow it had plowed. Steam rose around it like the truck was sitting in a cauldron. The guy must have found a concrete milepost or something hard beneath the snow. No one was out yet. Maybe the guy was knocked cold. Good to hurry. Singleton wrenched the first aid box and his flashlight from holders, opened the door and climbed down careful. The skidproof steps were iced. Going to an emergency was one time when you really had to be methodical.

It was cold. Cold. It was leather-stiffening, neck-clenching cold. The snow creaked where it was pounded onto the road. His breath was like an obstacle in front of his eyes, like it was solid. When he pulled air in, the moisture in his nose was frozen and the hair made it feel like he was trying to breathe through a mat. His teeth hurt. It was more than ten below. It was killing. Steam rose from his rig, normal temps that would not be remarked in other weather. He wondered if the heat in the markers would clear them and doubted it. At least there was no wind. If there was wind it would burn a man's face like freezer burn.

Singleton walked aft. Footing was good. The rig seemed like a worse casualty than it was, sitting in the steam cloud with the red glow of Singleton's stoplights illuminating the piled snow and steam. The headlights were covered. Broken most likely. The windshields were dark but unbroken. He knew what he was finding before his mind told him he had found it. The rig was a White painted Mack red. Somewhere under that pile of snow *Ben Singleton* would be painted on the door. No question. Why the delay? Ben was supposed to be an hour further down the road.

From inside the truck there was a bumping and desperate scramble. Singleton dropped the flashlight and first aid box to begin burrowing in the snow. It came away easy. The rig had torn up any freeze. It came away chunky, and he could feel the steam rising around him, freezing in his eyebrows and on his face. That front end was going to be frozen in solid. The cold came through his gloves like they were only a thin layer of skin. They kept freezing to the chunks of snow. He had to flip hard to get rid of it. The door was not jammed.

The thumping stopped. Now there was a whispering, a hushed and frightened and urgent pleading. The door pushed at the snow but it was still blocked. He cursed and worked, angry and then discouraged. The whispering was a girl's voice. The freeze was on his eyelids. He could hardly see.

He finally cleared the door. His gloves were stuck again. He forced the door, got it, and pulled it back against the snow far enough to climb to the cab. He reached over Ben and flipped on the cab lights, saw the girl and was less angry. He had met Sue once for about ten minutes, when he and Ben had teamed to Pittsburgh.

"Help him," she said. She did not recognize Singleton, and that was no surprise with his face iced up the way it was. She was a real little girl.

"You okay?"

"Yes. Help him." She was moving all right. She had probably been in the sleeper and the straps caught her. He leaned over Ben to see if any part of him was tangled. It would not do to force an arm or leg if he was busted up. As he leaned forward his pants legs pulled above the tops of his boots. Do it as quick as possible. The weather was killing.

The air pressure was not high enough. There must be a small leak opened in the line. It could be that the brake was the only thing holding them in position. When the pressure died the whole rig might drag over.

Ben was tilted forward and to the left. Ribs maybe, rising into the wheel. He got Ben's head up. There was a cut just before the temple. Maybe next time he'd listen and mount his fans low instead of high. No need to check for pulse, there was the cloud of his breathing. Concussion maybe. He felt the rib cage. It seemed okay. Then Sue was all over them, grabbing Ben, forcing his head back.

"Get off," he told her. "Head wound always bleeds bad. Always looks worse than it is. Get some snow."

[200]

She rolled her window, reached right into the snowbank and grabbed a fistful. She had recognized him.

"On his face, behind the ears, in the armpits." He picked Ben's knees up and swiveled him. Ben's head was pushed back and around into Sue's lap. His shoulders were on the doghouse.

Ben mumbled, started to sit up and almost kicked Singleton backward into the snow. Then he fell back again.

If he could almost sit up, and if he could kick, then probably nothing was broken. Singleton reached over, got him just above the waist and started pulling him out. He lost his balance, fell back and Ben slid out on top of him. Sue screamed.

Ben rolled over. He tried to get to his knees and fell on his face.

"Get down here." It was not necessary, she was already scrambling out. The brake-away signal started its high bee-buzz behind her, air pressure about gone.

"I've got him. You get up in my truck to help." He picked Ben up. He was a lot lighter than Singleton expected. He seemed to weigh no more than a tall girl. As he walked slow and methodical to the truck he heard Ben's rig settle. There was a slide and creak. No thump. It did not sound bad but he could not look.

Sue was strong. He raised Ben. She caught his shoulders and had him dragged into the cab almost before Singleton could hoist. He climbed up and together they settled him in the sleeper.

"Slap him awake."

"He's bleeding."

"Yeah, all over my sleeper. Slap him awake. I'll get something for the cut."

She looked at him like he was a monster.

"Sit right here and get warm." His voice sounded harder than he meant, but maybe that was good. Not easy to figure how to talk.

He climbed down. The job was to get them out of there before someone else came along, especially police. Police were out in every kind of weather. There was going to be enough administrative grief with this. They did not need to have cops see Sue.

He walked back to Ben's truck. The rig was tipped, the trailer had settled further toward the ditch and dragged the tractor around so one corner of the cab was in the roadway. The tractor was leaning bad. He hated to get up in it. The entire thing might lay flat. He should have thought to roll the window. No amount of money would get him on the downside of that tractor. It had pulled back enough that he could see the ice already formed on wheels, bumper and winter screen. A lot of local damage, but nothing serious.

The door came hard because he had to pull it upward. He slid into the tilted cab, gathered the log, bills of lading, back paperwork and Ben's gun. He searched for anything incriminating. They were just going to have to take a chance that the storage spaces would not be opened. Sue was bound to have clothing in there.

Singleton climbed down, felt an almost breathless relief, and walked aft in the snow-squeaking cold to spot the flares. Then he picked up the first aid box, flashlight, and returned to his truck. The back of his neck and his shoulders burned with being tensed up. No need to fear sleep now. He climbed up.

Sue was crying. "We've got to get him out of here."

He handed her the first aid box. "Put pressure on the cut. Hold a pad hard. Keep rubbing him with snow." His mind seemed as numb as his fingers. She would have to climb down for snow. She was climbing down now. He let her go. It would keep her busy.

You could head off a lot of grief if you let the cops know as much as was good for them. The ball pen fumbled in his fingers. He could not grab it right. In what looked like a five-year-old's lettering he got enough of it spelled out. Time, owner, destination, injury and place to contact. There would surely be a hospital in Jamestown. He listed the name of a stop and signed his name.

He had to get back down in the cold. No way out. Had it been this cold in Maine? He climbed down fast, and walked as quickly as the snow allowed to Ben's truck. He was not for any reason going to climb up into Ben's cab. He wedged the note between the door and the door frame. Then he returned to his own rig and climbed up. Sue was fooling around with Ben, but she took time to look at him like he was guilty of murder. He shoved the truck in gear and came away as fast as he could, which was not very fast. Ben was mumbling in the sleeper, breathing heavy but regular. He sounded more asleep than anything else.

"Get him awake and keep him awake."

"I can't. She was jiggling him, pushing him. Her voice trembled.

Sometimes guys kind of passed out when they were too tired. "How much sleep has he had?"

"Not much." Her voice was admitting more than she intended.

"How can that be, you're only out of Spokane?"

Her voice was small and apologetic. "We're ninety hours out of L.A., counting this load."

Now there, Singleton told himself, was a bunch of paper that he was not going to doctor. There was a mess. He was willing to bet that Ben had faked a co-driver. It was impossible. No, it was not impossible to do two loads and twenty-five-hundred miles in under four days. It was insane, but it was not impossible.

"Let him sleep."

"He hired guys to load and unload. Dropped the box and slept."

That meant that the kid had slept maybe eight hours out of the last four days. If they had been running like that he could just imagine the foolishness that had been going on before. No wonder Ben was thin.

"I took it for a couple of hours on the coast." Her voice was trying to offer some kind of justification, but her words were damning both her and Ben. Ben must be totally out of his mind. Women could drive trucks, no doubt, but they had to be women and not kids. Shirley in Harrodsburg could drive a truck. He looked at Sue. There was a wedding ring. Was it real or was it one of those used for overnight stands?

Her shoulders were thin, her hair long, and her face was girlishly pretty. It gave him a chill just to think of her behind a wheel.

"Yep," he said, "and when he wakes up maybe he'll be sane."

"I wish the police had found us." Then some of her surprise at seeing him worked through. "How did you find us?"

"Pure luck." Finding them was not a fluke. It was not as big a fluke as missing them for three months. If you really wanted to find a guy on the road it should not take three months, not if you knew the guy. Singleton had crossed after Ben twice, had known for two weeks that Ben was running west. That forced a different set of patterns.

"I'm sorry," he told her. He was not sorry for anything, and he was apologizing for nothing specific, but because of the girlishness he knew it would work. He was so angry he could hardly get his voice down where it sounded easy. "It's just that I can't imagine you kicking one of these things."

"Everybody's got to learn sometime."

He shook his head and shut up. Pushing fifty-thousand gross down a highway was not quite the same as driving a beat-up car to the grocery. Not exactly.

"I haven't seen him or heard from him since the day Grace called you." He was fifty years old. He was wet-nursing two kids who used their bodies like machines, and their machine like a plaything. "Tell me what's happened."

They were married. That was the first thing and the really big deal. Two days after trying to go to a whorehouse in Louisville. Well, the hell with it. Two days later Ben showed up in Pittsburgh and they were married. Singleton did not want to think about it.

And they were going to put together fifty thousand dollars. She explained that with enthusiasm. A three-year plan. It sounded like something they talked about in Russia. Ben needed that much to get started. It was obvious that Ben wanted to start again about where John had left off. It crossed his mind that John had not had fifty thousand. He started with one beat-up tractor and good judgment. Let it pass.

"Why didn't you call? We called you. We told you he was in bad shape."

She instantly became rigid with anger. Her mouth was set, like she was forcing herself not to scream.

He kept glancing at her, while he continued with the routine glances that covered road, gauges and mirrors. He wished he could turn down the heater, but it would not be good for Ben. The sleeper would cool off too fast.

Besides not answering his question, she was not watching him. She sat, almost tiny, and twisted at the ring on her finger. Once or twice her lips moved. Full mouth. Her cheeks were round and kind of flattened, with a high forehead divided by her long hair. Her prettiness was in her youth. He thought she would never be beautiful as a woman. Twice she turned to check Ben, to make sure the bleeding was still stopped. When she flipped around in the seat, her own seat in worn jeans pushed out. He could see that she was smaller than she looked. As thin as a person after a long illness. Maybe later she would be nice-looking. Right now her

[204]

face seemed disproportionately large for the rest of her.

"How old are you?" That could not be controversial.

"Twenty-five." Her voice was abstracted. She was studying on something else.

It was a lie, he thought. If she was twenty it had just happened.

"There isn't anything about Ben that I don't know." A challenge. Was she asking for information?

"Then you know one hell of a lot more than I do. All I know is that he ran off like a spanked kid."

"He didn't run." She was angry. You could find things out from a person if you got them mad enough. Her voice was scratchy with anger. "He didn't run. You people forced him out. Family." The last word choked her.

What had Ben told her? Wrong to tell her different, he supposed.

"You have a family."

"I wish the police had found us."

It was doing no good. She was not mad enough. Try another way.

"Sometimes people make mistakes without meaning to. Maybe we made mistakes."

"You're damn sweet right you did."

"But we were worried about him."

"Well, you don't need to worry now. I got him now."

It was too much. He swore to himself. If it was only freezing he would throw her out and let her walk. Cool her off a little.

"He just ran fifty thousand dollars in the ditch while he was in your care. Seems like we might worry some."

"After his dad busted him up and almost killed him." Her voice cracked. "He's all right. Ben's smart."

"Knows what to do," he grunted. This bullshit had been going on since September. Since September because of this bullshit he had gotten to see Catherine only once. Once. No woman was going to put up with that forever.

"You've got to help me. I can't stop him."

That was more like it. Now Sue was pretending he had won. She wanted something.

"We'll get it figured out."

There were lights in his mirrors. The snow shower tossed

behind him. He checked his watch. Two o'clock already. Supposed to drop today. No chance. Past time to call Catherine, though. He could certainly do that.

The lights were not closing very fast. If it was the state, they were in no hurry.

"We have to get a story you can stick to."

"What will they do?"

"Who?"

"Everybody. About the wreck?"

"The insurance company owns the load. The police will make a routine report. After the truck is fixed it will be grounded until it's inspected."

"Will he lose the insurance?"

What did Ben have, or what did she lack, that after a year's absence she would marry him overnight? She was scared now. He did not intend to use it, but he had a lever and it would not hurt her to know he had it.

"He could lose the insurance. Or he could get a letter of commendation from the insurance company. It depends on the story I tell."

"What about the story I tell?"

"And get him suspended? You're illegal as hell. You must know that."

She knew, but her face was set, ready to fight him. It made him feel better about her.

"If I say he drove to avoid an automobile, especially with three or more people in it, they'll pin merit badges all over him."

"Why?"

"Get this. Now get this. You drive to avoid. That's the first and biggest rule." This kid. Kicking an over-the-road truck and not even knowing that. "Claims on three people could go anywhere from a hundred thousand to half a million, depending on who died or what the injuries were, and juries almost always find against trucks. That means the insurance company would have to go the limit."

"What are you going to tell?" She was still ready to fight.

"Don't worry about what I'm going to tell. What you're going to tell is something else. You're going to say that you flew out here

[206]

when you heard, because no one is going to see you for a day and a half."

"He's my husband. You got to be with your husband." She repeated it like something she had learned in school.

Maybe he should let her screw it up. That way Ben would get a suspension. But he could not do that to another guy, even if it was best for the guy. No one would ever understand that.

"You turn with me to Minneapolis," he told her. "You hide in that sleeper all the way there and all the way back, because otherwise—," he looked at her with all the lack of affection he could muster so she would not misunderstand his intentions— "you're going to fix him up so he couldn't drive anything but a city bus."

Her face showed that he had won.

"He's just got a bump and he's dead for sleep. I've seen it before."

She sat back and he finished the last twenty miles. She fussed with Ben, cried silently and turned her head so Singleton would not see. She petted the wedding ring, twirling it the way a priest might take comfort from constantly touching a crucifix. Her face went pretty, almost ugly, then plain. At times she leaned far back in the seat and tried to check his speed without letting him know she was checking. Just a kid. He did not remember that Pat had been this dumb as a kid. What kind of woman would ever be interested in a blind man? Thinking of that, along with everything else. There ought to be a machine that when you were fifty it would blank your memory and you could start fresh.

He was glad to roll it off the road and into the stop. He checked for the rig that had done the fancy passing. It was not there but that made no difference. When you wanted a guy you could find him. Singleton set the brake and climbed down to get directions to the hospital. He was lucky. The guy on the pumps directed him, and in less than a half hour he had Ben registered. A little after sunrise, he and Sue were back on the road, and he was thinking of the night before.

Even on a perfectly dry night on a clear road, passing was no joke, not something to do without thinking. After long experience it became automatic, but a part of the automatic sequence was the thinking, sizing the situation. Singleton remembered a race he had been in one time outside Amarillo. There was a good quartering wind. He had tangled with a fine driver pushing a Jimmy. The load-to-power ratio must have been the same because the race ended in a draw. Each time one of them tried to pass, his rig cut the quartering wind, which supplied the other guy with about twenty miles per hour less resistance. Then the other truck would catch up. It was like a sailboat race at seventy. They had run that way for thirty miles, pulled into the same stop and joked. It had been a good time.

Other times you got a wind behind you. If it was a strong wind on a flat road, and if it was dead to the rear, it cut the fuel bill.

The passing of the night before had been so beyond his experience that he did not see how any excuse would make it right. For that reason his belly got tense and the adrenalin started to pump as he swung into the big stop outside of Fargo. He thought he saw the rig he wanted. It occurred to him that Sue had been in the sleeper and did not even know that another truck was involved.

They had dropped Ben at a hospital. The x-rays showed a small fracture and he was under observation but in no trouble. Singleton called the state, called a wrecker, and caught a couple hours of sleep. Then he called Catherine and she did not answer. Try her later. In fact, try it here from Fargo.

Sue sat beside him. She was feeling guilty for leaving although he had given her no choice. She was also mad, and Singleton figured she could stay mad or get over it. He was fed up with kids. Once. Only once since September had he seen Catherine, and that time had not been too hot, to tell the truth.

That driver had better have a good story. Singleton buzzed across the crowded lot. A lot of rigs were laid over. During the night clouds had formed, more snow most likely. There was no improvement in the road. The snow equipment must be cleaning the governor's front lawn.

He spotted his rig on the ready-line. "Something to eat?"

"No." She seemed extra small and extra sullen. "Just bring me some coffee."

That was a relief. He did not want to show up in any restaurant anywhere with a twenty-year-old. Halfway across the lot he stopped. His rig was running like always. If Ben had wired a car would that girl try to borrow a truck? He shrugged his shoulders. It was either close it down and make a point of the mistrust, or take a one-in-a-hundred chance. With all the snow she would not be that stupid, and besides, where was there to go?

The restaurant was busy. A lot of guys getting ready to go slug it out, because if all of them were laid over the restaurant would not be busy. The action would be in the garages.

He thought he had his man spotted. The guy would have to be one of three company drivers sitting at the counter. Their caps were different but their shirts were the same. As he walked toward them he saw that one was a guy he knew. One of John's drivers when John still had a company.

"Hey," the guy said. "Hey, hey." He was a Mex/Spanish/Negro guy, real skinny, with a face that twisted and seemed to joke by itself when he talked. On his left was a chunky driver of about forty-five with a bent nose and scars above his eyes. His shoulders were hunched over. Beside him sat a kid who was also chunky. The two men looked related.

"Sammy," Singleton told him, "I thought spicks went south in winter."

"I just now migrating Chicago," Sammy told him. "This here's the Shattuck boys, Paul and George. The ugly one is George." Sammy raised one corner of his lip, dropped the other down, and his eyebrows started making individual waves. "We a mean little flock."

"Steak and a plate of eggs," Singleton told the waitress who set coffee in front of him. Older woman, little heavy, but her hair was combed out nice. Good to see someone trying to look good.

"Where you tending?" Sammy said.

"Minneapolis and come back. Got a guy in the hospital. Ben."

"Ben." Sammy's eyebrows straightened out. "Who shot him?"

"No joke."

"He bad?"

"Busted up a little. Someone from your outfit ran him off the road last night."

All three men straightened, looked at each other, and Sammy looked at Singleton with apology all over him. The three guys looked guilty but it was a fooler. Any one of them could be, but now it seemed likely that none of them were.

"What time?" George said.

Singleton told them. He told about the lights. When he got to the spotlight part he could see that they were having a hard time believing it.

"It's a relief," Sammy said, " 'cause I just got in, and these guys were in jail at the time." Sammy was pleased that Ben was not hurt bad. His eyebrows started walking again. "Seriously, we're running together. I know it wasn't here."

"Who else is out?" George turned to the kid. What was his name? Paul?

"We can check with dispatch." When he spoke it was with the same implied authority as the other men. Singleton watched him. A professional was a professional whether he was twenty-three or sixty.

"That's the whole, straight-out story?" George was asking in a tone that wanted to know it all, because you had to know it all to justify what you might do.

"Ben was way too long without sleep."

"High?"

"No."

"We'll take care of it," Paul said. He was not excited or jumpy or eager or any other kid thing. Singleton found that he would take Paul's word as fast as he would the word of the others. Why had he been thinking bad about kids?

"He maybe had an emergency."

"He didn't, he's got one now." George finished his coffee, checked his watch, and stretched. "We got to go."

"John still alive?"

"Yeah."

"And Ben back on the road." Sammy pulled at his ear, grinned, and the other ear rode like a brown beetle crawling up the side of his head. "That Ben ain't got no luck."

"He's married."

"You see!" Sammy stood up.

"Keep the rubber-side down."

"Sure," Sammy said. "And look, don't worry about the other. They hired a bunch of dumb shits lately." The three waved back as they passed through the doorway.

Singleton sat mopping eggs, drinking coffee, and allowing the

[210]

warm feeling to last. He did not want to go back out there and tangle with Sue. He sure did not want to be back in the cold. The restaurant was warm, busy, and full of people who were either friendly or who would leave you alone. The road—he did not want to think of the road. It was a relief not to have to paste some guy. When Sammy said it would be taken care of that was a fact. He had not meant to pass the fight on, but he was glad it had happened.

Maybe the thing to do was sell out, buy a boat and fish, not out of Gloucester or some north Atlantic, George's Banks, freezing-water port. They took shrimp in the Gulf. A man could learn.

But who would go to the Gulf? Not Catherine. Go by himself?

Was that true? Catherine was different, ever since the trip to Atlanta last September. Really different, and he did not know whether he liked it or not. For one thing she was more independent. No, she was more happy about being independent, and she had scared the hell out of him the one time he saw her.

He bought coffee for Sue and walked to the door. It was going to be cold out there. The windows were glazed. He fumbled his jacket, tried to hold the coffee and get the zipper at the same time, told himself it was a short walk and shoved through the doorway.

At least she had not stolen the rig. He grinned. Ought not be so hard on them. He climbed up. Sue was in the sleeper snoring. He grinned again. She did not wake when he pulled. Later the coffee started to cool and he drank it against waste.

21

THEY came out of Minneapolis three days before Christmas with both rigs deadhead. The road had settled into a winter usefulness and their speed was good. Singleton led off. He was not going to get Ben pissed by insisting on following. His mind was not easy but it was getting easy about Ben. If only he could see Catherine, and she happy to see him, but about Ben he was learning a lot. Part of the learning gave him more confidence in Ben and Sue.

Ben had been the same as roped and tied in the hospital. Singleton had talked and persuaded and listened. Some of the explanations helped.

Sue was from a hill family that had never had anything, never expected anything, and did not want a whole hell of a lot. To Ben it seemed great that she had left home at sixteen, and Singleton could understand that, although he wasn't going to say anything to Ben. Sue was twenty-five after all. Hard to believe.

It had been a long wait with little to do. There was the repair and the administrative stuff. There was his own rig that needed sharpening up. It looked like the year would end fairly well, but he would not be rolling in success.

They took twelve hours to Chicago, which meant plenty of

stops. He did not want Ben to lay on it hard. Ben was acting very nice lately. The empty vans gave you a feeling like you were spending money for entertainment. They discussed the possibility of loads and said that just once, just this once, they would indulge themselves. In Chicago they laid over and rented rooms. It was like a holiday. He called Catherine and she was not home. She said she would be gone but he had somehow not quite believed it. The last time he called she seemed abstracted, while at the same time there was that disturbing warmth. She must love him or there would not be that kind of warmth. Of course she did. Of course.

Grace wanted them home. Women were sentimental about Christmas. The best part, he figured, was that when he delivered Ben and spent some obligated time, he would be free to leave. He wondered if Catherine was sentimental and doubted it, thinking that lately she would not even know it was Christmas unless someone told her.

In Chicago, early awake, he stopped troubling it for awhile and was caught by a sentimentality of his own. He felt warm and hopeful and believed that there were no problems in the future that would not be resolved easy and automatic. He lay in bed listening to the crossing patterns of engines and the far-off voices of men working, discussing, arguing. There was a puzzling noise out there. It intruded on the normal hum of activity, a heavy, slugging noise that was not as sharp as you expected from any truck he knew. When it finally pulled, the slugging changed to run cracking and high like any respectable diesel, but the padding on the edge of the sharpness was still there. It sounded sort of dirty, somehow. He lay under the warm blankets and wished he had seen it.

His face was scratchy but the sheets were clean and private. He did not want to get up. Then, realizing that he did not want to, he rolled out quick to shower and shave. While he was shaving Ben knocked on the door. Singleton let him in. With the warm and sentimental feeling he was glad to see Ben.

The kid was already gaining weight. He was not hiding his hands as much. A lot more confidence. Right now he seemed more aggressive than usual. He sat on the edge of the bed while Singleton shaved.

[213]

"Still as cold?"

"As a well-digger's ass." Ben was flipping cigarette ashes on the carpet.

"I heard a funny-sounding rig out there." Singleton watched him in the mirror. The punk was being pushy and it made the warm feeling go away. If this kid fouled things up now—.

"German rig," Ben said. "Some guy imported one. Looks funny, sounds funny, nice living spaces."

German cars. Now it was German trucks. Jesus bleeding Christ. Next it would be the Japs.

"I guess it's different in Europe. What do you want?"

Ben straightened, relaxed, and flipped more ashes on the rug. "Want?"

Singleton turned, aggravated. "You want something. Otherwise you wouldn't come grandstanding like an asshole and flip ashes on the rug." Ben ran his red-splotched hand behind his neck, grinned, and walked across the room to get an ashtray.

"I want you to go in alone," he said.

"Why?"

"Because I ain't going to be a kid bein' dragged home by the ear." He sat back down on the bed. "You know the whole story now. You know what I think, and what I think'll make it right. But, I am not goin' to be dragged home. Try it and I won't come."

"I won't try it." Ben was not asking a wrong thing.

"Deal." Ben stood. "You go ahead. We're going shopping. See you tomorrow afternoon, and you can tell her we're coming in."

"Shopping?" That was right. You did that sort of thing at Christmas. "Don't buy me a rocking chair."

"Buy you a toy fire truck that will pee against the wall." Ben was grinning and happy. "Drive careful," he said. He left.

Singleton thought he should be worried, and then told himself that the real thing to worry about was spending a night in that house with Grace. He would have to think about it. He secured his gear, checked out of the room and went to his truck. There was no schedule. He stowed his gear and returned to the stop. The roads would be good. A lot of guys would be home already, but there would be families driving long distance, the guys driving acting like total road experts after a year in city traffic. Figure it ahead of time and there would be no surprises.

[214]

Going shopping. There was practically nothing you could not buy in the new stops, and there were enough accessories that a rig carrying all of them would lose more payload than the accessories were worth. Still, he liked to look at them. There were lights. He did not need lights, but they were like red and white and amber eyes on the display boards, the fog lights, landing lights, hook-up lights, turns and markers and spots and van floods. Circles, ovals, squares. He liked it all, the rubbery smell of the tires, the neatly folded green-and-gray-and-tan work clothing. The mirror heads for the west coast, maybe twenty kinds of white-and-black, or striped with red and traffic yellow. The hundred other mirrors. He liked the heavy cast-feeling wheel parts, the red-painted jacks, the custom seats, air-horn covers, reflectors, gauges, tank caps, the tapes and wiring and padlocks. Coils of light, bristly manila line and the white hardness of nylon. The oil-smelling tarps, the fans, the hand tools in black cases like jewelry, and to him prettier than jewelry because of the use. The horns, all of it. And that did not even count the grocery off to one side, or the sporting goods in another section. He wandered through, looking, tentative, then went to his rig, climbed up and pulled.

It was a good and easy road. He was bringing Ben home, but what was best was that he had gotten himself in a mess when Ben ran, and now he was out of it. Free again. He thought of Catherine. Maybe too free. But because of Ben he could think affectionately of people again. It was almost like old times, when you saw a guy off the ship and into an ambulance, and you knew the guy was going to live and would not have lived except that you had been there and helped. He had helped save a lot of people in his life.

Pat. He sure as shit had not saved everyone. Singleton thought of Grace and Ben and Sue. He thought that he liked them all in spite of their faults; grinned and told himself that he had a few faults of his own, but that he did not really believe it. He leaned on the speed limits harder than was strictly necessary considering the empty van.

Grace was not at home when he rolled it into the yard. He did not know that at first. He only knew that she did not come from the house. He kicked the rig in a broad arc and brought it up facing the wind. Then he looked at the house, barn, and huge lot.

Part of it had been a field once. Once there had been a line of rigs—no good could come from thinking about that.

The house looked shabby. The heavy wind blowing across the fieldlike lot had aged the house. He seemed to remember a windbreak of poplar a long time ago, but as he looked across the wintering fields he knew that John must have taken it out when the lot was graded.

When he climbed down the wind was cold. It was like Dakota, but that was because of the wind. Instead of gathering his gear he ran to the house. The door was unlocked. He knocked on it, stepped inside and no one was home.

He wondered if something was wrong. Then he told himself to quit worrying. She was at the store, on an errand, doing something. It was nice to be in a silent and familiar place. Except for John, but John was upstairs.

Grace was sentimental but she was not wrong-headed. The house was clean and festive in a subdued way. There was a small tree in the living room and nothing else. He passed through the house and into the kitchen. She had left a note on the table, that she would be back soon and nothing needed doing. He was glad for the last part. Wondered if he would have looked at John if the note had not been there. He surprised himself. He had always done what needed doing. Coffee was hot on the back of the stove. He poured a cup and looked for his mail.

The old message and mail slots were gone. That was one of the first pieces of equipment she had junked. After searching cabinets and drawers he found it stuffed behind the toaster. There was a lot.

He got through most of it quick. A lot of trash. He opened the money envelopes first. Best to know right away if you were trimmed. He carried his ledger entries in his head. A good mail. There was a five percent bush on one check, charged to a new administrative gimmick. Something else to watch for. December returns were always good. Everyone tried to get their spending done, tried to get the tax work going for them. He fanned the checks. The year would end pretty well.

Three cards, one from Ann Arbor. He saved that one for last. The first one was from Shirley. When he was laid over because of Ben he had written a short, friendly letter and wished her luck.

Inside the card was a two-page letter. He read it and did not want to think about it. It was like she was using him for a diary of her loneliness. New mail address. Living with relatives outside Pendleton. A long way from the ocean.

The second card was from a truck stop off the Penn turnpike. They must be mailing against their lube record.

He opened the one from Pat. The handwriting on the address did not belong to Pat. It looked exact, almost mathematical, but it was more like a woman's hand. The writing inside was Pat's. It was not at all like the sprawling, bumpy writing Pat had once used for log entries. It said, "Merry Christmas." It was signed Pat Donner.

Singleton flipped it over. Nothing. He picked the envelope up, tore it across one end to make sure the letter was not caught inside. Nothing.

Merry Christmas. Pat Donner.

Singleton drank the coffee. He felt like it was going to choke him. He poured more, sat at the table and wished he was dead. There was no other mail except a postcard. Picture of a truck stop. He flipped it over. It said, "He was having an insulin reaction. Drive careful. Sammy."

He drank more coffee. He pushed Pat's card back and forth with his finger.

This road. This life-tearing, mind-warping, gray-haired road—this armpit-smeller, sock-sweater—this man unmaker that only killed halfway.

He walked across the kitchen to a window. Leaning far to one side of the counter he could see it out there, see it lying like a line across the flat, snow-filled land. He turned, looked out the other window, and saw his rig. Steam that was nearly invisible rose from melt around the winter screen. The steam was being blown back, along the sides of the truck. The truck looked like it was still rolling through light mist. Let the sonovabitch roll. His gut was sour. He sat back down.

There it was. The kiss-off. Didn't Pat know? Didn't Pat understand that he, Charles Singleton, always meant more with the occasional letters than he ever got said. Who was reading those letters to Pat? Was anybody?

Of course they were. Somebody else had addressed the envelope.

Didn't Pat know that he, Charles Singleton, was coming to see him? Going to drop by, talk careful, let him know?

Of course not. He faced it. It was not the road, not strictly speaking the road. It was himself. Always there had been time, and now eight, nine, how many years was it now, and there had been time. All the time it took a blind man to learn to read, to learn to work, to learn how to live.

What had he, Charles Singleton, done? Hauled freight. Bought a truck. Laid a few women. Finally mother-henned somebody else's kid, which was all right if you took care of your own. Pat.

He had carried Pat in his mind the way he carried Naomi in his mind.

He had been ashamed, afraid and guilty to see Pat.

Singleton stood, poured the last of the coffee, and put more on to cook. The routine chore seemed like miles on the odometer. How many pots, how many cups?

How many sunrises? Once, once, the sun rose over Seguin Island, the old man was below and Singleton had the bridge. Pat on the helm. Once.

How many sunrises did a man need, the sun coming off the flat reach of a prairie or over a distant chain of hills?

Maybe you only needed one of anything, as long as that one was perfect. Naomi.

Maybe one mile was better than a million.

Blowing chief, going to blow

"Blown and gone." He answered automatically, flipping the mail, wanting to sit down and stand up at the same time. He wanted to cry. He wanted to be not angry at himself. He wanted to get back eight years; to catch fish, to read books like Martha had once brought him, to help Pat—who didn't need any help now—and learn new things and do good.

Whatever that was. He did not know what that was, but he knew as firm as a tomb that the road was a fraud.

Eight years.

Nine years, how many years was it wasted

He picked up the checks, totaled them in his head, added the savings and checking deposits, estimated low on what he could get for the rig. It still came to almost twenty-eight thousand dollars, and that did not even count the retirement money, and there he was filing a mental note on how to avoid the next five percent nudge from a broker.

The road. It was like the base of his neck was telling him to climb back up, go have a drink somewhere and figure it out. It was that deep, for God's sake.

He told himself that he was done. This was quits, and he would find a way to show Pat. Done, but the back of his neck was telling him to climb back up, go have a drink somewhere, and the back of his neck, his shoulders, even his mind was bunching. There were sounds outside. Grace was coming just in time. For a moment he had felt almost crazy, and turning to meet her he did not feel much better. The advantage was that he had to act better.

She entered fast and afraid. Her voice was urgent.

"Where are they?"

"Christmas shopping." He did not tell her that they were doing it in Chicago.

Her relief was so great that she leaned against the table. The pot of coffee boiled over. Singleton stood to turn it off, then he turned back to help her with her coat. She smiled, whirled out of the coat, and did an extra whirl apparently for the hell of it.

Pretty. Her hair was messed up from the wind. She was wearing an almost girlish dress. He watched her and told himself that it was Grace who was girlish. He had seen the dress before, patterned, not girlish at all.

"Tell me." She sat at the table, chin in hands, her eyes smiling as much as her mouth.

He explained about Chicago and saw her fear.

"It's okay," he said. "I wouldn't have left them otherwise."

"Sure? Positive?"

"Absolutely sure. They'll be in tomorrow, just as sure as there's a road." It was good to have something positive to hang on.

She was delightful. She stood, came to him, kissed him on the cheek and whirled away and seemed to dive toward the refrigerator. "I like it hot." She put eggnog in a pan. The kiss had been as impersonal as a pat on the head.

"Tell me everything."

"I did on the phone."

"All over again. Right from the first."

He was trying to get the strain out of his neck and shoulders.

The mail was right there in front of him. He stacked it.

"The girl."

"Tough," he told her. "No bigger than a mouse."

"You mean hard?"

"Tough like a razor strop. They're doing fine."

Either she was not convinced or did not understand.

"Country girl."

"Oh, that tough. It's what he needs."

"If you say so." Maybe it was what Ben needed.

"And the other. Tell about the other."

He explained about the hub.

She was happy. Happy. He felt like hell. She poured the hot drink. "So it was foolishness after all?"

He let it pass. She was not going to understand, and if she did understand she was not going to allow it. Ben had been wrong. It was something he was going to have to carry. Pat. He had worked half the afternoon. Pat. Getting Ben one-third convinced that it was at least as much John's fault for not trading as it was Ben's fault for not replacing a hub. And they both knew better, but nobody would ever say anything about it again. Let it ride. Pat.

He had never seen her looking so relaxed, her mouth easy to smile, her hair unthought of. It was good to see someone so happy, and the tension in his shoulders seemed like some kind of payment for something.

"Is she pretty?"

"Ben thinks so."

"Then we'll think so. Does she go along about rebuilding the business?"

"At first I think she would have gone with anything. Now I don't know."

"It will work out." There was a sureness in Grace's voice as blatant as a seventeen-year-old.

Singleton felt for a moment that he was party to a hatchet job. Then he told himself to forget it. If that's what the kid got, it was exactly what he'd been asking for. That seemed truer than he could explain.

"I got my mail." He was pushing it around on the table in front of him.

"Good. You're certain sure they'll come."

"Sure."

"He didn't end up short because of the wreck?"

"I think he's got pretty good money."

She looked sort of disappointed. "We'll see what he needs."

"For my part, I'm getting sick of the road." He thought it sounded dramatic. It was to him.

"I was sick the first time I ever heard an engine start." She was pouring eggnog. "I wonder about her dress size. You'd better go shopping with me."

"I don't know about that stuff. I didn't undress her."

"Or me either, when you should have." She was smiling, happy, and reached to touch his hand. "I'm fine," she said. "Just knowing that he's back."

He was dumbfounded. The only thing he was sure of was that he did not have an invitation.

"I have to check John," she said. "Do me a favor. I'd like a fire in the fireplace. There's wood already in the barn. Split a little." She took one of his hands in both of hers, squeezed it like she was doing him a favor, and nearly danced from the room. Her footsteps on the stairs sounded as light as skipping.

Singleton gulped the drink, went for his jacket, and waited until he got outside before he began to swear. She had not said thank you, she had not said go to hell, she had not said, I'm glad you're here. About all she said was split some wood. He hunted through the tools in the shed beside the house. That axe was here someplace. It seemed like he was having too much to do with axes lately.

22

SHE had worked in October and her hands were better than her mind. Her eyes registered color, recorded, measured, estimated, picked up tint and tone, depth and substance. Then, rushing it all from her mind to her pigments, she found that her hands had known it all along. Perspectives boxed, circled, triangulated, moving sometimes past the end of the world, closing sometimes to the width of a fingernail. Her hands were teaching her. Her mind hurried after the hands, learning and testing. What her hands knew she came to know, and knowing, remembered firmly so she would never forget.

The hands were more ambitious than she, more daring, and the subjects dazzled her with pity and grandeur, horror and elation. A dead mouse, the weeds dying over her grandmother's grave. She felt that she could paint the wind, and found that you could paint the wind if it was firm enough and driving against either a tiny object or an illimitable horizon.

Breaking through. She knew it was happening, but she did not know what it meant and did not then care.

The work spun her into exhaustion, and finally into a rhythm of work, sleep, eat, work, sleep, eat; but not much to eat because there was no time.

[222]

Try the light. Hold the light. Her mind was getting stronger. She felt she could hold any light. She felt that she could work at the bottom of a mine.

The mind always knew, would always tell you when it was wrong, and she would go over the work until it was right.

In November the work broke, although she did not know it was November. It was cold, frost riming the window casings, water cold from the tap wind-chilled as winter worked beneath the house. Sometimes the dawn came like a rapidly igniting flare above the hills, and the valley lay on those mornings like a tunnel of red ice. On one such morning, rising with the dawn and nearly breathless to begin, she found that there was nothing to do. The brushes were like automatic pencils that had run out of lead.

She was exhausted, unbelieving, and returned to bed for a day and most of a night. The drive was gone. It would never come again. When she was painting she believed she would never stop. Now she was stopped and believed she would never work again.

Was this all? Was this to be the total production after half a lifetime? The following day she wept, endured fitful sleep, and woke to continue weeping. She went to bed again that night and slept twelve hours.

In the late morning she woke and smiled at the reflection in her mirror. She looked terrible. She smelled. The bed smelled. The clothing that lay on a chair was stiff with paint and dirt and sweat. Catherine watched her thin nakedness. Even her small breasts were smaller. She appraised herself: saw the body, the form, and felt the pressure, the working and driving impulse to paint. It seemed far away. She tried to provoke it, could not, but having felt it, was reassured. It was not gone after all.

The whole house smelled. At least the whole downstairs did. She bathed for an hour, then stood under the shower for five minutes. There was no clean work clothing. She found a thick robe, draped and tied it about her, and began making order.

She washed work clothes and hung them over the stove to dry. She swept, scrubbed, polished and cleaned corners that were seldom cared for. During that day she was compelled to order; worked many hours, slept again and rose to work. She washed walls, rolled back rugs to wash beneath them. Windows, appliances. On the third day she occupied herself with the small tasks. Order. Order. When the last mirror was polished, the last letter filed, the last stain washed from behind the old bathtub, she finally relaxed. On the fourth day she turned to herself.

There was nothing to do with the body except exercise and feed it. She cleaned her short nails and worked for two hours with her hair. When she finished she sat at the window watching clouds beginning to roof the valley. It was still early in the season but there might be a little snow.

She made lists. Food, supplies, tools. She checked her bank balance and it made her glad to know that she did not need much, because she did not have much. There would be no more income until the first of the year.

That night, the first night since the last time she had seen him, she felt a taste of loneliness, a bare touch of sexuality. He had called, had been calling, and she had more or less kept track of what he said. Her feelings were not very strong. They could wait.

But could his feelings wait? She had better think about that. She sat on the bed, a good wool blanket about her shoulders, black wool and gray and red, and tried to remember his voice. She knew he was having a difficult time. She was probably not helping.

Her long legs were thinner. She had not been walking enough. She ran her hands up the calves of her legs. They did not feel very pretty, but they felt strong and dependable.

He had been calling a lot lately. Time was mixed up. Maybe he had been calling regular like always and it just seemed like more. His voice was troubled, or else she was so wrapped up in the work that she heard it as troubled.

She was going to have to do better for him. The next time Singleton called she would absolutely have to make herself more direct, less abstracted. Meanwhile, tomorrow she had errands.

The next day snow threatened, withdrew, threatened again. She got the old car moving and went into town and back in a hurried dash. The roads were lined brown, umber, and in the cold they did not feel sure or permanent beneath the wheels. She was glad to be home. Her house felt like a fortress against cold and even against loneliness.

She wondered if it was time to return to work.

It was time and not time. Now it was different. The eye estimated, judged, moved with confidence, but it no longer rushed. It lingered. The foundations became more exact, more appropriate, and for awhile she feared that she was getting mechanical. Then she found the problems of mechanics were insisting that they be solved, but the other parts, the feeling, intuitive parts, seemed to ride above the mechanics.

Completed work was another matter. Most of it would never sell. The subjects were bad. She would view the work, study it. At times her depression was absolute. At other times she wept and could not say why she was weeping.

In December Singleton called once a week. He sounded anxious. She did not know whether he was anxious about them, or about the situation he was working with in Dakota. Ben was found. Soon it would be over. She was glad for him, for herself, but all through December, with the work, she really knew that she was not doing well. The work compelled her. It laid life aside and she had no controls that would enable her to handle it. Her mind, moving less than free, tried to take time to construct a coming world. She was not lonely yet, but she knew it was coming; could feel it coming, and Singleton became more gentle, knowing and dearly held than her mind knew could be true. The trouble was that she was having a hard time telling him that.

Then the restlessness hit. She did not recognize its meaning at first. It caused the work to slow. When it finally took shape and explained itself she was afraid.

The work could only be done alone, but if you worked alone and saw no one, you had no standard. She figured her money, figured when she would work at teaching and when she would be paid for the Christmas sales of her weaving. She found that her margin was seventy-five dollars. A person could do a lot with restlessness and seventy-five dollars.

The world was in chaos. There had been Congress and communists. A war was coming. A race war was almost certainly about to start. Just because you learned new things, did not mean that you completely forgot old things. She was still timid, and the work was calling on her for an act of courage.

She would visit with her brother in Winston, which she always did at Christmas. She would walk through Winston, and she would not avoid the slums, or the men on the streets. She would stay with the crowds. That was not much, but it was enough to start with. When Christmas was over, it might be that the work would require her to do other things or go other places.

When Singleton called a few days before Christmas, apologetic because he was obligated to be in Indiana at Christmas, she told him that it was just as well. She would be away from home for a few days. He made her angry in a small way, because he was apologetic. In a larger way, he made her angry because he was once more being vague, like he could not put words to his situation. He could not just say that he was caught by a situation and hated it, could not say that he felt an obligation to her, even if he had none. She felt slightly cruel, and awfully stupid.

When he asked, not asking well, where she was going, it was her turn to be intentionally vague. Mostly, she told herself later, because she did not really know. She was defensive. She could hear his unhappiness on the phone, and yet she could only plead a visit to relatives in Winston.

"I could call you there."

She gave him the phone number. "I may not be there all the time." The conversation was one of those terrible phone conversations they had been having a little too often, lately.

Later, she would tell herself that she had lied. She could have been more kind and less on the defense. It should have been easy to tell him that her work was making big, new demands. He might have even understood that, because he certainly understood about work. She had not deliberately attempted to deceive him, but she had lied by not telling him what she was doing and why.

Her preparations to leave were inadequate. She had never locked her house, could not find the key, and so left it open. Her two and a half months of work stood available to any intruder, although she was ninety-nine percent sure that no one would intrude. This was, after all, rural North Carolina.

There was a dusting of snow on the road. She would not take her car. She had a good dress, plenty of work clothes and enough money to buy bus fare, food, and a bed in a YWCA if one was needed.

THE elderly outcast, Charles Singleton, borrowed Grace's station wagon on the morning of the day before Christmas and went to Indianapolis. He was feeling sorry for himself, he was angry at Grace, he was sure he was being cuckolded, and he did not know whether he wanted to get drunk, laid, shot or run over. All he knew was that he had best stay out of his truck. He had called Catherine twice, and had twice been told that she was out. Of course people did go out at Christmas, shopping; but she had not called back.

It was a lousy mood and it lasted until he found a bar off the circle in downtown Indianapolis. He drank cheer for an hour and was not cheered, but after an hour he felt better.

A lot of guys were talking along the bar. He wished women, the women who belonged to the guys, could hear the talk. By New Year's the bar would be back to the gutter, back to the sex talk, the business talk, the horse-betting talk. On the day before Christmas it was slob sentimental. It was nice to know that guys had that in them once in a while.

He left with a pleasant buzz. Probably it was going to be okay. Probably she really was going to visit relatives—and what right did he have to bitch anyway—but why was she so mysterious?

That was the best bet. If she really was seeing somebody else she would have had a story all worked out and it would have been a good one. He was just being suspicious. Right now it was going to be fun to spend some money. He could figure the other stuff out when he met her.

Something for Ben was no problem. He bought a fifty-dollar pair of fancy stitched boots and disliked the salesman because the guy moved too fast and did not have anything more expensive.

The women were a problem.

"What do you want?" he had asked Grace.

"Nothing. I bought you a tie."

At the time he had believed it. At the time. It had been a lousy time. She was so happy, and he—he didn't want to think about Pat. Or Catherine.

Now he did not believe it. He started looking in windows; at sterling silver chickens, fur-lined pizza cutters, eighteen karat ashtrays, Nubian bookends—he must have hauled an awful lot of junk in his life—imitation hand-carved chess sets with the machine marks still visible, genuine hand-made blankets from Scotland with machine-made wool and the border sewed on a hand sewing machine, dreck from Europe—some Jew guy had called it that once, putting it over, catching a price; the stuff was dreck from everywhere; early American design that was as near to being that as a garden tractor was to being the Mayflower, mink earmuffs, genuine imitation diamond-encrusted dog collars. That was it. He decided to buy her a pup. Collie pup. Living on a farm you needed one.

He telephoned Grace and told her to expect him late. The phone was in a joint. He drank one to the new dog.

Something for Sue. Young girl. Clothes, he guessed. What size? He poked through the stores and was bumped, jostled, elbowed, damn near kneed and nearly beaten into the ground by fat ladies, every one of whom seemed to have a wart on her nose with a hair growing out of the wart. It was a lousy mood and it was almost coming back. It was hovering.

No clothes. The only thing he knew about style was did it look nice on the person wearing it.

Twenty-pound box of candy, seven-foot stuffed giraffe, new set of skis, and what in the name of all that was wonderful were they doing selling skis in Indiana?

She was just married. Think of something.

He bought an expensive set of china and grinned. There was a feeling of domesticity about it that was just going to set Ben on his ear.

He went to another joint, burdened with the box of china, the box of boots and a still unsatisfied thirst. He had a beer, a shot and a sandwich. Then he got a pocket full of change and began calling through the list of shops and breeders. After a half hour he was reconciled to the fact that buying a pup at Christmas was not going to be a breeze unless you wanted something for five thousand dollars with an unpronounceable name. He stepped outside and bought a paper, stepped back inside and began calling the classifieds. He finally came up with a collie twenty miles out of town. Going back to the car he picked up a half-dozen beers. Shopping was tolerable if you cultivated the right attitude.

Traffic was mean. Mean. He finally got free of town and on what he thought was the right back road. It turned out to be the wrong one. He stopped in a joint to ask. They were having a pretty good time in there. As he walked back to the car he was half sorry that he could not stay.

When he finally found the place he also found that the kennel owner was an elderly lady dog-lover, the kind who manicures poodles but runs over small children and old men. She smelled his breath and told him that no one was home.

He explained that he had to have a pup for his seven-year-old niece. He was just high enough to want to start a story of a resolute, slowly wasting child, bravely smiling from a hospital bed. Some last shred of good sense told him nix.

"Come this way." She led him around the house, through a steel-fenced compound and into the kennel. It was heated, clean, and the runways inside were nearly as long as they were outside. He boosted her a peg or two in his estimation.

They were good pups. He could tell before he picked them up. When he chose the best one she raised the price.

Nothing was too good for his dying niece. He paid. The woman wrapped the pup warmly in a shard of old blanket. The pup licked him in the mouth. The pup did not gag but the woman looked like she was going to. He left as quick and as gracefully as possible.

[229]

Once out of sight of the house he pulled to the shoulder and opened one of the beers.

The pup whined and peed on the seat. It occurred to Singleton that he had incurred a responsibility. He did not blame the pup because he understood the feeling and started hunting for a filling station. Station wagon seats were washable.

It was five o'clock. A bad time to be driving. He pulled into a station, filled the tank, went to the john and bulled with the kid on the pumps. He was a nice kid and he eyed the pup and the beer enviously. Singleton opened two and the kid joined him. It was really quite friendly. The bad feeling chased him back to the road but did not catch him.

"C'mere, pup," he said.

The pup was not buying any of it. It crouched in the corner, whining and unhappy. The poor pup was hungry, poor little pup. That was it. Singleton found a grocery and bought a pound of hamburger. He gave the pup half of it and the pup did not get sick. Encouraging. Very. Singleton put the other half of the hamburger in the back seat and drank the next to last beer.

Things would work out. Everybody saw relatives at Christmas.

He turned the radio on. Jingle bells. He turned the radio off.

It was a little, warm, fuzzy pup. He picked it up, looked around carefully, then rubbed it against his cheek. The pup liked that. The pup liked him.

Things would work out.

It was a big grocery store in a new shopping center. He went back, bought more beer, a dog collar, some paper towels and a leash. Then he drove the car to a container at the far end of the parking lot to empty beer bottles, ashtrays, and clean the seat with the towels. The pup was interested. It sat on the seat and watched. It did not try to run away.

Singleton was about to take his dog for a walk. He caught a chill instead. He recognized that it was serious. Really cold. He climbed back in the car, started the engine and ran the heater high. In a little while it was all right. He realized that he was pretty drunk. He was indignant. Almost always he could drink much more. It was catching him funny.

The pup was friendlier now. It cuddled against Singleton's hip, snuggled in, not whimpering. Singleton rubbed the pup's ears.

He was surprised to find that he was crying, smacked the side of his face, looked all around. No one was near. He cried some more for the hell of it, for the self-pity of it. Drunk on Christmas Eve and almost the only person he had ever cared for in the world— he thought of Pat. He thought of Naomi. And Catherine. He loved them all so much.

Sobs started rising in his throat and he told himself that was enough. That was as much as you could indulge yourself. The sobs did not want to stop but he got them stopped.

He looked at his watch. His eyes were focusing perfectly. He was drunk all right, but he was not as drunk as he was acting. It was six o'clock now. His belly felt all right. It was his head that was bad. His head was not spinning, it just felt bad. Bad. It felt like there were a million thoughts trying to snake in there and grab him.

Do you run from me

"Don't take all the credit," he told her.

It was time to pump bilges again. He cruised through the parking lot, onto the road and looked for a filling station. He found a bar instead.

The bar was open which was merciful. Everything else was closing. All the Nubian bookends were nicely wrapped, ready to push their cans against dictionaries, their Nubian boobian front ends—forget it. The kids were being tucked.

Jolly old saint nickel ass

Some sailors would make a joke of the Last Supper.

Life and property

He had to get away from them. They were ganging up on him. He ruffed the pup's fur, rubbed its ears, and locked the car when he got out. No one, by God, was going to steal his pup. When he walked to the bar he did not stagger. It made him feel good. It also made him feel ashamed. He had acted drunker to himself than he was. Inside the car the pup was crying. The pup did not want to be left. It did not want Charles Singleton to leave.

In the bar he ordered a beer and headed for the can. Emergency. When he got back his beer and change were sitting there. He tasted the beer and looked around.

Losers, and only a few of them. The bartender was thin, pot-bellied with a long red nose and no teeth in front. He had hairs growing off the bottoms of his ear lobes, three black scraggly hairs per ear. Except for that he was bald.

"Cold," Singleton said.

"Up." The guy was watching a news broadcast. The television above the bar was flyspecked. The announcer looked like he had measles.

Singleton swiveled around. Losers. Woman of not more than thirty seated in a booth. Red cheeks, red nose, thick ankles. Pretty once, you could tell. Alcoholic now. You could tell that, too. Old guy seated across from her drinking wine. Knobby, broken-looking hands that were big for a thin old man, VFW badge, or Moose or Beagles or something on his coat lapel. He seemed to broadcast a sour smell clear across the room.

The television said that two hundred people were dead on the roads. .

"Is worst'n Europe," the guy seated down the bar said. Singleton looked at the guy. He looked interesting. Young guy with a real snootfull. His sports jacket was two sizes too small.

"It's pretty bad here."

"Sure buddy," the guy said. "C'vilyuns know ever' fuckin' thing."

"GI?"

"Ex. I discharge yesterday. Knox." He swung around and almost fell off the stool. "Parish," he said. "A—a—reeeely outta getcha in Parish."

Singleton turned back. The guy was too drunk. In the far booth was an old woman with yellowing white hair wearing a black dress. She was nursing a beer and talking to herself.

The television drooled a commercial. Apparently the right hair cream made your pecker longer.

"Another beer," Singleton said. One more and he would have to go. Have to.

The ex-GI fell off his stool, looked astonished, curled up in the cigarette butts, the spit and crap, and went to sleep. Singleton stood to beat the bartender to him. He picked the guy up and stuffed him in a booth. The bartender was coming as fast as a hammer toss. Singleton turned, pushed his hand against the guy's chest, and shot him backward. "Stay there," he told the guy.

Who did the guy think he had been shitting? Singleton pulled out the GI's billfold and counted the money. A little over four hundred dollars. He stuck it back in the billfold and put it in the guy's pocket. Then he went to the phone. The VFW man was protesting, yelling something at the young alcoholic. The girl was blubbering. It burbled through the bartender's toothless screaming. Singleton called for a police ambulance, made sure that the cops knew how much money there was; made sure that everyone heard him making sure. He watched the old woman sitting alone in the booth. She was carefully explaining something to somebody. The television showed the violin section of an orchestra. Being joyful.

Singleton hung up the phone and walked out to the station wagon. He started the engine, petted the pup, and watched the interior of the bar until he heard a siren. Then he popped a beer, took a nourishing slug and pulled away. If the sonovabitch lost his license it was just what he had coming.

Finally there was nothing left to do but go back to the house. He checked his watch. Not much past seven. Very bad.

Catherine was visiting relatives. Yes. There was no place in the whole world for Charles Singleton to go except to his brother's house.

In all the world there was no one but him who could make a decision about Charles Singleton's worth. That was the point wasn't it? Wasn't it?

A blind man had finally shown him his worth, but it was up to Charles Singleton to admit it.

What did you do when you came off the road? He honestly did not know, and yet he honestly had to do something. More waste made all of the perfect times untrue. He drove carefully along the deserted roads that were still iced in spots where the graders had not hit. He drove with one hand and alternately petted the pup and drank beer with the other.

It was a long way to John's house and he drove it slow and careful. There was bound to be a bunch of drunks out. When he got there lights were on in the kitchen, but he figured they were in the living room. Smoke from the wood he had split was coloring the darkness at the chimney. A few sparks. Good, dry wood.

Ben's rig was pulled in beside his. It was a relief. He had known certain sure that Ben would come, certain sure. That did not keep it from being a relief.

Singleton pulled the car alongside his rig, which hid it from the house. He was not ready to go in there yet. Besides, the pup was a surprise. How did you take care of a pup until morning? He sat for a few minutes, then picked up the pup, climbed out and walked to his truck. He climbed up.

The cab was cold but it shielded him from the wind. He would get cold and then gradually he would get warm. That had happened a lot of times before.

Catherine's picture was pasted to the dash. He struck a match and looked.

"I picked this life myself," he told the pup. "Got no one to blame but myself."

The pup wagged its whole rear end and whined. Cold. Singleton picked it up and tucked it under his jacket.

"You aren't going to live forever," he told himself.

Something flicked across the darkness around the sparking chimney. Was he seeing things? He looked. It flicked again. He continued to look but nothing more happened. He could have sworn it looked like a bird or maybe a bat. Impossible. A maverick. It would die.

What could he do, coming off the road?

All of his life he had worked. He could not remember not working. As a child his first job had been caring for one shed of chickens. His first serious whipping had been for leaving a door open, although the shed had not been raided. Weasels. Foxes.

Life was supposed to be about something. Once it had been about something. He would have stayed in if that had not happened to Pat. It had been about something then.

He remembered his father and leaned toward the door of the truck. There was no light. He switched on the markers. In the driving mirror, as he leaned against the door, there was a shadowed image. He knew that the image was his but the memory of his father was strong.

Make us proud

"Balls," he told the voice.

He switched on the cab lights. The brakes still had good pressure. They were tight. He switched off all the lights.

"Truck," he said. "Old truck." The truck was not old. He knew it. "Damn fool," he muttered. He wondered if he had pulled his last

[234]

load and told himself that it had to be true. He wondered if he could sell the truck.

With the ships it had been different. You left a ship knowing that when you saw it again the guys would have it clean. It would never be a scow.

On the road it was not the same. A man made his own rules, enforced his own regulations. He was not sure he could sell the truck and turn it over to another man's rules. Maybe to Ben.

That was a good idea. Think about it.

Sometimes, you know, it's like you are the truck you know

"You were drunk," he told the voice.

The windshield was frosting from his breath. His hand dropped naturally to the gears, the extension of mechanical contrivance that spelled movement. He felt like crying again. Was he that big a fool?

The pup was snoring. It was kind of funny to hear. Singleton figured that the best way to keep the pup a surprise was to not go inside the house. He climbed into the cold sleeper, snuggled the pup under the blankets and eased off. The voices were still coming at him, but some of the songs and stillness were also there, the way it was sometimes when he dreamed. It was good, because it was familiar, to get warm in a cold sleeper, gradually working your way toward sleep. He did not want to go back into that house, anyway. He drowsed at first, waiting for and trying to enter the songs and stillness, and he slept nine hours. He woke early feeling pretty grim. The pup had crawled from beneath the blanket, pissed on top and then crawled back underneath. It was snuggled under his arm. His beard was scratchy and his mouth was sour with beer. Ordinarily he would have reviewed the night and been ashamed. This time was different. In spite of the wet spot and all the rest of it his mind got easier as he got fully awake.

The dawn was there someplace obscured by snow clouds. The light was just coming. Singleton climbed down, found the hamburger in the back seat of the car. It was not frozen very hard. He fed the pup. Then he let the pup out for a walk. It stayed close, but at least it shit outside the cab. He put the pup back up, drank the one remaining beer, and found that the cold air was making him feel pretty good. He turned and walked to the house.

The door was unlocked. No one up. He headed for the john,

showered, shaved, and dressed in clean clothing. He made coffee. By then he heard movement upstairs.

The smell of the coffee seemed to draw Ben. He was rubbing his eyes and yawning.

"Hah," he said. "You're going to get it."

"Why?"

"They worried about you. Sat up til midnight."

"I was here." Singleton poured the coffee. "I was outside drinking."

Ben grinned. "I know. You were in way before nine."

"You let them sit?"

"Your business." Ben was like a diver poised over the coffee cup. He seemed rested.

"Thanks."

Ben gulped. His face said that the coffee was too hot. He got it down. "I'll tell you something," he said, "because I haven't told you yet and they won't. I want to tell you thanks for getting me."

It was good of him. It was a good way to close a thing out and Singleton said so. Then the conversation dead-ended. Grace and Sue came in five minutes later looking like buddies, looking like old friends, looking like two cats who had caucused over a cageful of mice.

Singleton saw that he had been on the downside of the caucus. Both of them were smiling at Ben.

"We worried about you." Sue's twenty-five-year-old, nineteen-year-old-sounding voice gave the impression of a mother's disapproval. She was looking at Ben but she was talking to Singleton.

"I'm glad you're here," Grace said. "We sat up late."

"Did you have enough firewood?" If she wanted a fight he figured they might as well have it right away.

She smiled at Ben instead. "Eggs and bacon and toast. Okay?"

"We'll just step out of the way." Ben winked at Singleton. That made it better. He walked from the kitchen holding his coffee and Singleton followed. Ben kept going until he was outside.

The sky was bleak and unexciting. The snow clouds were doing none of the fancy flying and scudding like when there was a good wind. The wind was low and light. Later it would pick up. Later it would snow and make the roads bad. It was always good to have really bad weather on holidays. It cut the traffic deaths even if it raised property damage.

"When I was a kid," he told Ben, "we'd get up excited and early and the old man would work to keep us in line. Opened the stuff before breakfast."

Ben was nursing the coffee and looking over the fields. The two rigs looked lonely, closed down and sitting together in the middle of the big lot. Maybe later in the day they could pull them into the barn.

"There were just the three of us," Ben said. "I was expected to act like a kid. Got kind of hard to do by the time I was fourteen."

"What took you so long?"

"I don't know," Ben said seriously. "It's like I've always been the last to catch onto anything. I learn it then I've got it. Book stuff is easy. It's the other."

"You got company." He could hear the pup crying out there. Ben heard it too. He was looking, trying to find where the noise came from.

"C'mon," Singleton told him. They walked across the yard and climbed up. Ben made a fool of himself over the dog. Singleton wondered if he should not give Grace the boots and Ben the dog.

"It's for your mom."

"Best kind of deal. I get the pup and she gets the responsibility."

Singleton thought about that. "She's down on me for some reason."

"They got to talking last night. I was fooling around in the other room, wrapping stuff. They think you're a bad influence." He was petting the pup, rubbing its ears like he was trying to wear them out.

"That gets to me. That really pisses me off."

"Sure it does." Ben set the pup on the seat and it did a double bounce, then landed in Singleton's lap. "They're trying to get me off the road. What more do you expect?"

"Are you coming off?"

"I left once. I'll leave both of them." There was a quality in Ben's voice that had not been there before. "No matter what you say I'm convinced that the only way to make it right is to build this business back up."

[237]

"I don't get your reasons."

Ben stole the pup back. It licked his face. The pup liked Ben as well as it liked Singleton. "You don't need reasons when you're convinced."

"I guess." Singleton decided to tell him. "I'm quitting," he said.

"I don't believe it."

They talked for awhile. Sue appeared in the open doorway and called them.

"Got to go in a minute. How much will you take?"

"Twelve."

"You're crazy. The tractor's worth that."

"I know it, but I'd rather you had the rig."

Ben did not say anything embarrassing and that was good. He understood, his understanding a clean thing you could almost touch as you sat in the cold cab. "We'll go to the bank the first of the year."

"We better go in."

"We can't leave this pooch. They won't open stuff for hours."

"I guess a surprise is as good one time as another." Singleton tucked the pup under his shirt. "Let's eat."

They walked back across the lot. The pup wanted out. The pup did not want to miss anything. It was not sleepy and private like on the night before.

They entered and he set the pup on the floor. "Surprise for you," he told Grace. The pup started bouncing against Ben's leg. Ben had a slob look on his face, bending over, playing with the pup.

Grace turned, did a double take, and looked like someone doing a quick and it-better-be-accurate computation. That took two seconds, just enough for the picture of Ben and pup to get registered. She began to act like Singleton had given her a gold mine instead of a seventy-dollar dog. She walked to him, hugged him, hugged him again, knelt to play with the pup and then fed Singleton an extra-big breakfast. Even Sue was more enthused than any woman ever was over any dog. Singleton felt like he had just given Ben a hatchet job.

It was after breakfast, after they were having coffee and talk in the living room that Sue tied another knot. The fireplace was going with Ben-cut wood this time. Everyone was comfortable, friendly, about to give things to each other. Ben was stretched on the sofa, hogging the softest spot in the room. The pup was curled beside him.

"I've got the best surprise of all," Sue told them.

Singleton was uncomfortable. There was nothing to do. Talk when it was only talk bored him. He wished he had a newspaper.

"Umph, oomph," said Ben. He was not holding up his share of the conversation. He was trying to get back to sleep.

"Tell us quick." Grace's voice sounded like Jingle Bells.

Maybe Sue had decided to try for an interstate license.

"I'm going to have a baby."

It was Ben's show. He did not oomph. He sat up like someone had goosed him with a hot spike. Speechless in spite of it. It was almost impossible for a six-two guy to break his neck falling off a twenty-inch sofa but Ben almost made it. He looked like a guy who had just pulled in, run a routine check, and found that for some horrible reason he was three quarts down on oil.

The women were kissing each other.

"Congratulations, dad." Singleton figured that the kid's name would be John. If it was a girl he figured that Sue was prepared to do it all over again. He stood to shake somebody's hand, saw that Ben was not acting like a father, and decided to shake with Ben. He pulled him up and whispered that he was supposed to kiss the bride, which was not exactly accurate. It was as close as he could get.

Ben did everything pretty well. Grace beamed approval. It was obvious that she had known it beforehand. The whole deal was a heist.

But what was there to say?

24

HE HAD to climb down and go inside pretty soon. Otherwise his mom would start thinking he was brooding again.

But what was there to say? If you got wired into thinking about something over and over, it took hold of your mind like a cheap song that you hummed while you hated it. Ben sat in his truck and looked across the wind-swept, snowy fields. Part of his view was blocked by his uncle Charles' truck parked alongside. It cut the wind and made it seem like he was in a cave looking out onto a stormy plain. The fencerows that lined the long drive down to the road were drifted, but the heads of dead weeds stood out of the drifts like quills, or like you had ruffed a dog's fur backward. It was a thumping wind, the kind that would just kick you all over the road. He would not care, though, if right now, Christmas day, he could catch a load. Wind was tough, but it was not all that tough. It wasn't as tough as living.

He did not know whether he had been had or not. Sue was not talking. Maybe she had deliberately not used the diaphragm, or maybe they really had been caught.

He rolled the window. A rush of air twisted and boomed between the two vans parked side by side. Cold out there. A butt-freezer. He rolled the window back up.

But he loved her and people had families. Wasn't that what it was all about, anyway? Whether she had done it intentional or whether they got caught, was something he was never going to know.

And he was ninety-eight, no, absolutely ninety-nine percent sure that it was his. Course, he had been flat on his ass in the hospital for a while, and she had been with his uncle and God knows who else around the truck stops, but that didn't mean anything. He knew for sure that it was his. His uncle Charles would have kept an eye on her, and he knew his uncle Charles well enough to know that he would never mess around.

Besides she *was* his wife. Nobody, nowhere, could be such a liar that they could snug up against you that way and still be making it with anybody else. Ben told himself that he ought to be ashamed of himself, and he was ashamed of himself. There were some things you shouldn't let yourself think.

He turned on the radio. After it warmed up he ran the dial. Maybe the Russians had started a war and bombed New York or something. Christmas carols. Choirs and Liberace vocals. He turned the radio off.

Funny how things worked. If you looked back you could not figure whether it was all luck and accident, or whether there was some kind of design.

If Fonnie had not had somebody big like a congressman up there, and if he, Ben, had not been so drunk because he was mad and trying to prove something, then he could have just gone to some girl and got it out of his system. If he had not been so drunk then he would not have been so hung over. There would have been no blowup. He could have gone back on the road quiet and pretended that everything was okay.

An engine was sounding from someplace a long way off. He rolled the window again and listened. Airplane. Some guy up there in the overcast looking for a place to light. Dangerous. He only needed to make one mistake and he would die.

That road down there was deserted. If he sat long enough, something would come by. Even on Christmas the stops were open, and there were enough guys in the world without a place to go that somebody would come by. Furniture guy, probably.

Of course you could never know a hundred percent. Not unless

[241]

you were with them every minute.

The windows were frosting. The defroster fans were mounted low, now. One more thing to remember about setting a rig up. The west coasts were clear, with just little drifts along the edges. He leaned out and looked at himself. It could be worse. His face wasn't all smooth like it had been. It was getting creased, but not as much as his uncle's. He figured in another twenty years he was going to look just like his uncle, which was okay.

He was going to have to go upstairs and see his dad pretty soon. No way out of that. Nobody else might understand or care, but he did. It seemed like something a person ought to do on Christmas no matter what else you did.

Well, those days were gone. There was going to be no more running together, and with his uncle quitting there was no chance of that, either.

Of course she had laid other guys. She even admitted it, but not since she had been in love with him. You had to guess that all of them did.

Why was it so important to them that he come off the road? Why couldn't they get it through their heads that the road was what kept anybody straight?

Because they didn't understand it, that's why. Even Sue didn't understand, and she had been out there. Practically nobody understood it, but they wrote songs about it and books. Like that stupid Polack beatnik or whatever he was. You could not trust that guy with a '47 Plymouth on a back street. That was a nowhere guy who could not find his ass with both hands. The road wasn't all that stuff he wrote.

The road was real. You could trust the road. It wasn't going to throw anything at you that you could not handle if you paid attention to the rules — and that is what got him and his dad — and that is what ditched him back in November. From now on he was going to pay the strictest attention to the rules. Maybe things between people were always slipping but the road was real. You could depend on it.

The air pressure was steady on one-twenty. A good, tight system, good'n'tight.

He had to climb down pretty quick. His mom would think he was brooding. If she said anything he was just going to ignore it, because even she must know the kind of crap that was working in that house right now. He wouldn't blame his uncle Charles for just telling both of them to go fuck themselves. It was a force-out. Nobody was even pretending, hardly.

He looked toward the house, the smudge of smoke at the chimney. It would get dark soon, and the dark would come all at once. Maybe he would split some more wood. Maybe if things got too bad the next couple of days the two of them, he and his uncle, could go bring in some more from the grove. Snow nut deep to a tall palm tree, but it would be better than sitting around. Have to hire somebody to paint that house next summer. If they didn't maintain it they were going to start losing it.

The door opened while he watched, and his uncle stood there looking out into the yard. He was looking at the trucks, and then back to the barn and the grove, and then out across the fields. His uncle stood like he was extra tired. The wind was whipping his clothes and blowing his hair back but he wasn't braced against it. It would make you tired, all the bullshit that was going on.

Or maybe his mom had asked his uncle to step outside and get him.

No. That wasn't it. His uncle opened the door, reached back in, and pulled out his bag of gear. He was heading out. Heading out, by God. Something had happened. Maybe he finally had a belly-full. Ben checked the cab to make sure everything was tight, just an automatic thing you did even when you had not been running. Then he opened the door and climbed down. Find out what was going on, what had gone wrong. The steps were snowy and close to slick in spite of the nonskid surface. He braced himself and hung alongside the truck for a minute feeling the wind. Felt tired himself, by God. This sitting around was enough to make anybody feel like that.

[243]

25

You felt it first in your gut, and then it moved to your head, and then it got to your heart and made you want to yell and kick and scream. They were a bunch of murderers and liars back there. They were killing each other and pretending that everybody loved everybody. No one, not one of them, was saying what they thought or felt. He bet they weren't even saying it to themselves. Knew it, in fact. Singleton had figured out fast why he was no longer welcome and was a bad influence.

Even Ben was acting. Ben found some pretext to follow him down to the stop, when it would have been more honest of Ben to say that he was coming along because he wanted to. Ben's rig was like a red shadow in his mirrors, and the white road was going dim and gray as night came on. Singleton kicked on the markers and saw Ben's markers come on a half second later. At least he was not inattentive.

Grace had received a phone call that afternoon. It made her look just as happy as she had looked when she came in with wind-messed hair. Grace had found a man. Not that he cared, but it was interesting.

The other part was not interesting. He could not bring himself to think about the other part, at least not until he got rid of Ben.

For the best part of an hour now his mind had been numb and he wanted to keep it numb. First his mind just froze. Then it got numb. When everything was worse than bad, numbness was a pretty good thing. Having Ben follow him down to the stop might even be a good thing. It would keep him from having to figure this out until he got on the road and way away from them.

And even if it—it—it—had not happened, he probably could not have hung around. The women were getting to him. They were putting a noose on Ben and they were not even subtle. So he just had to say the hell with it, and tell them he was headed for North Carolina. Catherine would not be home, but they did not know that. Grace could explain if anyone was interested, which they were not.

The fancy stitched boots that Ben had given *him* were stiff and slick. The really good leather workjacket that Grace had given him put a new smell in the cab that he knew he would probably come to like.

He wheeled it into the stop and put it on the readyline, what little line there was this time of year. No need to buy fuel until he found where he was hauling from.

Hauling? He had forgotten that he was going to quit. Was he going nuts?

Ben pulled in beside him. They climbed down and headed for the restaurant. The lot was almost empty. There would not be much work for the balance of December.

They took a booth and in two minutes he had his hands wrapped around his—he shook his head—millionth cup of coffee, probably. He did not even want it.

"Don't go away mad," Ben said.

The numbness saved him. "Not at you, anyway."

Leave these blues behind me

"They're just excited. You'll be back around the first?"

Let that tandem call

"As near as I can tell."

"If you change your mind."

"I don't think I will." He did not know what he was going to think. Fake it. "I'm fifty years old. Time to find something else."

Start that road to windin'

"It doesn't sound right."

[245]

From it all

Singleton looked at him. It wasn't right. It was dead wrong. Ben did not even know, and if Ben had been a kid once, he had better be a man now, because he had a man's problems. It was just crazy the way Grace and Sue meshed. They fed lines to each other like they were rehearsed. Both of them country-raised. Well, Indiana had bred a lot of killers.

Make your bad news

"I think it's right," Singleton said. "I've got a fella to look up, maybe a bridge or two to burn." He wondered if it was true. He had nothing to do.

Chasin' that lonesome road

Now it was going to be embarrassing. Ben was looking at him the way Pat had looked once. Would it be all right to help Ben? Would that make it right?

Cried to see me go

"You pulled me out when I needed it."

Now these stacks are boomin'

Ben should not have said that. As near as he could see he had helped pull Ben right into a marriage, a baby, a worse problem than he hoped Ben would ever know about. There were not going to be many free miles for Ben.

Let 'em blow

"Don't think about it." Now he just wished Ben would leave. He was getting feelings like when you used to leave a ship. The next time he saw Ben they would be strangers and Ben would be changed. Strangers would surround them. Maybe he would never see Ben again. Or, if he did see Ben again, it would be on the road. Coffee. News. Goodbye. He did not like thinking that way. Besides, he was quitting the road.

Take a guy who smokes and wears glasses, take a day's run, he'll be straining through three layers of fogged glass on the inside, plus whatever he's collected on the windshield, then add dirt to his headlights

"Maybe I'll write a book about how not to get killed on the road."

"Somebody ought to." Ben was uncomfortable and you could tell he didn't even know why. The hell with it. Let him go home. He would get back in time for the funeral.

[246]

"Better get back, I guess."

"See you in a few days," Singleton told him. "Keep it in the road."

"You, too." Ben was backing away. Then he turned and left.

Goodbye, Ben, he thought. If I helped you, I hurt you. He wanted to run after Ben, stop him. He wanted to tell him that you carried it with you, wanted to say that it was a thing a man came to expect and the only way, the only way out—but he did not know what that way was.

An' then we drove along the river there. Low fog. River would be foggy in hell and Mike was driving. Nice fella, Mike. You know him? Yeah, nice fella but he was snakebit that night. Started hitting things. Lights like silver discs in the fog. Couldn't cut her back, couldn't kick her. Fog collecting and running on the windshields like rain.

Hit a rabbit. Felt syrupy when we rolled him. Then it started. Two minutes later we hit a possum. Minute after that another rabbit. Old Mike was goin' tight around the mouth. He started breaking back the speed. Listen, Mike, I said, some jerk will come from behind and asshole you. He picked it back up a little. Mouth hard.

Can't miss 'em all, I told him.

Can't miss any of 'em, he said, and he was right. Some guy in a car came fishtailing in behind us. Scared to pass, bright-lighting us. We hit a possum and then a rabbit and then another rabbit. We were wholesaling, man, Mike, white as cottage cheese, and then it got bad. Like every animal in the county was on that road. We ran into a pack of rabbits, maybe fifty of them looking up all surprised at those disc-silver lights. It was like floating, man, and later on I picked a bunch outta the trailer frame. It was too much for Mike. He started to pull over and hit a dog. Big old mongrel dog but pretty. Ol' Mike just set there sweating and I took the flashlight and gun back and shot it. Lying half across a bob wire fence, hindquarters messed up, guts hanging out. Snakebit, man. I took it the rest of the way. We didn't have any more trouble.

He did not know the way out.

"We'll see what happens," he muttered.

"What?" The waitress was just passing. Tall girl. Plain. Legs too thick.

[247]

"More coffee."

He could get drunk. It seemed like he had been doing that a lot lately. It was boring. He could haul another load, but what good was that when you already had enough money. He could roll Ann Arbor. No, better to get it all settled first.

When they bright-light you, turn on your cab light and be willing to give ten percent on the speed, a little trick, it diffuses the light in the mirrors

"Go away," he told John. "You're dead, because your woman is screwing someone else."

He did not want the coffee. He tossed change on the counter and left. Just in time. Some idiot was plugging the juke.

His truck *was* the readyline. A few rigs were parked at the far end of the lot, closed down, silent, standing in the gathering dark like square-nosed monuments. His rig sat surging, warm, alive. Its markers were kind of like a symmetrical galaxy of bright stars, and the trailer was framed against the black sky. The sure, certain lines of the trailer were as definite as a well-planned lie.

If only he did not always have these feelings of being responsible. Then he would not have known anything, and maybe there would still be some place in the world that looked like home.

Around two that afternoon he had lain down to take a nap. There was nothing else to do. The women were cooking things. The new dog was busy pissing on the floor. Ben was the hell and gone off somewhere. He went to the back room, shucked off his boots and lay down. He even believed he was sleepy.

The voices did not come at him. Probably he could have handled that. The songs and stillness did not come, either. What came were worry thoughts. He had lain thinking of Catherine, trying not to think of Pat, and then he thought of what you did when you came off the road. Nothing. He had come up with nothing. Except the fishing boat idea. It seemed like an honest thing to catch fish and bring them in and sell them for people to eat. It wasn't doing anything important, but at least it was honest. A man could not be ashamed of using his time that way. What time there was left.

He did not want to think about that. Even when he pulled the pillow over his head, the thoughts did not go away. It was a loss. The brave times were fine, but they were past, and a used-up sailor who was a used-up truck driver was no good to this world or himself. They were lousy thoughts and they had finally rolled him back out of the sack and onto his feet.

He pulled on his boots, walked down the hall, and from the kitchen came voices of the women talking about cribs and baby clothes and nurseries and colors of paint. He did not want to get into that.

Ben was not in the living room. Maybe he was out splitting more wood. Singleton would never know why he did it, and he wished he had not done it, but on an impulse he hung a left and walked upstairs to see John. If he was coming off the road he might not see John again for a long time. Besides, it was Christmas.

It seemed like the smell was not so bad, not nearly as bad as he remembered. A man healed. Things got into a routine. The routine was what made things tolerable and was what cut the smell. Singleton stood in the hall and remembered his brother and all the plans and hard work. Probably he should not go in there. Probably it was better to leave John alone. He had leaned against the frame of the door. The lousy thoughts hovered in the back of his mind. It was because he wasn't moving, that was the reason. When things stopped, when there was nothing to do, then all the stuff that was laying back waiting for you attacked.

Something bothered him and he could not quite get hold of it. It was the kind of uneasy feeling you had when your ear picked up a small, unexplained sound in the rig that happened so irregularly it could not be traced. Like a sound that could be saying something important, but did not come steady enough to tell you where it was.

But this was not a sound. He listened and heard nothing. Maybe far off, the distant murmur of the women in the kitchen, and at the end of the hall the slight pressure of the wind vibrating the window. Those were normal, everyday sounds and they did not mean a thing. It was not a sound.

He stood and tried to empty his mind. The lousy thoughts came at him and he pushed them back. He did not even know how long he stood there, but it must have been three or four minutes. His mind got almost empty. The uneasy feeling was searching, puzzling, like it was asking questions of itself, and he let the feeling have his mind because it seemed like he could trust it. Lots of times you did that on the road, trusted what you felt even more than what you knew. Instincts could tell you things. Instincts actually were something you knew, they just operated different.

When he finally caught it he was so shocked, that for a moment he could not move. He caught it not with his face or hands, but with his left leg that was feeling the draft from beneath the door as he leaned against the frame. It was not a heavy draft, but it was there and it was cold. Then he was able to move and opened the door quiet and fast.

One of the white curtains was moving easy and silent like a fat ghost. It was not flapping or being blown hard, it just rose and swelled fat and collapsed and rose again. The room was not hot like last time and his brother lay stretched on the bed uncovered like last time. The diaper arrangement was the only thing he had on him. The curtain fell and sort of hovered, and collapsed and hovered, but not nearly as much after he closed the door.

Singleton walked to the window. It stood open about two inches. An old-fashioned framed window with heavy gaskets pressing all around the frame. No possible way in the world for the wind to have blown it open. He closed it fast, had to push twice because the gaskets pressed so hard. Then he turned around.

If anything, his brother was thinner, although that did not seem possible. The afternoon light was dim. It did not cause enough shadow to give John any extra substance. He looked like a thin pole lying on a bed that was now too large. Breath slurped in and out of his open mouth the same as always. This time the hand was not plucking at the sheet, the eyes were unfocused.

You could see that deterioration had taken place since just last fall. Singleton noticed it most when he looked at John's feet. The legs had been thin before, but now the feet were skeletal, like the pictures of the Nazi-concentration-camp people. You could tell that the man was gradually dying, too, anybody could tell that. Singleton looked around the room and began to get mad.

On the steel shelving there was a layer of dust. It was not thick, but it was not just a two-or-three-day accumulation. Along the bed, stains on the tile floor showed that the place had not been flushed down for a while.

Yet the smell was not as bad. The whole room gave him the

feeling of half-ass maintenance, or the way a rig looked when you had been out too long and there had been no time to clean up. It was still efficient, it still ran and was dependable, but the edge was off. Either the smell was not as bad because he had been expecting it, or there was less smell.

He stood before his brother and his mind got cold and then it froze. Not much could move in such a mind, and Singleton could think feelings but not have them. He could not think ideas. Later, he understood that his mind told him then everything he needed to know. He just did not analyze it at the time.

These good country people. Salt of the earth. Hot to tell you about your responsibility, eager to explain what your morals should be.

His mouth tried to say something to his brother. It would not work. He did not know, and nobody else knew either, including the doctor, if John understood anything. Better to say nothing. Better to go. If John was getting better, then pneumonia would probably not hit him. It was obvious that John was getting worse.

He knew them. Knew their country tricks and their country ways. Grace was not thinking of murder when she did it. She was careful not to think at all. She had made some excuse to herself, then she had deliberately tried to freeze her mind the way his mind was frozen now. When John died Grace would cry and she would mean it.

Oh, he knew them. No goddamn wonder a man had to get out, had to go to sea or hell or someplace.

She would cry like her heart was broken, and one part of her heart would be broken. Maybe she would even cry while her new man held her, and then the holding would get her interested in other things. He turned from it. He understood her and did not care. The whole thing was finally who and what you were, and sometimes even where you were. He could not take some troubles from Grace, not if they belonged to her. No more than she could have taken those that belonged to him.

He had lived with burdens all his life. It was a part of living. When people could not take care of themselves, you could not just pass by. No sea was so bad, no storm so heavy, that you could not pass a line to another man. If it was too heavy and you could not, then you lost the cutter trying. That's how it was, and anybody

[251]

who was different was good country folk. Made no difference where they were or what they did or how smart they thought they were. In the Guard guys sat Grummans down in the open sea because they had people in the water.

He remembered a kid named Tommy, harbor patrol, tide at flood, people in the water beyond the bridge in Portland. There was not enough room under that bridge to move the boat through. So Tommy gunned it and took off the superstructure and got the people. Only broke some ribs and one arm when the wheelhouse exploded around him.

The old thoughts and hurt got him moving. His mind was still stiff, but the numbness was beginning and the old thoughts moved slowly in the numbness. Naomi was back there someplace, and Catherine, and they were all gone now. It was past.

His mouth moved and tried to make words. He looked at his brother who was better off dead, who was having a favor done for him, a favor that Charles Singleton knew was logical and so wrong that the wrongness was like a scream. He had to say something.

"Keep it in the road," he whispered, knowing the stupidity of it, knowing the uselessness of it, but not knowing what else to say. He crossed the room and got into the hall and closed the door quiet. The numbness was really helping, and he had gone to the back bedroom, packed his stuff and left. He did not say anything to the women. He did not even say goodbye, and it was Grace who had done it for sure because at least Sue came in to see what was wrong. At least Sue seemed like she cared a little bit, even if she was relieved. Ben was just dumb. Ben did not even catch on that anything had happened. But of them all Ben would know and understand that there was only one thing to do, and that was climb up and drive.

26

THE pain was red like the sky. It was red like the watered blood from the death wound of a rescued corpse. It got hot when the numbness went. He drank the numbness back into him, but drinking, sleeping, waking, the pain waited and was ready. It had been dulled but waiting and then it surged like a spurting artery; and like an artery, it was intrinsic and interior and pumped a history of blood. He drove and the empty trailer was beaten hard by the wind. Once on interstate, the wind kicked harder.

His direction was south. The road at first ran on a slant and for a little while he faced a sky of red. He checked, without knowing that he checked, the direction of wind gusting across the dead fields. Above the land, high, there seemed to be a great wind roaring far above the tops of trees. Naked branches beyond the right of way were bent by surface gusts.

Against the red a small bird flew, rising high, pushed into the upper air, falling, rising, fighting the sky.

He caught overdrive and the truck bellowed into the wind. The tunnels of the exhaust stuttered and boomed the overspeed as the tach red-lined and showed the engine full out. He watched it curiously, feeling the rapid, heavy throb of the first time the engine had ever been in overspeed. It seemed that the engine would break, that no metal forged could stand that strain. His mind merged with the engine and it was filled with hammers.

He did not know what love was. He did not know why you would want it or look for it or remember it. He dropped back the speed. For a while the engine was rough, the engine was settling in, the harm that might be done already done. Singleton found himself panting, looking left and east, finding another sunrise. The sky was deeper red.

He whipped off the exit to 127, not lifting his foot. The empty van jumped and danced its tandem across the roadway. He applied more power to correct.

It was all gone. If it had ever been there, if it had not been a joke or a fraud, it was all gone. There was nothing left. There was not enough of him left.

Going to blow

It had blown and gone. It was gone.

The two-lane macadam ran like a black river. He drove it fast and wild and pushed hard on the curves. Outside of Lawrence- burg he lifted his foot and bowed his head over the wheel, not looking at road, not looking at anything. The truck boomed onto the four-lane streets, riding the yellow line. He raised his head and corrected.

"I'm sorry," he told the truck. He rolled the rig through Law- renceburg and back onto two-lane. His eyes were stinging. The sun was yellow on his left quarter. It was not far to Harrodsburg. The tandem jumped across every curve. He wondered if he was going to kill himself.

He pulled into the deserted stop in Harrodsburg, his mind blanking in and out. Perception came, faded, returned. Dark and bright, echoes of red, and then for a while it was black like the belly of night and the voices talked and muttered, roared and wept, advised and cautioned.

His forehead was pressing the wheel when the voices faded. He tried to raise his head and found that he could, but it was almost impossible. Then the voices dwindled even more and he was surprised by the sunshine.

The stacks muttered. They soothed him. Singleton turned to the sleeper and fumbled beneath the pad. He pulled the gun out and laid it on the front seat beside him. A forty-five automatic.

John had kidded him about it. Too big to carry, but a forty-five was the only pistol he had ever known. Now it lay on the seat, flat, black, well oiled. He always maintained it the same way he maintained the rest of his tools.

The voices seemed to wait. He picked up the pistol and released the magazine. It was fully loaded. The stubby, fat, dull-gleaming top bullet was pressed hard by the spring. He tried to rock it with his thumb. It moved a little. The gun had been fired through one magazine. Tested when he bought it. The gun was a joke, part of the importance-feeling that guys got. Hardly anyone got highjacked any more.

You did not kill yourself because someone else was a killer, but enough could happen that it might not be possible to live.

His breathing was better. The gun seemed to help. He sat thinking of guns. His first one was a twenty-two when he was a kid. He shot a squirrel and since then had never shot another living thing. The squirrel was different from butchering a hog. With a hog there was use. How much could you get to eat off a squirrel?

There were forty-fives, thirty calibers, fifty calibers, twenty millimeters, three-inch-fifties. Depth charges. That was a kind of underwater gun.

Verey pistols. There was one that made sense. But the other, the one that made the most sense was the line-throwing gun that put out a messenger attached to a heavier messenger that was attached to a towline. A gun was not the way. The voices were still. He reloaded the forty-five and shoved it back under the pad. He sat knowing that soon he would have to taste the loneliness, and that drove him back onto the road.

When you were dead you did not feel. The loneliness caught him where 127 connected with 150. It started like his old friend who he had known so long, the partner that rode with him and helped kick off loads in hot sun or freezing wind. He had always been able to handle it, but now it changed and was awful. It was a gulf, vast, vast; like a shrouded night at sea with the bellowing lonely cry of the horn that trumpeted your presence into fog; a fog so thick that you did not trust the radar as water hissed at the bow and you began to think of the depths from which the fathometer received no echo. The trumpeting like the last soul in a perplexity

[255]

of night. It was deep, like falling through space into a canyon. It was like every withheld sob you had ever choked, like standing a remote night watch on a winter beach where the wind was cold and there were no cities anywhere.

He began searching the road. One-fifty connected with 25 in Mount Vernon. Every trace, every mark of error interested him. Outside of London was the right trace. Before the approach to Dive Bomber Hill and two hundred yards beyond the gully bridge, there were heavy marks where a car had braked hard. They would serve. They would fool the police, the insurance company, and anyone who cared to remember him.

A long living in the world stirred in his mind. He made no difference to anyone. He tried to think of Catherine and could not.

But there was no hurry now. He turned and went back to Livingston. He went in for coffee. The stop was like a thousand stops. The waitress was a lanky hill woman with an honest, ignorant face. She smiled. Nice smile. Country smile.

He warmed his hands around the coffee cup. Another driver sat at the counter. The waitress spoke to the driver like she wanted his attention.

The coffee was good.

Singleton finished, threw a dollar on the counter, and walked out. He climbed up and began to look at road. The voices were all of them laughing.

Blowing, chief

He had failed. He could not name how, and he could not name what the standard was for success, but he had failed. Blowing. Blowing. The rush of the exhaust was a great wind intermingled with the wail of the drive.

Catherine's picture was on the dash. He looked at the picture and crested the last hill. It was a half-mile run on the steep side. The long living stirred in his mind as he sought gears and saw the gray-white of a cutter in the fog, slipping through a complete silence of mist and water. A song from an island spiritlike among the splashes of surf. The long sand beaches of Nantucket where you dropped the pick and rowed ashore to walk through the crowded, narrow streets.

A myriad of old-fashioned homes and firehouses, churches,

stables, storefronts. Men forking fish in the heat of a Maine summer. Pat smiling at him, and the turbulence of water that rushed high about the boat deck as you ran against the gale, too unsteady to reverse course. The bar women, the fisherwives, who were like other women, but who watched the weather reports as other women have huddled in cellars listening to distant cannon.

The crest was past. The hill was a slide.

Trucks passing up a long four-lane, the guys blinking their thank-yous as they got the come-over sign. The tall red-and-yellow lighted vans, going and going away.

The road, gravel, macadam, concrete. The scenery that was a part of the land, but he was not part of the land, and so it was only scenery.

The west, hills like you could check them with framing squares

Hurt men sitting in twenty-five cubic feet of space staring into the sun.

Do you run from me

That stuff

See a train in the road, okay, see a house, okay, see a big ol' barn with the doors opening to let you through and it's time to pull her over

He was onto the bridge. On the far side he had the marks in view and watched them carefully to gauge the distance. He tensed his arms, his hands, the truck thundering at the marks, rolling at them fast, closing, and passing over them to roll hard against the hill. The truck lost speed, dragged, fell off on the grade and Singleton leaned on the wheel gasping. His hands would not do it. His hands, his mind, his arms were spastic. He could not shift and he could not kick the clutch and finally all he could do was let the truck die along the shoulder.

He could not do it. He sat stricken. Numb. Then the loneliness made its demands and he screamed, wept, tore at his clothing, completely demented, and then he passed out and even the restless voices had nothing to say to him just then.

The road ran like a tangled line, looping back, snarled and twisted, reaching past the heart of dark hills by skirting the mountains and following the wandering courses cut by streams. It eased along bluffs and through badlands, it turned and reeled its way through lake country, it bridged gorges and swamplands. It

[257]

drove straight lines across prairies and it rose on high overpasses above cities. The road followed long-forgotten routes that were originally the trails of Indians; had then become corduroy, and after that, gravel, and, finally, asphalt. The road map of the country had been laid before roads, before cartographers; and as he came to consciousness it seemd to Singleton that his mind was sorting its way through the map of a foreign land. The routes were confused, the familiar colors lost in a confusion of pink and brown and gold. No road map was ever colored that way. His eyes did not focus for what seemed like minutes, and he wondered if he would ever see again. When his eyes finally did focus, he realized that he was looking through the truck window at sunlight on the winter-covered land. He stared for moments, afraid to close his eyes, and then he closed them and sat waiting until his legs felt strong enough to kick the clutch and brake. He got the truck started and came away slow, his mind doing the automatic things, moving his glance to mirrors, dash, and down the road. His hands were ten-two on the dish wheel, and his driving was perfect. His mind asked nothing of him, so he thought of nothing. He made no stops for fuel, he made no stops at all, until hours later he arrived at Catherine's darkened house and backed into the drive after three pull-ups. His mind had behaved very well, but now it began to assert itself. It was making him climb down, it was making him go in there. He walked across the snow that was unmarked by anything except the tracks of small animals.

Once he was inside, he stood for minutes, unable to move, and wondered why he had come here. He began to walk through the house, paused before the open bedroom door.

He was old. Old. He stood before the mirror in Catherine's cold and empty house, where he would surely not have come had he not been certain it was empty. He did not know how much time he had. He figured it was not much.

The skin on his face had collapsed, and it made his nose narrow and knobby, like the crooked noses of old men. His cheeks sagged. The wrinkles, the creases, the old scars were like pits and wounds on his weather-beaten skin. He looked at his hands and the veins stood out blue. He did not know all of the reasons why he had to come here, but he figured that the mirror was one of them. His clothes did not fit. They seemed too large ever to have belonged to him, yet two days ago they had been the right size. His muscles felt shrunk around his bones.

Without her the house was different. The room was different. Always before he had looked at the house and thought its oldness good. Now he saw that it was not just old. Catherine must be poor. The rugs were as thin as drop cloths. The furniture was the kind that people gave to charity. The bedroom was like a cell. It had not seemed that way before.

He walked through the house to the kitchen and turned the faucets. They were not frozen. He looked around. The hinge on the oven was broken. The linoleum was worn. It was like seeing a secret, shameful thing. His intrusion was a crime.

He considered. He could wire the bank, get a thousand dollars. He could go to hell. No woman could bear up under a thing like that, even if he left a note.

He understood now. He had always known that you always had choices, but now he knew that if you stalled on making a choice long enough, then it went away. Good intentions were something you fooled with.

Of course Catherine was not with a man. Or if she was with a man, it was not for a wrong reason, because Catherine was honorable. Of course. Of course, if she came here right now, she would love him. Probably. She would try.

It was just that she would soon discover that there was not enough man left to be worth loving. The mistakes and the responsibility and the failures added up over years. The heart wore out, like it grew thin and tired. You tried to love them right, and you worked; you made the ships run and the trucks, and you saved people from dying, and you lent people money—and the heart wore out and if she came back right now, right now, right now there was nothing left.

He figured that it all started with Naomi, with dreaming the past instead of taking care of what was happening right now. He thought of Naomi and could not remember her, how she looked. What she meant. He realized that for better or worse she was finally out of his mind, she was gone.

He walked to the window. The rig stood there, churning exhaust into the gray sky. It was a machine, a machine. He knew that he had to say goodbye and did not know how. He did not want to say goodbye. He did not see that he had any other choice.

Singleton walked to the living room and stood in front of the cold fireplace. There was a draft down the chimney. If they were together he would install a moveable closure if he had time. The room was colder than the kitchen. He looked around, moved toward the front door and looked out. There was no one on the road. The truck had made tracks in the drive. Maybe it would snow. Maybe it would cover the tracks before she returned.

There was another room off to the right. He had never been there. He was already guilty of breaking in on her privacy. It was bad enough, and he hesitated. Then he entered the room.

All of the paintings were hers. There were canvasses and drawings and sketches all around the walls, on chairs, in stacks. He looked at them. The colors did not look right, not natural. Some of the shapes could be recognized: people, trees, grass, but they were like the main lines of a shape instead of the shape itself. He did not understand what he was seeing, but he supposed she did. There was one painting that he looked at, and caught his breath. That did not make any sense. It was just a bunch of pinkish white, and silver and red, but he could not look at it again. He turned and saw his own face. It was pinned to the wall along with a half-dozen other faces.

He examined the picture of himself. It looked like him, like he had been, but there was something about it that was better than him. It was the way he might have liked to look, but which in his mind he knew he never had looked. Not like that. Not for years, anyway, not since the road.

He unpinned the picture and carried it back to the bedroom. He looked in the mirror. Maybe this was the goodbye.

This, this was what she saw, what she remembered. Singleton walked through the house and replaced the picture. Then he went to sit in front of the fireplace.

There was not much to say. There was not much to think. He could not stay here. There was no place else to go. The chair was soft and it would be nice, nice, to light a fire and sit in that chair. Sit through the cold evening. You did that if you were old.

Shirley was in Oregon. She might be glad to see him. But that was another beginning, that was dream stuff.

If Catherine came home would she want him to stay? He stood, walked to the front door and looked out onto the road that wound like a black hem along the bottom of the mountain and then began to climb.

It was not friendly, the road. It killed and it maimed and it laid fires behind your eyes. It rolled and turned and twisted. It burned the juice in your kidneys and soured your gut. It turned friends into strangers and strangers into bed-partners. There was no excuse you could give the road. It forgave nothing.

He stepped through the doorway, tested the knob to make sure it was shut even if it would not lock, and walked to his truck.

Singleton climbed up, shoved it in gear, and headed out. The exhaust cracked and fluttered, the gears sang with the thumping cadence of the wheels, the wind tore and shrieked against the horns and mirrors; the winter roadside rolled past, and in the drive and flight and thunder of the rig the restless voices complained and cried and admonished, they cautioned and blamed and sobbed; and when he came to a choice of main routes he was surprised and frightened because the voices drove him north.

27

V<small>AN</small> Gogh was *sane*. Catherine was *sane*. If Van Gogh ever did a crazy thing it was because of the sanity. When he was working he showed the awful clarity and intenseness, the crystal, un-rhythmic, straight-lined and piercing sanity of saneness. He had been the only sane man in a world of greengrocers.

More than anything else Catherine returned with that knowledge. She wanted to shake the bus-riding fat man beside her, this casual stranger who seemed to carry his autobiography around his waistline. She wanted to explain to the young girl in the seat ahead of her, or to the old woman across the aisle. She wanted to shake that fat man until he rattled, joggle him from his newspaper, his fat, his bland and possibly well-fed world. She wanted to weep on his shoulder and explain how much he did not deserve, exhort him to show how much he could deserve. He seemed like a primitive, harmed and unholy creature.

The fat man could become sane. He just did not know it. She did not know how to tell him, at least not until she returned to work. The work might tell him.

Their governments and wars and race wars meant nothing. Their religions were silly. Their morals were infantile. If the universe was made up of nothing but electrons that made no difference, either. Not even if their ridiculous gods were a net of confused electrons. It was the human capacity for sanity that was the most important thing in the universe.

She had not eaten for a day because of the money and because she could not have eaten anyway. Her brother thought she was crazy, really crazy, but for now that was all right. Her belly was still tight with thrill. The energies of her discoveries would not go away. Her brother probably thought she was seeing a man, and that was all right. It was easier for him to believe that than to explain what she had learned.

She had nearly lived in the streets, walking the streets with an abandon that no lady was allowed, not even in these changing times. Any teacher would be fired if she were caught doing such a thing. She walked without apparent purpose on her own great purpose.

Somewhere among the crowds of well-dressed men and women, or the ill-dressed black men and women, or the tobacco men and women who were farm-dressed, she had discovered how uncommon each one was. They sounded so much alike. It was not until you listened, watched, listened again—and then they were not alike at all. They only *thought* they were.

Now, when a man spoke to her on the street she was able to smile, or to tell him to go to hell. Both were unladylike things to do, but both were possible. When a man spoke to her on the street she was able to hear his voice, instead of automatically fleeing from it. Now when a man spoke, she could hear what he said and she knew how to answer.

Her eyes seemed brand new. She had not only forced herself to be with people, with crowds, but she had watched what they valued. Most of what they valued was trash, but some of it was not.

In the museum and in the stores that sold handwork, she had not been moved by the successes so much as by the huge failures. She had seen a patchwork quilt with perfect stitching, stitching that even she, Catherine, could not do. The thing was ugly because the woman had a sense of design but no sense of color. She had seen paintings where the painters had been brave. She estimated forces in the products of work. She found that viewing the work allowed her to know the worker. She knew not only the

[263]

feelings that pressed the work forward, but the very sense that had put motion into the working hands. She grieved with the brave painters, because the work had gone confidently to the point where the task exceeded their skills.

She understood a lot, now. She understood how the old-time mystics had fashioned separate and complete towers of beauty and understanding. Their lives, the process of their discovery and living, had been works of art. Their sanity had been perfect, true, but too private. They were largely the viewers of their own art.

She, Catherine, had not done as well, but she had been nearly as reclusive. Almost, she had wasted her perfecting eye because of shyness and privacy. Almost, she had wasted her life.

Catherine left the bus in Asheville and took a local bus home. There was more work to do than she would ever get done. There was more thinking to do than ever before in her whole life. It was awesome when she stopped to consider it, and she had been considering it a lot. Her job, she thought, was to be one more center of sanity, one more sane voice in a world that was hungry for sanity.

It had snowed and tracks were in the drive. They could only have been made by Singleton's truck. She walked along them to keep her feet dry. Two people. Marriage was nothing. Sex was not much except when it was happening. She would be for Singleton, maybe, what he had been for her. He had, whether he knew it or not, wakened her into looking at the qualities of her isolation. A catalyst. Maybe she could be the same for him.

She went to her storage room and stood before the door because she was afraid to go in there. That seemed common and cowardly, unworthy of her. She was not afraid that her work was bad. If it was bad, you could do something about that. She was afraid that it was common.

She opened the door and turned on the light.

The relief unfastened the tension and she was free. Now she was hungry. Now more than ever it was important to eat and sleep. Her hands were shaking from the relief, or maybe from hunger. She closed the door and went to the kitchen. She was grateful and not sure who or what to thank, but she was willing to think about that as well. The house felt different. It was like someone had been there. She supposed that Singleton had come inside.

She worked well for the first week, the snow-covered valley serene with winter, the old house warm with a low fire and her own activity. Instead of her earlier frenzy, she set up an intelligent work schedule that actually produced more work.

Singleton did not call during that first week. When he did not call during the second week she became uneasy. In the third week the uneasiness changed to fear. He had always made light of hazard. He had always said that he was safe on the road. Now she imagined him dead in a ditch or already buried or in a hospital. She tried to shove the fear away but it began to absorb her dreams. The work began to slow and then it stopped.

He was almost unreasonably important. When she was still confident that he loved her, that he would show up, she thought his absence a good thing. It allowed her to get the schedule working. She dreamed and planned and the work went well.

He was tied to movement. She understood that, at least she did now. He would always be that way. It was all right. Living together was not nearly as important as being together when you actually were together. The understanding that she had to give him, to bring from him, was going to be a matter of long process. That was all right, too.

Once he had given her a phone number. She searched, found it, called Indiana.

Life changed. She did not know if her intuitions were better, but she trusted them more. She knew from the first that she was on the edge of a great height and was in danger of falling. The voice on the phone was Grace. She had no address, she had not heard from him. It was like him, Grace said, to abandon everybody when they needed him most, when his brother was in the hospital and they were all nerved up about it.

The voice said other things. Not even the remove of the phone could hide the intonations of that voice, or what it implied. It implied that Singleton's absence was all Catherine's fault, and then it implied something else. Grace did not actually call her a whore but the intonations did. At some other time she might have been nearly destroyed by such a thing. This time her intuitions

[265]

saved her. They told her to listen.

Something was making that voice afraid. It was saying more than it intended: that Grace did not want Charles Singleton, she did not like him, she did not want to think of him, but she did not want any other woman to have him, either. There was a curious edge that kept creeping in. It was the sound of someone telling lies about things that were important to them.

"If he calls, if you get an address?"

The voice promised to give him a message. What did she want to say?

"Ask him to call. Tell him to please call." As she said it she knew it was hopeless. The hatred in that voice was not concealing its fear.

What had Singleton said about her and to whom? She hung up the phone, stunned, her mind like rock. No experience was as bad as this. He was gone without explanation. If there was an explanation it was not going to come from the only other people who knew him.

It took a while to figure it out, and she never did get it completely figured out. She had lied to him; not about where she was going, but about her need and intent. At the very time in her life when she had understood that she never needed to lie again, she had lied.

She blamed herself because there was no one else to blame. She wrote letters and did not mail them. The work stopped. Now Catherine stopped.

Everything big that she had discovered was submerged beneath loss. It was like there had been a grand structure of knowledge, and in the structure there had been one weak place and that place was her. The tension of work that she had been riding, even cultivating, for so long, now combined with fatigue and she was mad.

She was in blind flight before her own ignorance. All things that she feared seemed like thunders rolling behind the hills. Her parked car in the drive crouched like a hunting beast. The telephone became an evil presence. For a while the telephone symbolized every violence and mistake and cupidity she had ever known.

She hallucinated, thought she did, could not be sure. The

telephone rang perpetually. Words moved through her head like a chromatic scale of color and light dancing across the face of a blind person. Ringing. Ringing. Once it was her boy husband, dead these many years. Once it was her dead mother who started speaking of sin. Sometimes there was no voice at all, and those were the times when she knew that Singleton was calling. She did not go to the schools.

She began to walk. On some days the day would resolve itself into sunset as she huddled in the glade. On others the day would fade around her in the forest, transitory into evening gloom, transitory into night. Mornings opened on the eastern hills and were red on the snow-covered land. On one morning she woke to the thunder of guns and walked in the pasture to find the snow stained with black blood, the marks of frenzy in the snow, and the leaping tracks of deer fleeing from hunters. The world was in flight.

Her movements, which in her madness seemed simple, pressed her to exhaustion. She found herself in places with no memory of how she got there. Along the top of a ridge. Kneeling beside an ice-rimed spring.

She walked the valley, sometimes kneeling beside the stream. The wind sifted her hair. The voices of the valley that might ride such a wind were silent, remote or abandoning her. She knelt listening.

It could not last. Her body rebelled. She found herself in a fight to save her life. In bed, blankets piled high, trying to eat, to drink. She fought for survival and won. Her body insisted on days of convalesence. Her emotions were frozen. Then rationality pecked at her like a small bird. There must be reasons for him to be gone. Some mistake. Hers. His. She loved him. By the end of February the madness was not gone but it seemed under control. She was able to walk, but not far. She scorned herself for weakness. Life, which was supposed to treat her like a lover, had treated her like a painter instead.

There was no excuse for weakness. She had food, clothes, work material and shelter. In early March, with more courage than she remembered she had, she entered her storage room. Some memory of the clarity of true sanity returned. She left the room nearly terrified with the realization that something more would yet be required. She fled to the ridge and wandered. The second message came. The younger growth of scrub and trees had survived the winter.

That evening she was finally in control. The wind was spring-raw, pressing around the house, occasionally back-drafting the chimney so that small puffs of sparks and smoke threatened to leave the fireplace and dart at her. She went to her storage room and got his picture.

She had lived alone for so long. She looked at the work and he momentarily seemed present. The face was colored by the fire. There was nothing false in the work. If this face was true once then that once was still true, and maybe the present and future could be true as well.

You had to live. Dying was when you failed. No one held the copyright on pain.

She asked herself if she still wanted him. Did she want him enough to take a chance on one more bout with hope? She did not believe that she was worthy of him, and she did not think that he could ever fill her world as she had once hoped. Did she want him?

More exactly, she told herself, she did not want anyone else. That was true, but it was partly a lie because there was a part of her that wanted only him. She made her decision and the next day drove to Asheville to look through telephone directories of over fifty places where she had never been. The road was clear but icy in spots by the time she returned home after dark. Melted runoff formed spots of glare in the low places. That night she wrote letters.

After that she was able to work and the work went methodically but well. The work was the first and most important thing. It might well be, anyway, that all of the rest of it was either echoes or smoke.

28

Buying time to beat confusion. Running the circle of days, the tandem pounding and throbbing on the concrete route from New York to Chicago and return. Two rounds a week, the tandem smacking the jointed concrete as he bought time. He passed below Ann Arbor ten times, a dozen, twenty times. The money he made was steady and big and the job was like driving a taxi.

Her first letter caught him in the truck stop just across the bridge in Chicago. Guys were all around him, the roar of engines, guys passing back and forth to the shops or john or restaurant or store. He almost did not get her letter. He would not have gotten it except for the sharp cashier who remembered the name when she saw it on his shop bill.

She searched the mail stack. She was blond and tough, but there was kindness under the toughness. You saw that sometimes with experienced women.

He was expecting no mail, so he figured it was a forwarded check. There were still a couple of those out that would have first gone to Indiana. He had already written them off. Maybe it was an advertisement, although usually the stops just discarded crap like that. Some of them even discarded mail. When he saw it was a letter he thought it might be from Ben, or maybe from Shirley.

Then he saw it was not. He fumbled the letter, dropped it, picked it up and looked at the blond woman. She looked back, startled, almost afraid. Then she reached to touch his arm. She smiled like she was glad, even if she did not know why. He did not know what was in his eyes, what they said, but they must have said something. He was not breathing well as he stepped through the doorway and walked to his truck.

He climbed up, the stacks muttering to themselves like always, and he laid the letter on the seat beside him. Then he sat. Confused. He had been confused a lot lately, having trouble deciding anything that did not have to do with the road. In the center of the confusion was fear. When he began to get confused about the road he was done. It would be all over when he got confused about the road. He did not know what he meant when he said it would be all over. Apparently this pain was not going to kill him. But what could he do if he was not dead. He had already failed to kill himself.

Some cowboy sonovabitch snapped a beat-up Jimmy onto the readyline beside him. The paint was peeling and the truck looked like a thousand miles of patchy road. He felt more than heard the raw edge of the engine and knew that the thing was muttering smoke. The guy climbed down and headed for the restaurant. Jeans, work shirt and baby-blue cowboy boots. The guy switched his ass like some girl who was selling, and the movement looked even more whorish as sun hit the big windows and reflected light and darked the guy into a silhouette.

The reason his breathing wasn't any good was because he was holding his breath. Stupid. He picked the letter up. Put it down.

It could be anything. Anything. He had never known her to complain although sometimes she got mad. He did not know what she would do. Maybe she had waited this long to write him off. He told himself that he knew what it could be, but he must not hope it was that.

When he opened it, the letter was a lot like the ones he had left for Ben. She did not know what was wrong. Had she done something wrong? Please call.

Please call. He shoved it in gear and headed east. Winter was beginning to lose its hold. The road was patchy with melt in spots. In other places it was winter-broken. Melt along the roadside.

Confusion. Traffic boomed past and he did everything right. He always did everything right, and the rig was solid in the road and you could depend on it like being in church. The rig was as solid as your father should have been.

Her second letter caught him six hours later in Toledo. He got that letter because he asked for mail, standing nervous and timid while another girl, with brown hair this time and popping gum, searched the stack. This girl did not touch his arm and she did not look at him. All afternoon he had been afraid. Now, the afternoon gone and the floods greasing the asphalt before the readyline, he climbed back up and went through the same drill. He was afraid of that second letter. There was one good sign. It was postmarked the same day as the other.

It was the same letter. When he found that out, he let himself feel a little of the hope lying back of his neck, back in his head where he pushed it because he was afraid. It was the same letter as the other. She was mailing blind to the stops.

He could almost see her. She who knew nothing of the road, going to library or telephone office or searching out some dinky southern truck stop for telephone books and addresses. The first letter was not a fluke. It was not something written just once when she was feeling bad or lonesome.

Her picture was pasted to the dash. He had tried not to look at her picture, but he had not been able to get through the confusion and take it off. Now he looked at it. At her.

Do you run from me

"Yes," he said. "But not mostly."

Maybe she had been with another man. Maybe she was with him now. He looked at her picture, smoothed the letter and then folded it careful. He sat thinking about it, really thinking, and really trying to feel everything about it. Maybe he was the world's biggest horse's ass. He had never known her to lie. Never. She must really want him.

If she loved him and really wanted him then he didn't care if there had been another guy.

He did not care. He did not care if she was with somebody else right now, right this minute.

Was that all? He put the folded letter back in the envelope and placed it with the first one.

[271]

Of course it was not all. She remembered him the way he had been, but something was cold in him now. When she knew him he had not yet failed, even though he could not name the failure.

He pulled out the log, the record of time and miles and lies. The record of incident and downtime; of the circle of road, the land rolling past, or the road like a river through the land. Nothing was settled and he did not know what to do. Lately he had known less and less what to do. He logged himself in.

What he should do right now was bull New York and drop. Then he should call, and if it went right he should go see her. And maybe then he would know what to do. He could see Pat and say goodbye, but the first thing, of course, the very first thing was to get the van empty.

He shoved it in gear and sat waiting for his foot to come off the clutch, and his foot would not come. He shoved it back out of gear. A White mustang pulling a grainside cruised in front of him, the guy running the readyline for a place to light, searching, and the guy slumped into the wheel in a way you knew was fatigue and not booze.

The web of routes was in his head. He knew the routes like a salesman knows the stock in his store. The north-south, east-west, the secondaries where you could pick up time. The routes rolled through his mind crisscrossing and paralleling, black and blue and red like a wiring diagram that you searched to run down a short in your markers.

His foot knew what to do. Or his foot knew what not to do. He did not want to think of going north, but there did not seem to be any other choice. He shoved it back in gear and this time his foot was working right. He ran it fast on the low side, pushing it pretty hard until he found his route, and then he hung a left and headed north; the night road was busy with car guys hauling the new junkers down from Detroit like spawn that would hatch from the trucks and flash onto the roads, swarming. Swarming like his thoughts, his fears, and he found out something about fear.

Fear was almost always worse than the facts that you feared. Because next morning when Pat got it through his head who was calling, he actually, really sounded pleased and even eager. Singleton had not expected that. He hung up the phone, committed now, and glad to have stalled long enough for a shower and shave.

He climbed up and pulled from the lot to start unwinding the last little jag of road before the Ann Arbor city limits. He was not much further north than he had been, and he was inland from the lakes, but the weather was no prize. The wind was kicking the van. The sky was gray and cold and ready to spit snow even this late in the season. His gross was sitting in around fifty thousand. Good freight gross that any basic transmission could handle. Especially the Chicago-New York route. Like driving on an ironing board.

The wind was still popping him when he got into town. Ann Arbor was tough for driving when you got down by the college. He ran it slow along neatly laid out streets and when he found Pat's house it was small and white with unmelted patches of snow lying in shaded places beneath well-trimmed shrubs. A guy was standing on the porch in his shirt sleeves waiting. The guy had to be Pat but it did not look like him.

Singleton closed it down quick. Even before he could get out of the cab the truck felt out of place back here on a side street. Not like a bull in a china shop. More like an oil tanker surrounded by pleasure boats, its grace and power and beauty held in because it was too close to delicate things. And why was he worried, anyway? Pat could not see the truck.

His heart was beating fast. He could feel it, and he was nervous and shy. He sat for a second before climbing down, but sitting made it worse, so he opened the door. The wind was cold up his pant legs as he climbed down. He walked around the cab quick because if you moved that way maybe you would not have time to get clumsy and do something dumb. He went up the walk to the house, and in spite of wanting to do it efficient and well the timidity caught him and he slowed down.

Pat had picked up weight, filled out. He was not fat, just bigger, and there were traces of gray in his crewcut hair. It was partly the haircut that made him seem heavier. He was almost jowly, and maybe he did weigh ten percent too much. His face was still dark and he was not wearing glasses. The dark eyes were looking straight at Singleton and it was hard to believe that Pat did not see him.

Pat's hands were not as heavy as he remembered. It was like his hands had refined themselves. The fingers were long and spidery and narrow the way musician's hands looked.

"Chief." The voice was nearly firm, but there was a tremor in there.

Singleton got up the four steps to the porch, took Pat's hand to shake because the hand was sticking out there, and then Pat felt how and where he was and reached around with his other arm and hugged him. Hugged him. Right there on the front porch. It was surprising and personal but it was just right.

"You're pretty thin," Pat said. "Come on in and we'll feed you up." He gave one more little jolt to his hug, then turned and went into the house like any other man would go into a house.

Inside the house it was about the same as other houses. Furniture sat around. Wind kicked the curtained front window. Lights were on against the grayness of the afternoon and Pat walked around the end of a couch, headed back through a small dining room and toward the kitchen. He walked without any hesitation. Awful hard to believe that he could not see. In less than a minute Singleton was seated at the kitchen table with a cup of coffee. Pat poured the coffee by sticking his thumb over the edge of the cup. A cute trick, but Pat had always been sharp. He sat at the table across from Singleton and there was a kid look on his face that made the strange kitchen feel familiar and like old times. Up close you could still see the traces of scars, but they were so thin that, except for the long one on the neck, you had to look to find them.

"Now that I have you here I'm going to make sure you stay for a while." There was nothing bullshitty in Pat's voice. He really meant it.

That truck and that load were supposed to be in New York right now. He thought for a moment and could not even remember what was on the truck. Dry freight of some kind.

"I can stay for a day," Singleton told him. Something about a load of freight no longer seemed important. He had hit enough schedules on the minute, sometimes way ahead of time. If some wholesaler had to wait twenty-four hours for some junk inventory it did not mean much. After forty-eight hours the shipper and the insurance company might start to howl.

"Stay for longer than that," Pat said. He had hesitated before he said it, almost like he was asking for something.

"I'll come back. Got a load to drop, but I'll come back."

"In how many years?"

"Right back."

Pat actually relaxed. Like he was actually relieved by the promise. What did he, Charles Singleton, have that would make Pat
want him around after all this time? Maybe Pat was lonesome.

"And I have a surprise," Pat said. "She'll be along in a little
while. Right now she has a class." His face softened, and there was
just a touch of a smile around the heavy lips. Did being blind let
you show more of yourself?

"You married?"

"Going to be," Pat said. He was grinning like a punk.

Catherine. He thought of her and felt automatic loss, and then a
little hope, and then fear. "I think I'm immune."

"Would have said the same about myself six months ago. Then
this smiling lady showed up in class."

"Smiling?"

"You can hear a smile," Pat said. "And you can touch it." He
drained his coffee. "You empty?"

"Uh huh."

"Push me your cup."

Singleton shoved it to him and Pat reached and picked it up
without a fumble. Then he tossed it in the air, wheeled out of the
chair and caught the cup behind his back.

"I got to tell you something chief. The sooner we get it out of the
way, the better off we'll be together."

Then Pat said that there were as many kinds of blind people as
there were other kinds of people. That was the first thing he
always had to get straight with his friends. Lots of blind people
were not cripples at all, which is what everybody expected. When
he, Pat, was on his home ground, nobody had to walk soft and try
to take up slack that wasn't there. As long as Singleton didn't
shove some piece of furniture out of place — and maybe not even
then — or leave stuff laying around, he did not even have to think
of Pat being blind.

"And it isn't an easy way to think," Pat said. "It takes practice,
but now that you finally showed up let's hope you get some
practice." Pat was like Catherine in one way. He could put words
to important personal things and not be embarrassed. Even that
was going to be hard to get used to, but after Grace and Ben and

[275]

Sue it seemed like a hell of a good way to learn to live.

"You fight against it," Pat told him later. "Maybe for a couple of years it isn't real—like lifers in prison who constantly read law books to find a loophole. Then one day you understand that it is real. You start working your way back into the world."

Pat was fixing lunch by that time, working and talking. On his home ground he was like anybody else. He worked with tools, knives, pans, heat, with motions as sure as if he had sight.

"I don't think I'd do so good."

Pat turned like he was looking right at Singleton.

"That's bullshit, chief. You always did what you had to do." Then he turned back and started slicing a tomato. He was kind of talking to himself, or lower, rather. He was still talking to Singleton.

"This world is just as real as any other world. As real as the Guard, as real as that truck of yours."

If Pat only knew. The truck was real enough, but the world it ran through did not seem real any more. He was about to say something, backed off from it, and was glad because there were scuffle sounds at the door and a girl came in. She was carrying books and puffing, and her scarf had slipped around so that it was not doing any kind of job at all. Her hair was black like Pat's, the scarf was bright red, and that was all he saw at first except that she was tall. She yelled a hi to Pat and disappeared through the dining room and off to the front hall or bedroom.

"A true hot sketch," Pat said. "Name of Judith, and for god's sake don't call her Judy."

"Don't like nicknames?"

"Well, not that nickname." Pat turned as Judith came steaming back through the house and into the kitchen. Pat cupped his ear, then raised his hand like he was fending off an attack. "Is it the Dragon Lady," he said, "or is it Mrs. Roosevelt?" The girl grabbed him and hugged him. From the back she looked shockingly like Catherine. Long hair and all.

Then she turned and she did not look anything like Catherine. Pat was right about the smile. It was the best thing she had going. This girl was Italian looking, swarthy and not a girl after all. She must be about the same age as Catherine—acting like a girl, though. The open smile and easy movement made him feel like a grandfather.

Pat pointed at him. "Just showed up," Pat said with mock sorrow. "Lot goes on around here when you ain't home." Then he introduced Singleton and turned back to work. Judith sat at the table beside Singleton.

"He's glad you're here. I'm glad you're here. What took you so long?"

Everyone was glad to see him. Either it was a put-on or they were nuts.

"I was just passing through."

"In a pig's ass," Pat said. Then he let it drop.

"You got a bad mouth," Judith told Pat. "You going to have to do something about that mouth." She turned back to Singleton. "Stay for a few days?"

He could not. He had to deliver that load. He wanted to stay, and said so, and then he promised to come back.

"How soon?"

"Soon." As soon as he could figure out what the hell to do.

"And if you don't we call the police." She nodded at Pat. "Too much for any one person to handle—and then, there's that potty mouth." She was laughing as she said it but her eyes were not laughing. Her eyes seemed to be trying to say something important, but he did not know what it could be. It made him uneasy. When she looked at him it was almost like she could pull him toward her with her eyes. Get it figured out when he had some time alone.

"And wise to be so young," Pat said. "Pay attention, for I have a master's degree in psychology and a Mexican omelet." He came to the table and sat down. Judith stood, served and brought the plates. Whatever she was trying to tell him was lost for now. He would figure it out later, when he was back in the truck.

But that is not how it went. She was not going to let him get away with that.

"I want to talk to your friend," Judith said to Pat. "He can walk me to class." She had an exact way of speaking when she was serious, the same way that her hand motions seemed more exact when she ate or poured or used utensils. Singleton liked the way she looked at Pat, and he liked the way they talked straight across to each other.

"Need company?" Pat's question was a little edgy. Not like he

[277]

had his feelings hurt, exactly, but still edgy.

"Nope," she said. "Tonight, baby. Tonight I'll want company."

And Singleton was slightly shocked.

Judith could move, and she did move until they got down the block and around the corner. The wind was dusting winter-crap along the streets. Here and there the grass was showing a first hint of green, but mostly it looked dead. A gray day. For a moment it almost seemed like he could see the wind, and the wind was also gray.

Judith slowed and took his arm. She had been walking like she was pushing the world ahead of her, or else running to catch up. Like she was making everything real through her determination. He had known people like her before and sometimes they made him uncomfortable. Not because they were devious, but because they could only see one side of a thing. Her hand on his arm told him by its feel that she was comfortable having it there, even it if made him a little uncomfortable.

"We have time," she said when she slowed down. "We'll take time. If I don't get to class that's all right." She looked across at him, as tall as he was almost, and her dark hair under the red scarf looked so like Catherine's that for a moment he honestly suffered in wanting to touch it. "I'm sorry," she said, "but I have to put you through something. At least it isn't dumb."

Her face was not pained. She did not seem afraid or sad, but she did seem determined. Catherine's features were fine. Narrow. Judith was what people sometimes called handsome, or striking, but she was not beautiful. Her eyebrows were thick, the lips and nose not thick but big. If it were not for her vitality, her intensity, she would look kind of mismatched. Her face would be like an accumulation of spare parts that almost, but did not quite fit.

"We'll go someplace and talk," she told Singleton. "He's your friend, too."

"More than that."

"I know. At least I know about him. We all have heroes, and you don't live with a man without knowing where he hurts."

She was shocking the shit out of him. He did not like that word, hero, and then he found himself wondering how many men she had lived with. Then he told himself to shut up and pay attention.

She took him to a small restaurant and a back booth, and then she shucked out of her coat. He found himself once more paying attention to her hands. They were kind of like Pat's. Long and narrow and efficient looking, but her arms were a little bit heavy and disproportionate to her hands. He found himself wondering if she was in love with a blind man just because he could not see her. Then he told himself that he was thinking bad. Most any man would be interested in this woman.

"Pat is one of my heroes," she said. "Not just because I love him." She looked directly at Singleton. "Because I know the fight he's made, is making. Because I've been there."

"Hurt?"

"Blind."

Her eyes were suddenly the most impossible and important eyes he had ever looked into.

"From the time I was thirteen until the time I was twenty-eight. But mine got fixed. You don't need the story."

He did need the story, but he did not need it then.

"I mean that I know what he goes through," Judith said. "I know it, and there is still not much I can do to help."

"I thought he was doing good." What she said made him afraid for Pat.

"He is doing good. Sure. He's a good teacher. A good thinker. The way these things go he'll be head of a college department by the time he's old enough to retire."

"Then what's wrong?"

"He's never accepted that that's all there is. He's never accepted being blind."

"He said he had." He distinctly remembered Pat saying he had accepted it.

"You never lied to yourself?" She knew she was being personal and direct and she was talking without any apology at all. Her voice was saying something though, the undertones were. Her voice was asking him to be honest.

"Most of my life," he said. "Yep. Most of it."

He could actually see her relax. Now her speech slowed. He could actually see her start trusting him more.

"What often goes wrong," she said, "is that you get uneasy. It's a limited world. There are only so many things you can do. No matter what you do, or how well you do it, you get to feeling fat

[279]

and useless."

He could trust her. He did not even know why, except he had watched her accept that she could trust him.

"You don't have to be blind to feel that way." His voice was lower than he meant. Timid.

"No."

"You can go all over hell and gone and still feel useless."

"Then you understand," she said. "Pat either has to do something else, or do something more." She touched his arm again. When most women touched your arm you figured it was a sex thing or a sister thing. Judith touched his arm like it was another way of talking, like she could say things with her fingers.

"It's important to be a teacher," he said. "I never learned all those things. I couldn't teach anybody anything."

"That probably isn't true. I don't know you except for what I've heard and what I'm seeing, and that's good, mister."

She was a stranger. He had not known her for more than an hour, yet he found himself talking. It was all hesitant and he did not say anything about Ben or Catherine. Talking about the road. About its endlessness and uselessness. About wanting to quit and not knowing what to do. As he talked he began to feel good. Something started working deep in his mind, something that did not connect just yet. Then it did connect.

He could quit winners. If he had something to do that was right, not just something to run to. You could figure out what was right if this woman was part of it, if Pat was part of it.

His imagination seemed like it was about ready to start working hard and well. For the first time in years, years, he felt the power of energy. It was real power, and it was energy that did not come from some kind of mechanical combustion. This was real energy. It had nothing to do with shoving stuff on or off a truck.

"You're a moral man."

She frightened him saying things like that. People did not say things like that. At the same time it hurt you like you wanted to cry that anybody could say something beautiful like that.

"I thought Pat had written me off."

"He thought the same about you." She touched his arm. "Pat knows. He knows you blamed yourself, but he never thought there was anything to forgive. But he knows you never forgave

[280]

yourself, either."

These people. It welled up in him, the secrets and emotions that he had never told anyone, except he tried to tell them to Catherine once. They welled like the tears that if they came to his eyes then the hell with them. He looked at her eyes, at the silence that was deep as a cavern behind her laughter. The silence of memory, of blackness, of hope.

These people. They understood. It was right to believe in stuff that was invisible. Catherine. She knew it too. She had been trying to say the same thing. He could see that now, see it clear as a probing, switching searchlight over black water. Just because things were invisible did not mean that they were not right.

The energy was not just in his mind. It was all over him, in his chest and legs, just sitting and pressing and waiting for a direction to point.

"I'll think of something," he said. "I don't know what yet, but I'll think of something."

"I think you will," she told him. "Because you love him too."

"If I'd had an education. If I'd learned that stuff." There was so much he could have done. The past was just loaded with ideas. All around him were ways of making those ideas work, if a man had an education like Pat had an education. There were new machines, stronger metals and concrete; but he had always thought of those ideas like you thought of dreams. A long time ago somebody should have started a mountain rescue outfit because of floods. The rivers and creeks swelled, taking children and sometimes whole families in the rush of water. People became lost in those forests, and planes went down. And that, a mountain rescue service, was just one of a hundred ideas he had but thought were dreams. All over the country, and it was not just some stupid preacher thing about doing good. It was about being good, and that was the big difference.

"I'll think of something," he told her. "I'll think of something perfect."

"Just make him part of it. Even a little part. Me too."

"Depend on it," he said. "Depend on it the same like it was Pat telling it to you." He stood. "I think I have to take a walk. I'll be home for supper." It was nice to say what you felt without feeling obligated to explain or alibi. He walked the length of the room, shrugging into his jacket as he went. He got out the doorway before he started blinking really hard.

The cold lay across the city like the very father of the wind, and the wind probed his clothes, probed around windows, poured through cracks of houses, and wrapped itself around buildings. He was in it, of it, and did not feel it. He walked and he thought, and the excitement would build and grow and then he would think of something even better and would start all over again. The excitement would not leave. It would not leave him alone and it was the best thing that had ever happened to him. Ever.

He walked until darkness began to gather, and it would soon be time for supper; and he realized that the restless voices that should ride this wind were gone.

He had to get back to Pat's house. Drop that last load. More talk. More ideas. He had to get back, but for a few minutes he could take some time for himself.

It was not easy like at the truck stops. He had to go to four different stores before he could wring out enough change to make a pocketful. The last store was just across the street from a filling station. He waited for traffic to ease up, and then he walked across the street and into a phone booth where he firmly closed the door against the wind.